By the time they reached the cabin, Elizabeth's head was whirling, her humiliation and confusion melting into a flame of hatred for the man whose brutal grip was bruising her wrist. Alexander Burke grimly closed the cabin door and shoved Elizabeth roughly away from him. She stared at him in mute fear. He tossed clothing at her.

"Put them on."

"You can't mean. . . ."

"I do." His voice was hard. "I don't have the time to tolerate spoiled society bitches like you. Now take off those fancy clothes."

This was impossible—it couldn't really be happening to her! "I won't! You can't make me, you. . .you Yankee filth!"

He took one quick step toward her, and the blow knocked her back on the bed. She lay there sobbing, but he yanked her to her feet. "Do as I say or I'll rip that dress from you myself!"

Trembling, she turned her back to him and began to unfasten her gown. His voice cut at her like a sword blade.

"Turn around!"

She did as he told her, feeling oddly deadened, detached, as if none of it were real. . . .

Alexander Burke stared down at the girl sleeping there, and cursed under his breath. He remembered the magnificent loveliness of that body as she had stood naked before him that morning; how he had had to fight to retain his mask of composure. Damn, damn! He had enough troubles as it was, without some golden-haired goddess to complicate things.

TO DISTANT SHORES

JILL GREGORY

ace books

A Division of Charter Communications Inc.
A GROSSET & DUNLAP COMPANY
360 Park Avenue South
New York, New York 10010

TO DISTANT SHORES

An ACE Original

First Ace Printing: January 1980

Published simultaneously in Canada

2 4 6 8 0 9 7 5 3 1
Manufactured in the United States of America

This book is lovingly dedicated

To my wonderful husband, Larry, who believed

To my father, my brother, and all those friends and relatives who gave me their support and encouragement when I needed it the most

And, especially, to my beloved mother, whose joyous memory I shall always cherish.

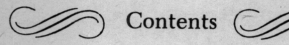# Contents

Part I.

Journey

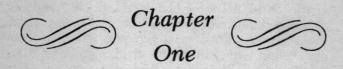

Chapter One

London, October 3, 1777

The ballroom was alive with music and laughter and light. Huge chandeliers bedecked with thousands of winking candles dangled from the vaulted mosaic ceiling, bathing the room in a soft, splendid glow. Lords and ladies reclined on gold brocaded sofas or gathered in elegant bunches like so many perfect flowers; the old oak floor, polished to a high gleam, was crowded with dancers whirling in a rainbow of lush silks and satins. Jewels glittered, laughter tinkled, and the finest wines flowed freely.

The host and hostess of this festivity drifted smilingly about the room, overseeing the enjoyment of their guests. Lord and Lady Carrington were well noted for the lavishness of their parties, and this gala was no exception. The surroundings were beautiful, the music soft and lilting, and the re-

freshments as ample as they were delectable. The
evening was proceeding exactly as all of London
society had expected.

And, as usual, Elizabeth Trent was the star of the
party. From the moment she made her entrance,
Elizabeth was the center of rapt attention, a
slender, enchanting vision in rich turquoise satin,
her soft violet eyes glowing in the candlelight, her
golden ringlets framing her face in a cascade of
gentle curls. All eyes had fastened on London's
most sought after beauty, though the expressions of
the observers varied greatly. Young gallants, their
eyes bright with admiration, flocked to her side in
a manner less than sedate, while young women and
their worried mamas watched in jealous dismay.
Lord and Lady Carrington greeted her with open
affection, for in addition to her own sweet, charming personality, she would add liveliness to their
ball: it was widely known that Elizabeth created a
stir wherever she went. Indeed, ever since her coming out the previous year she had captured the
hearts of dozens of suitors and become accustomed
to reigning over a court of admirers at every public
function she attended. The Carrington ball proved
no exception.

Her chaperone, Mrs. Hampshire, had long ago
given up trying to shelter Elizabeth from her throng
of suitors. It was impossible! The impudent girl
flirted outrageously! She actually encouraged the
attentions of those poor young men and gave every
indication of delight at their bewitchment.

But thank heavens, (Mrs. Hampshire sighed to
Lady Evans, as Elizabeth danced by with young
Lord Penrith) dear, sweet Elizabeth was never

bold. Though she enjoyed holding court over the young men, she possessed an air of refinement and taste which prevented her from ever appearing vulgar, or fast. The stout matron to whom these remarks were addressed was forced to agree. Despite her prim, disapproving nature, Lady Evans had to admit that the dashing Miss Trent, for all her laughing and fluttering of eyelashes, was always a lady.

"Of course, there is no reason why she should not be," she sniffed to Mrs. Hampshire, her eyes following the young couple with the piercing stare of a hawk. "Her breeding is of the finest. I knew John and Margaret Trent quite well, you know."

"Yes, indeed," Mrs. Hampshire agreed. She was a plump, amiable woman with graying hair and moist, bright eyes that darted frequently about, noting everything which went on amongst her companions and supplying her with information with which to enjoy her favorite pastime—gossip. She was a kindly woman, a distant cousin to Elizabeth, who had taken on the charge of chaperoning the girl when her own husband had died three years before, leaving her not exactly penniless, but in a less than comfortable economic situation. Grateful for the position she enjoyed in the Trent household, where she earned a handsome salary and attended the finest parties, she was as fond of Elizabeth as she was proud of her. Now she answered Lady Evans promptly, with undisguised pride in her voice.

"Elizabeth's birth and position are unquestionably fine, my dear, as you've said, and her fortune, well, everyone knows she inherited *everything* after John's death. And I must say, Charles has taken wonderful care of her, given her everything, as though she were his own daughter instead of his niece." She smiled with satisfaction. "That girl has had nothing but the best."

Lady Evans nodded and turned back to watch the blonde girl flash a smile at her partner as he led her toward a gold brocaded sofa at the other end of the glittering ballroom. She wondered shrewdly what lavish compliment he had visited upon her to merit such a smile.

Elizabeth, meanwhile, was unaware that she was the subject of so much discussion. Her mind was absorbed with a delicate little problem of her own and she was thinking fast.

"I assure you, Miss Trent, I shall be totally despondent if you don't promise me the next dance as well. Surely you won't pain me with a refusal? I beg you to consent!" Thomas Penrith took her hands earnestly in his, his blue eyes regarding her eagerly as she gazed innocently at him.

"But Lord Penrith, I fear you will grow tired of my company! And then imagine my loneliness! No, I think I had better prolong our friendship by declining your very gallant offer. But I would be honored if you would pay me a morning visit tomorrow or the next day." She smiled at him and the warmth of that smile made young Lord Penrith blush with pleasure.

She went on sweetly, "You see how I wish to draw out the length of our friendship? In small doses it will last much longer. I dread the day you will cast me off!" She lowered her lashes sadly, but he could see the irrepressible smile curving her lips.

Penrith was laughing now. "You are so absurd, Elizabeth. I will always adore you. However, since

I see that my pleas are quite useless, I won't plague you with them any longer." He grinned boyishly. "But I will accept your invitation. You may expect a morning call from me tomorrow." He raised her hand, his lips brushing it in a gentle kiss.

"Would you care for some wine, Miss Trent?" The voice at her elbow was deep and slightly familiar. Elizabeth glanced up quickly, aware that her heart had begun to beat faster. Lord Richard Milburne towered over her, resplendent in burgundy satin.

This was the man she desired for her next dancing partner. It was because of him that she had so steadfastly refused Thomas Penrith's invitation.

Of course, it was a tricky business, for she didn't want to hurt Thomas Penrith's feelings, but she had been certain from the way Lord Milburne's eyes had followed her and Penrith about during the last dance that he intended to ask her for the next one. And Elizabeth had already determined that Lord Richard Milburne would be her next conquest.

She smiled demurely into his eyes and accepted the proferred glass of wine. Lord Penrith rose, staring coldly at Milburne.

"I see you are in good hands, Miss Trent. If you'll excuse me, and you also, sir, I will leave you now." He bowed formally and was gone.

Lord Milburne settled himself beside Elizabeth and watched as she sipped the wine, her eyes lowered. What a little beauty she was. Golden hair, ivory skin tinged with pink, and those glorious violet eyes, so wide and expressive. Her turquoise gown, cut fashionably low in the bodice and trimmed with ivory lace in the latest vogue, showed off her slender, curved figure to perfection.

Ah, here was a woman to notice. The body of a goddess and the face of an angel. He was determined to see her alone, away from the strict eyes of society.

Elizabeth was equally well aware of Lord Milburne's physical attractions. He was a handsome man with broad shoulders beneath his well-cut clothes and a commanding air about him. Not only was he one of London's wealthiest bachelors, but he had a renowned reputation as a swordsman and was rumored to be something of an adventurer. Vaguely, Elizabeth recalled that he had a cousin living in America working as a spy against the rebels. This even further enhanced the aura of romance surrounding him. It was not difficult to see why all of London considered him a prize catch.

Not that Elizabeth wanted to snare him into marriage. Nothing was further from her mind! She had absolutely no desire at the moment to be tied to one man. Why should she? Barely nineteen, beautiful, and a considerably wealthy heiress herself, she was not in the least ready to exchange the dashing life she led as London's most sought after debutante for the humdrum existence of a settled married lady. As far as she was concerned, the more suitors clamoring for her attentions, the better she liked it. But she *had* determined that Lord Richard Milburne would be her newest and most devoted suitor. In furtherance of this goal, she bestowed on him her most charming smile.

"How kind of you to bring me this wine, Lord Milburne. It was just the thing I needed after that dance."

He smoothed his blond mustache with one gloved hand and smiled back at her. "Perhaps you would also like a stroll in the garden? I believe the evening is not too chill and the night air can be very refreshing."

This was not what she had planned. The idea of a stroll with Lord Milburne in the dark garden was certainly appealing, but she glanced in the direction of Mrs. Hampshire and hesitated. It was not right, she knew, for a young, unmarried girl to go out alone with a man, especially one she hardly knew. They had only been introduced that evening! Yet it was tempting. It wasn't as if she needed to be afraid of him. He was a gentleman, after all, of good family and background. And so handsome!

"A walk sounds lovely, Lord Milburne, but the music is beginning again and I do so love to dance. Isn't the orchestra wonderful?"

He said smoothly, "Yes, indeed, but I wish to speak with you privately and fear that the music and the dance shall distract us. Will you walk with me? Please?" His strong hand covered hers. "I promise you will be quite safe."

His faintly mocking tone made Elizabeth look at him sharply. He was daring her! Well, she certainly wasn't afraid of him, and after all, it would be exciting to be alone with him. She smiled prettily into his gleaming eyes.

"Very well. I should like a breath of cool air. If," she added mischievously, her eyes lightening from violet to a clear, sparkling blue, "Mrs. Hampshire doesn't stop us first."

He laughed. "I assure you we will slip away quite unobtrusively."

He led her to the candle-lit, linen-draped table where wine and tiny cakes were being served and deposited her crystal goblet upon it. They drifted casually toward the French windows which opened onto the garden and before Elizabeth had barely realized it herself, he had whisked her outside.

The night was cool and starry. The faint scent of summer's final flowers lingered sweetly in the air, and the grass whispered softly in the feathery breeze. Milburne led her a short way down the neat, shrub-lined path, his hand on her elbow. As they walked, they chatted gaily, an undertone of flirtation beneath the casual conversation. He informed her of his intention to visit his Loyalist cousin in America shortly, and Elizabeth wondered privately if her allure could persuade Lord Milburne to remain in London. The challenge intrigued her.

"What was it you wished to speak with me about?" she inquired lightly.

His deep voice answered her, sounding suddenly strange amidst the quiet of the garden. "I wanted to tell you how beautiful you are," he said softly.

Elizabeth, though pleased with the compliment, began to feel a trifle uneasy. They were now a considerable distance from the house and the garden was quite dark. . . and very deserted. Moreover, his hand on her elbow had tightened.

"You're very kind. But surely, Lord Milburne, we've gone far enough."

"Have we?" he murmured.

Elizabeth stiffened.

"Not far enough for me," he continued, and turning her head quickly, Elizabeth saw that his eyes glinted and a tiny smile played at the corners of his mouth.

Alarm showed in her face. "I'd like to return to

the ballroom now, if you please," she said in a voice that trembled ever so slightly. "I'm beginning to feel chilled."

A low laugh escaped him. He reached for her. "I can solve that problem for you, my dear."

Elizabeth hurriedly backed away, saying as sharply as she could through the panic now enveloping her, "Don't touch me! I said I would like to return to the ballroom!"

Milburne had not really intended her any harm when he had suggested the garden walk. All he had in mind at the time was a light flirtation to pave the way for a more intimate, if not respectable, relationship. He had a feeling that the ravishing Miss Trent possessed as much passion as she did beauty and he had his own notions of how to woo her. But he hadn't expected anything much to happen tonight. He found, however, that being alone with her was having its effect. He loins grew heavy with hunger as he stared at her, golden hair tousled by the wind, fear widening those brilliant eyes, and the bosom of her dress swelling with her heavy, frightened breathing. Before he quite knew what he was doing, he grabbed her slender arms and dragged her from the path into the shadow of a huge, gnarled oak. His eyes gleamed with amusement and excitement as he grinned down at her.

Elizabeth struggled to free herself of his iron grasp but he held her easily, effortlessly, and she gasped furiously, "What. . .what are you doing? Let me go at once!"

His grip tightened and he laughed. "Why must I let you go, Miss Trent? I am enjoying our present position immensely!"

"You said you wanted to talk to me! How dare

you treat me in such a fashion! Let me go!" Her
eyes in the faint light shone dark and stormy above
flushed cheeks. Her breasts rose and fell against his
chest as she panted with the exertion of struggling
against his grip. But he only laughed again.

"It is your own fault, my dear. I cannot resist
your charms. And in addition, I am well aware that
you have no protector to call me out for my scandalous behavior. Your uncle and guardian, General
Charles Trent, is stationed in India, I believe, and
you have no other male relative to serve as protector. I know I am quite safe in stealing a kiss from
you. Which is exactly what I am about to do."

He pulled her closer and said huskily, "If you
will only relax, you might even enjoy it. I am not a
repulsive man. Many women find me quite attractive. I daresay you do also."

"I no longer do so, if ever I did!" Elizabeth hissed
furiously, straining to break his vise-like hold. "You
are revolting and despicable! Release me at once or
I shall scream and bring the entire party out here to
witness your abominable conduct."

"Surely you would not wish to create such a
scandal?" he said softly.

"I would infinitely prefer it to the continuation
of your company!" she flashed at him. Cold with
fury, she opened her mouth to scream.

Milburne pulled her roughly to him and pressed
his mouth over hers. She strained to pull away but
he was much too strong for her and his lips cruelly
bore down upon hers. It was a long kiss, and a violent one. Only moments before, inside the brightly
lit, festive ballroom, with the glitter of jewels and
chandeliers and the gay music and chatter, Elizabeth had fantasized pleasantly about what it

would be like to be kissed by Richard Milburne, but now she was totally revolted. His lips burned into hers, his tongue ravaged her mouth, and she felt nothing but rage and repulsion.

Was this what passion was like?

She had once let a young man kiss her lightly on the lips, although this was generally forbidden unless a couple were formally engaged. But he had been charming and so polite, and the kiss quite spontaneous. He had kissed her lightly, quickly, just once. It had been nothing like this—nothing at all!

While Milburne finally released her, Elizabeth was gasping for breath. Her body shook uncontrollably. She put the back of her hand to her lips in horror and wiped away the wetness his mouth had left. Her eyes lifted distressfully to his and were met with a bold mockery. He grinned at her.

Elizabeth raised her hand and hit him as hard as she could across the mouth.

Immediately, a red blotch appeared where her hand had struck, and his grin faded, replaced by an ugly hard gleam in his eyes. But Elizabeth did not wait to see what he would do next. Whirling, she caught up her skirts in her hand and ran up the path toward the lights and the music.

Mrs. Hampshire hurried toward her, frowning worriedly.

"My dear, where have you been?" She stopped abruptly, staring at her charge's pale face. "Why, Elizabeth, what is the matter? Are you quite well?"

"I. . .I stepped into the garden for a moment, Loretta. Forgive me if I worried you, but I felt a trifle ill, perhaps from the. . .lights. . .and the noise. I wanted some fresh air."

Even to herself, her voice sounded weak with the falsity of her words.

"Well, of course, my dear, but you should have told me. You look positively ill, child! Perhaps we should leave. I believe you ought to go straight to bed." She grasped Elizabeth's hand fretfully, noting in dismay its cold clamminess.

"Yes, I do feel rather ill. Perhaps it would be best if we leave immediately."

It seemed an eternity before they had said their formal farewells to their host and hostess, but at last they escaped into the cool night air and Elizabeth settled into the cushioned seat of the private chaise, eyes closed wearily. She had decided that it would do no good to create a scandal now that the dreadul incident was over. After all, she had allowed it to happen by behaving so improperly! She never should have taken one step outside with Lord Milburne, nor even considered it! It was her own fault for being so naive and trusting.

What was more, even if she did create a scene, and ruined her reputation in the bargain, there was, as Lord Milburne had so crudely observed, no one to defend her honor. Her uncle was indeed stationed in India and she had no one else.

No, there was nothing to do but go home and try to forget the whole horrible incident. But, she vowed silently, she would never trust a man again! From this moment on she would guard against them with all her strength and all her wits.

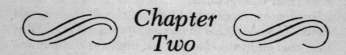

Chapter Two

"Thomas, you seem to attract misadventure like a magnet," Elizabeth laughed.

They were in the Blue Salon, an elegantly appointed parlor overlooking Trent House's south courtyard, where as a child Elizabeth had played hiding games amidst the shrubs and statuary. Tea had just been served.

"May I pour you another cup?"

"No, thank you." Lord Penrith leaned back and rested his arms on the finely carved arms of his chair. He watched as Elizabeth gracefully refilled her china cup from the gleaming silver teapot, and then said, grinning, "I daresay you don't believe that all these adventures actually befell me during my term at Cambridge. I swear to you it is true."

"I would never insult you by disbelieving your words," she smiled. "I do wonder, though, what scrape you will fall into next!"

"That is all behind me now," he assured her. "I was nothing but a green boy then."

Elizabeth surveyed him frankly. He certainly didn't appear to be a green boy this morning; he looked quite handsome and extremely fashionable in a blue satin embroidered waistcoat, white satin small-clothes, and blue silk stockings encasing his muscular legs. His shoulder-length brown hair was lightly powdered and tied back in a queue, and his manners were as polished and engaging as always. Elizabeth was glad they had been seeing so much of each other; since the Carrington ball three weeks before his attentions to her had increased markedly, and she found that he was a delightful companion, always amusing and never stepping over the line of respectability.

Unlike certain other English *gentlemen,* she reflected bitterly. Since the Carrington ball she had tried desperately to block from her mind the unpleasant memories of her encounter with Richard Milburne, but they persisted in haunting her maliciously. Last week, however, she had learned of some good news: Milburne had sailed to America in search of adventure. He intended to aid his Loyalist cousin against the rebels.

"I hope a Yankee kills him," was Elizabeth's first venomous thought upon hearing this report. Since then the unsavory memories had receded, only returning occasionally to cause her a twinge of discomfort.

Her thoughts were interrupted by a polite knock on the heavy oak door.

"Come in," she called.

A footman in full blue livery bowed himself into the parlor. "I beg your pardon, Miss Trent, but a messenger has just this moment arrived from the harbor with a billet from General Trent. Hopkins instructed me to deliver it to you immediately."

"Yes, of course!" Elizabeth glanced from the billet to Lord Penrith as the servant departed. "I don't mean to be rude, Thomas, but I am terribly anxious for news of my uncle. It's been several months since I've heard anything at all from him. Would you be very offended if I were to read this letter immediately?"

"Read it, by all means," Penrith said cheerfully. "According to the reports I've heard, things are going quite smoothly in India. No problems at all for our forces. Now, in the Colonies it's a different matter!"

"Oh yes, I'm so glad Uncle Charles is not stationed *there!* They say the war is not going at all well!"

"I daresay the problems are only temporary. The Colonies cannot hold out for long against the Royal forces! But," he smiled apologetically, "forgive me for boring you with this political talk. Go ahead, Elizabeth, open the billet at once."

Breaking open the seal, Elizabeth retorted, "You aren't boring me in the least! You know perfectly well that I'm interested in what is going on in the world. You gentlemen are so tiring to persist in believing that women are indifferent to the state of things."

Penrith regarded her with mingled amusement and admiration. Here was a girl who cared to talk of more than fashions and society gossip! During the past few weeks she had often turned their conversation to topics most women fastidiously avoided. The war in America, the political situation in India, and even the subject of finance. Admittedly, Penrith always felt uneasy when she steered the conversation to these topics—it seemed so strange to discuss such things with a woman! He couldn't help but feel uncomfortable about it. At the same time, he found himself admiring Elizabeth's thirst for knowledge and her intelligent understanding of subjects ordinarily discussed only by men.

What a marvel she was! So clever, and so beautiful. He noticed that she looked especially lovely today, like a slender, fragile flower. Her golden ringlets were tied with yellow ribbons and fell in soft curls about her shoulders, and her dress of yellow satin, trimmed with white bows, temptingly accentuated her slender waist and generous breasts. Her fine, high-cheekboned features might have been chiselled from white marble, were they not warmed by the pink sweetness of her smile and by the way her large violet eyes shone when she laughed. The sunlight flooding through the wide windows of the parlor bathed her in shimmering gold light like some radiant princess. Really, Penrith decided with unconcealed admiration, she presented a most fetching sight. Fantasies of sweet kisses and tight embraces crowded in his head.

Elizabeth opened the letter with pleasurable anticipation, eager for news of Uncle Charles. It was unlike him to be so long in corresponding! She intended to give him a good scolding when she wrote her reply. But as she began reading the smile faded from her lips. The neat scrawl on the paper bore no resemblance to her uncle's bold, fluid script. With tightened throat she scanned the contents of the missive and her fingers grasped the paper convulsively as its contents became clear to her.

"Dear heavens!" she gasped on a sob, her eyes darkening distressfully.

"Why, what is it?" Penrith asked as he hurried to Elizabeth's side. "Are you ill?"

"No. . .no, but Uncle Charles is ill. . .most dreadfully ill! This missive was written by his steward on his behalf!" She was white with shock, and she pressed her shaking hands to her face as her thoughts whirled and tumbled in wretched confusion.

Penrith frowned, clasping her hand soothingly. "How distressing for you! I'm very sorry, Elizabeth. What is the nature of his illness?"

"A. . .a foreign disease, it seems, common in India. He is apparently quite weak, and often delirious." She lifted her eyes to his suddenly.

"Oh, Thomas, I must go to him at once!"

She broke away from him and started toward the door, but his astonished voice stopped her.

"Elizabeth, what do you mean? You can't possibly intend to go to India? It's absurd!"

She stared at him. "I must! I couldn't bear to sit here doing nothing while Uncle Charles is suffering!"

He took a step toward her, arms outstretched. "Come, listen to me. You don't realize what you're saying. Such an excursion would be most improper for a lady."

Elizabeth eyed him with rising anger. She had no patience with such silly arguments. Uncle Charles needed her—that was all that mattered! "Improper, you say!" she began indignantly. "Wouldn't it be much more improper to sit here comfortably in England while Uncle Charles suffers alone in a foreign country, without any one who cares about him to nurse him?" Her voice quivered with increasing fury. "Charles Trent

cared for me ever since my parents died, Lord
Penrith, ever since I was a mere child in the
schoolroom. He did everything in his power to assure my comfort and happiness. And now he is ill
and needs me, and you suggest that I sit comfortably by and do nothing. You shock me! It is you,
Lord Penrith, who has no notion of propriety!"

He flushed under her angry stare and biting
words, but tried valiantly to control his own
temper. She was upset, indeed, almost beside
herself. He tried to reason with her once more.

"Please calm yourself, my dear, and listen to me
for a moment. If your uncle had married, surely it
would be the duty of his wife or children to go to
him, but no one can possibly expect you to do so! A
young woman, not yet twenty years old, journeying
alone to a foreign country in the midst of a war?
Why, rebel privateers and naval ships haunt the
seas. It is unthinkable, you must see that. Please,
Elizabeth, be sensible."

Elizabeth's eyes sparkled with anger. There was
haughtiness in her aristocratic, chiselled features as
she drew herself up straight and regarded him coldly from the doorway. Her voice was edged with
icicles.

"I appreciate your concern for me, and for my
reputation, Lord Penrith, but I intend to join my
uncle as soon as possible, despite whatever misgiv-
ings *you* may have." She gave him a tight little
smile. "I beg your pardon for leaving you so abruptly, but as you can well imagine I have many arrangements to make. Good day!" Whirling swiftly,
she left him there, torn between amazement and
disapproval of her behavior.

Elizabeth flew up the stairs and down the dim,

carpeted corridor to her suite of rooms in the south wing of the house, wondering bitterly how she had put up with Thomas Penrith's stuffiness for so long. Just a quarter of an hour earlier she had thought him charming, but his attempt to dictate to her had brought back all her resentment toward the male sex. His patronizing attitude was almost as insufferable as the physical mauling by Lord Milburne had been! She was a grown woman and very well able to make her own decisions! Why was she treated like a child just because she was a woman? She had as much sense as any man, probably more than most, and she refused to be tyrannized. Especially in this situation, with Uncle Charles ill and needing her. She reached her sitting room, her thoughts spinning wildly in her head, and tugged the bell to summon Anna, her maid.

It was true that Uncle Charles had not requested that she come; the letter had only stated that he was seriously ill, and had contained instructions for her to contact Melby, Charles Trent's man of business, in the event of future misfortune. Elizabeth knew that her uncle was trying to assure her that, should he die, her financial future was safely in the reliable hands of Mr. Melby. She was well aware that she had inherited a considerable fortune after the death of her parents. This was in trust for her until she was twenty-one, but in the meantime Uncle Charles had arranged for her to receive a sizeable quarterly allowance from the inheritance, permitting her to live in total luxury. If Uncle Charles died she would inherit the bulk of his estate as well. He had few other living relatives; indeed, she was the closest, as he was hers. Mrs. Hampshire, of course, would receive a generous sum, enough to allow her to live comfortably for the rest of her days, but Elizabeth would receive the lion's share.

Not that she wanted it! All she wanted was to join Uncle Charles immediately and nurse him back to health. She refused, for the moment, to face the dread prospect that he might not recover.

When Anna entered the room Elizabeth was busily selecting suitable gowns for the journey. She leaned out of the wardrobe and addressed the girl rapidly.

"Anna, please ask Mrs. Hampshire to come see me as soon as possible. Tell her it's extremely important."

"I'm sorry, miss, but Mrs. Hampshire has gone off to do some shopping. She said she would be back in good time to have a bite to eat with you." The girl's dark curls bounced as she bobbed a curtsy, her brown eyes watching Elizabeth curiously. Her mistress seemed so excited—and upset. She wondered with eager interest what was afoot.

Elizabeth ordered the girl to wait and promptly sat down at her writing desk to dispatch a short note to Mr. Melby, requesting his presence at Trent House at his earliest convenience. She sealed the note and handed it to Anna.

"Give this to one of the footmen at once. Tell him to take it to Mr. Melby's place of business in the City, and then come back here immediately. I need your help!"

The girl, her eyes big with wonder, scurried away.

A short time later Elizabeth descended the stairway to greet Mr. Melby. He was a short, mustachioed man, inclined to perspire, who beamed at her over his spectacles. Little beads of perspiration formed at the top of his balding forehead and he dabbed at them with a clean white handkerchief, saying, "Ah, Miss Trent. How nice to see you. What may I do for you this morning?"

Having steeled herself for this interview, Elizabeth was able to greet him with tolerable composure. "Thank you for coming so promptly, Mr. Melby. Won't you step into the library with me? I have some urgent business to discuss with you." She glanced over her shoulder as he followed her across the hallway. "Would you care for some refreshment?"

He declined, and followed her into a panelled room lined with thick, linen covered volumes. Heavy brocaded draperies covered the windows so that no sunlight leaked in, but the room was warmly lit by a generous fire and several well-placed candles flickered in their bronze wall-brackets.

Elizabeth settled herself behind the massive oak writing desk, hoping that the position would give her an appearance of authority. She had no doubt that Mr. Melby's sentiments on the subject of a journey to India would be identical to those of Thomas Penrith, but she was determined to win him over. She would simply have to convince him that she was traveling to India with or without his help, and hope that he would relent. Taking a deep breath, she began in what she hoped was a businesslike tone.

"I received very startling and unpleasant news this morning, Mr. Melby. About my uncle."

His somewhat protuberant eyes widened and he leaned forward in his chair. "Oh, dear. I'm quite sorry to hear that, Miss Trent. I hope the General isn't ill?"

"Indeed he is. Quite seriously ill, I'm afraid. That is why I am leaving England as soon as possible to join him in Calcutta. I would like your assistance with the arrangements, if you please. I shall need passage on a ship, as well as. . .why, what is the matter, sir?"

Mr. Melby had turned pale and was gaping at her, his moist lips parted in astonishment and such a look of amazement on his round face that Elizabeth felt almost like laughing.

"You surely do not intend to journey to India alone?" he demanded.

"Certainly not. Mrs. Hampshire, and my maid, Anna, shall accompany me. Do you have any objections?"

He dabbed nervously at the beads of perspiration which were now coursing freely down his face. "My dear Miss Trent, you must be aware of how unthinkable a scheme this is! It is not at all the thing for a young lady, with or without a *female* chaperone, to travel without *male* protection. Especially now, when the seas are unsafe. It's absolutely out of the question."

"Very well, then, sir. Would *you* care to accompany us?" Elizabeth asked evenly.

He blinked at her. "Impossible! You know quite well that since I am not a relative it would be totally improper for me to travel with you. Really, Miss Trent!"

"Well, as *you* know very well, aside from Uncle Charles I have no male relative. Therefore," and her voice became steely, "I have no choice but to set out for India in the company of my chaperone and maid. Under the circumstances it seems to me a perfectly respectable and reasonable arrangement."

There was a pause while she waited for his reaction, but he merely stared at her disbelievingly so she continued briskly.

"Now, I'll be very grateful, Mr. Melby, if you will elect to assist me in the preparations for the journey. Otherwise. . ." She shrugged. "I'll merely have to ask someone else to help me."

Mr. Melby was obviously taken aback. He stared at her almost dazedly, his mind crowded with varying emotions and thoughts. To his dismay he was now faced with a most difficult decision. If he helped Elizabeth Trent book passage on a ship for India, he would be contributing to her improper and foolish behavior. Yet, if he refused to have anything to do with her scheme, she would find another man of business who would gladly offer his services to a wealthy heiress; a man, perhaps, with fewer scruples who might not handle the affair correctly or, worse, who would take advantage of his innocent employer.

Another thought occurred to him. The foolish girl might even bamboozle one of her many admirers into assisting her, and who knew what scandal might erupt from that?

The usually mild-tempered little man cursed inwardly. One way or another, the silly girl would have her way. She had always been a stubborn, headstrong creature. With a sigh, he made his decision. Since he couldn't stop her, he might as well make certain the arrangments were proper. It was the least he could do for poor General Trent.

Elizabeth refused to let herself dwell on the unpleasant possibility which had occurred to her earlier, that due to the several months required for a voyage between England and India her uncle could even now be dead, or that he could die while she was en route to him. Cold horror filled her at the thought, but she quickly dismissed it from her mind. It was a risk she would have to take. When she arrived in Calcutta she would find out all she needed to know.

Loretta Hampshire's reaction to Elizabeth's plan was to be nearly as horrified as Lord Penrith had been, but she too was eventually won over by Elizabeth's determination. She finally gave her reluctant consent, deciding that with Anna and herself accompanying the girl, she would be properly supervised and cared for, despite the lack of male protection. No sooner had she agreed than Elizabeth sent word to Mr. Melby to book passage for three persons on the next ship bound for India.

Bad news at this point interrupted the household's hurried activities. Mr. Melby returned with the information that the next ship to India would not depart for at least two months. He had booked advance passage for three persons, the finest accommodations available on the vessel. There was no other ship available with an earlier departure date except, he reported disdainfully, a merchant craft bound for Calcutta, which departed at seven o'clock the following morning.

"And," he added, "even if that vessel were suitable, which of course it isn't, there is only space for one additional passenger."

Elizabeth bit her lip. "Do you mean we must wait two months before setting out?" she asked in a low voice.

"It is unavoidable," he apologized.

Mrs. Hampshire patted her arm comfortingly. "Elizabeth, my love, I know how disappointed you are, and how worried about poor Charles, but at least now you will have adequate time to prepare for the journey. Think how much more comfortable it will be for that reason."

Elizabeth thanked Melby and excused herself quickly, returning to her bedroom where she closed the door behind her. It was dusk now and the silk curtains had been drawn about the windows. A wood fire burned cozily in the grate and the room was rosy and pink in the candlelight. She sank down thoughtfully upon the bed, with its pink satin coverlet and lacy pillows, and kicking off her slippers, tucked her legs beneath her. She gazed about the room, remembering the hours she had spent here, comfortable, happy, secure. All due to Uncle Charles. He had taken her in when she was ten years old, after her father had been killed in a hunting accident. Her mother had died giving birth to a stillborn son when Elizabeth was three years old; she barely remembered her. But Uncle Charles had given her a home when she was orphaned, and more than that, he had given her love. She owed everything to him.

She remembered their summers in the country, when he had taught her to ride and they had spent hours galloping about the peaceful green countryside with Alice and Philip Harwood, children from a neighboring estate. It was Philip Harwood who had secretly taught her to fence; she had always been fascinated by that graceful art. Uncle Charles never said anything, but she had always suspected that he knew of the secret lessons and was amused by them. He had been a good and always generous guardian and, as Elizabeth lay curled on her bed, lost in memory, hot tears came to her eyes and ran unnoticed down her cheeks. But after a while the tears stopped. She made her decision. She would not wait two months. She would go at dawn.

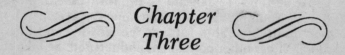

Chapter Three

The last shadows of night still clung to the sleeping trees when Elizabeth rose silently from her bed and lit a single candle on the bedtable. In the uneven, flickering light she dressed quickly, donning a soft, peach-colored gown with long, loose sleeves and a high, lacy ruffle about the throat. She pinned her shining curls on top of her head in a neat chignon, and then checked the items in her portmanteau: several gowns of muslin and silk, the necessary undergarments, a few toilet accessories, and the jewels which she had inherited from her mother. She glanced longingly at the beautiful silver gauze ball gown draped temptingly across the vanity chair. Last evening she had inwardly debated whether or not she should include the gown, and had decided rather severely that it was a frivolous notion. It was impractical—an unnecessary luxury. When would she have occasion to wear it? But another side of her had argued that, should Uncle Charles recover speedily and resume his duties as commander of his unit, she might have good occasion for the garment. It was inevitable that they would be invited to balls or parties for the diplomatic and military corps serving in India. In such a case, the gown would be indispensable. Last night, her sensible side had won out and she had resolutely decided against including the dress, but now, she reached out impulsively to stroke the soft, gauze netting—so delicate, so beautiful. She bit her lip. It wouldn't take up *that* much space in the portmanteau. She folded the gown carefully amongst her other possessions and secured the lid of the trunk.

Surveying the room briefly, Elizabeth was satisfied. All was in order. She moved to the writing desk and stared down at the note she had so carefully composed last evening. As she carried it to the bed her eyes ran quickly down the page, a painful tightness constricting her throat as she read the neatly etched words for the final time.

"Dearest Loretta,

I hope you will find it in your heart to forgive this ungrateful behavior, for by the time you read this note I will be en route to India on the merchant vessel to do my duty by my uncle. Necessity prompted me to go against what I know your feelings to be in the matter and indeed, what I myself know to be proper. However, my uncle's welfare is to me more important than all the proprieties, so I have abandoned them in favor of serving him.

I beg you to forgive me and to understand why I have acted thusly. Do not fear for my well-being; I am able to fend for myself and will take the utmost care. And Loretta, I beg you to cancel the arrangements for the later ship. Please, do not follow me. Once in India, Uncle Charles will see that I am chaperoned and attended, and I promise you I will assure him that my scandalous behavior was not due in any part to lax supervision by you, but due instead to my own wickedness in deceiving you.

Please thank Mr. Melby for his kind troubles on our behalf. I thank you also, my very dear Loretta, for your willingness to accompany me on what I know would have been an unpleasant journey for you. I have the comfort of knowing that my actions have spared you the necessity of *that* and I only hope that this letter shall help to spare you anxiety on my behalf. When I return from India, you may scold me to your heart's content. Until then I remain:

> Lovingly,
> Elizabeth"

Gently she laid the missive on the pillow. She hoped with all her heart that Loretta would not be too upset, but she had the strong fear that her chaperone would blame herself for her charge's behavior. Elizabeth was sorry, but she had no choice. She knew perfectly well that if she had told Mrs. Hampshire and Mr. Melby of her intention to travel via the merchant craft, alone and unattended, that they would have forbidden her and even made it impossible for her to do so. This was the only way —still, she did not like it.

Sighing, she turned from the bed and took up the long, white furred cape Uncle Charles had given her for her nineteenth birthday. It was satin lined and warm, and would be ideal for a cold sea voyage. She flung the cape about her shoulders and tucked the hood about her head. Then she blew out the candle, and clutching the portmanteau tightly in one hand, and the white fur muff containing the money pouch in the other, she made her way to the door.

Outside, dawn's first light shimmered over the dew as Elizabeth, a white, fur-framed figure in the morning mist, peered about for a hackney. Summoning a passing one was easy, fortunately, and a moment later she was settled in the dark, cramped coach and traveling at a brisk pace toward the harbor. She gazed out the window, wondering how long it would be before she again saw the cobbled streets of London. A sadness crept over her like a chill fog. She shook herself, and setting her lips together firmly, forced herself to think instead of the journey ahead. After all, she had never been to sea before. It would be exciting! She began envisioning handsome sailors, and romantic moonlight strolls on deck. And at the end of the voyage, she would be reunited with Uncle Charles. That was the most heartening thought of all.

Her spirits lifted still further as they neared the harbor. The sea was smoky green in the early morning light and it looked mysteriously alluring. Alighting from the coach, she paid the driver and replaced her money pouch inside the fur muff; then, ignoring the driver's curious glance, she moved resolutely toward the pier. No doubt he was unaccustomed to depositing well-dressed young ladies at the seaport in the early hours of dawn, but he was too awed by her obvious rank to voice the questions that must have been hammering in his head, and Elizabeth was too well bred to offer a hackney driver any explanations of her business. It was probable that the merchant captain would be equally astonished, but Elizabeth felt confident that by maintaining a cool command of herself she could brush past any possible obstacle without undue trouble.

As she approached the pier, she gazed about, eyes wide with wonder. She had never before viewed such pandemonium. The dock teemed with activity and noise. Merchants crowded the pier, bustling with self-importance as they bought and sold their wares, dodging the brawny seamen who rolled seemingly endless barrels of tar and produce and cargo to and from the ships. Street harlots strutted boldly up and down the waterfront, brazenly displaying themselves for all to see as their shrill calls and laughter rang in the tangy sea air. Ragamuffin children darted about with gleeful shrieks, trying to snatch an apple or peach from the open crates. Forming a background for this bustling panorama were the ships, long, lumbering vessels rocking gently on the green sea, their proud white sails billowing in the morning wind as the hazy mist slowly lifted and disappeared into the azure sky. It was a colorful scene of tumult and confusion, of flurried excitement, of raucous, shouting voices above the ever present roar of the sea.

A young boy, perhaps twelve years of age, was dragging a wheelbarrow laden with potatoes across the wooden shingled pier. He was covered with grime and grease, from the tip of his shaggy head to

the rags which served him as clothes, and on down
to the worn boots where unsocked toes showed
through the splitting soles. The dock workers, noisy
and unkempt, leered openly at Elizabeth as she
made her way across the pier, but she ignored them
as she had the hackney driver and addressed the
boy instead.

"Excuse me," she called, and he lifted his head to
her in amazement.

"You talkin' to me, mum?" he asked incredulously.

"Yes, I am indeed." Elizabeth smiled at him.
"Would you be so good as to direct me to the captain of the merchant vessel sailing for India this
morning?" Beneath the impassive calm of her voice
she felt a wave of compassion for the child before
her. For really, he was no more than that. Beneath
the dirt on his face she could see that his cheeks
were thin and pinched and his eyes had an empty,
hungry look to them. She had at first taken him for
a twelve year old, as he was fairly tall, but upon
closer inspection she realized that he couldn't be
more than nine or ten. She thought back to her own
childhood and a twinge of guilt stabbed her as she
compared the life she had known to the one en-
dured by this child.

"Aye, mum, he's right over there." The boy
pointed a cut, bleeding finger toward a group of
men further down the pier. They were standing
before a sturdy-looking vessel and one of them, a
short, husky man in loose-fitting trousers and a
shiny-buttoned waistcoat, was waving his arms, apparently giving instructions to the others.

"Captain Mills, that's who you want, all right,"
the child informed her wisely. He added with a

touch of pride, "That's my brig, the *Windhammer*, he's afront of."

"Your brig?" She regarded him with some surprise. "Are you sailing on that ship?"

"Aye, mum. And now I'd best be loading these here potatoes on, or the Captain'll flog me sure." He smiled shyly. "Mornin', mum."

"Good morning. And thank you." Elizabeth watched as he steered the heavy wheelbarrow across the pier, dodging the rowdy dock workers. Then she herself followed briskly, to all appearances unconscious of the stir her presence created among the seamen. She picked her way single-mindedly toward the knot of men indicated by the boy, giving no sign that she saw the frank, admiring stares of the sailors about her, or that she heard their crude remarks and lewd invitations. She kept her eye resolutely on Captain Mills as one by one the men about him saluted and withdrew. As he was about to turn away, toward the water, she hailed him.

"Captain Mills! May I have a word with you, sir?"

The Captain turned back and Elizabeth saw the flicker of surprise in his pale blue eyes as she approached him.

"Yes, miss?" he inquired politely, his eyes taking in every feature of her appearance. Captain Edward Mills had no idea what a lady of obvious quality was doing on the harbor at dawn, or why she sought speech with him, but he knew that it behooved him to treat her with the most careful respect. Many a career had been ruined because a sea captain, accustomed to despotic rule over his crew, failed to readjust to society's class structure when on land, unthinkingly behaving with less than proper civility to a member of the upper ranks. Captain Mills had no intention of joining that unfortunate company. So it was with some wariness, as well as respect, that he regarded the fur-caped young lady before him.

Elizabeth inspected his appearance as critically as he had observed her own. What she found satisfied her. Although his attire was far from elegant, his white captain's trousers and blue waistcoat were in good condition and surprisingly clean. The silver buckles on his flat leather shoes were highly polished; his stockings did not sag. Blue eyes stared out of a ruddy, weather-lined face, and though he looked a far cry from the splendid gentlemen she was accustomed to speaking with, he had the appearance of a decent, respectable man. Under the circumstances, that was all she required.

Elizabeth spoke pleasantly. "I understand, Captain, that you are sailing this morning for India. Am I correct?"

"Yes, miss, bound directly for Calcutta." Captain Mills gestured with his thumb at the vessel bobbing on the water behind him. "That's my ship, the *Windhammer*. We'll be leaving shortly now." His tone was respectful, but he could not keep a note of curiosity from creeping into his voice. For the love of the sea, he couldn't figure out what this girl, looking like a fairy princess from the story books, wanted of him. He experienced a vague uneasiness, which deepened considerably with her next words.

"I also understand that you have space available for one passenger. Is this also true?"

"Well, yes, miss, I must say it is, but it's not much, just a spare cabin and cot."

A cot! Elizabeth's heart sank. She hadn't expected luxury, but what the captain said suggested a lack of even minimal comfort, something for which she wasn't quite prepared. At the very least she had expected a proper bed! Nevertheless, she regarded him steadily and replied without betraying a trace of the doubt his words had created.

"Very well. Captain, my name is Elizabeth Trent. I would like to obtain passage on the ship. . .with your permission, of course." She gave him the smile that had melted so many other male hearts. "It so happens that I must journey to India immediately and your vessel offers the quickest transport."

Incredulity flooded Captain Mill's features, but Elizabeth continued smoothly. "Naturally, I will pay generously for my passage, as well as for any additional supplies required for an extra passenger."

"Miss, you can't mean that you want to travel with *us*?"

"Certainly." Elizabeth had been through this argument before, but this time there was a marked difference. Yesterday she had been dealing with people whom she knew and to whom she was close; moreover, they had been people reasonably near to her in rank. Captain Mills, a merchant seaman, was not. This alone made her situation easier. For although he might be shocked by the idea of giving her passage on his ship, he could not seriously refuse her demands. Both her position and her wealth made it difficult for him to defy her wishes, lest he incur the wrath of what the common called a "swell." She knew as well as he did that he had little choice in the matter, so she waited out his desperate protest patiently.

Captain Mills cleared his throat, but his voice emerged hoarse and nervous. "Beggin' your pardon, Miss, but do your parents know about this? I mean, I could get into a pack of trouble if it ain't all right and tight with them. I don't mean any disrespect or nothing, but. . .I don't want any trouble!"

"There won't be any trouble, Captain. I am journeying to India to visit my uncle, who is also my guardian, and I promise you he will be delighted that you have been so obliging. He'll be most generously grateful to you for assisting me in reaching him quickly." Elizabeth gave him her sweetest smile. She knew, of course, that Charles Trent would be outraged if he knew she was conversing with a merchant seaman, much less traveling on his craft, but she had no intention of telling that ailing gentleman the details of her journey—at least, not at first. There would be plenty of time for explanations after he was well again, and then, although he would be furious when he discovered how she had made the voyage, his anger would be directed at her, not at Captain Mills. Charles Trent was familiar with her stubbornness, and he knew just how persuasive Elizabeth could be. No, he would not blame Captain Mills.

So, airily dismissing the lie she had just told the Captain, she turned her mind to studying the effect her words had had on him. To her amusement, he looked like a hunted hare who recognizes his fate but still hopes desperately for escape.

"Miss, the cabin I have to offer isn't fit for the likes of you, if you'll pardon me for saying so. Wouldn't you be more comfortable waiting for a regular passenger ship? Sure now, your business with your uncle could wait for a regular ship?"

She spoke coolly. "My business with my uncle, Captain, is not your concern. It is my wish to set out immediately and I am willing to pay for my passage." She eyed him with raised brows. "Do you mean to refuse me?"

Under Elizabeth's haughty stare, the last of Captain Mills's protests died a quick death. "No, miss, I sure don't mean to refuse you," he said hurriedly. "Not a bit, you're most welcome."

He was rewarded by a cool smile.

"Now, right this way, miss, if you please. We'll be setting sail pretty soon, but I'll send Hawkins, the purser, to see you about extra provisions you might want, and we'll see that you get 'em quick-like. Watch your step now, Miss Trent."

Elizabeth hid her relief under a mask of calm composure and followed him sedately on board the ship. The *Windhammer* was a rambling, lengthy, three-masted merchantman with huge, billowing sails and an ornate carved figurehead of a flowing-haired, unsmiling woman at its bow. Crossing the wide, main deck with its hardwood floor and solid railing, crowded with spare sails, coils of rope, and barrels of tar, Elizabeth noticed two sets of stairs at both ends of the ship, one set leading up to the quarter deck and the other down into darkness. Captain Mills led her toward those in the stern, explaining that the other set of stairs was the forecastle companionway, leading to the crew's quarters below deck, as well as to the galley. He lit a wall-bracketed candle and led her down the steps through a narrow corridor. This section contained his private cabin, a supply room, and the cabin she was to occupy, which proved to be the first one to the left of the corridor. As Captain Mills fished about for the key, Elizabeth wondered wryly just what degree of hardship was in store for her. She took a deep breath as he swung open the door.

The chamber into which Captain Mills ushered her was barely larger than her wardrobe closet in Trent House. It consisted of a narrow cot with a lumpy mattress, covered by a rough woolen blanket of an indeterminate shade of grey, a small wooden chest with three shallow drawers, and a single yellow candle in a brass holder above the chest. The floor was bare, though the wood was scrubbed clean, and the wooden walls were also empty, save for a pair of crossed swords hanging over the cot. They were the only items of decoration in the room.

Elizabeth struggled to hide her dismay upon viewing such bleak surroundings, but something of what she was feeling must have shown in her face, for Captain Mills's voice held a faint but unmistakable note of satisfaction as he said:

"I told you it wasn't much, Miss."

She turned to face him, chin uplifted. "It will do very well, Captain. If you'll be so kind as to send the purser to see me, so that I may supplement a few items, I'm sure I'll be most comfortable." She moved to examine the crossed swords more closely. The metal gleamed sharp and silvery, and an intricate design bordered the blades.

"These swords appear to be very fine. Do they belong to you?"

Captain Mills grinned. "No, sad to say. They're Collins's. You see, my first mate, Collins, usually beds here. But his sister, no more'n a chit of a girl, ran off and eloped with some rascal, and Collins, he was madder'n fire. Begged leave to go after 'em, and I knew he'd be little use to me if he was frettin' and fumin' all the time. So I let 'im go. That's the only reason this cabin is available right now." He chuckled softly. "Thunder and turf, he was in the worst pucker!" He seemed to recollect himself suddenly, for the toothy grin faded from his face and he continued rather stiffly.

"Collins picked up those swords in France, after the war was over. Prizes 'em higher than anything, I expect."

"I don't blame him," Elizabeth responded. "They're very fine."

He bowed slightly. "Yes, miss. Now, if you'll excuse me, I've other business to attend to. Hawkins will be down directly to see you, so if there's nothing else. . ." His voice faded into a polite question.

Elizabeth had been thinking rapidly. Now that she had intimidated Captain Mills into taking her on as a passenger, she decided it would be wise to cultivate his friendship. As commander of the merchantman, he could make her journey pleasant or unpleasant in many small ways, depending on his whims. It was to her own advantage to see that he looked upon her with favor. With this in mind she smiled warmly, allowing a tone of friendliness to creep into her voice.

"Thank you, Captain Mills, you've already been more than kind. I have every confidence that with you in charge, the voyage will be both speedy and comfortable."

The Captain warmed noticeably. He rubbed his stubby hands together and his ruddy color deepened. "Well, now, thank you, miss. You just let me know if you need anything. Anything at all."

"I certainly will," she answered brightly.

When he was gone and she was alone, Elizabeth sank down on the cot. Wearily, she removed the heavy cape and tossed it beside her on the rough woolen blanket. The room was chill from lack of a fire, but she hardly noticed. Her head throbbed with the strain of the morning and she could think of nothing but that she was to be a prisoner of this tiny room for months to come. For a wild moment, she thought of calling Captain Mills back, of telling him that she had changed her mind. It was still early, perhaps she could even creep into her own house without anyone noticing. They would never have to know what she had attempted. But this desperate impulse faded as quickly as it had arisen. No, it would not do. She had made her decision and she would stand by it.

Outside, the sounds of tramping feet and men's shouting filled the air, telling her that the final preparations for departure were in progress. But it was quiet in the cabin. The ship swayed slightly with the rhythm of the sea and the air in the room was tinged with the smell of salt. Elizabeth sat up and took a deep breath. This was only the beginning, she warned herself. Once the ship left port she would be subject to all the hazards of sea travel. Long, chill days awaited her, filled with nothing but dreariness and the monotony of this horrid little room. The nights would be cold and lonely at best; at worst, ravaged by wild storms and raging winds. She wondered briefly if she would find that the nightmare of seasickness awaited her also. Well, she would face it, all of it. Whatever Captain Mills, or Mr. Melby, or Lord Thomas Penrith thought, she was as hardy as any man and she would prove it.

She stood up and dragged her portmanteau from the center of the cabin where Captain Mills had placed it to the wall where the chest stood. She began unpacking, concentrating on the reward that would be hers when she reached her destination. Whatever she had to face would be worth it, tenfold, if only she could help Uncle Charles. That was her purpose, and that was what she must think of. Nothing else! Determination swept through her, clearing her weary brain like fresh air blowing through a musty room.

She had nearly finished unpacking when a sharp rap sounded on the cabin door. That would be the purser, Hawkins. She straightened and moved to the door.

"Miss Trent?"

The man facing her spoke politely, softly, but something in his voice made the blood run cold in her veins.

"I'm Hawkins, the ship's purser." There was a pause, and then he continued with the faintest note of contempt. "What can I do for you?"

Elizabeth stared into his face, and felt a shiver of ice down her back. He was a tall man, with thin, greasy black hair plastered to his head, and a smooth, oily voice. His eyes, like two black olives, gleamed at her beneath thick dark brows, and beneath his right eye a jagged scar showed white against sallow skin. His mouth, smiling faintly, was thin-lipped and cruel. Beneath the dull blue seaman's uniform he wore, sinewy muscles bulged with obvious power, and the hair on the back of his hands was coarse and black.

For the first time since she had made her decision to leave England alone, Elizabeth was afraid.

"I. . .I would like to give you a list of items to procure for me," she stammered, with a vain attempt at composure.

"May I come in?" Again, that soft, insinuating voice.

She hesitated uneasily, but he was already edging forward into the room and she took a hurried step backward to let him by. As he passed close to her, the heavy smell of fried fish and oil met her nostrils. She took another step back and spoke rather breathlessly.

"Mr. Hawkins, would you like a written list, or should I just tell you the things I want?"

He smiled leeringly. "Why don't you just tell me what it is you want, Missy? I'll be happy to oblige you, any way I can."

Those black olive eyes ran over her from head to foot, taking in the graceful flow of her gown over her slender body, resting greedily on the place where the muslin tightly hugged her breasts. His tongue came out and licked the corner of her lower lip. Then his gaze fell on the open portmanteau at her feet.

Elizabeth saw it at the same time, and with a little cry, bent to close the lid over the lace underclothes still tucked inside. But he moved too quickly for her and before she could stop him he had grabbed a petticoat and was holding it in front of him, grinning appreciatively.

"Now this is real pretty, Miss Trent. The Captain told me a fine lady was on board, but I wasn't sure I believed him. I do now, though. You can always tell a fine lady by her clothes."

He laughed and ran his fingers over the white

lace, his mocking eyes fixed on Elizabeth's outraged features. With a cry of fury, she snatched the garment from him and thrust it behind her back.

"Get. . .get out!" she gasped. "Leave this room at once!"

He took a step forward. "But what about the list, Missy? You're forgetting that you asked me to come here." He sneered at her. "You need my help, remember?"

Elizabeth backed away, cheeks flaming, and fear stabbing through her like a finely honed blade.

"Candles. . .and bl. . .blankets! That's all I need! Please, just get out!"

The last words were almost shouted, but he paid them no heed. He advanced upon her as if she hadn't spoken.

At that moment, a noise at the door caught her attention. Hawkins heard it, too. He froze momentarily, then swung angrily about to face the open door.

"What do *you* want?" he snarled.

The boy to whom Elizabeth had spoken on the pier stood in the doorway, his mouth gaping. Dimly, Elizabeth recalled that he was sailing on the *Windhammer*.

At the sight of a harmless and familiar face, relief flooded through her and she gasped a little breathlessly, her eyes still on Hawkins whose sinewy body which seemed to fill the tiny room.

"Come in, boy!" She spoke quickly as the child hesitated, his wide brown eyes flickering uncertainly between her and the purser. "Mr. Hawkins was just leaving!"

Hawkins glared at him. The boy swallowed and

spoke in a high, frightened voice.

"We're hoisting anchor, sir. The Captain wants to see you."

"I'm going," Hawkins growled. His black eyes gleamed at Elizabeth.

"I'll get those candles and blankets you want, Missy," he hissed softly. "Anything else you want, too. After all, it's going to be a long, cold voyage."

With a knowing grin, he swaggered to the door, shoving the boy out of his path as he went.

The child went sprawling to the floor and as he fell, his head struck the wall beside the bed. Elizabeth, forgetting her own disquiet, rushed to kneel beside him.

"Are you hurt?" she asked anxiously. To her relief he seemed merely dazed by the blow, mumbling quickly enough that she shouldn't bother with him. She helped him to his feet, anger now replacing the panic she had felt earlier.

"I'm going to report that man to Captain Mills immediately," she stormed. She was trembling still as a result of her own scene with Hawkins but her voice was cold with fury. "He has no right to treat you in such a way. I shall see that he answers for it!"

"Oh no, miss!" The boy looked up at her in alarm. "Don't say nothin' about me, I beg you. I don't want no trouble!"

"But that man struck you," Elizabeth cried incredulously. She stared at him. "Surely he must be reported for such conduct?"

It was his turn to look surprised. "Oh no, miss. Why? I'm only the cabin boy."

"What difference does that make?" she demanded. "He has no right to beat you, particularly without cause."

Fear welled up anew in his face. "He didn't!" he cried hoarsely. "He didn't beat me! I'm not complaining, not at all! Please, don't tell the Captain!"

She understood then. "It will be worse for you if I do report it," she said softly. "Is that correct?"

The boy looked down. He mumbled something incoherent, and Elizabeth, after a moment, went on briskly. "Very well. I shan't say anything."

The ship lurched suddenly and a great shout went up from the deck above. Elizabeth felt the floor sway violently beneath her feet and then a gentle rocking motion took over. They had set sail.

The boy raised his head. He swallowed. "I've got to go, miss." His face brightened with a smile. "I'll be back later, though. I'm to serve you, did you know?"

"No, I didn't know." She returned the smile. "If you're going to wait on me, perhaps we should exchange names. I'm Miss Trent."

"Call me Henry," he offered. "Henry Davies, that's me." Then, tentatively, "You won't forget not to mention nothing about. . .before," he said, his eyes meeting hers earnestly.

"I promise you, I won't say a word."

With a grin of relief he was gone, whisking out of the room like a mouse in search of cheese.

Elizabeth bolted the door behind him. She stared at the lock, wondering if it would be strong enough to keep out Hawkins. Or anyone else, for that matter. The full danger and vulnerability of her position struck her suddenly like a heavy blow. She was marooned at sea, a woman alone, with a crew of rough, hardened seamen. She wondered now why she had taken lightly Mr. Melby's belief that she needed protection. These men were not like the gentlemen she was accustomed to associating with! Where those men had been diamonds, jewels of culture and refinement, these seamen were rocks— hard, rough, uncut. She remembered the hot breath and wet, ruthless kiss of Lord Milburne that night under the stars. Then she thought of Hawkins's greasy advances a few moments before. Repulsion gripped her with both memories, and her eyes swelled with tears. She had pledged after that night at the Carrington ball that she would never again be prey to the animal instincts of a man, and now, here she was, trapped and helpless at the mercy of a merchant crew. Blind and stubborn as she had been, she had fled the safety of her home for the prison of a ship, and the danger not only of the sea, but of the hardened seamen surrounding her.

For a good cause, she reminded herself desperately. For Uncle Charles!

Fresh tears welled in her eyes as she wondered what her fate would be on this voyage. What condition would she be in when at last she was set down on the shores of Calcutta?

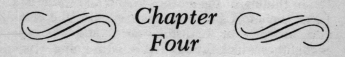

Chapter
Four

It was midday. The ship bustled with activity
and noise as the seamen scrubbed and swept the
deck, hoisted and maneuvered sails, checked ropes
and other gear. Captain Mills's voice boomed orders as he patrolled the deck, and the men shouted
in coarse, rough voices among themselves as they
worked. Elizabeth stood alone at the railing, tightly
gripping the slippery wooden bar as she gazed out
at the winter sea. The first week of the journey had
been fairly smooth, with the wind warm for October, and the ocean rippling with relative tameness
beneath the ship. Then, yesterday, a storm had
blown up, seemingly out of nowhere. The howling
wind had whipped the swirling green sea into a
mad frenzy until white peaks crested on the
monstrous waves and the ship was tossed about like
a helpless child in the hands of a giant. The storm
had raged relentlessly through the entire night, but
now, at last, its fury seemed to have subsided, at
least temporarily, and Elizabeth had taken advan-

tage of the opportunity to leave the chill bleakness
of her room and view the open sea before her. It
was the ninth day of her journey.

She took a deep breath. The air smelled strongly
of salt, and it left a tangy taste on her tongue, but
she found this invigorating rather than unpleasant.
She was draped again in the furred cloak, but it was
no longer the pure, dazzling white it had been at
the beginning of the journey. Wind and water had
taken their toll, but worn and soiled as the cloak
had become, it was still warm, and she was
thankful for thick fur and heavy satin lining which
helped to protect her from the bite of the wind.

Wondering anxiously if the storm had really
passed or was only gathering strength for a fresh
attack, she peered at the sky, leaden grey and thick
with scudding clouds. A heavy mist hung over the
atmosphere, and she could barely discern the inky
blackness that was the sea, with its restless waves
slapping greedily at the ship. Elizabeth had an uneasy feeling that the storm would return to ravage
them further.

But it wasn't the storm itself that concerned her.
She was dry enough in her cabin, and although the
tossing and rocking of the ship was uncomfortable,
she had found, to her relief, that she wasn't prone
to seasickness; that, at least, was one nightmare she
had been spared. No, it was the storm's effect on
the voyage that disturbed her. Already the
journey's length had been considerably extended;
their earlier speed nullified by the foul weather.
This was what gnawed at her: the knowledge that
each time nature's fury unleashed itself upon them,
the day when she would be at her uncle's side was
dismally postponed.

The deck creaked near her. Startled, Elizabeth spun about and looked into Captain Mills's ruddy face.

"Oh, Captain, good day!"

He studied her closely. "Were you expectin' someone else, Miss Trent? You sure looked surprised, and I might say, scared, when you heard me." His voice hardened suspiciously. "Any of my men givin' you trouble?"

"No, Captain, not at all," she assured him quickly. It was true; since that first day she had managed to avoid Hawkins, and to her relief, he had made no effort to seek her out. The cabin boy, Henry, had brought her the additional blankets and candles she had requested, and she had made it a point to spend as little time as possible on the deck where Hawkins, or one of the other seamen, could approach her. She dined alone, in the cabin, served by Henry, and only occasionally, when she could no longer bear the close confinement of the bare little room, did she venture onto the deck. The seamen sometimes called crude compliments to her, or stared boldly as she passed them, but she pretended not to notice, and so far, no one had dared to touch her. She knew that she owed much of this to Captain Mills, as well as to her own precautions of keeping to her room. She had discovered that the merchant captain was a strong commander, who tolerated no shred of disobedience from his crew, and Henry once confided to her that the Captain had made it very plain: no one was to disturb the "lady passenger." Elizabeth was grateful for his concern, and they had become friends. She knew that he respected her for not complaining about the conditions on board ship, and indeed, she made it a point to be undemanding. The conditions were miserable enough, with only briny salt pork, a meager ration of potatoes, and dry, hard bread for sustenance, not to mention the discomfort of the hard cot and the chilly room, but she knew full well that she had brought these discomforts on herself when she made her decision to embark on the merchantman, and she resolutely resisted complaint. In turn, she respected the Captain for his firm command and efficient management of the crew. He was a gruff, demanding leader who worked his men hard, but he gave them fair treatment and provided decent rations, unlike more mercenary captains who squeezed the maximum amount of work from their crews in return for the bare minimum of food and comfort necessary for survival.

"Do you think the storm has passed?" Elizabeth asked hopefully.

Captain Mills scanned the cloud-laden sky. "For now, perhaps. I expect it'll come up again later tonight, though. Those clouds don't appear to be goin' anywhere." He gave Elizabeth his rough, crooked smile. "Don't worry, though, Miss. We'll make it to Calcutta all right and tight, and without too much delay. Just so long as we don't meet up with any of those privateers, I'll be satisfied to put up with a few storms."

Elizabeth nodded vigorously. "You're right, of course. At any rate, I imagine we're safe enough in weather like this. Who would want to battle in this weather?"

The Captain rubbed his leathery cheek with a sunburned hand. "I wouldn't put anything past those rebel pirates, Miss. This fog would be nice and concealing if they wanted to get up real close to us before we even realized. . ." He broke off abruptly at the alarmed expression on her face.

"Beggin' your pardon, Miss Trent, I shouldn't have mentioned that to you. It's just the fretting of an old captain." He patted her hand in a fatherly way. "There's nothing to be worrying yourself about. I've got men posted to watch out for other ships, just like always, and they haven't spotted any sign of trouble. None at all."

Elizabeth thought his voice overly hearty; she glanced at him sharply. He was hiding something from her, trying to protect her in some way. Fear pricked her, but she remained outwardly calm.

"Well, if you're not worried, then I certainly shan't be," she said brightly, although her mind was racing, trying to remember all she had heard about the privateers.

She knew that they were legalized pirates, men authorized by the rebel colonies in America to disrupt British trade. Colonial trading merchants would outfit a ship with men and guns, and send it to sea, with the express purpose of capturing British trading vessels, both cargo and crew, By disrupting trade in this way, they hampered British morale as well as economy, and forced Royal Navy ships to patrol the seas in search of them, thus diverting warships from their offensive maneuvers. Royal Navy ships, instead of attacking colonial warships or capturing rebel ports, often found themselves assigned to patrolling the seas, protecting merchantmen from attack by private colonial craft. They were a nuisance, the privateers, whose job it was to disrupt and distract, but they were not to be taken lightly. The men who manned the privateer vessels were the cream of the adventurers—bold, daring, dangerous men who relished a fight and who had much to gain from the capture of British ships. Prize money was awarded to the crews who captured British vessels, whether merchant or warships, and many men had made their fortunes in this way. During these days of war, the rewards were temptingly high; rumor had it that cabin boys, who received the smallest percentage of the prize, often earned the equivalent of several years' wages from a single successful expedition.

Elizabeth remembered Thomas Penrith's warning about privateer ships that "haunted the seas." At the time the threat had seemed remote and impossible, but now, surveying the thick mist enveloping them, Elizabeth shivered. The threat of attack suddenly seemed very real, particularly with Captain Mills's unguarded words echoing in her ears. She wondered uneasily if he had reason to suspect impending danger.

Her thoughts were interrupted abruptly by the sounds of a scuffle behind her. Captain Mills heard it, too, and glanced sharply over his shoulder.

"What's this?" he demanded, even as Elizabeth stared, fists clenched, at the scene before her.

Hawkins approached them, dragging Henry alongside of him, his thick, hairy hands cruelly gripping the boy's worn shirt collar. Henry, struggling wildly, and with his face blotched red where he had obviously been struck, tried in vain to break free.

"I didn't do nothing!" he cried, half sobbing, as the purser hauled him up before Captain Mills. "I didn't, I didn't!"

"Captain, I caught this scum-rat with his claws

in the supply room," Hawkins rasped with satisfaction. "Looked to me like he was stealing extra lemon juice for himself, leavin' that much less for the rest of us." His fingers tightened on the boy's collar. "Admit it, you cur!"

Henry yelped with pain and Elizabeth gave a cry of protest.

"That's enough," Captain Mills commanded sternly. "Let him go, Hawkins."

Henry slumped to the floor as the purser loosened his grip, and Elizabeth bent over him anxiously, murmuring soft words of comfort. She raised her head to stare at Hawkins with blazing eyes.

"For your information, Mr. Hawkins," she spat out, "Henry was procuring the lemon juice on *my* behalf. He informed me at breakfast that Captain Mills ordered him to increase my intake, since my resistance to scurvy is probably lower than those more accustomed to sea travel." Scurvy was the dread disease of sailors, responsible for countless deaths. Even when death did not occur as a direct result, the weakness induced by the disease often laid the unfortunate victim open to the contraction of other illnesses. Lemon juice, however, was believed by many to successfully combat the disease, and large supplies of this substance were bottled and kept on board the ship, to be imbibed daily by the crew. "I believe Henry intended to serve me an extra portion at my midday meal," she continued furiously. "Have you any objection to that?"

Hawkins was scowling now, a look of pure venom in his eyes. He wet his lips with his tongue, his black olive eyes flicking from Elizabeth to Captain Mills, who stood frowning, with his legs planted solidly apart, hands on his hips.

"Well, Hawkins?" Captain Mills demanded in a dry, hard voice.

Hawkins cleared his throat. "I didn't know, sir," he offered rather lamely.

"You do now," the Captain said curtly. "The boy was following my orders. However," he paused, studying the purser with his shrewd blue eyes, "even if the boy had been stealing, you had no authority to discipline him. You should have reported him directly to me."

"I did, Captain!" Hawkins protested, his face reddening. "I brought him right up to you!"

"After striking him, and nearly choking the daylights out of him," the Captain barked harshly. "I'm the captain of this ship, Hawkins, and I decide when a member of my crew is to be punished. I won't have you, or anyone else, taking over the authority that belongs to me." His voice boomed across the deck, reverberating with anger. "Is that clear?"

"Yes, sir!" Hawkins's lips compressed together tightly, and he glanced toward Henry, who, with Elizabeth's help, was now sitting up on the floor.

Elizabeth read the hatred in his eyes, and with a tiny shock, realized that it was directed as much at her as at the boy. Why? Because she had championed him? No, deep inside she knew that, worse than taking the child's part, she had committed the unpardonable sin of witnessing Hawkins's humiliation. He was an arrogant man, and not likely to bear a reprimand with good grace, particularly when a woman was present. She suspected, with an uncomfortable twist of fear, that he would never forgive her, or the Captain, or Henry, for that singular humiliation. He would plot vengeance if he could, perhaps not against Captain Mills, but somehow, against her, or Henry, or both of them. They were vulnerable targets. More than ever, she realized, Hawkins was a man to avoid.

"You may go." Captain Mills nodded at him, and Hawkins saluted, departing with a final venomous glance in Elizabeth's direction. The Captain turned his attention to Henry, who was stumbling weakly to his feet.

"Are you all right now, boy?"

"Yes, sir," the child managed to say in a small, pitiful voice, but Elizabeth noticed that he was fighting back tears.

"Captain," she put in quickly, "may Henry come to my room and rest before he goes about his duties? He'll be bringing my meal soon, and perhaps he can take his meal with me—just for today, until he feels a little stronger." She gazed beseechingly at him, and the Captain nodded.

"Very well, miss. He's not much use to me in the state he's in now." He smiled kindly at Henry. "There boy, perk up. Miss Trent will see to you and then you can go back to work." He turned to Elizabeth. "Good day, miss. Don't you forget that extra portion of lemon juice!" He bowed slightly and strode away, loudly admonishing the gaping seamen who had ceased their work to watch the scene with Hawkins. With a flurry of activity, they resumed their duties, none wishing to incur their Captain's wrath, as had the unfortunate purser.

Elizabeth led Henry silently to her room. She sat him down gently on the bed, dampened a handkerchief in the cool water of the basin he had brought her earlier, and tenderly bathed the bruise on his face, which was swollen now and, she was sure, must be throbbing painfully.

"It's all right," she told him soothingly, as tears trickled down his pale cheeks. "That man will never dare to touch you again."

"I. .I'm scared," he confided, gamely attempting to gulp back the tears. "He'll be madder'n anything now!"

"Yes, but you heard what Captain Mills told him," she reminded him. "Believe me, he'll be too frightened to harm you again."

He peered up at her, his wide child's eyes curiously trusting. "Do you really think so, miss?"

She smiled. "I'm sure of it. But Henry, if he ever does hurt you in any way, or threaten you, I want you to tell me immediately. You know that Captain Mills won't tolerate such treatment, and there's no reason to be afraid of telling him. He'll know how to put a stop to it." She lifted his chin so that he met her eyes with his own brown ones. "Do you promise to tell me if there's any trouble?"

He nodded, the tears gone and a happy smile uplifting his mouth. "Thank you, miss," he breathed, and threw his arms around her neck. Elizabeth held him for a moment, then gave him a squeeze and let him go.

"Now, if you're feeling better, why don't you fetch my meal, and your own, and bring them both straight back here? We'll have a picnic together."

He was gone in a flash, his feet pattering hurriedly down the corridor toward the galley.

Elizabeth rose and paced around the room. Hawkins's face, livid with rage, floated in her mind, a permanent, ugly image. She wondered uneasily just how he would seek his revenge—and when. Well, at least his brutal mistreatment of

Henry would come to an end as a result of the incident on deck. She thought again of the little boy's position, an apprenticeship of virtual slavery with no time to spare for the enjoyment of childhood. It was so unfair! She reflected almost bitterly that his was the same fate shared by countless other British children who were unfortunate enough to have been born into the lower classes. The leisure and luxury she had known as a child were reserved solely for the aristocracy; those less well born never knew the pleasures of pony rides and Sunday picnics. And Henry's later life, she knew, would consist of only more drudgery and toil. A low born cabin boy could never hope to rise far in the world; at best, he might after years of apprenticeship, rise to a seaman's rank, but certainly not much higher. His position in the world had been determined at the moment of his birth, and there was virtually nothing he could do to improve his status.

It's shameful, Elizabeth fumed, that a child so bright and eager should be shackled to such a miserable existence. She wondered suddenly why the injustice of England's class structure had never before occurred to her. Not once in all her years of luxury had she questioned the system that allowed her to live in splendor while others eked out a squalid existence. Indeed, until this voyage she had never come into contact with those less fortunate than herself. Her circle had been select, a composite of England's most prestigious and pampered citizens. She smiled wryly, considering the reaction of those same ladies and gentlemen if they could read her thoughts at this moment.

The storm returned at midnight that evening and

raged feverishly until dawn, when it subsided into a steady torrent of rain. This continued most of the following day, forcing Elizabeth to keep to her room. Upon serving her evening meal, Henry disclosed that the rain had ceased, and she determined to have a quick stroll on deck before retiring for the night.

It was dusk when she ventured out. The wind had vanished with the rain and it was very still. Above, the sky was unlit by stars or moon, and the sea whispered below like a thousand dark creatures stirring in the night. Elizabeth shivered. The mist, if anything, was even thicker than before, a heavy, impenetrable cloak over the winter sea, muffling both sound and sight.

Huddling against the rail, Elizabeth wondered wistfully what gaiety was commencing in London at this very moment. No doubt an Assembly at Almack's, or a theatre party was in progress, or perhaps an evening of whist at one of the more stately mansions. Her London life seemed so far away now, a memory of a distant past, instead of, what? Ten short days ago? Something akin to regret touched her, and quickly she gave herself a mental shake. It would do no good to think of the past, to ponder what could have been, what could be at this moment. She had made her decision and it was the right one, of that she was certain. She must allow no room for doubt or futile regret, but must think only of the future. After Uncle Charles was well she would return to England, and resume her comfortable, happy life. She would forget this dreadful journey, with all its discomforts and privations— she would forget it had ever taken place!

Sighing, she turned from the rail, pulling her

cloak tightly about her as she moved toward the stairs leading to her cabin. It was dark in the passageway, and damp, and she picked her way carefully down the slippery wooden steps. The corridor was deserted and uncommonly dark. Why hadn't the candles been lit? She edged along the rough wooden wall toward the first door on the left —her door—a sense of uneasiness crowding in on her even as she fumbled in the sash of her blue muslin dress for the key she had placed there. Her fingers found the key, and she groped for the keyhole above the door knob. The darkness was thick, suffocating, and a sudden draught of terror crept along her spine. The next instant she knew why, as the pungent smell of fried fish and oil met her nostrils. But even as she opened her mouth to scream, a hairy hand clamped brutally down over her lips, and Hawkins's voice, a whispered hiss in the darkness, taunted her.

"Now, Missy, you don't want to make no noise, do you?" He chuckled softly in her ear as she tried to swing away from him, and his free arm pulled her roughly to him, pinning her back to his chest.

"You just give me that little key, and you and I can have a nice private talk!"

Elizabeth struggled desperately, but Hawkins wrenched her arm up and grabbed the key from her stiff fingers. He fitted it into the lock, still chuckling, and thrust her roughly before him into the cabin.

The candle she had lit earlier had burned low, but in the wavering light she could see his sallow face, gleaming with sweat, and the black eyes glowing triumphantly as he kicked the door shut behind him.

Elizabeth, one hand to her mouth where his fingers had bruised it, backed away. This couldn't really be happening, not to her! She read the hatred in his eyes, and with it something else. Lust—excitement. She knew that he meant to have her—now, tonight. Faint with terror, she managed to gasp, "Get. . .get out! You'll regret it if you don't!"

"I'll regret it if I do!" he sneered, and with a sudden lunge, gripped her arms in a vise-like hold and shoved her backwards onto the bed, tumbling heavily with her. Elizabeth tried to scream again, but he hit her across the mouth, once, twice, until she sobbed with pain. The narrow room was a black-edged blur; her head throbbed as if a million needles of light pricked her skull; dimly she felt his weight on her, pinning her to the cot, his breath hot on her face. . .her neck, and suddenly, his hands found her breasts. He attacked them greedily, his fingers ruthlessly tearing at the bodice of her dress and the lace of her petticoat beneath, until her full, creamy breasts, rose-tipped, were exposed. He gasped with pleasure and his wolfish fingers rubbed and fondled eagerly as Elizabeth bucked frantically beneath him, sobbing with pain and revulsion. His lips found her nipples and began to suck and bite at them; desperately she struck at him. Her fingers entwined themselves in his greasy hair and she pulled with all her strength. Cursing, he raised his head and struck her again, full across the mouth.

"I'll give it to you rough, if you want it that way," he panted.

"Please, just let me go," she begged, dizzy and half-blind from the force of the blow. "Please . . . don't do this!"

He laughed with brutal satisfaction. "So, the fine lady can beg, can she? Well, it's not going to do you much good, Missy. I want you, and I'm aiming to have you." His lips came down on hers in a wet, crushing kiss and he seemed merely amused when Elizabeth squirmed frantically beneath him. His hands moved once more to her breasts and began squeezing them, while his lips planted wet kisses on her throat.

"No. . .no!" she moaned, but he laughed again and his hands wandered slowly down toward her thighs. A fresh wave of panic washed over her, and with it, a flood of helpless despair. Her hair had loosened from its neat chignon, and tumbled, damp and tangled, about her face and throat, almost choking her. She struggled on with desperate strength, and as his fingers probed between her thighs, she gave a cry of sheer terror.

Suddenly there was a rush of feet above their heads, the sound of men running. Hoarse shouts and heavy thuds met her ears. Could it be that someone had heard her cry, that at any moment Captain Mills or Henry or another seaman, anyone, would burst through the door to her aid?

Hawkins had heard it too. He stiffened and sat up, straddling her, listening to the clamor and commotion above.

"Damn," he hissed savagely. "They must have struck at last!"

He heaved himself off the bed; his hand slid to his hip. A dagger gleamed there. Hawkins patted it with a grunt of satisfaction as he loped toward the door, but then he stopped, turning back to Elizabeth who was now sitting up, disheveled and bewildered. He gave her a final, leering stare.

"Missy, you can bet that when those privateers are finished with you, you'll be wishing mighty hard you were back in this cot with me!"

"Privateers!" she whispered hoarsely.

He nodded. "One of the lookouts spotted 'em before the storm two days ago. Captain hoped we'd lost 'em in the bad weather, but me, I've just been wondering when they'd strike." He grinned evilly at her horrified expression. "Lots of luck to you, Missy! You'll need it!"

He swung out of the cabin, and Elizabeth paused only long enough to straighten her torn gown so that it covered her breasts before she flew after him, racing up the steps of the companionway to the main deck. Attacked by privateers! Nothing could be worse! She knew full well the slight chance a merchantman would have against a sleek, powerful private craft. The *Windhammer* sported only six guns and a limited supply of powder, and besides, it was a heavy, clumsy vessel and couldn't hope to maneuver away from a more agile, heavily weaponed colonial ship. The privateer craft was sure to win!

At the thought of being taken prisoner by the rebels, her head swam, and she leaned dizzily against a wall, weakly surveying the scene before her.

It was a scene of confusion and clutter which met her dazed eyes, with men rushing about, daggers in hand, positioning heavy guns and dragging kegs of powder into place. Some brandished swords, all were sweating, and their eyes held a mixture of fear and grim resignation. Henry scampered by, pale and excited, and Elizabeth saw Captain Mills on the quarter deck, shouting at the men below. She fought her way to his side, unnoticed, even in her disheveled and nearly revealing state, by the throng of seamen swarming over the ship.

"Miss Trent!" Captain Mills barely glanced at her; he was peering alternately into the fog and below at the toiling men. "Go to your room, girl, and pray for a miracle!" he barked.

"Is there anything I can do?" she shouted.

"Stay out of sight!" he ordered tersely. "If those privateers get a glimpse of you, they'll fight like devils! We've got enough problems already! Now, listen to me, Miss, get down to your cabin and bolt the door. And don't come out for nothin'!"

She raced back the way she had come. Just as she reached the lower deck, a great shout went up and, whirling rapidly, Elizabeth saw the grey mast of a ship looming out of the heavy mist. There was a quick intake of breath among the seamen, and then all at once, a deafening roar, and the *Windhammer* shook like a naked tree in a winter blizzard. For a wild moment, Elizabeth thought that the storm had returned and that the noise was thunder booming. Then, as she saw smoke curling and men sprawled on their bellies all about her, she realized with a sickening thud that they were under enemy fire. She clung to the wall, horror spilling over her, unable to move. A cold, clear voice rang out of the ghostly darkness from the grey-masted ship.

"Yield!" it called with powerful, unmistakable arrogance. "Yield, sir, or take the consequences!"

Elizabeth turned her eyes toward the quarter deck, straining to see Captain Mills through the misty darkness. She wondered what his response would be to the privateer's imperious order. Her heart hammered in her throat, and she became suddenly aware that her nails had dug into her hands where she had clenched them. But she barely felt the pain; her mind was too crowded with nightmare thoughts and an unspeakable dread.

Captain Mills's answer was prompt and unmistakable. He shouted an order, and a barrage of fire from the guns lined alongside the *Windhammer*'s deck rattled in the night: the challenge had been met. Suddenly, confusion broke loose again as both sides fired together with violent zeal, and men fell, spouting blood on the deck from great, black gashes, and screams of agony sounded chillingly amid the din of gunfire. Elizabeth stared with horror-filled eyes at the scene of smoke and blood, her ears ringing with the clamor of battle. Barely ten paces away, a seaman collapsed in a heap of tangled limbs, his face contorted in anguish as he writhed helplessly before her eyes. An instant later he lay limply still. A ragged sob escaped her, and she shuddered uncontrollably. The stench of burning gunpowder and fresh blood filled her nostrils, choking her, but she couldn't move. She felt as if she were welded to the wall, a helpless, terrified witness of the spectacle before her, both fascinated and repelled by the awful violence of battle.

A hand tugged at her sleeve. Peering down through dazed eyes, she saw Henry, panting, his face even more pale than usual beneath the grime.

"The Captain sent me to tell you to get out of sight!" he babbled. "He's madder'n fire, seein' you still on deck. Better do as he says, miss, or we'll be in worse trouble!"

"I'm going," she told Henry weakly, and with a nod, he was off, dodging fallen bodies and flying sparks with incredible agility.

Elizabeth stumbled hastily back to her cabin, where she bolted the door. She knew immediately that it was a silly gesture. If by some miracle the *Windhammer* emerged victorious from the skirmish, or managed to escape, the bolted door would be unnecessary. Captain Mills would see to her safety, and no doubt incarcerate Hawkins for his attack on her. She would be safe, with or without a bolted door. But if the privateer should win the battle raging above, no door, no bolt, however strong, could protect her. They would storm the ship, taking all who survived as prisoners, and Elizabeth knew she would be worth more to them alive, as an object of their lust, than she would be dead. With a shudder she recalled Hawkins's words: *When those privateers are finished with you, you'll be wishin' mighty hard you were back in this cot with me!*

She paced frantically about the tiny room, listening to the tumult of battle above as suspense pounded through her body, building to a painful, almost unbearable tension. It seemed as if the battle had been raging all through the night—an endless, desperate struggle. Oh, when would it end? What would be the outcome? She yearned for some hint as to what was happening, but she could detect nothing, beyond the thunder of the guns and the cries of the wounded. From these she derived no comfort.

Just as she felt she could bear the suspense no longer, that she must risk everything and rush up to the deck to see for herself how the battle went, the night grew strangely quiet. She strained her ears for some sound, but there was none. No gunfire, no shouting, nothing.

She waited, hands clenched. And then, finally, it came—the sound she had been waiting to hear. Boots stamping down the stairs, the rasp of voices. Desperately she tried to distinguish them, praying that it was Captain Mills coming to tell her all was well.

The doorknob turned, rattled. A voice spoke. Then she knew. It was the same voice that had spoken out of the darkness from the grey-masted ship. A cold voice, arrogant and authoritative.

"Hand over the axe! We'll break it down!"

They were flailing at the door then with huge, lusty blows, and the wood was already splintering. It couldn't hold for long. Elizabeth's heart pounded wildly. She was trapped, penned into the tiny cabin, with the privateers' raucous voices filling her ears, and terror wholly consuming her.

"It must be that wench we spotted early on," a deep, bawdy voice rang above the others. "Hurry up, Simms. I've been thinkin' about her all night!"

With the words, something broke inside her. A little bit of the terror seeped away. It was replaced by anger, a hot, bursting fury that swelled inside her, pulsing through her veins like a powerful fever.

"Very well," she thought savagely. "If they want me, I suppose they'll have me. But I won't make it easy for them!" Her eyes flew about the room for a weapon, and eagerly fell on the crossed swords above the bed. With a cry she sprang forward and drew a long, shining blade from the scabbard. At that moment, the bolt splintered and with a shout of triumph, the men kicked open the door. Elizabeth whirled to face them, sword in hand.

The privateers spilled into the room, gaping at

her, their eyes bright and eager. They were a motley bunch, dressed in soiled, bloodstained breeches and striped jerseys, with sweat gleaming on muscled arms and dark growths of beard on their leering faces. Elizabeth barely noticed them, however; her eyes were glued to the man who stepped past them and stood, legs apart, facing her. He was a tall, powerfully-built man wearing black satin breeches and a white silk shirt, with ruffles gathered at the sleeves. The shirt was damp with sweat and clung to his body, revealing bulging muscles in his arms and shoulders. His hips were slim above thick, powerful thighs, and the hands placed solidly on them looked strong, with long, well-shaped fingers. His hair was black, and his skin tanned bronze, but it was his eyes that held Elizabeth's attention so firmly riveted. They were light grey, and cool, under black brows, and as they observed her, standing there with her hair shimmering rosy gold in the dying candlelight and her blue muslin dress revealingly torn and only barely concealing her generous bosom, they held something like amusement not unmixed with admiration. She flushed under his frank scrutiny, and tightly gripped the sword.

He raised an eyebrow. "It seems the wench wishes to do battle," he said to the men about him, his expression amused. There was a hearty burst of laughter.

"I shall, of course, oblige her." He drew from the scabbard at his hip a long, gleaming sword and bowed mockingly to Elizabeth. He raised the sword above his head. "*En garde.*"

Elizabeth's eyes shone like blue fire. The man thought to make sport of her! Well, she would show him! Her secret fencing lessons with Philip Harwood had not been in vain; she knew herself to be a deft, skillful swordswoman. Proudly, she raised her weapon, her dark blue eyes burning with stormy brilliance into his cool grey ones. He smiled at her, a smile full of arrogant mockery.

She attacked then, moving with swift agility, and he parried her attack only just in time. The grey eyes lit with surprise, one brow raised in acknowledgment of her skill, and then he in turn moved with amazing speed, cutting beneath her sword and dangerously close. Elizabeth parried at the last moment, her heart filled with a sickening dread. As they fought on, with quick, lightning strokes, her terror increased. She realized sinkingly the futility of her position. She could never hope to defeat this man, much less the gleeful, chortling mob surrounding him. She had been foolish to have even considered resistance; she saw that now. The man facing her, calmly parrying her thrusts, was a master swordsman, graceful and strong. His skill was far greater than hers, his agility remarkable for so large a man, and his strength overpowering. She was already tiring—she couldn't even keep up her defense much longer, much less strike offensively. She fought on desperately, trying not to heed the bawdy remarks called to her by the grinning men, and focusing all her weary attention on her opponent's movements. She knew she couldn't go on much longer.

The privateer struck then—a blow like lightning, but with the strength of a battering ram. Her sword flew from her aching hand to clatter hollowly on the wooden floor. Elizabeth's head flew up to meet her opponent's eyes; they were smiling faintly, and he pointed his sword at her breast.

Pale with terror, she slowly backed away. He advanced upon her, sword level, those grey eyes cold and deadly. He intends to kill me, she thought wildly. He actually means to kill me! She backed as far as she could, until the wall brought her up short, and she clung there, trembling, her eyes on the gleaming blade that moved steadily toward her. He stopped at sword's length from her, and raised the blade to her slender white throat. She stared at him with wide, terrified eyes. The men were strangely quiet.

"Yield!" he commanded, in that same arrogant, icy voice he had used before. "Yield to me, Captain Alexander Burke, as my prisoner—or face the fate of the vanquished." He smiled coldly. "Death!"

Elizabeth tried to speak, but the words stuck in her throat. A cold, empty sensation swept through her.

"What is your choice?" he barked harshly, and moved the sword so that it pricked at her throat.

"I yield," she whispered weakly. It seemed as if the room reeled and blurred before her eyes. Dimly she saw the gleam of satisfaction in his eyes, and then darkness clamped down, as she crumpled forward into a sea of blackness.

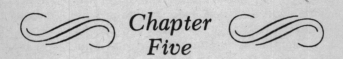

Chapter Five

She was lying on her satin sheeted bed in Trent House, with the pink coverlet pulled tightly up beneath her chin, and a warm fire glowing in the hearth. She was warm and comfortable and safe, and Uncle Charles was calling her, waking her for a morning picnic. His voice drifted to her as through a fog. . . .calling. . . .calling. No, it wasn't Uncle Charles's voice after all, it was. . . .another voice, oddly familiar. It was calling her. . . .calling. . . .

"Girl! Here, girl, wake up!"

Slowly, she opened her eyes. Memory crowded back, painfully, as she saw that she was not in her own room at Trent House, but in an utterly strange one, lying on a huge, walnut four-poster in a lamp-lit chamber. A black-haired man stood over her, his face dark with a forbidding scowl. At sight of him, a sob rose in her throat.

"Ah, you've come about," her fencing opponent remarked calmly. The scowl vanished, to be replaced by a cool, slightly amused expression.

"What. . . .happened?" Elizabeth tried futilely to control the quaver in her voice.

"You fainted. Fortunately for you, my reflexes are sharp, and I was able to withdraw my sword before you could fall upon it. As it was, you only fell upon the floor."

Elizabeth said nothing, but stared fearfully at him, and at the room in which she found herself. It was a fairly large, wood-panelled cabin, adequately lit by an oil lamp which rested on the sturdy walnut desk across from the bed. Behind the desk was a high-backed chair, and in the corner of the room, near a tall mahogany chest topped by a washbasin, sat a small round wooden table and another high-backed chair. The bed was covered with a patchwork quilt and several plump pillows. It was a modest, but comfortable cabin, much nicer than the one she had been occupying on the *Windhammer*, and Elizabeth realized with a start that the man before her must be the commander of the privateer ship. Dimly, she tried to remember. Yes, he had called himself. . . .Captain. Captain Alexander Burke.

Unnervingly, as if he could read her thoughts, he drawled, "You *do* remember what passed between us a short while ago, don't you? You yielded yourself as my prisoner." The grey eyes gleamed. "I hope I need not refresh your memory by drawing my sword once more?"

"No!" Elizabeth cried, so suddenly that he smiled and she bit her lip angrily. She hated herself for letting him see her fear, and resolved to show a braver front. Her chin lifted and she spoke with cold hauteur.

"I remember what happened, Captain Burke.

Pray be good enough to inform me what has occurred *since* I fainted."

The amusement in his eyes deepened. "Ah, the fine lady," he commented dryly. "Well, madam, I slung you over my shoulder like a sack of potatoes and brought you on board the *Hornet*, to my private cabin, where you presently find yourself. Your belongings were brought over by one of my men."

He nodded toward the corner. Her portmanteau rested there, with bits of clothing sticking out as if someone had crammed them in. "Do you wish to know what became of your fellow sailors?"

Elizabeth nodded. She was sitting still, her hands clasped tightly together.

"They are imprisoned in chains below. In the morning, I shall seek out the commander of the vessel, who merits special consideration, and will thus be locked alone in a guarded room. A small group of my men shall remain on the merchantman to steer her alongside of us." He paused. "There will be quite a pretty sum paid for this prize," he said speculatively. "But you, my dear, are the most valued prize of all."

He reached out to touch a blonde curl.

Elizabeth drew back, her eyes glittering like blue diamonds. "Do not touch me, Sir," she said coldly.

Burke stared at her, lying among the bedsheets, her hair flowing golden about her shoulders, her cheeks flushed a becoming pink. He laughed.

"I assure you, my sweet, that I shall touch you often in the days to come. But do not worry, you won't dislike it."

With a cry, Elizabeth sprang off the bed and rushed to the opposite end of the cabin. He did not try to stop her, but merely watched as she paced about the room, like a golden-maned lioness trapped in a cage.

"Why must you do this?" she cried, whirling to face him. "Why can't you let me go? I've done nothing to you."

His voice was cold, impassive. "Let you go? Where, you silly wench, in the middle of the ocean? Be my guest, if that is what you like."

She bit her lip, staring at him in tormented silence. She had never met a man like him before, so cold, so much in control. She was reminded faintly of Lord Milburne that night he had tricked her into walking in the garden with him. This man, this Alexander Burke, had something of the same cool, sophisticated charm. But there was more to him than that. He was undeniably attractive, a strong, rugged man with a lean, hard muscled body, that shock of raven black hair, and those grey eyes, so clear and keen. She had heard that Americans were a crude and boisterous breed, but this man had the quiet grace and the smooth, cultured voice to rival any English aristocrat. She sensed a sharp intelligence, and there was stubbornness in his jaw, a slightly malicious curl to his lips. He couldn't be more than thirty years old. She wondered suddenly how a man like this should come to be in command of a privateer ship, for there was something about him that spoke of wealth and refinement and she could easily imagine him the lord of a fine estate. She studied him silently, until he spoke again in a voice edged with mockery.

"And now, my sweet, I would like some information from you. To begin with, what is your name?"

She raised her chin proudly. "Elizabeth Trent."

"Now tell me, if you please, how did a lady of obvious quality come to travel on a common merchant vessel? For despite the wretched condition of your gown I can easily recognize that you are a lady of birth." There was a spark of curiosity in his grey eyes as they shrewdly raked her slender form.

"Necessity compelled me," she replied stiffly.

He made a gesture of impatience. "Do you forget your circumstances? I am not one of your servants, to whom vague statements are satisfactory. I am your master, commander of this ship, and you are my prisoner! I want to hear the entire explanation, and I want to hear it immediately. Is that clear?"

He took a threatening step toward her, the grey eyes alive with anger, and Elizabeth nodded quickly, fearfully.

"Very well! Continue."

She then told him the entire story, of Uncle Charles and his illness, the need for a ship sailing immediately to India. She stood straight, forcing herself to speak in a cool, distant voice. Despite the length of the room which separated them, she was intensely aware of his physical presence, of the strength in the lean, rugged body and the temper that had flared so suddenly and frighteningly a few moments ago. She had an awful suspicion of what it meant to be a prisoner of such a man, and fear was gnawing at her even as she talked, eating away at the calm she fought to preserve.

He listened attentively. When she had finished there was a short, tense silence.

"You must care deeply for this uncle of yours to go to such lengths for his sake."

"I do," she replied quietly.

"It is unfortunate that your ship crossed our path," he continued in that smooth, impassive voice she was beginning to know. "Unfortunate for you, and for your uncle. However, that is your problem and I cannot help you with it." She uttered a brief protest, and he silenced her with a frown. "My country is at war, Miss Trent, and I am doing my damndest to help her win that war. No price is too high." He paused, removing a gold enameled snuffbox from the drawer of the desk. He flicked it open and took a pinch of snuff. "My job is to capture British merchant vessels, or when feasible, small warships, and bring them back with me, thus disrupting British trade, and at the same time, diverting enemy battleships from American ports. The merchantman we've just taken, the *Windhammer*, is no exception, and its seamen are our rightful prisoners." He closed the lid of the snuffbox with a snap. "You, Miss Trent, have gotten in the way. But, again, that is your problem, not mine. You remain my prisoner, and I shall personally see that you don't forget it."

He turned away from her to seat himself at his desk, and began shuffling through some papers. For all his unconcern, he might have been alone in the cabin. Rage and frustration mounted in Elizabeth's breast. He had dismissed her, just like that! As casually and indifferently as if she were a puppet—a toy without feelings and rights. The cruelty and unfairness of her situation almost choked her. His prisoner! His prisoner, indeed!

"How typical that you brave Americans should choose to attack harmless merchant vessels and helpless women!" she taunted furiously, unable to contain her growing rage.

He lifted his head from his paperwork to regard her with raised brows. "We are a small people fighting the largest, most powerful empire in the world. We attack where and when we can, no matter how insignificant the target may seem."

"Why don't you attack a battleship if you're so eager to fight for your freedom?" she retorted.

He looked bored. "The *Hornet* is equipped with only twenty guns. Yes, I know, that is more than the merchantman carries; however, it is less than half the number sported by the average British warship. Oh, we attack Royal Navy vessels when the opportunity presents itself, and when we have a reasonable chance of victory. But in the meantime, we must content ourselves with less. . . .uh, spectacular quarry." He turned with an air of dismissal back to his paperwork, leaving Elizabeth speechless, with her cheeks flaming and her breasts swelling with indignation.

She wasn't at all satisfied with his calm response to her taunts; her anger remained unabated. Another thought formed in her mind, though, as she gazed restlessly about the room. Where was she to sleep? Several hours had passed since the battle, and she guessed it must be nearly midnight. Soon, Captain Alexander Burke would finish his paperwork and retire for the night. And she? She thought she knew the answer, and felt the terror once more pounding in her blood. This evening had been an interminable nightmare. Was it to hold even more horrors for her, in the bed of this strong, hardened man who looked at her with mockery and coldness?

She didn't have long to wonder. After a few minutes of shuffling through his papers and making brief notations with the tall quill pen at his elbow,

Burke shoved the chair back and moved away from the desk. Ignoring Elizabeth, he began unbuttoning his white silk shirt, until she gave a stifled shriek, and he stared at her in mild surprise.

"What. . . .what are you doing?" she asked hoarsely.

"Undressing. Do you object?"

"Please. . . ." she began, but he cut her short.

"I have no intention of raping you this evening, if that's what you're afraid of," he said impatiently. "I fought a long, hard battle tonight and I'm exhausted. I'm going to sleep. You may join me in the bed if you wish, or, you may sleep in the chair in the corner. It means nothing to me, one way or the other." He grinned at her, his eyes glinting with amusement. "When I take you, Elizabeth Trent, it will be when I am rested, and at my full strength, so that I can savor the experience to the fullest. Believe me, you are safe tonight."

Elizabeth stalked to the chair in the corner and sat down upon it. It was straight-backed and uncomfortable. She sat stiffly, her eyes averted from the man casually undressing before her.

"I'll take no chances," she flung at him savagely, studying the grain of the wood on the floor.

He laughed. "It will grow quite cold in the night, my sweet. You will stay awake shivering if you choose the chair."

She maintained a stony silence, and he shrugged, naked now, and dimmed the oil lamp on the desk. He settled wearily into the huge bed. Elizabeth glanced up from the floor. The room was as black as a pit; she could see nothing. She heard him though, settling comfortably between cotton sheets and thick quilt, adjusting them to his comfort, with the bed squeaking beneath his weight. Perched rigidly in her straight-backed chair, Elizabeth became even more achingly aware of how hard and uncomfortable it was. Her body ached from the strain of the evening's events, and she longed desperately for the warmth and softness of the bed. For perhaps half an hour she sat there, feeling the cold creep down her spine, and hearing the cabin grow quiet as the man in the bed stopped shifting, and his breathing became even and regular. Then, tentatively, she eased herself out of the chair. The floor groaned gently beneath her feet as she moved cautiously toward the bed, hardly daring to breathe. Slowly, carefully, she lowered herself into the four-poster. She still wore the torn blue dress, but she pulled the woolen blanket and heavy patchwork quilt up to her chin, devoutly grateful for their warmth, and for the heavenly softness of the bed beneath her. There had been no sound, no movement from the man beside her. Their bodies were not touching, but she sensed his nearness, and smelled his warm male flesh close beside her. Then his voice came out of the darkness, husky and disturbingly near, and she froze in terror.

"How did you tear your dress, Lizzie?" he asked softly.

Apprehension gripped her. "A. . . .a man on the ship. . . .Hawkins. . . .tried to. . . .He attacked me just before your ship appeared," she whispered.

There was a long silence while Elizabeth tensed herself, waiting for what would come next. Any moment she expected him to grab her, as Hawkins had done, using her to satisfy his animal lust.

"Hawkins, eh?" His voice was oddly quiet.

The bed creaked, and she stiffened, but he had

only turned over. She heard him settling the quilt about him once more, and soon, the steady, even breathing resumed.

She let out her breath in a long sigh of relief. He was asleep. For the present, it seemed, she was safe. And at least for tonight she had a warm, comfortable bed to sleep in. The four-poster was much roomier and softer than the cot she had been sleeping on for the past ten days, and she felt her weary body relax and snuggle into the downy plumpness. She knew she should be tense and worried, for she had no idea what new horrors the following day would bring, but somehow, she felt strangely relaxed. She found the soft breathing of the man sleeping beside her oddly soothing. As she lay there, sensing his presence in the big, cozy bed, the edginess and fear drained from her body, and she drifted off to a deep, dreamless sleep.

The bed, and the cabin, were empty when she awoke. Elizabeth lay still for a moment, getting her bearings, and then sat up with a jolt as she remembered where she was. She peered about the room. He was gone.

She had no idea what time it was, but from the sounds of flurried activity outside the solid oak door, she decided it must be midmorning. Scrambling out of bed, she rushed to the door and put her ear to it, listening. The scrape of feet and noisy shouts greeted her ears, and she turned away. Those sounds of shipboard activity were familiar; she had heard them every morning on the *Windhammer* for ten days. Yet, today it was another crew performing similar duties, not the seamen she had known. Those sailors, with the exception of Captain Mills, were in chains below. All of them—

Hawkins, Henry. . . .

Henry! She had forgotten all about him last night! Memory rushed back, and with it, dismay, as she envisioned the ragged little boy chained in a damp, filthy pit with the likes of Hawkins for company. Her blood froze at the thought. He was only a child, serving an enforced apprenticeship on the *Windhammer*—why should he have to suffer because of some silly war waged by adults?

Something had to be done.

Elizabeth paced nervously about the cabin, trying to choose her best course of action. Although her first impulse had been to sneak down to the hold in an attempt to free the boy, she immediately realized the futility of this plan. She would probably be stopped long before locating the hold, and even if she weren't, how could she hope to free Henry from iron chains? Besides, where would the child escape *to*? There was nowhere he could hide. No, the only solution was to approach Alexander Burke and plead for the boy's release. She set her lips together grimly. It wouldn't be pleasant, nor easy, but *somehow* she must convince Burke to be merciful with the child.

Rushing to her portmanteau in the corner, Elizabeth rifled through its contents in search of some presentable clothes. The white cloak had been crammed into the case, as well as the silver gauze ball gown she had foolishly elected to bring, and her other garments were in similar untidy condition. She shook out the dresses and the cloak and hung them in the wardrobe near Burke's desk, reflecting bitterly that if she was to be imprisoned in this cabin she may as well take advantage of its facilities. With critical eyes she surveyed the few morning dresses she had brought with her. There was a rose colored muslin, and the yellow satin with white bows, but she shrewdly decided that these were too simple, too modest, for her purpose. She needed, more than anything else, to appear elegant and cool, and completely in control. She must impress Captain Burke with her wealth and social position. He must see that he ought to treat her with respect! Only by commanding his respect could she hope to influence him with regard to Henry's fate.

A basin of clear water and a plump towel rested on the mahogany chest, and stripping off the torn blue gown, she rinsed first her face and hands, and then her throat, breasts, and arms in the cool water. It wasn't nearly as satisfactory as a bath, but it *was* refreshing, and she patted herself dry with the thick towel almost gaily. She turned briskly back to the wardrobe, drawing forth a violet silk dress with long, tight-fitting sleeves and a high, lacy ruffle about the throat. She donned the gown over a clean white petticoat, gaining confidence from the rustle of the silk as she straightened the bodice. She searched once more through the portmanteau until she found her hairbrush, and when the tangles were gone and her hair was smooth and glossy, she pinned it up with practiced expertise. Finally she surveyed the results of her efforts in the oval mirror beside the mahogany chest.

Gone was the tousled girl who had faced Burke last night with blonde hair straggling about her shoulders and a tattered dress only barely concealing her bosom. The woman who gazed back at her now was elegant and composed. The only sign of her previous ordeal was a faint, reddish bruise on

her cheek where Hawkins had struck her, but it
was barely discernible. She smiled at herself,
pleased with the results of her efforts. The violet
dress fitted snugly, emphasizing her full breasts and
slender waist. Moreover, the high lace ruffles circling her throat added a touch of sophistication.
Wide violet eyes, their brilliance enhanced by the
matching color of the gown, smiled back at her
from a delicate oval face, and her hair, piled high
on her head, with only a few sausage ringlets
dangling about her ears, shone brightly gold. She
moved away from the mirror feeling happy and
confident. Now she would see what Captain Alexander Burke had to say to Miss Elizabeth Trent of
London.

The deck was crowded with brawny, busily
working sailors, but Elizabeth saw no sign of Captain Burke. She paused at the head of the companionway and gazed about her at the sparkling beauty
of the day, her breath escaping her in a gasp of delight. Never had she viewed anything more splendid.

The last of the mist had lifted and vanished, and
the sun now shimmered silver in a satin blue sky
dotted with puffs of snowy clouds. As far as she
could see, the ocean sparkled a bright diamond
blue, until it met at the distant horizon with the
magnificent sky. The breeze fluttering the masts
above smelled invigoratingly of salt and sea, and
the pleasant, tangy taste of salt was on her tongue.
She savored it, blinking her eyes against the dazzle
of silver and blue about her.

It was the third of November and the weather
was unusually mild. Although the afternoon would
be chilly, the morning sun was warm, and she was

glad, after all, that she had decided against donning the soiled white cloak, whose worn and dirtied condition would add nothing to the elegance of her appearance. No, it was better like this, with the rustle of silk about her legs, and the wind tickling the hairs on her neck. She felt alive and strong, and sure of her success with Alexander Burke.

She swept regally along the deck, ignoring the open-mouthed stares of the sailors. Chin uplifted, she glanced coolly about for the Captain. He was nowhere in sight.

A short, wiry seaman approached her somewhat hesitantly, his straggly brown hair falling in his eyes and a confused, almost apologetic expression upon his homely face.

"Excuse me, miss," he began, his brown eyes embarrassedly meeting hers. "Does Captain Burke know you're. . . ."

"I wish to speak with Captain Burke immediately," Elizabeth interrupted him haughtily. "Please direct me to him at once."

The man licked his lips nervously. "He's on the quarter deck, miss, but I don't think you'd better go up there. . . .Wait, miss! I wouldn't do that if I were you. . . .the Captain won't like it!"

But Elizabeth had already swept away toward the flight of wooden steps leading to the quarter deck. She mounted them swiftly, without so much as a backward glance at the distraught seaman. The Captain won't like it indeed! If she was to survive this journey unscathed, she must show Alexander Burke that she was not his puppet—his prisoner!— to be treated in whatever way he wished. Her rich attire and the aristocratic, polished manners she had cultivated since her birth were her only weap-

ons. She must use them to intimidate Burke as she
had Captain Mills and the sailor below; somehow,
she must force him to treat her as was her due. This
was the first step, and if he didn't like her seeking
him out on the quarter deck, it was too bad for him.
She would show him that she did not fear his dis-
pleasure—indeed, he must learn to fear hers! The
splendor of her gown and the brilliant beauty of the
day gave her confidence and strengthened her
hopes. In the light of this glorious morning, defeat
seemed impossible. . . .

As she neared the head of the stairs, Elizabeth
became conscious of an odd, hissing sound, and
heard the murmur of subdued voices. A moan
reached her ears, low and agonized. What was
that? What was going on? The sound punctured
her spirits, causing a little bubble of tension at the
core of her composure. Breathlessly, she reached
the top of the flight and stared in amazement, and
with growing horror, at the scene that met her
eyes.

A knot of men stood on the far side of the quarter
deck, their clothes torn and stained with dried
blood, their hands crossed together in heavy chains.
Elizabeth recognized them as the *Windhammer*'s
crew. Behind and around them stood other seamen,
obviously from the *Hornet*, for they carried evil-
looking bayonets, pointed levelly at the chained
prisoners. But the attention of both prisoners and
captors alike was centered, not on each other, but
upon the man lashed to a post before them. His
back was naked, except for the rivulets of blood
which ran down it, tracing a pattern like that of
raindrops on a window pane. With a gasp, Elizabeth recognized him. It was Hawkins.

Twenty feet away from him stood Alexander Burke. He was clothed in black breeches and a white silk shirt which was open at the throat, revealing an expanse of muscular, tanned chest covered by crisp black hair. His boots were black and gleaming in the morning sun. A wicked-looking leather whip glistened in his right hand. He was just about to raise it, but at the sound of Elizabeth's gasp, he turned his head slightly and saw her. His eyes narrowed.

"What are you doing here?" he demanded.

All eyes turned toward her. She noticed that Captain Mills, his arm in a sling, waited beside Burke, and ignoring the latter's question, hurried forward to address the *Windhammer*'s commander.

"Captain, I'm so sorry to see you injured. Is it serious?" The calm concern in her voice masked a rising nervousness.

Captain Mills cleared his throat. "It's nothing, miss, nothing at all. I'm glad to see you looking so well."

"Forgive me for interrupting these civilities," Burke's sardonic voice broke in. "But Miss Trent has not answered my question. *What are you doing here?*"

She met his gaze then and with a shock saw the blazing anger in his eyes which belied the coldness of his voice. In spite of herself, she found herself stammering. "I. . . .wanted to speak with you. . . .about something. It's. . . .important."

"I don't recall giving you permission to leave my cabin," he replied. There was a glint in his eyes. "But since you're here, you may remain. It may do you good to witness the punishment for a prisoner who disobeys my commands."

He turned grimly back to Hawkins and raised the whip above his head. With cruel, nearly incredible force he lashed it forward, and Hawkins gave a little sob of agony as the leather ripped into his flesh.

"Twenty-one," Burke said impassively.

Elizabeth closed her eyes, feeling waves of nausea wash over her. Hawkins was a villain, it was true; she had not forgotten his brutal attack, and she still had a bruise on her cheek to remember him by. But he did not deserve *this*—nobody deserved this! She wondered weakly what he had done to merit such a severe punishment. Burke had said he wanted her to witness the punishment of "a prisoner who disobeys my commands." Was he warning her that she might share the same fate?

Again and again the whip fell, until finally Burke pronounced: "Twenty-five!" in that same, terrifyingly calm voice. There was a pause. "Tucker, cut him down. Get some ointment from Doc Blake and have one of his fellows see to him." His deep voice rose to include the other men. "Dismissed!"

Elizabeth opened her eyes. Hawkins, half-dragged by a tall, husky youth, was being led past her down the stairs, his face ashen, the black eyes she remembered so well dazed and blood-shot. After him, accompanied by their guards, filed the prisoners, head down, chains clanking. They smelled of filth and sweat, and Elizabeth's head swam as they passed her. She swayed slightly, and Captain Mills grasped her shoulder with his good hand.

"There, miss, it's all over now. Are you all right?"

She nodded and tried to smile at him, fighting

back the sickness. She must get a hold on herself! Her dealings with Burke must be from a position of strength, not one of fainting submission. She summoned the remnants of her courage and turned to face him.

Burke's cool grey eyes studied her face, but he spoke to Captain Mills. "Captain, you may go," he said politely. "Don't hesitate to send for Doctor Blake if your arm pains you."

The rival commander nodded curtly. "Thank you, sir." His voice trembled with the effort of civility toward this Yankee upstart who had beaten him. He hesitated. "I'd like to say a word or two on behalf of the young lady, Captain, if you don't mind. She's been through a bad time. . . ."

Burke cut him off coldly. "My business with Miss Trent does not concern you, Captain Mills. Now, if you'll excuse us. . . ."

A hawk-faced sailor standing behind Captain Mills reached forward and tapped the older man on the shoulder. The captain, his face like stone, gave Elizabeth's elbow a final squeeze and turned abruptly away on his heel. He strode down the steps, closely followed by the guard.

Elizabeth watched him go and then turned back, white-faced, to Burke. He was really angry, she could see that. Beneath the impassive set of his features a muscle twitched in his jaw, and his eyes were like blazing steel. They were alone, except for the seamen working single-mindedly on the rigging. The cheerful sounds of whistling came to her ears, curiously incongruous with the mood of uneasiness which had settled upon her. Her violet eyes met his, and widened at the expression of fury they encountered.

"Now, if you please, tell me what matter was so important that it led you to leave the cabin without my permission." His voice seethed with anger.

Elizabeth lifted her chin. "I was not aware that I needed your express permission to leave the cabin."

His eyes narrowed to grey slits. "You are my prisoner! You do not have free run of this ship. I see that I must teach you what that means!"

"It was important!" she retorted. "How was I to know when you would return so that we could discuss it?"

"Tell me what was so important," he ordered grimly.

Elizabeth faltered. Up to this point, the encounter was not going at all as she had planned. Instead of being impressed by her fine appearance, he seemed merely angered. His eyes, wandering down her body, taking in the clinging silk, the richness of her gown, seemed to grow even steelier, his lips clenched more firmly together. He still held the whip in his right hand, and for one awful moment, she feared he might strike her. But he just stood there, piercing her with his eyes, waiting tensely for her reply. Why had she sought him out? For a moment she could think of nothing but her plan to impress him, to intimidate him into treating her properly, and she wondered wildly why she had ever entertained such a foolish hope. Then, ashamed that she had forgotten for even a moment, she remembered the original cause of her venture.

"Captain Burke," she began pleadingly. "I believe there is a boy, a child really, chained with the men below. . . ."

"The prisoners were here a few short moments ago," he interrupted. "Did you see a child among them?"

She stopped as if he had struck her. Frantically, she tried to recall the scene of a few moments earlier—the prisoners bunched together, surrounded by armed guards. Henry had not been one of them, she was certain. She would have noticed him if he had been present! A horrifying thought crossed her mind as she had a mental vision of him the last time she had seen him, dodging gunfire and fallen bodies on the deck of the *Windhammer*. Perhaps, in the course of battle, Henry had been. . . .

"No!" she gasped. "Oh, no—not killed!"

Alexander Burke smiled grimly. "Was this child a friend of yours?" he suggested mockingly.

Her eyes flashed. "Yes, he was!" she retorted. With a start she realized that they had both spoken in the past tense.

There was a short, awful pause during which she felt the color drain from her face. Then Alexander Burke spoke calmly. "Allow me to relieve your mind, my sweet. Your little friend is safe and in my care." He laughed at her outraged expression.

"Why. . . . why did you lead me to believe. . . .?" she sputtered.

"That he was dead? It amused me."

"Where is he?" Elizabeth demanded.

"Suffice to say that he is not in chains," he replied smoothly, and then a frown came over his face. "Which is where you may shortly be if you do not accept your status here a little more readily."

It was Elizabeth's turn to be blazingly furious. He had deliberately frightened her about Henry merely because it "amused" him, and now he was threatening to chain her like a common criminal! Her violet eyes became a deep, stormy blue and she felt her cheeks grow crimson as the boiling anger spilled out. "Captain, your treatment of me thus far proves beyond all doubt that you are the worst kind of a beast and barbarian! For your information, I am English and I am a lady. My family is one of the finest in Britain! Your treatment of me as a common criminal is outrageous, and I won't stand for it any longer." Her voice shook with open contempt. "I have a fortune in trust for me in England, and if it's money you want, I can see that. . . ."

The back of his hand struck her full in the face, and she tumbled backwards, sprawling on the deck. All about them the sailors stopped their chores to stare, but Elizabeth was aware of nothing but the throbbing pain in her head, and the tall, dark man looming over her, whip in hand. She gasped in pain and shock, and fought back the tears which were straining to spill from her dazed eyes.

"You are speaking of Miss Elizabeth Trent," he flashed. "But Miss Trent is no more. You are now only Lizzie, my prisoner and my servant."

She stared up at him, her eyes wide with disbelief, her heart pounding like waves in a storm. Lizzie! He had called her that last night, before falling asleep, when he had asked her how her dress had been torn. Then she had barely noticed, but now the name rang with insult. She wanted to cry: "I'm not your common Lizzie—I'm Elizabeth Trent, belle of London society!" but she said nothing, merely staring at him with parted lips, one hand to her swollen cheek.

"You may begin by scrubbing the main deck," he said, in that same hard voice. "That was Jack Hill's job, along with Tucker's. Hill was killed in the skirmish last night, so it seems almost appropriate that you should take over for him." He studied her mockingly. "His clothes come close to fitting you, too. Now get up."

Slowly, unsteadily, she began getting to her feet, but not quickly enough for Burke. His arm shot out and jerked her upright, his fingers closing cruelly over her slender wrist, and then he stomped down the stairs to the main deck, dragging her ruthlessly behind him and shouting for Simms, his lieutenant, to fetch Jack Hill's clothes on the double.

By the time they reached the cabin, Elizabeth's head was whirling, her humiliation and confusion and anger melting into a flame of hatred for the man whose brutal grip was bruising her wrist. Simms, a burly, red-haired man, appeared in the doorway and silently handed Burke a pile of worn-looking clothing. He was dismissed with a curt nod and Alexander Burke grimly closed the cabin door. He released Elizabeth's wrist and shoved her roughly away from him. She stared at him in mute fear. He tossed the bundle of clothing at her.

"Put them on."

"You can't mean. . . ."

"I do." His voice was hard. "I don't have the time or the inclination to tolerate spoiled society bitches, Lizzie. The sooner you learn to do as you're told, the better off you'll be." He made an impatient gesture. "Now take off those fancy clothes."

This was impossible—it couldn't really be happening to her! She clenched her teeth, and unable to help herself, shouted, "I won't! You can't make me, you. . . .you Yankee filth!"

He took one quick step toward her and the blow this time knocked her back on the bed. She lay there sobbing, but he yanked her to her feet. The biting note in his voice stung her like a whiplash.

"Do as I say, Lizzie, or I'll rip that dress from you myself."

She stared tearfully at him. He meant it. Of course he meant it. He had already shown himself to be a brutal, ruthless man, capable of anything to achieve what he wanted. She hated him—hated him with all her heart! Yet, she had no choice. She must do as he said. Trembling, she turned her back to him and began to unfasten her gown. His voice cut at her like a sword blade.

"Turn around! This way."

Slowly, with the tears streaming down her pale cheeks, she turned to him. His face was like a mask, the features set and impassive, all except for his mocking eyes, which held a glint of satisfaction. With shaking fingers she slowly unbuttoned the front of the dress, and the bodice fell away to reveal her frilly white petticoat. The violet dress fell with a swish about her feet, and with a tiny sob, she slipped off the petticoat, standing before him exposed and terrified. Barely able to see through the blur of hot tears that burned her eyes, she reached hurriedly for the clothing that had belonged to Jack Hill, and pulled the grey and yellow striped jersey over her head to cover her bare shoulders and breasts. She grabbed the grey woolen breeches and pulled them up. They were loose, but a rope sash tightened them so that they would stay up, and although the jersey fit loosely also, it provided complete coverage. That was all she cared about. Her hair had come loose from its chignon when Burke had hit her on the quarter deck, and now it streamed about her shoulders. She didn't care. It didn't matter anymore.

She felt numb, dazed. She hardly noticed when Burke led her out to the main deck, introducing her as "Lizzie" to the tall, husky youth who had led Hawkins away after the whipping. The boy's name was Ben Tucker, and he showed her what to do. How to dump the ragged mop in the bucket of soapy water he brought, and to mop the deck, and rinse it, and polish it on her hands and knees. She worked all afternoon side by side with him, bent over the floor until her back ached and her knees and hands were red and sore from kneeling and scrubbing. She did as he told her automatically, feeling oddly deadened, detached, as if none of it were real, as if it were only a strange, grotesque dream.

At dusk, she returned to Burke's cabin. Simms brought a silver tray laden with food for Burke, and a separate tin one with a small portion of salt pork and potatoes for her. Even when Burke seated himself at the little round wooden table and calmly ordered her to serve him, she felt nothing. The hatred she had felt for him this morning remained, but it was still, motionless—like a raging river that has suddenly become a glassy pond. She served him, and stood behind his chair while he ate, and when he had finished and retired to his desk, she sat in a wooden chair and ate her own meal, tasting nothing. Simms came to remove the trays, and she moved like a sleepwalker toward the bed. Burke's voice froze her.

"Don't climb into that bed in those filthy clothes," he warned. As she halted in confusion, he rose from the desk and crossed to the mahogany chest, drawing forth one of his own silk shirts. He tossed it to her. She put it on silently, aware only of

how soft the silky material felt against her skin in
comparison to the rough wool she had been wearing all day. She climbed wearily into the soft bed,
unmindful of the man working at the desk less than
five paces away, and pulling the thick coverlet up
to her chin, fell into a heavy, exhausted sleep.

Alexander Burke rose from his desk and strode
over to the bed. He stared down at the girl sleeping
there, her blonde hair tangled on the pillow,
blankets pulled snugly about her shoulders, a bruise
on her cheek. He cursed under his breath. Why had
he behaved as he did? He was angry, deeply angry,
but this time it was directed against himself.
Strange feelings churned within him as he gazed
down at her, experiencing a jumbled mixture of anger, shame, and desire. She was beautiful, yes; that
he could not deny. There was an aristocratic quality
to her features, a grace and dignity that even the
shabby clothes he had forced on her could not disguise. But there was more than beauty to this girl.
Beneath the cool, composed exterior smoked a passionate nature; he was sure of that. He had seen her
eyes glow with anger, her cheeks flush. That had
been rage, it was true, but he sensed that she was
capable of passionate responses in other ways, as
well. There was a fire in this girl, a flame which for
some reason he had tried to extinguish today.

At present, he reflected grimly, it seemed he had
been successful. She had been like a shadow tonight, a pale image of the vibrant girl who had
whirled to face him last evening with a sword in
her hand and battle in her eyes. Somehow, though,
he suspected that the flame had not been ex-
tinguished, only gutted temporarily. Half smiling,
he wondered when it would flare up again. He

longed to pull back the coverlet and gaze at her slender white body beneath the sheer silk of his shirt. He remembered the magnificent loveliness of that body as she had stood naked before him that morning, and how he had had to fight to retain his mask of composure, to suppress the almost over-powering desire to take her in his arms and tumble her backwards onto the bed, to take her quickly, brutally, and to release inside of her the torrent of rage and desire that swelled within him. But he had mastered that desire, and somehow, tonight, he had watched her under veiled lids as she moved me-chanically about the cabin. Now he felt the desire swell within him once more, and he quickly turned away. Damn, he had enough troubles as it was, without some golden-haired goddess to complicate things.

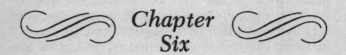

Chapter
Six

A week passed, and then another. Elizabeth barely noticed. Her days had become a pattern of work and sleep, and she barely remembered a life other than the one in which she was now immersed. Every morning she was hauled out of bed, clad in nothing but the silk shirt Burke had given her, and commanded to serve his breakfast. When he was gone, she dressed quickly and hurried out to the deck, where Ben Tucker handed her the mop, pointed to the water-filled bucket, and told her what portion of the ship to clean. She had become so used to the shabby breeches and striped jersey she wore day after day that she hardly noticed their roughness against her skin anymore, and the cold blasts of wind which whistled about her in the afternoon seemed barely to affect her; she was too damp and warm with sweat from the effort of mopping and scrubbing to notice the chill. She didn't even bother to pin up her hair in the morning—it would only come down, and besides, why should she bother to look neat? Instead she let it swirl freely about her shoulders as she worked, concentrating only on completing the day's labor before dusk so that she could return to the cabin, and after serving dinner, go to sleep. She had become more or less used to the grueling, rigorous work she did every day, and she was no longer as wearily exhausted in the evenings as she had been at first, but she preferred sleeping to spending time with Alexander Burke. So far, he had not touched her since that first day. In fact, he had treated her with icy civility, merely giving her orders and going on about his business without so much as a glance at her. She, in turn, obeyed his commands quickly and silently, whether they be serving his evening meal or fetching a bar of soap from the supply room. There was a wall of ice between them, and as far as Elizabeth was concerned, that suited her just fine. The less she had to do with Alexander Burke, the better.

Ben Tucker, though, was another matter. He was a tall, strapping boy with a wide, disarming grin, a thatch of curly blond hair and mischievous blue eyes. Elizabeth guessed that he was about her own age, perhaps twenty at the most, and she was well aware of his boyish appeal. He had the same kind of gay, happy-go-lucky charm as Thomas Penrith, without the intolerable stuffiness that had angered her so when last she had seen that proper young Englishman. Elizabeth liked Ben, and she was grateful for his company. It had been a long time since a young man had made her laugh and flirted with her; her days in London as the toast of the town now seemed distant and unreal. She barely remembered a life where she had known total leisure, and had nothing to do but attend parties and charm eager young men. Ben Tucker and his cheerful good humor were now her only diversions. As she worked side by side with him, an easy friendship sprang up between them.

One cloudy, blustery afternoon they were working on the quarter deck. Far below, grey and forbidding waves crashed against the sides of the ship, and Elizabeth, fascinated by the endlessly changing colors and motions of the sea, had paused from her scrubbing to lean against the wooden railing and peer down into the chilly, mysterious depths.

"I had never seen the sea before I set out for India," she mused aloud. "I never imagined it could be so. . . .marvelous."

"I know what you mean," Ben agreed, glancing up at her from where he was cheerfully polishing the wood with a soft cloth. "It's my first journey, too. I had to *beg* Mr. Burke—I mean, *Captain* Burke—to let me come." He laughed. "At first he wouldn't hear of it."

Elizabeth stared at him curiously. "Why did you call him Mr. Burke?"

"Well, actually, Lizzie, I've known him all my life as Mr. Burke, and it's not easy to begin calling a man something different after so many years." He paused at her expression of confusion. "He's not a real ship's captain, you know. He's only been doing this since the war started. I guess he decided that if he was going to outfit a privateer he'd better go along in charge and see that the thing was handled right."

He broke off as a step sounded on the stairs and Elizabeth whirled guiltily to see who was joining them. For a brief moment she feared that Burke would catch her resting, but to her relief, it was only Henry, scampering across the boards toward them, a smile lighting his small, round face.

The flushed, beaming child who approached them bore little resemblance to the dirty, ragged boy Elizabeth had first seen on the London dock. His torn clothes had been replaced by a clean, if somewhat oversized jersey and a pair of brown cloth breeches with patches on the knees, both of which belonged to Ben, who at Captain Burke's request, had given them to Henry, and seen that the baggy breeches were secured by a rope sash similar to Elizabeth's. Ben had also scrubbed Henry from head to toe with a thick brush and a cake of strong soap; consequently, the saucer-eyed boy skipping toward them, rather comically dressed in enormously oversized clothes, appeared cleaner, healthier, and in much better spirits than Elizabeth had ever seen him before.

Captain Burke, it seemed, had taken Henry under his wing. Elizabeth discovered this on the second day of her enforced labor on deck, when Burke had strolled up with Henry tripping along at his heels, like an eager puppy following his master. Despite the humiliation of her position, she had felt a strong desire to laugh at Henry's astonished expression when he saw her kneeling, rag in hand, beside a bucket of water. He had swept down upon her, his arms clinging to her neck as he bubbled over with declarations of happiness at seeing her. She hugged him and responded in kind, only to learn that "the Captain is a first rate fellow!", who knew everything there was to know "in the whole world." He had followed this naive pronouncement with the information that: "Captain Burke's going to see I'm taken care of when we get to

America!" At these words, Elizabeth had shot a
startled glance at Burke, who lounged calmly
beside her, looking relaxed and amused.

"America?" she had faltered. "Is that where
we're going?"

"You heard what Henry said," he replied lazily.

"Isn't it grand, Miss?" Henry exclaimed. Then
he seemed suddenly to again notice her odd appearance. He glanced uncertainly from her to Captain
Burke. "Miss, why are you. . . .I mean, Captain,
why is Miss Trent. . . ."

"Miss Trent is following my orders, Henry. And
I'm afraid we must not disturb her any longer; she
has much to do. Come along, boy, I want to show
you something."

Elizabeth had glared after him as they sauntered
off. Oh, if only she were a man—she'd break that
arrogant Yankee's neck! How dare he treat her so
insolently! And yet—the same man showed kindness to Henry. It was strange that he had taken
such a benevolent attitude toward the cabin boy,
and such a cruelly unreasonable one toward her.
What had she done to deserve his malice? She had
found no answer to this question and had turned
drearily back to her scrubbing. Henry's excited
words echoed in her head. Were they really headed
for America? If so, she would never see Uncle
Charles again. A sob rose in her throat, but she
choked it back. Crying wouldn't help. If she was
headed for America, nothing would help her now.

That had been two weeks ago, and she was still
no closer to knowing their destination. Ben was
close-mouthed and evasive whenever she broached
the subject, and she had not had an opportunity to
further question Henry about it. Pride forbade her

to plead with Alexander Burke for a straight-forward answer.

Now, as Henry skidded to a halt before her and Ben, she smiled at him. "Good afternoon, young man. Haven't I warned you about running across these wet floorboards? One of these days, you're going to break your neck!"

"I have a message for you," he announced importantly, dismissing the scolding with perfect unconcern. "From the Captain!"

"What's up, monkey?" Ben tugged affectionately at the youngster's ears, eliciting a delighted squeak of laughter. Ben, it seemed, was only second in Henry's idolatrous eyes to Captain Burke himself. When he wasn't trotting at Burke's heels, he attached himself to Ben, who treated him like a favorite younger brother.

"The Captain wants you to finish up here straight away," he informed them wisely. "There's a storm brewing, 'cording to Simms, and the Captain says you're to help Richards and Daws with the rigging, Ben. Miss, he wants you to wait for him in the cabin. He's planning an early supper."

Elizabeth and Ben scanned the sky. "Simms is most likely right," Ben sighed. "Sure is getting cloudy out there. Well, thanks for the message, monkey."

Henry laughed and with a wave, ran back the way he had come.

"I don't mind finishing early," Elizabeth said with relief, gathering up the damp rags and the mop as Ben lifted the half-filled bucket. They started down the steps, moving slowly and carefully over the stairs they had scrubbed that morning. Her thoughts, however, were not about the impending storm or the welcome treat of a shortened working day. She was pondering again how strange it was that Alexander Burke should show such extraordinary kindness to Henry Davies. It did not seem possible that the cold, hard-hearted man she knew could be the same one who treated the boy with tolerance, even indulgence, or who, for some unfathomable reason, had won Henry's worshipful adoration.

"Ben," she said suddenly, "isn't it odd that Captain Burke should show Henry such kindness? He doesn't seem at all the type of man to care for children."

Ben continued steadily down the steps. "Captain Burke? Why, he's always going a step out of his way for folks not as well off as he. You don't believe it? Lizzie, I could tell you stories. . . .and I know, too, seeing as I've known him all my life, and worked for him almost four years now. You'll never meet a better man."

Elizabeth was silent, pretending to be concentrating on watching her feet as she negotiated the narrow steps, clutching the mop and rags in her arms. She digested Ben's words confusedly. They were high praise from an outspoken young man like Ben Tucker who certainly wouldn't be afraid to voice his criticism aloud. She said stiffly, "Really? He appears quite differently to me."

"Well, you just don't know him real well. Besides, Captain Burke isn't overly fond of women. My ma has said for as long as I can remember that Mr. Burke'll never take himself a wife, not after what he's been through." Ben broke off abruptly, and Elizabeth, seething with curiosity, was about to ask him what his mother had meant, but he changed the subject hurriedly. "Not that there haven't been a pack of women trying to prove her wrong!" he grinned. "That fellow's a regular devil with the women. They swarm over him like a nest of wasps over a strawberry tart!"

"Oh?" Involuntarily, she spoke more coldly than she had intended, for Ben flushed and shot her a quick, embarrassed glance.

"I beg your pardon, Lizzie. I was forgetting about you and the Captain. . . .you know, sharing the cabin and all. . . ."

"It's all right, Ben." She felt the hot blush steal into her cheeks to match his own embarrassment. Ben, along with the other privateer seamen, believed that she was Alexander Burke's mistress as well as his deck servant. She was well aware that they had been warned from the first against molesting or insulting her, and she knew that she owed this sanctuary to Burke's protection. But along with that protection went the humiliating conjecture that she was "the Captain's woman." The men all knew that she and Burke shared a cabin and a bed, and it would never have occurred to them to doubt that Burke did not seek his pleasure from such a tantalizing source. She herself had wondered almost resentfully why, since that first evening when he had promised to "take her", he had never approached her or given any indication that he found her desirable. Not that she wanted him to, of course! The idea was revolting—she abhorred him more than any man she had ever known! Still, it irked her that he appeared unaware of her charms. But Ben and the rest of the crew took it for granted that she and Burke were lovers, and Elizabeth was too embarrassed by the subject to discuss it with him and correct that faulty impression.

They continued down the stairs in uncomfortable silence, until Ben, upon nearing the landing, jerked the bucket accidentally and some water sloshed over the rim onto the floor at the precise spot where Elizabeth was setting her foot. With a cry, she slipped and would have fallen, but Ben grabbed her arm and held her upright, overturning the bucket and spilling almost all of the dirty water at the foot of the steps. Elizabeth, supported by Ben's strong, bronzed arm, turned to meet his eyes, a combination of dismay and laughter widening her own. They stared at each other for a full moment, and then amusement overcame consternation. They began to laugh, holding on to each other and rocking back and forth in the puddle, the previous strain between them forgotten in the absurd hilarity of their situation.

It was in the midst of this riotous scene that Captain Alexander Burke came upon them. He watched for a moment in frowning silence, his grey eyes narrowing to dagger points. When he spoke, his voice was edged with anger.

"Well, well, isn't this a pretty scene? Really, Lizzie, I had no idea you would find a servant's life so amusing."

Elizabeth froze as if she had been turned to marble, and Ben hastily removed his hands from her shoulders. The grin with which he faced Burke, however, showed neither fear nor guilt.

"We had a little accident, Captain," he explained easily. "Lizzie nearly fell on some spilt water."

"That *is* amusing," Burke replied with biting sarcasm.

Elizabeth raised startled eyes to his face, surprised at the bitterness and anger in his voice. It was a dramatic departure from the icy civility with which he had treated her in the past weeks. Was the truce over then? Why? What had caused him to speak so, and to regard her with such a hard, piercing stare which made her flesh seem to shrink?

"It was an accident, Captain," she said quietly. "We'll clean it up straight away."

"Ben will clean it up," he contradicted harshly. "You will come with me."

His strong fingers gripped her elbow and bore her irresistibly along with him. Ben began to offer further explanations, to place the blame on himself, but Burke cut him off and stalked away, sweeping Elizabeth along with him.

Confusion and anger battled within her. She cast an apprehensive look at his features as he dragged her along with him. The grey eyes were alight with anger, and a muscle twitched in his jaw. His mouth was grimly set. He flung her before him into the room and kicked the door shut, his eyes never leaving her face.

"Now tell me," he said, in a voice of steel. "What was that little scene with Ben Tucker all about?"

Elizabeth tossed her head defiantly, and began to rub her elbow where his fingers had bruised it. "Ben told you. Some water spilled and I nearly fell. He caught me, and the rest of the bucket overturned." She glared at him. "It seemed quite amusing, since we'd spent all morning cleaning that very spot. I do hope, Captain Burke, that laughter is not forbidden to one so lowly as a deck servant."

Burke's fists clenched, but his voice was even enough, and filled with contempt. "*I* hope, Lizzie, that you have not forgotten your position on this ship. Your job is to clean the deck, not to indulge in vulgar flirtations with my crew."

Vulgar flirtations! That was too much! A spark of fury caught fire somewhere inside her, making her eyes sparkle like blue sapphires. "How dare you!" she cried wrathfully. "You twist and distort an innocent friendship, perverting it with your own foul mind! We were laughing, do you hear me? Laughing!" Her voice had risen to a hysterical pitch as the weeks of dreary labor, of drudgery and obedience, took their inevitable toll, aided by her torturing doubts about the future. She lunged suddenly at Burke with wild, clawing fingers, screaming her rage and venom.

He grabbed her wrists as she threw herself at him and held her tightly. Elizabeth struggled madly to break free—to strike out at him, to claw his face—but she was helpless beneath his powerful grip. Finally, in fury and despair, she began to sob, her diatribe never ceasing, but becoming a shrill, hysterical recitation of the wrongs inflicted upon her.

"And now you won't even tell me where we're going, or what's to become of me! It's tearing me apart, this crazy uncertainty, can't you see that?" Her sobs became louder, more convulsive. "What's to become of me? Haven't I a right to know even that?" She choked on a rising sob, and broke off, still fighting his cruel grip.

Burke watched her closely, his expression undergoing several changes during her outburst, but Elizabeth's vision was too blurred with tears for her to see. Though the softening of his features escaped her, she heard with surprise the quietness in his voice as he abruptly released her wrists.

"Sit down and calm yourself. I want to talk to you."

She collapsed on the bed, still sobbing uncontrollably, and he stood over her for a moment in some uncertainty until a knock at the door drew his attention. It was Simms, with the dinner trays.

Burke took them from him, ignoring the red-haired lieutenant's curious glance past him at the weeping girl upon the bed. "Thank you, Simms," he said shortly, almost closing the door on the lieutenant's bulbous nose. Burke set the trays down upon the table and said in a mild voice, "Come sit with me, Lizzie. I wish to talk with you over dinner."

Elizabeth raised her tear-stained face to peer at him. He had already seated himself, and made a gesture for her to do the same in the chair opposite from his. She stared at him incredulously.

"Come, girl," he said impatiently. "You heard me right, come take your dinner with me. We must talk."

She rose slowly and moved toward the table, sitting down gingerly at the seat he had indicated. A smile touched his eyes at the caution with which she took her place.

"I'm not going to bite *you*," he teased, almost gently. "It's my dinner I want to bite."

Elizabeth was under control by then, but she felt weak from the release of tears and all the pent-up emotions which had plagued her for weeks. She ate silently, not glancing at her companion, who kept up a steady flow of conversation about the repairs needed by the ship, the impending storm, the consequences of bad weather on their progress across the Atlantic. He studied her intently all through the meal, and when he had finished, he leaned back in his chair.

"Lizzie, you said you would like to know where we're going," he said slowly.

Her head flew up, interest sparking in her still swollen eyes. She said nothing.

His eyes never left her face. "Our destination at the moment is Madagascar."

"Madagascar?"

He nodded. "We'll be arriving there before too long. As I said, there are some necessary repairs to be made to the ship, and to the *Windhammer*, as well as fresh supplies to be bought before we head back to America. Also, I'm hoping to intercept another merchant ship in the area. It's a popular route." He smiled. "I'm not quite sure what to do with you once we're back home, however. It would be absurd to put you, a private British subject, and a mere girl at that, in a prison camp, and there will be quite a scandal, I'm afraid, if I bring you home with me." She flushed and the amusement in his eyes deepened. "Much as I would like to, of course."

The blush deepened, but she lifted her chin proudly and made no reply. Burke laughed. "Lizzie, it amazes me how even in those rough, dirty clothes you're wearing, with your hair loose and tangled, and your face swollen from crying, you can still look like a damned princess any time you please."

"And you, Captain, despite your elegant speech, always look like the ruthless pirate you are!" she retorted, taking in the black hair falling over his dark brow, the cool grey eyes, and strong, stubborn jaw. His silk shirt was open at the throat, revealing his broad, hairy chest, and his hands, resting on the table, were tanned and strong-looking. Elizabeth had known many men in her days as London's pet, but she had never encountered one to match the dark, powerful virility of this American privateer. She had observed him giving orders to his men, supervising the running of his ship, and had marveled at the vibrant, dominant power he exuded. He was an unmistakable leader, a hard, shrewd commander capable of quick judgment and astute decisions. When he was with the crew or working at his desk, there was a warm, vibrant sense of power about him. With her, she was conscious of an icy reserve. He still exuded, unquestionably, the aura of the authoritative commander, but the intensity of his personality, of his whole being, was subdued, like a wild stallion held in check. He was a puzzle to her, a mystery, a man of contradictions. Now, although she expected him to be angered by the insult she had just shot at him, he responded with amusement, his eyes gleaming.

"Lizzie, you astonish me. I expected at least some measure of gratitude for informing you of our destination." He shook his head. "Your lack of gratitude wounds me more than any insult you could hurl."

"Thank you!" she spat out sarcastically.

A great laugh burst from him, and slowly, involuntarily, a smile tugged at her lips. For a long moment there was a pause. Their eyes met, and Elizabeth was intensely conscious of the rain pounding on the deck above, of the howl of the wind rushing above them. The ship had begun to rock giddily, and the pewter dishes and tableware were rattling about on the table, but she hardly noticed. Her eyes were locked on those of the dark-haired man opposite her, and for one long moment, she could not look away.

There was a sudden, startling roar of thunder and the mood was abruptly broken. Hastily, she stood up and began to gather the soiled dishes and knives and forks together on the trays. Burke rose also, but slowly, leisurely, his face thoughtful as he moved to his writing desk. It was some time before Elizabeth could bring herself to glance at him again, and when she did she saw him, head bent, apparently absorbed in his reading. She looked away quickly, aware of the silence except for the raging storm outside, and of his presence, disturbingly near. It seemed as if they were the only two people on the ship; indeed, on the sea itself, and it occurred to her suddenly, electrifyingly, that it was going to be a long, tortuous night.

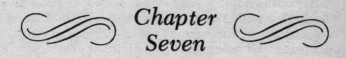

Chapter
Seven

The morning dawned dim and cheerless, with a steady drum of rain and the wind whipping relentlessly at the *Hornet*'s battered sails. Elizabeth awoke to find Burke already gone from the cabin, and she wondered bewilderedly why he hadn't awakened her as usual. She dragged herself from the bed to pull on grey breeches and jersey, sifting in her mind the events of the previous day and night.

Ben Tucker's words about Alexander Burke particularly interested her. She was not surprised by the fact that women "swarmed over him", as Ben had put it. After all, he was an undeniably handsome man, with a definite air of elegance, despite his rugged, tough appearance. No, his magnetism with women didn't surprise her one bit. What baffled her was the statement Ben's mother had made, predicting that Burke would never marry, not after "what he's been through." What had Alex Burke been through? Even Ben admitted that the older

113

man was not fond of women. Why not? Perhaps, Elizabeth mused, he had been jilted by some girl; that would explain why he was so cold and reserved with her, why he treated her with distrust and hostility. A seething curiosity burned within her as she searched for an explanation of her captor's behavior. She had an overwhelming desire to understand him.

His behavior last night only added to the contradictory nature of his personality. He had been furious after discovering her and Ben on deck, laughing and holding on to each other. Then, after her own outbreak of unleashed fury and despair, his mood had altered strangely; he had become a quiet, almost sympathetic companion—even inviting her to dine with him! The remainder of the evening had been one of odd tension, with Burke working at his writing desk, giving Elizabeth brief, restless glances from beneath his brows, and she in turn busying herself with mending her blue dress, all the while stealing nervous, puzzled glances in his direction. They had lain in the great bed that night, as the ship danced about on the wind-lashed sea, listening to the rain beating overhead, acutely conscious of each other's presence. Every nerve in Elizabeth's body was stretched taut, and her eyes stared wide at the wood beamed ceiling. She knew that Burke, too, was far from sleep, and fear vied for supremacy with some other, less easily definable emotion in her breast. She was confused and more than a little alarmed by her own feelings, but she refused to explore them. She only knew that it was many hours before she slept, and sleep, when it came, was fretful and disturbed. She didn't know that Alexander Burke, beside her, didn't sleep at all.

Now, after dressing, she shook out the sheets and coverlet, smoothing them over the four poster. She found she couldn't stop thinking about the previous night. Her thoughts were interrupted, though, by the creak of the cabin door, and her heart began beating a little faster. Alexander Burke strode into the room, wet and dripping. His face looked drawn and tired beneath his tan, and his black hair clung damply to his head.

"Good morning, Lizzie," he said wearily.

"Good morning. You didn't waken me today. Is something wrong?"

"Wrong? No. It's still raining, though, so you won't be able to work on deck. I've some shirts that need mending; you can work on those."

She nodded and turned back to tidying the cabin. The iron mask was back in place; the wall of icy civility had clamped down between them once more. At least, she reflected, he wasn't angry with her. And it had been kind of him not to awaken her as early as usual. She wondered if he knew how little she had slept last night.

As the morning continued, so did the rain. Elizabeth worked at her mending, and Burke came and went, returning to his desk between supervisory inspections about the ship. In the early afternoon, Elizabeth took advantage of his mild humor to risk a request she had been considering for some time, but had not dared to broach. Quietly meeting his piercing gaze, she asked to be allowed to visit Captain Mills in his guarded room. Burke looked thoughtful for a moment and then shrugged.

"I see no harm in it. I'll tell the guard to expect you this afternoon."

Eagerly, with something close to optimism, Eliz-

abeth later made her way across the slippery boards
of the rain drenched ship. She huddled tightly in
her white cloak, which still provided a warm shield
against the icy wetness of the winter storm, even
though its onetime splendor was lost forever. She
must have looked a ridiculous figure to the staring
seamen she passed, a slender form draped in a
soiled cloak, with grey woolen breeches and stockings showing beneath when the wind blew the
folds of the cloak away from her body. She stomped
along in the brown leather boots that were several
sizes too big for her, holding the hood about her
face while several strands of gold hair escaped to
swirl in the wet, driving wind. But Elizabeth
wasn't thinking about her appearance as she made
her way, almost blind from the rain striking her
face, to the cabin where Captain Mills was kept
under guard. She was thinking only how good it
would be to see the ruddy, dependable face of a
man she liked and trusted.

The prospect of the visit accounted partially for
her raised spirits, but in addition, there was the
knowledge of the *Hornet*'s destination, and a tiny,
unformed plan which had taken root in her head.
Elizabeth had decided, one way or another, to
make her escape while the ship docked in
Madagascar. As of yet she had no clear idea how
she would manage to flee the ship and seek hidden
shelter on land, but she was fully determined to
find a way. She would think and plan, and once
they had docked she would watch for her opportunity. It was this inner resolve which uplifted
her spirits, igniting a spark of hope in her breast.
The feeling of helplessness and despair which had
engulfed her during the past weeks faded under the

knowledge that she could, in time, take action to save herself. Soon, if all went well, she would be free of Alexander Burke and his damned privateers!

The guard nodded politely and stepped aside as Elizabeth reached Captain Mills's door. She opened it and stepped quickly inside.

The room where the old merchant captain was imprisoned was really a storeroom. Coils of rope, spare sails, canvas, flannel for cartridges, flints, and copper sheathing took up almost all the space. A corner had been cleared, and a cot set up in it for the Captain, but aside from that, the tiny room was crowded with ship gear, so that she had to pick her way carefully across the floor to where Captain Mills was rising with alacrity from the cot, an expression of unbridled pleasure brightening his face.

"Well, miss, if this isn't a dandy surprise! Come right in, now, and set yourself down." He beamed at her, but all at once became aware of her clothes beneath the cape, and of the heavy boots on her feet, and he stared at her in astonishment.

Elizabeth laughed, settling herself on the hard cot. It reminded her of the one she had slept on while traveling on the merchantman. The four-poster she slept in now was a great deal more comfortable, and she wondered briefly how she had ever grown accustomed to the cot. Then her attention was recalled by the dumbfounded expression upon Captain Mills's face, which was rapidly being replaced by one of outrage.

"Don't tell me that rebel captain has made you wear those clothes, miss!" he exploded.

Elizabeth nodded ruefully. "Yes indeed, Captain. I'm afraid my circumstances have undergone quite a change since I set out upon this journey. I'm

now only a common deck servant to our illustrious
Captain Burke."

The ruddy old sea captain slammed his fist
against the wall. "That bloody devil ought to be
horse-whipped!" he ejaculated.

"I agree with you perfectly." She forced a smile.
"But speaking of horse-whipping, I recall that the
last time I saw you, when Mr. Hawkins was
being. . . .disciplined. . . .by Captain Burke, you
had a sling on your arm. It's gone, I see, but tell me,
are you fully recovered?"

"Yes, thanks be said." He rubbed his right arm
vigorously. "It's as good as new, I'm happy to say.
I hope Hawkins has healed as well."

She regarded him curiously. "Captain, what happened that morning? I never understood why Burke
was beating him. Did Hawkins try to escape?"

"No, miss, that wasn't the way it was at all. After
we were captured that night, I spent what was left
of the evening in the hold below with my men."
He shook his head ruefully. "Compared to that hell
hole, this room here is a paradise. Well, at any rate,
early in the morning, we heard boots stomping
down the steps and suddenly torches were shining
in our faces. It was Captain Burke and a handful of
his men, armed to the teeth, let me tell you. Burke
ordered us all to stand up and give our names and
ranks. As soon as he heard I was the Captain, and
saw my arm was in bad shape, he saluted me and
said I was to see the doctor. Then he turned back to
the others. He was as cold as ice, that fellow.
Looked 'em all over real slow, and then says in that
high'n mighty way of his: 'You—Hawkins!' Well,
Hawkins turned paler than a grounded fish. He
opened his mouth, but nothing came out! Burke

just smiled, cool as you please. I've seen a lot of tough characters in my day, miss, but this Yankee, he's a dangerous one. I could tell right then, just by that lazy old smile, with the steel showing in his eyes. He said he wanted Hawkins to help him out with a little demonstration—of what happens to prisoners who misbehave. I swear, miss, I'll never forget it; those men were as silent as death itself, and Hawkins, all he could do was croak. I guess you know the rest." He rubbed his jaw with the familiar gesture she remembered. "You can believe that those men will think not twice, but three times, before they try to make any trouble on *this* ship. Burke sure showed himself as a man who'd tolerate not a speck of nonsense."

"I see," Elizabeth said slowly. She wasn't sure that she did. Ever since that first morning she had wondered why Burke had given Hawkins twenty-five lashes with his whip. Captain Mills's explanation that it was a means of intimidating the prisoners was reasonable, but it didn't explain why Burke had singled out Hawkins for his victim. Could it have something to do with the fact that she had told Burke the night before of Hawkins's attack on her? Somehow, she couldn't believe that he had punished the purser on her behalf. Still, why else had Hawkins been selected out of all the other crew members?

"He's a hard man, all right," Captain Mills continued. "But his treatment of me has been none but fair, I grant him that." His shrewd blue eyes scanned her face. "And you, miss? How are you faring?"

Elizabeth blushed. Captain Mills, like everyone else on the *Hornet*, must assume that she had become intimate with Burke. Confusingly, she wasn't certain whether she was more embarrassed to confess that he hadn't molested her than she would have been if forced to admit that he had. She shrugged, trying to appear casual, although she felt the heat of the blush burning her cheeks. "I'm well," she replied, avoiding his gaze.

The old sea captain leaned forward and patted her hand with his gnarled one. "Begging your pardon, miss. I sure didn't mean to be embarrassing you. Damnation! Doesn't that scoundrel have an ounce of respect for a fine young lady like yourself? It's barbarous!"

"I'm afraid Captain Burke doesn't share your gallant sentiments, Captain," she said, with a rueful smile. "I matter no more to him than a common scullery maid."

"Speaking of scullery maids, have you seen Henry of late?" He chuckled gruffly. "That boy runs in and out of here, serving my meals, you know, full of talk about 'America' and that 'Declaration of Independence' the colonists flung in our faces. It seems Captain Burke has been telling him a lot of stories about how even a common born boy like himself can become rich and powerful, like that Mr. Benjamin Franklin who went up before the House of Commons some years back. I don't know if you remember, miss, but there was a big to-do about the Stamp Act in the late sixties, and that Mr. Franklin came to London and spoke against it." He shook his head. "Burke has been filling the boy's head with stories of how Franklin was a candlemaker's son, and how he rose up to be such an important man. Now Henry seems to think America's just the place for him to make his fortune, too."

She laughed. "No wonder he's so full of high spirits. And he seems to hang on every word Captain Burke says."

It was late when she returned to the cabin and the dinner trays had already been served. Elizabeth glanced apprehensively at Burke, fearing a reprimand, but he merely raised an eyebrow and inquired mildly if her visit had been pleasant.

"Yes, very pleasant," she replied, and then, hesitatingly, "Thank you for permitting me to see Captain Mills. It was very kind."

He shrugged indifferently. "As I told you before, I saw no harm in it." He turned impassively back to the food on his plate.

Elizabeth felt the angry color rise in her cheeks. He had rebuffed her! She had made an effort to be genuinely civil, to ease the strain between them, and he had answered her with that cold, unbearable indifference! She stalked across the room to hang her damp cloak upon a peg, vowing never again to make an even remotely friendly gesture toward him.

After they had both dined, Burke informed her that Simms was ill, and requested that she return the trays to the galley, since the lieutenant had been ordered to bed. She silently gathered up the tableware and dishes and stacked them on the trays, moving stiffly to the door, unaware that Burke's keen grey eyes followed her.

The rain had ended, but the night air was chilly. Elizabeth shivered as she returned from the galley, hurrying through the darkness along the main deck. Suddenly, a shadow detached itself from the blackness and she gave a startled gasp.

"Sorry," Ben Tucker grinned, looming before

her. "I didn't mean to scare you, Lizzie."

"You succeeded, nevertheless," she replied with a relieved smile. "What are you doing here, anyway? You're not on watch tonight, Ben."

"No, I've been checking our ammunition, and then, it being such a nice night, I thought I'd take a little stroll before joining the rest of those gambling fools below deck."

"Nice night?" Elizabeth said incredulously. "I'm nearly frozen."

"*That's* because you didn't put on your cloak before walking out here." He took her arm, leading her toward the railing. "Come on, take a look at the sky. Don't worry, I'll keep you warm. Now, tell me, have you ever seen anything like that?"

She had to admit that the evening *was* beautiful. The sky stretched above them like black velvet, and the moon shone mistily, a perfect, gleaming pearl. Here and there tiny stars studded the soft velvet blackness like glittering diamonds, and the sea below made its own gentle music. The deck was empty but for the two of them, and as Elizabeth gazed out at the night she felt a kind of peace settle over her. Ben wrapped his arm around her shoulders and drew her warmly close to him. She sighed with something almost like contentment. It was nice to be here with Ben; he was so solid and strong, so kind.

When he turned her to face him, she responded almost automatically, smiling up at him. He leaned forward, a strange light glowing in his eyes. His lips fastened on hers in a kiss that was awkward and sweet at the same time. Relaxed and peaceful, Elizabeth responded instinctively, moving closer to him, placing her arms about his neck, and returning the kiss almost as if she were in a dream.

Alexander Burke paced restlessly about the cabin. He knew he ought to be planning the ship's approach to Madagascar, determining the precise location of the bay in which he intended to dock, and studying his maps and instruments, but his mind kept straying to the girl. Try as he might, he couldn't shake off the vision of Elizabeth Trent which intruded mercilessly on his thoughts.

From the very beginning he had tried to maintain a detachment where she was concerned, and from the very beginning he had failed. She had the power to infuriate him when he was determined to be indifferent, to intrigue him even when he thought he had dismissed her from his mind. Her cool beauty and passionate spirit tortured him; he longed to see them merged, to see the cold, haughty features transformed into a face burning with passion and desire. That first night, he had made a decision to leave her be. He had never taken a woman by force—had never had to. He could have his pick of women. But this one was different. She was disturbing, fascinating. And a virgin, he was sure.

Burke slammed his fist down on the writing desk, scattering his papers. He had done a lot of ugly things since this damn war began, but raping women, especially virgins, wasn't one of them. He'd keep that record, come hell or high water. Yet. . . .he ran his fingers through his hair in a gesture of frustration. It was sheer torture to sleep beside her every night, to see her slender, tempting body so near, so accessible, yet so forbidden. "I ought to get her out of this cabin," he thought savagely. "Or better yet, off the ship!" An idea occurred to him. Madagascar. He could leave her there. She'd eventually get passage on to India, and

live happily ever after with her uncle. Or she could
go back to England and marry some titled aristocrat
who'd keep her in diamonds and furs. "At least
she'd be out of my hair!" He laughed mirthlessly.
Somehow, the idea of Elizabeth as the wife of some
faceless English lord was less than satisfying. More
unsettled than ever, he stalked about the room.

"Where is the damned girl, anyway?" he wondered angrily. "She could have made the trip to the
galley and back half a dozen times or more already!" A thought crossed his mind. Perhaps, in the
darkness, she had fallen down the steps leading to
the galley. Even now she could be lying there, hurt
or unconscious, unable to call for help. This fear
grew in him, and with a sudden movement, he
wrenched open the cabin door and flung himself up
the stairs, heading toward the main deck which led,
on the opposite end, to the galley companionway.

Despite his hurry, he must have moved with considerable quietness, or else the couple at the railing
were too engrossed in each other to heed the outside world. For as he reached the main deck, he
saw them, two figures dimly perceptible in the
shimmering moonlight, their arms wrapped tightly
around each other, their lips locked in a kiss.

Burke stopped short. He drew a sharp, painful
breath, his body stiffening as if he had been turned
to ice. His blood, though, had begun to boil, the
heat of fury coursing through his veins, blotting out
all else save the rage flowing through him like lava
through a volcano. But his voice, when he spoke,
was controlled and even.

"Now, tell me," said Alexander Burke, with terrible, deadly calm. "What have we here?"

Chapter Eight

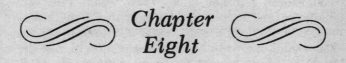

Elizabeth gripped the back of the tall, wooden chair for support, as pale and trembling, she faced Alexander Burke. She barely remembered getting back to the cabin, or the dreadful scene on the deck. All she remembered was Ben's flushed face and his stammered attempts at apology or explanation, and Alexander Burke, his face set as if it were carved of stone, but with that strange, frightening light in his eyes, curtly dismissing the boy, and dragging her away.

Now, as she watched him, she felt her heart begin to pound with a nameless fear. She had never seen him look quite like this before.

"Captain Burke. . . ." she began, with a slight tremor in her voice.

"Shut up." His words sliced through her like a knife blade. "I've had enough of your mealy-mouthed explanations. I don't want any words from you."

Her eyes flashed at that. "I wasn't going to offer

you an explanation," she spat at him. "There is no reason for me to explain myself to you!"

"Quite true. No explanation is necessary—your conduct speaks for itself. Actually, Lizzie, I'm delighted to know that you're not the virtuous young lady you claim to be. However, from now on, I must insist that you bestow your favors on me alone, rather than on the members of my crew."

Elizabeth felt her knees grow weak. This was madness! She had been caught kissing Ben Tucker —that was all! Of course, it was a little improper to kiss a man one wasn't formally engaged to, but the dark, starry night and Ben's sturdy, friendly presence had seemed to weave a spell about her. She didn't understand exactly what had happened, but she understood even less why Alex Burke was in such a deadly rage about it. A cold finger of apprehension brushed her spine as she met his glinting eyes. Never had he looked so formidable.

"It was a kiss. . . .nothing more. . . .I've done nothing unvirtuous. . . .as you say." Her voice trailed away under his hard scornful stare, and he laughed bitterly.

"Oh, yes, I'm quite certain you're still a virgin. But that condition is going to be remedied shortly." With that he began slowly to unbutton his silk shirt. All the while, his piercing eyes never left her face.

Her knees buckled beneath her and she clung to the chair for support. "What. . . .what do you mean?"

Coolly, Burke sat down upon the bed, pulled off his boots, and began to unfasten his breeches. "I've waited long enough," he said coldly.

"No!" Elizabeth knew then the reason for the nameless fear which had descended upon her when she had seen his hard, bright eyes. Instinctively, she had sensed that something—something she had said or done—had pushed him too far. But surely. . .surely. . .he couldn't mean that tonight. . .after all this time, he was going to. . . .

"No!" she cried again, terror rising in her throat to choke her.

Then he stood before her, magnificent in his nakedness, his bronzed body powerfully muscled, the broad shoulders, slim hips, and strong, thick thighs where his male hardness now rose and swelled, all terrifyingly revealed before her stunned eyes. She backed away unbelievingly, as all power of speech ebbed away before the sight of his manhood. This couldn't really be happening. . . .he wouldn't. . .he couldn't. . . .

Alexander Burke laughed harshly. With leisurely deliberation, he strode closer and closer, until Elizabeth felt the hard wood-panelled wall against her back. He confronted her, standing so close that she was dizzyingly aware of the tension in his body, taut like a whipcord, and of the suppressed excitement behind the hard grey eyes. With a sudden movement, his hands shot out and entwined themselves in her hair, pulling her toward him.

Spurred by a burst of sheer terror, she struck out wildly at him, trying to wrench past him, away from the wall. But Burke only chuckled, pinning her arms to her side, holding her effortlessly despite her desperate struggle to escape.

"Let me go," Elizabeth gasped, writhing in his iron grip. "You can't do this to me!"

"Can't I?" Burke mocked her, tightening his grasp so that she winced. He drew her closer, wrapping his arms about her body, and his eyes shone into hers with that unsettling glow. Then his lips crushed down upon hers with a violence that robbed her of all power to think or move, blotting out everything but the burning of his lips upon hers. Fiercely he kissed her, and long. Afterward, when he raised his head at last, the room swam before her eyes and she could only dimly perceive his face bent over hers.

"It was my intention to leave you go in Madagascar," he whispered huskily. "But now, Lizzie, my sweet, I don't think I'll ever let you go." He smiled with glittering malice as her eyes widened. "Until I've had my fill of you, that is."

"You. . . .you monster!" she hissed, her eyes becoming stormy and her body stirring once more with desperate fury beneath his restraining hands. "I hate you!"

Outraged, she kicked out at him, catching him in the shin with her booted foot. Burke grunted in pain, his eyes narrowing.

"Bitch!" he rasped. He thrust her violently across the room and she fell upon the bed, but before she could spring up he had pounced upon her, pushing her full upon the four-poster, his weight pinning her helplessly and his laugh adding fuel to her fiery rage as he began with strong fingers to rip her clothing from her body. Elizabeth bucked frantically beneath him, trying to throw him off, to stay his hands which tore so brutally at her garments, but her efforts were negligible against his onslaught. Finally, she was lying naked beneath him, and her squirming only seemed to add to his enjoyment of the situation.

"Now, you beautiful bitch, I'm going to teach you something you'll never forget." He lay full upon her, his breath rustling her hair as he spoke in her ear.

"No! Please!" Elizabeth begged, tears spilling down her flushed cheeks.

Burke seemed not to have heard her; he began to kiss her eyelids, her throat, her lips, with fierce, hungry kisses that scorched her flesh. His hands found her breasts and began to fondle them, exploring, caressing until she moaned aloud. Somewhere inside her something strange was beginning to happen. Liquid fire seemed to be running through her veins; her flesh seemed to tingle beneath his strong, yet somehow gentle touch, and her lips were melting under the flame of his. She had never, ever experienced anything remotely like this before in her life. A sharp memory of Hawkins's greedy, grabbing fingers and wet kisses remained etched permanently in her mind, but that attack bore no resemblance at all to what she was experiencing now. Then she had felt nothing but pain and revulsion; now, against her straining will, her body was responding eagerly and readily to Burke's touch. His hands made her quiver with excitement, and she found herself returning his fervent, demanding kisses with an equal passion of her own, one which she had never suspected she possessed. Elizabeth became aware of an ache—growing, gnawing between her thighs, a strange, savage hunger coming from her very depths. Suddenly, Burke spread her thighs with his knees, and then he was inside her, surging with one awesome thrust, and a blinding, searing pain stabbed through her, so intense that she would have screamed, but that his mouth muffled her cry, and then the pain was gone and she was aware of nothing but his churning, thrusting movements deep inside her. Instinctively, she matched her movements to his, throwing her arms around his neck and arching her back, opening herself to receive him as tears of agonized ecstasy escaped from her burning, feverish eyes. The room —the ship—reality itself—faded to nothingness, replaced by an overwhelming joy and fulfillment which crowded all else into oblivion. . . .

Afterwards, she lay in Burke's arms, dimly conscious of his soft whisperings, his lips brushing her ear, his powerful hands stroking her with infinite tenderness. She lay, dreamy and contented, in the shelter of his hard, muscled body, as the memory of their lovemaking lingered sweetly in her mind. She sighed.

"Is something wrong, sweet?" he said softly, and she gazed into his smiling eyes.

"Um. . . .no," she replied, still dreamily. She began to snuggle closer to him, but as she moved her legs she became aware of something sticky on the sheets beneath her. Elizabeth froze, then, with a quick movement, pulled back the coverlet and saw, smearing the white muslin sheets, a dark red stain of blood. Blood! Her blood! Full realization of what had happened struck her, shattering all her dreamy peacefulness. She raised horror-stricken eyes to Burke's face.

"You. . . .you've ruined me!" she whispered throbbingly. "Look what you've done!"

"Lizzie," he began, reaching out for her, but she struck his arm away and threw herself back upon the pillow, sobbing uncontrollably.

"Don't touch me!" she cried between her sobs. "You filthy pirate beast! I hate you—I hate you!"

Burke stiffened, his eyes hardening. "That is unfortunate for you. You're going to be spending a great deal of time in my company—here in this bed."

Her sobs grew louder, and more violent. Burke heaved himself out of the bed and began to dress with quick, angry movements. Scowling, he strode to the door, but paused to glance back over his shoulder at the weeping girl, her golden hair loose and flowing over the damp pillow, her naked body gleaming in the lamplight.

"I'll expect you on deck as usual at first light," he said grimly. "I want this ship in first-rate shape before we reach Madagascar, or what's lacking will come out of your hide as well as any other slouchers!" The door slammed behind him.

Elizabeth wept for a long time, the knowledge of her defloration causing waves of despair to wash over her. What would become of her now? She was ruined, destroyed. What man would want her, now that she was no longer a virgin? Many, surely, she reflected bitterly, but none for his wife. And even if she succeeded in escaping while in Madagascar, her purity could never be recovered.

But even worse than this knowledge, more humiliating by far, was the realization of her own response to Alexander Burke's caresses. For she had given herself to him as fully and eagerly as he had taken her. The blissful memory of his male hardness, deep and powerful inside her, was now a memory of shame, causing the blood to flow to her cheeks, not this time from passion, but from the most degrading humiliation. With this shame came a new, previously unknown fear. Now, more than ever before, she feared Alexander Burke, the one man who could stir her to such dizzying heights of passion, who had the power to arouse her as she had never known she could be aroused. She feared this power, and she feared the man who wielded it, but more than that, she feared her own weakness, knowing that despite all her efforts to school her body and her heart, she would fall easy prey to his advances whenever Alex Burke desired it. Why he, of all the men she had met, possessed this power— that she didn't know. She only knew that the attraction she had previously begun to feel for him and had tried so hard to extinguish, had now been irreversibly kindled. Her only hope lay in not letting him discover his power, in keeping from him the knowledge that he could fan the flames of her passion at will.

While Elizabeth lay in anguished solitude on the blood-stained bed, Alexander Burke sought the solace and quiet of the open night to soothe his tormented brain. Even at the rail of the ship he loved, looking out at the restless sea, he found no comfort. The echo of Elizabeth's sobs and her hate-filled words haunted him, mingling with the sweeter memories of their impassioned lovemaking. He had yearned to see her face alive and burning with passion, and to feel her soft body raging beneath him. These desires he had attained tonight. But he had not counted on the feelings which tormented him now, for even as he stood in the cool night breeze, he felt the heat of longing beating through his blood again, and he knew that he wanted her. Now that he had had her once, he knew it would be impossible not to take her again, and again—endlessly, continually. He had never felt this way about a woman before; he had wanted them, yes, but not with this fierce, hungry need he experienced now for the golden-haired English girl who claimed to hate him. She was like a drug in his system, a drug of which he could not get enough.

Burke slammed his fist against the wooden rail, cursing. He refused to explore his feelings further. There was a physical desire, yes, but there was something more, something he did not care to probe. At all costs, he must not let the damned girl suspect his feelings, lest she use his weakness against him. Beautiful women had a talent for that, as well he knew. Whatever happened, he would be damned before he became a puppet for her to manipulate as she chose. Determinedly, he hardened his heart, blotting out as well as he could the memory of her eyes burning like blue fire, and her face flushed and glowing while her body merged violently and totally with his.

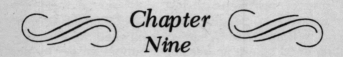

Chapter Nine

The island of Madagascar, located two hundred and fifty miles off the Southeast coast of Africa in the Indian Ocean, had long been a stopping point for English and French, as well as American pirates, who preyed on the European trading vessels traveling to India, Indonesia, and China. Unfortunately for these buccaneers, more British and French naval ships began patrolling the area during the latter part of the eighteenth century, and pirate activity became more sparse, though it was still very much in existence. The Malagasy accepted and even encouraged the use of their coasts by these pirates, and it was for this reason that Alexander Burke had deliberately steered his ship in their direction. He intended to capture another British trading vessel before returning to America, and Madagascar promised him a safe haven, as well as an opportunity for replenishing his supplies and repairing the damage inflicted on his ship during the battle with the *Windhammer*. And above all, it provided an excellent ambush point for capturing his next victim. Trade was so heavy between India and Britain that Burke was certain it would not be long before an unsuspecting merchantman passed through the area.

The *Hornet* reached port in a bay near the village of Tamatave on a February afternoon when the tropic sun blazed overhead after a morning of steady rainfall. Long before the ship had actually entered the Indian Ocean, its passengers had become aware of the radical change in climate. Elizabeth had begun working barefoot on the deck, shedding her thick, heavy boots, and often rolling up the sleeves of her jersey to bare her perspiring arms. These adjustments did little to relieve her discomfort, however; the hot sun beat down unmercifully, parching her throat and scorching her skin. Ben Tucker no longer worked beside her on deck; Burke had replaced the boy with a thin, scrawny sailor named Greye, who kept to himself and barely glanced at Elizabeth, much less providing her with the friendly comraderie she had found in Ben. Her days working on deck had grown more and more unbearable, until finally, one blistering afternoon when the sky was electric blue and the sun unusually fierce, she had fainted, mop in hand, and been discovered by Henry, who had run frantically to fetch the Captain. Burke had carried her to the cabin himself, bathed her face in cool water, and sternly ordered her to remain in bed the rest of the day. After that, her deck duties were discontinued.

"You'll provide me no nightly pleasures if you're dead of sunstroke," Burke had explained with his mocking smile.

The ship docked without incident in a small, wooden-platformed harbor. Elizabeth listened stonily from a corner of the main deck as Burke issued curt orders, instructing Simms and the *Hornet*'s purser, accompanied by Henry, to purchase supplies in the village while the other sailors began the ship's repairs. A third group of selected men were dispatched as lookouts, ordered to maintain a sharp watch for other vessels. The small crew which Burke had assigned to sail the captured *Windhammer* joined him on the *Hornet* after securing the battered merchantman alongside, submitting a list of repairs for that battle-scarred vessel. When all orders had been given and arrangements made, Burke approached her with long, easy strides and informed her abruptly that she was to accompany him.

"Where are we going?" she demanded sullenly.

"To the village. I have the name of a man to contact there."

"Is it safe to roam about among these. . .people?"

He laughed. "These people are quite civilized, I assure you. They're not going to boil you in oil for their supper."

Despite his words, Elizabeth felt a quiver of apprehension as she followed him off the ship, warily eyeing the Malagasy natives standing about on the pier. To her discomfiture, they returned her appraisal with unconcealed curiosity. The men were brown-skinned, with thick, straight black hair and dark, somber eyes, their features having a Polynesian accent, but the darkness of skin suggestive of Africa. Wide shawls were draped about their shoulders, beneath which hung a long, brightly colored garment, similar to a loose fitting dress, which cov-

ered baggy white trousers. They were barefoot.
Broad-brimmed straw hats covered their heads, apparently as protection against the hot, tropical sun
when it appeared intermittently amongst the
almost continuous rain. Just now, it sparkled overhead, although the ground beneath Elizabeth's
bare feet as they reached a grassy path was moist
and springy, as if it had rained recently.

"How far is it to the village?" she gasped breathlessly, trying to stay as close to Burke as she could as
they made their way past the staring natives.

"A short distance." He neither glanced at her nor
slackened his pace but continued rapidly along the
steep, craggy path.

Elizabeth tossed her head and concentrated on
keeping up with him and not losing her footing.
Her uneasiness about the strangeness of her surroundings gave way to an awed admiration for its
exotic beauty as they made their way through a
dense, wooded forest, where the steep path they
were following was almost overrun by tangles of
sinewy green plants and shrubs. The forest was
alive with the chirps of a thousand birds, splashed
with color as they swooped overhead, and the sensuous, fragrant scent of orchids filled the warm air.
Impressed as she was by this luxuriant tropical
spectacle, Elizabeth took care to note the direction
they were heading, as well as the distance. The
more familiar she was with the local territory, the
better her chances for successful escape.

After a short while, the path led them to a clearing, where a group of wooden buildings on stilts
lined both sides of a reed covered track. A wide,
green river wound behind the buildings on the far
side of the track, curling into the distance, where

the forest gave way to rising hills. Brightly garbed
men and women passed about them, staring openly
at Elizabeth and her companion. Burke approached
a stout, black-skinned woman with crinkly hair,
and after a brief exchange, with the woman nodding and gesturing vigorously toward one of the
wooden houses on the far side of the street, Burke
again turned back to Elizabeth, taking her arm as
he led her toward the indicated building.

"Don't tell me you understand their language!"
she exclaimed in astonishment.

He shrugged. "Very little of it. But fortunately,
this man I'm going to contact knows a fair spattering of English, so we should get on fairly well."

"Who is this man?"

A wicked grin lit his face. "His name is Kee
Narunda. An acquaintance of mine who, uh, dab-
bles in piracy, told me to contact Narunda when I
asked his advice before embarking on this journey."

"What charming company you keep!"

"Thank you. At any rate, the natives here are
sympathetic to pirates for some reason, and this
man, Narunda, should be able to tell me if there are
any British ships in the area—and that's what I
want to check out first."

He stopped as they drew up before the house. It
appeared to be a sturdy structure, built upon a wide
platform, and supported by thick poles. There was
no one in sight.

"Narunda!" Burke called. There was a short
pause. "Kee Narunda!" he repeated, in that strong,
authoritative voice she knew so well.

A thin, elderly man emerged slowly through the
doorway to stand on the wooden platform, peering
down at them through eyes almost lost in a face full

of wrinkles.

Burke spoke a few words to him, none of which Elizabeth could make out, except for the name "Fredericks," which sounded absurdly out of place in this exotic land. But the name had a powerful effect on the tiny, old Malagasy, who began to smile, showing chipped yellowed teeth, and to nod his head so vigorously that his sparse hair, still dark despite his age, fell in thin strands across his eyes.

"Fredericks!" he repeated, with apparent delight. "Mandrosa, mandrosa," their host said, gesturing for them to use the rickety ladder leading up to the platform and to enter his house.

Once inside, Elizabeth sat quietly down on a reed mat indicated by the old man, while he and Burke conversed haltingly at the other end of the room. She had plenty of time to stare about her at the odd little house, with its bamboo covered walls, thick reed mats over a hardwood floor, and strings of beads hanging from doorways which led, she supposed, to adjoining rooms. A loom sat in the corner, some bright orange material draped across it. Noting these things, and recalling the bright, colorful garb of the people she had encountered that day, she felt a rush of surprise at the degree of civilization in this presumably primitive coastal village. It was, of course, nothing like the sophisticated society of England, but she couldn't help feeling a little silly about her earlier fears of the natives, whom she had expected to find little better than savages. She began to realize just how absurdly sheltered her existence in England had been. She had been raised in complete ignorance of any society other than her own, taught to condemn those who were different for no other reason than that they *were* different. Her own ignorance made her ashamed, and deep within her came a new urge, the urge to expand her scope of knowledge, to learn more about the many peoples of the world. She found herself strangely excited by her unfamiliar surroundings.

Just as she was about to rise and examine the material draped across the loom, the beads parted from the doorway nearest her and a girl entered the room. Elizabeth stared at her. She was beautiful. Tall and willowy, with rich brown skin and long, straight black hair which swirled over her shoulders. She wore a bright yellow sarong which emphasized the gleaming darkness of her skin; her eyes were long and almond shaped, with thick dark lashes and delicate brows, and her lips were pink and sensuous. She moved with lithe grace as she entered the room, pausing as her almond eyes took in first the old man, then swept to Burke's strong, muscular form, and finally traveled to Elizabeth, crouched on the floor. Her gaze shifted slowly back to rest upon Alexander Burke.

The old Malagasy spoke to her rapidly and the girl nodded, moving to seat herself gracefully at the loom, tucking her long legs beneath her.

Elizabeth saw Burke's eyes follow the girl, who glanced up suddenly, caught his gaze, and smiled. White teeth showed. Burke said something to his host and the old man laughed, Burke joining him as he turned to stare boldly at the girl.

Elizabeth felt the color rising in her cheeks. She was suddenly overwhelmingly aware of her own dirty, ragged appearance, with her grimy breeches and sweaty jersey, her hair dirty and tangled about her sunburnt face, and her bare feet muddied from the trek through the forest. It was now she who felt like a savage—a filthy, smelly savage who hadn't bathed in months. At that moment, she didn't know whom she hated more, Alexander Burke, his cool grey eyes fixed on the dark-skinned girl with unconcealed admiration, or the girl herself, immaculate and lovely.

"How long are we going to stay in this hovel?" Elizabeth had meant to sound coolly contemptuous, but even to her own ears the words sounded merely petulant.

Burke turned his gaze on her, and it hardened. "Even though our host cannot understand you, I request that you speak more respectfully," he said coldly. He stroke across the room and yanked her to her feet.

"Are we going?"

"No. Narunda has invited us to dine with him this evening, and to accept his hospitality for the night."

"You mean we're going to *sleep* here?" Her voice rose dangerously, and there was a hard, bright sparkle in her eyes.

He smiled maliciously at her. "Of course. I would not insult our host by refusing. As a matter of fact, I'm looking forward to the evening."

"I can well imagine you are!" she retorted, her eyes flickering contemptuously toward the girl working the loom with quick, slender fingers.

"Ah, yes. Narunda tells me she is a slave. She attends to the household chores, and. . . .any extraneous duties he may require."

"I suppose he'll loan her to you for the evening?" she exclaimed scornfully.

"She is available," he replied, his eyes cold on hers.

Elizabeth's fingers itched to claw at his eyes—

she wanted to spit in his face—but she merely met
his cool gaze with her own burning, angry one, refusing to look away, to give in to his icy, mocking
stare.

Finally he laughed. "Lizzie, it pains me to tell
you this, but you need a bath."

Her eyes flashed. "No more than you do, Captain!"

"True. Narunda has told me of a place by the
river where we can bathe in private. Come along;
we must refresh ourselves before the evening
meal."

He pushed her roughly toward the door, pausing
only to speak a few parting words with their grinning host.

The place by the river was a shady bank behind
the village, where wild orchids burst with color and
a rich, pungent scent, and the grass was thick and
luxuriant, and greener than any she had ever seen.
At first sight of the clear, rippling river, Elizabeth
gave a shriek of delight, and began immediately
stripping off her damp, dirty clothes. The day was
hot and humid, and her hair clung damply to her
neck. Her whole body felt sticky and uncomfortable. It would be a pleasure to bathe in that
sparkling water. She gave not a thought to Alex;
her nakedness was nothing new to him. He had already seen and touched every inch of her body during those long nights at sea following that fateful
evening. Her virginity was gone, as well as her innocence, and Elizabeth had realized long ago that it
was no use trying to regain lost modesty. She shed
her clothes carelessly and raced naked for the inviting water. As she plunged in, she laughed de-
lightenedly, letting the cool liquid rinse away the

sweat and grime of her months at sea. Burke, standing with legs apart on the bank while she played and splashed, watched her with an unreadable expression in his eyes. After a few moments he pulled from his breeches pocket the cake of soap he had brought off the *Hornet,* and tossed it to her. It landed beside her with a splash that sent water into her eyes.

"With my compliments," he called, as she glared angrily at him. With a burst of laughter he began stripping off his soiled garments.

By the time he had stripped and waded into the river, Elizabeth had massaged the bubbling suds through her hair and all over her body. She felt wonderfully, deliciously clean. Then her gaze fell upon Burke, wading toward her. His tanned chest gleamed with sweat, the muscles bulging in his arms as he moved easily through the water. His black hair tumbled over his brow, and there was a dangerous gleam in his eyes as he drew near. Elizabeth quickly waded away from him, throwing the bar of soap in his direction. She watched him uneasily, but he only laughed, took up the soap, and began to scrub himself. With a scathing glance she turned away and began rinsing the suds from her hair.

"This is a perfect day for a bath," he remarked.

"Yes, it's lovely now," she retorted, "but I suppose it never occurred to you that we're just going to have to put those filthy clothes on again before we return to the village. It seems to me that it will quite defeat the purpose."

"Not at all, Lizzie. Mika, the slave girl, will bring fresh clothes to us in a short while. I arranged it all with our host."

"You mean that girl is going to come *here*?" she demanded incredulously. "To find us like *this*?"

He laughed. "Don't be melodramatic, Lizzie. You've no need to play the outraged innocent with me. I know better."

"Oh! You're insufferable!" she cried, and with a flounce, turned away from him to begin wading back to shore.

The swoosh of parting water warned her, but she had no time to react. Before she could move, Burke had grabbed her from behind, with one arm encircling her waist, and the other wrapped around her throat. He pushed her downward. Elizabeth barely had time to gasp a protest before he had dunked her unceremoniously under the cool, rippling water. He let her up after a moment, and cursing him, she struggled indignantly against his restraining arms, but his grip was unbreakable. Still laughing, he dunked her again, this time holding her under until Elizabeth felt as if her head would burst and little lights exploded in her skull. Finally he let her up, and gasping for breath, she clung weakly to him, unable to support herself as she tried to clear her waterlogged eyes and nostrils. Burke, chuckling, dragged her ashore and threw her down on the grassy bank. He stretched out beside her, resting on his elbows as he watched her struggle to regain breath and strength.

Elizabeth coughed and gasped. She felt wretched—weak and dizzy and helplessly furious. She lay quietly, summoning her strength, while her breathing returned to normal. Beside her, Burke chuckled softly.

Suddenly, she threw herself at him, her nails digging at his face, a scream of hatred in her throat. He grabbed her wrists, but not before she had the satisfaction of seeing a jagged scratch show blood on his cheek. He rolled over with her and threw his weight upon her. Elizabeth fought with the strength of an angered lioness, her golden hair streaming about her bare breasts and shoulders, her cheeks flushed, her eyes like blue fire, burning with hatred. She was no match for him—she knew it even as they wrestled in the grass, but still she fought with desperate strength, striking out in her fury against this man who had so often and so viciously wronged her.

Burke laughed again as he drove her flailing wrists to the ground, his body pinning her helplessly. Beneath him, she panted and squirmed in frustrated rage. "You're superb, Lizzie," he murmured. His lips brushed her eyelids, which made her struggle even more. "Yes, indeed you are. But you could learn something from our friend Mika. She is a slave, too, you see, but only perceive the difference. How docile she is, and obedient. You're by far too high spirited, my sweet. It is clearly my duty to tame you."

She opened her eyes at him, hissing, "You'll never tame me, you rebel filth! You're a beast—a monster! You're. . . ."

His lips crushed down upon her mouth, smothering her words, and he began making love to her— rough, violent, demanding love, bruising her body with the violence of his lust. He entered her without preliminaries, thrusting deep, driving her with his own need, and to her shame, Elizabeth found herself responding with a fervor that matched his own. So it always was, her body, young and alive, refused to obey the desperate dictates of her mind. Despite all her resistance, her betraying body surrendered, and then, thought and reality vanished, replaced by a blinding sensation of ecstasy that left her limp and exhausted. This time was no exception.

When it was over, she lay in his arms, tears of shame trickling down her cheeks. It was very quiet. The sun shone brilliantly overhead in a sapphire sky, making little silver lights dance on the water, and only the faint rustle of the waving grass disturbed the silence.

Burke stroked her hair, which was clean and dry now, feathering softly about her face and shoulders. "You're wise to enjoy your time on land while you may," he said. "We sail again in the morning."

"In the morning?" she brushed the tears away and stared at him in surprise. "But I thought you intended to wait here several days. Aren't you planning to intercept another trading ship?"

"Yes, but Narunda had some rather disturbing news. There was a British frigate in Tamatave last week, and rumor has it that more are in the area." He grinned ruefully. "Even the pirates at St. Marie are up in arms, and that's a pirate stronghold if ever I saw one. My wisest course, in light of these facts, is to get the hell out of here."

Elizabeth sat up, struggling not to betray the excitement his words stirred in her. "Then you believe it's possible that another British ship could land here at any time?"

"It's possible, yes." He placed his fingers under her chin and tilted her head up to look at him. "But don't let it upset you, Lizzie," he said softly. "We'll be off in the morning, so you needn't fear that you'll be rescued and thereby deprived of my company."

" You're despicable!" She pushed him away and would have scrambled to her feet, but he pulled her back and began to kiss her again. Legs and arms tangled as they rolled about, but they were interrupted by soft footsteps in the grass, and Elizabeth saw with dismay that Mika was approaching them, carrying a large bamboo basket laden with clothing, a half smile curving her lips. With renewed struggles, she tried to free herself from Burke's embrace, but he held her fast, merely smiling up at the slave girl and speaking a few words which caused her to utter a low laugh deep in her throat.

She placed the basket of clothes on the bank, and looked quizzically at Burke. He spoke again and she flashed him a smile. With a graceful nod, she turned toward the village, returning as swiftly and quietly as she had come.

Elizabeth, who had blushed crimson at the girl's approach, sputtered furiously, " You! How could you do this? And what did you say to her?"

His eyes mocked her. "Why, Lizzie, I merely promised her that tonight she should have her turn with me."

She stared at him, speechless. He stood up, pulling her to her feet. "I've thoroughly enjoyed the afternoon," he said urbanely. "However, we owe our host the consideration of arriving promptly for dinner. I believe you'll find something suitable to wear in this basket, but first I suggest you wash our dirty clothes in the river."

He gave her a shove, ignoring her incensed protests, and ordered her, still naked, to wade knee deep in the water and to scrub the clothes, while he lay on the bank, his head propped on his hands, calling instructions from time to time and teasing her. When she balked, he threatened to dunk her again, and she hastily renewed her efforts. When she had finished, he spread the garments on the grass under the still bright sun, then threw Elizabeth to the ground and made love to her once more, long, lingering love this time, driving her wild with the subtlety of his caresses, arousing her to tormenting heights before satisfying her throbbing desire. The sun was setting and the clothes were dry when they returned to Narunda's house.

Upon their return, they encountered Simms, who conferred briefly with Burke about the morrow's plans. As Alex told the lieutenant of his intention to sail in the morning, Elizabeth bit her lip. Her hopes for escape faded with the setting sun.

Their meal that evening consisted of a large bowl of rice, meat stewed with ginger and aromatic leaves, and grilled fish covered with sauce. Fresh tropical fruit finished the repast. To Elizabeth, draped in a flowing white sarong, her hair loose and golden, it was a feast. After months of salt pork and potatoes, the fresh meat and fish were delicious, and the rice was a welcome change. She attacked the fresh fruit so eagerly that Burke was moved to inform her that she had the appetite of a horse, rather than of a delicately bred young lady. She spat an angry answer, and continued heaping berries on her plate, undaunted.

Shortly after dinner, it began to rain—a hard, streaming torrent which Narunda assured them occurred nearly every evening, and most days. It grew dark and quiet outside, save for the streaming rain. All at once a strange sound intruded: the beat of countless drums, and low, eerie chanting. Elizabeth's head flew up in alarm.

"It's nothing," Burke assured her. "The Malagasy love music. This goes on every night, according to what my pirate contact told me."

At length, Narunda retired to another room, and Elizabeth and Alex were alone, save for the slave girl working the loom, her fingers moving as rhythmically as the steady sounds of the beating drum outside. Burke unrolled a lengthy mat from the corner and threw it down beside where Elizabeth still sat upon the square reed mat she had occupied during dinner. "You'll sleep on this," he told her. "But first, take off the *saimbo*."

"What?" Elizabeth gasped, with a quick glance at the slave girl in the corner. "Have you no sense of decency? Must you rape me in front of that child?"

"I'm not going to touch you. Mika and I are going into the next room. I want to be sure that you don't lose your head and run off into the night!" He grinned. "Not that I really expect you to, with the rain, and the restless natives and all, but I'm not going to take any chances. Take off your clothes."

"I won't!" she hissed in outrage, but with a quick, angry movement, he pulled the *saimbo* over her head and held it carelessly in one hand, smiling coolly down at her.

"I suggest you get a good night's sleep. We leave for the ship at first light."

In shocked dismay, she watched as he strolled over to the girl at the loom and extended his hand. Mika smiled at him, rising, and followed him meekly through a beaded curtain into another chamber. Neither of them glanced back at Elizabeth, fuming, naked on the floor. She stared after them, fighting a wild impulse to bolt across the little room and out

into the night, despite the rain, despite her nakedness—and to keep running and running until
she could run no more! She had to get away! But
even as these thoughts whirled through her brain,
she knew they were hopeless dreams. Where was
she to go—to whom? She couldn't survive alone in
the forest, and there was no one to whom she could
flee. She didn't know the language, and besides,
Alex Burke would find her. Somehow, she knew he
would find her, no matter where she hid.

Hopelessness descended upon her, making her
shut her eyes hard to press back the tears. Here in
Madagascar she was maddeningly near to India, yet
for all the good it would do her she may as well be
back in London. Alex Burke would take her home
to America with him and she would never see Uncle Charles again. She would never see anyone she
loved and cared about again. Her whole life, since
the moment when Alexander Burke had boarded
the *Windhammer* and strode into her cabin that
foggy winter night, had become a never ending
nightmare, from which there was no hope of ever
awakening.

A giggle, quickly muffled, sounded from the next
room, and she stared in mounting fury at the
beaded curtain. She knew everything that was happening in that room, from the hungry, demanding
kisses, to the caress of Burke's hands, the press of
his thighs, and the knowledge made her so angry
she found it difficult to breathe. She clenched her
fists. Why should she be so furious just because Alex
was making love to another woman? She should be
delighted, relieved that he was not bothering her.
Tears crept from between her eyes and rolled unheeded down her cheeks. Tears of anger, frustra-

tion, despair. . . .and something more. An emotion she didn't understand, an overpowering feeling of hatred and betrayal which reminded her dangerously of jealousy, welled up inside her. Jealousy! Over that vulgar, despicable pirate! Never! Against her will, a tiny voice inside of her chided that, of all things, Alexander Burke was not vulgar. Despite his rudeness and his heartlessness, he always spoke and moved with an undefinable elegance, an air and manner that marked him as an educated, well-bred man. And, the voice continued, he wasn't really a pirate. He was a rebel, yes, who was fighting the King, but his lawlessness was that of a man at war, not that of a common criminal. He was a privateer, with a letter of marque from the rebel government. For whatever that's worth, she reflected scornfully. A piece of paper from a body of men disobeying their King! It occurred to her for the thousandth time that she still knew almost nothing about the man who had enslaved her and made love to her for all these months. He was always so coolly evasive whenever she tried to question him about his background in America—his family, friends, business. Alexander Burke was as mysterious and inscrutable to her this day as he had been the first night she had met him.

The jungle noises continued: the beating of drums, the low chanting, the rush of rain and wind through leafy trees. The other room was quiet now. Elizabeth lay in tortured silence as her body stirred to the primitive sounds of her surroundings, coming alive with a need that had grown in her these past months, a desire that filled her with shame.

She must have drifted off to sleep for it was out of a hazy fog of restless dreams that excited voices pierced her consciousness. She opened her eyes to see Burke stumbling through the room toward the door in response to frantic calls from outside.

"Captain! Captain!"

"What the hell is it, Simms?" he shouted, hastily pulling on his breeches.

Elizabeth sat up, one hand to her sleep-misted eyes. Burke's tall frame filled the narrow doorway ahead.

"It's the British, sir!" The lieutenant's voice from outside trembled with urgency.

"Damn! What about them?"

"The lookout just spotted 'em. Three frigates, Captain, armed to the teeth—and a merchantman. Heading straight for us! And coming fast!"

Part II.

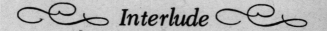

Interlude

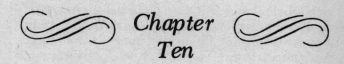

Chapter Ten

The door opened and a tiny olive-skinned girl padded softly into the room, peeking shyly at Elizabeth from beneath a thin veil. She was draped in a loose, flowing *sari* of bright scarlet and beneath her veil she wore a black beauty mark in the center of her forehead. Her feet, on the gold embroidered Persian carpet, were bare. Many bracelets of polished metals jangled on her brown arms, and in her dainty hands, adorned with gleaming rings of copper and brass, she carried a silver tray of tea and cakes.

The servant carried the tray to Elizabeth, reclining amidst a fluff of pillows on the feather four-poster, and nimbly set her burden down upon the finely carved nightstand beside the bed.

"Thank you," Elizabeth smiled.

She didn't know if the girl understood or not, but the servant smiled timidly, bobbing her head as she backed toward the door. Alone once more in the solitude of the cheerful yellow room, Elizabeth sighed deeply and reached for the silver teapot.

It was the afternoon of her arrival in Calcutta. She had been escorted by the three British frigates which had rescued her, the merchantman, *Red Snow*, which they were guarding, and the *Windhammer*, with Captain Mills once more its proud commander. The captured *Hornet*, on which Elizabeth traveled, had sailed alongside, manned by a crew of victorious Britons. It had been a proud procession that had swept into Bengal harbor, triumphantly displaying the British banner for all to see. And though it was a searingly hot, cloudy day, with the humidity soaring so high that her hair clung damply about her head in feathery wisps, Elizabeth had perched at the railing to watch Calcutta come into sight.

Her first impression of Calcutta had been of an enormous, sprawling village crowded with mud-thatched huts, palm trees, and strangely clothed men and women, but as the ship had docked sedately, she had forgotten the city itself, consumed instead by a sudden, feverish impatience, now that the seemingly interminable journey was over, to see Uncle Charles.

Captain Mabry, the handsome young officer who had captained the *Hornet* after Burke's surrender, had driven her directly to the military offices in Fort William, along the banks of the wide, brown Hoogly River, and together they had learned that Charles Trent was indeed still alive, although in uncertain health. Upon receiving directions to General Trent's mansion, Captain Mabry had insisted upon driving her there himself and so, in a very short time, Elizabeth found herself in one of her

uncle's handsome sitting rooms, greeting Dr. Shifnal, Uncle Charles's attendant physician. Here,
however, she had been greatly disappointed, for
she had wished to see her uncle immediately, but
the doctor regretfully informed her that Charles
Trent was sleeping under sedation, and would be
for the next few hours. If she could wait just a short
while longer, so as not to disturb him, surely, by
dinnertime. . . .

"Of course," she had responded instantly. "I certainly don't want to disturb him. But tell me, Doctor, what is the precise state of my uncle's health?
Will he recover?"

The doctor's prognosis had not been encouraging. Charles Trent's health was declining rapidly,
and the only course now was to make his remaining
days as comfortable as possible. Dr. Shifnal had
moved into the suite adjoining Charles Trent's so as
to be always near him, and a special nurse had been
engaged to see to his needs. But, the doctor had
assured her kindly, the sight of his lovely niece
should do a great deal to restore the invalid's spirits,
if not his strength. After some discussion, Dr. Shifnal had suggested that she rest during the remainder of the afternoon, and visit her uncle before
his evening meal. She had accepted this advice
gratefully, and after bidding good-bye to Captain
Mabry, who was waiting in the study, she had followed the bulky Hindu housekeeper, Freela, up the
marble stair to the pretty yellow bedroom where
she now reclined.

Elizabeth sipped her tea slowly, savoring its
flavor. A brief nap, the tea, and her new surroundings had bolstered her spirits considerably. A short

time ago she never would have believed that she would once again experience the attentions and luxury she now found showered upon her. She remembered that final night on the island of Madagascar, when despair had closed in suffocatingly. It seemed a long time ago. From the moment the British had taken command she had once more become Miss Elizabeth Trent, lady of London, a position she had been born and bred to hold. She sighed and leaned back against the pillows, setting the empty teacup into its saucer. Only one small thing nagged at her. She owed some measure of her respectful treatment, irritatingly enough, to Alexander Burke.

The events which had taken place after Simms's dramatic announcement of the British approach seemed unreal to her now: the frantic race with Burke back to the ship, his crisp, shouted orders to the crew, the moment when he had shoved her rudely into the cabin and commanded her to pack her belongings and to don the finest dress she owned. Breathless, her heart pounding, she had obeyed him, donning the violet silk dress she had worn the first morning of her imprisonment, the same gown that had been intended to impress Alexander Burke.

The deck was a scene of frantic confusion. Men scrambled madly about, hoisting sails, rolling barrels into place, shouting in hoarse, tense voices. Elizabeth found Burke on the upper deck, arms folded, his eyes squinting against the sun as he gazed out to where the full-masted sails of four long ships billowed in the morning wind.

Elizabeth's heart had hammered uncontrollably.

Rescue—undreamed of, unhoped for—was upon her. There was no way Alexander Burke, with his single privateer vessel, could defeat three heavily armed frigates. Moreover, he could not escape to the sanctuary of the open sea, for the *Hornet*, although scheduled to sail that morning, had been caught unaware. The hurried repairs that had been made the day before had left many necessary supplies and tools on the dock which had to be repacked and loaded onto the ship; the sails which had been mended had not yet been replaced; and although the crewmen worked frantically to prepare for sailing, there was simply not enough time to get away before the British ships could fan out to intercept them. Alex was trapped. The grim expression on his face told Elizabeth that he knew it. As if he had read her thoughts, he glanced at her and smiled coldly.

"Yes, it seems you shall soon be free," he said. His voice was hard. "Resistance and escape both seem futile at this point. That leaves one option."

"Surrender?"

He nodded.

"How unlike you," she remarked mockingly, studying his face with satisfaction. "You're by far too arrogant a man to seem capable of surrender."

He shrugged. "The inevitable must be faced. It would be silly to have my ship destroyed and my men injured or killed in a futile gesture of resistance. I may be arrogant, Lizzie, but I am also practical. My decision is a realistic one."

Her eyes sparkled maliciously. "Captain, it gives me the greatest pleasure to know that you will shortly be a British prisoner, and will most likely

spend the remainder of your life in a filthy hellhole.
I hope you spend one year in prison for every single
time you've called me Lizzie. By heaven, you'll live
to regret it!''

"Perhaps." Disconcertingly, he laughed, and
turned his gaze to rake her slowly in the way she
hated, the way that made her pulse race so uncomfortably. "But there are certain aspects of our acquaintance, my sweet, which I shall never regret."
His strong fingers brushed her cheek and traveled
lightly on down her throat. "You are a superb
woman, Lizzie. Beneath that spoiled, fairy princess
exterior lies an exciting, passionate woman—a real
woman, capable of more than drawing parlor flirtations and flighty coquetry. You're alive—on fire!
But you fool yourself into believing that you're a
lady—no, a princess—some kind of marble statue
incapable of blood and guts feeling. But I know
better, don't I? I've seen you explode like one of
these tropical storms. . . ."

"That's enough!" she broke in, her voice shaking
with fury, her cheeks crimson. "You'll pay for this,
Alexander Burke, you'll pay dearly. I swear it!"

He shrugged again. "As you wish. But I think
you'll decide otherwise."

"What do you mean?"

"It would be to your advantage, I believe, to
keep your. . .loss of innocence a secret, don't you
agree? I hardly think such knowledge would increase your standing with British society."

Her breasts rose and fell as she struggled to contain her anger. "You know it will ruin me!" she
cried. "But it is a little late to alter the situation!"

"Not at all. I have already seen to it, as a matter

of fact. Captain Mills has been removed from the room he's been occupying these last months, and is prepared to swear that he spent the entire voyage chained below with the men. He's quite fond of you, incidentally, and is more than willing to cooperate. When the British board the ship they will find you, most properly dressed and coiffed, in the cabin Mills has been occupying. You will assure them that you've been respectfully treated, provided with all the privacy and consideration demanded by your station. My men will not betray you, and I will support your story. So you see, my pet, your reputation will emerge from the whole experience with negligible tarnish."

Elizabeth's heart beat faster. This was her chance —the one hope she had to save her name and reputation—her future! It would work, too. Alex had planned it well, and surely the British officers would not doubt her story if she greeted them as he suggested: well-dressed, calm, with a favorable account of her treatment. No one need ever learn the truth! There was only one flaw with the plan. It denied her the pleasure of exposing Alexander Burke for the monster he was, of revenging the abuses she had suffered at his hands by watching him punished for his crimes against her. She clenched her fists. It was a dear price to pay for her reputation.

"How very thoughtful of you to arrange matters on my behalf!" she flung at him venomously. "Pardon me if I refrain from thanking you! I think we both know perfectly well that you have arranged matters in this way, not out of any compassion or concern for me, but only to save your own damned skin! You know full well what would happen to you if I were to betray you for the brute that you are!"

A strange, hard look came into his eyes, a look which made her falter in uncertainty. She was at a loss to read what was in his mind. Then he bowed stiffly, and said with simple, cutting mockery, "As you say, ma'am." He turned sharply on his heel and walked off.

The last time Elizabeth had seen him, he had been in chains. Standing beside young Captain Mabry, she had watched with a queer wrenching of the heart as Alex was herded roughly into the hold with Simms, and Ben, and the rest of the crewmen. His face, hard and grim as granite as he marched in line with his men, both hands chained behind his back, had scorched her memory every day of the journey to India. She deliberately avoided walking on deck when the prisoners were exercised, and she did not have even one more glimpse of him while they were at sea, but somehow, that last, heart-shaking vision would not fade from her tormented mind. She was freed and her ordeal was over, but still, she had no peace.

With a start, Elizabeth recalled her thoughts to the present. It must be nearly dinnertime. At last, after all these months of waiting and worrying, she would see Uncle Charles. She sprang up from the bed with buoyant energy and began to dress, shaking off all thoughts of Alexander Burke.

Dr. Shifnal opened the door in response to her soft knock. "Come in," he smiled. "I've told him of your arrival and he's anxious to see you."

She stepped past him into the dim chamber, softly illuminated by flickering candlelight. The room smelled of sickness. It had a dry, musty odor, like that of dead leaves, mingled unpleasantly with a pungent, medicinal scent. As her eyes adjusted to the faint lighting, Elizabeth perceived her uncle across the expansive bedchamber, reclining upon a mahogany four-poster, and propped up by an abundance of pillows. A warm, if somewhat weary smile, trembled on his lips as he greeted her with precariously outstretched arms.

"Oh, Uncle Charles!"

She flew across the room and into his arms with a little sob of pure joy. She leaned over to kiss his cheek, noting in dismay that it felt feverish. He was very pale, and what once had been a strong, handsome face was now a thin, haggard one, with watery blue eyes bereft of their twinkle. His hands dangled cold and limp in hers.

Nevertheless, he managed to say heartily enough, "What a naughty child you are to come all this way for a troublesome old man! You should know better, my dear, indeed you should!" But there was no mistaking the pleasure in his eyes as a telltale tear escaped to wander down his cheek.

"Oh, Uncle!" Elizabeth laughed, hugging him. "It was nothing, I assure you. I had the most pleasant journey, so you are not to be worrying. And you see, it has all turned out well, for now we are together again!"

"Impossible child!" He smiled weakly at her, then fell silent, a shadow of pain crossing his face.

"What is it, Uncle Charles?"

"It's. . .nothing, my dear. A passing twinge." He spoke with an effort. "I suppose the doctor here has told you about my condition."

"Y. . .yes." Elizabeth hesitated. She did not

know if her uncle was aware of the hopelessness of the situation. His next words enlightened her.

"It seems I'm not going to recover," he began, but upon hearing these words, Elizabeth protested uncontrollably. "Now, now," he continued, patting her hand. "We must both accept the truth, my dear. I've never believed in skirting the issue, you know that."

Elizabeth nodded, unable to speak. Tears trickled down her face as she clutched his hand, wondering at the courage and strength which permitted him to speak so easily about his forthcoming death. She could do nothing to alter his destiny, but she could make his final days as pleasant and easy to bear as possible, and this she silently vowed to do.

Charles Trent gave her a wan smile. "Now, my dear, since everything is out in the open between us, we can have. . .a nice talk. Tell me all about your journey, and what has been going on in London. You can't know how I've yearned for news of you."

She told him then, gaily recounting the parties and balls she had attended, chatting entertainingly about their mutual London acquaintances, and finally, about the journey to India.

"Yes, my own Anna accompanied me, and she has taken the greatest care to see that I have every luxury," she lied blithely. She had already decided that Uncle Charles need never know the truth about her journey. He would never again venture beyond the bounds of his bedroom, and no one who entered it would betray her story. Dr. Shifnal had agreed that the truth would cause him unnecessary and dangerous distress, so it was with free conscience that Elizabeth invented a tale of a delightful, carefree voyage aboard one of His Majesty's frigates, where she had been given the most comfortable private accommodations imaginable.

"And Captain Mabry is the most complete gentleman, Uncle," she assured him. "I find him extremely charming."

"And why not?" he demanded, with a trace of his old gruffness. "Any man who didn't try to charm you, child, would have to be more than a little out of his head. A gentleman knows a lady when he sees one, and a beautiful one at that."

Elizabeth lowered her eyes. She had a sudden, startling vision of Alexander Burke standing barechested before her, hands on hips, his cool grey eyes raking her slowly, as they had done so many times before. *He* had not treated her like a lady, she reflected with painful bitterness. But then, he was no gentleman.

With an effort, she tried to concentrate on the conversation. As the lighthearted words sprang automatically to her lips, her mind strayed in a more disturbing directions.

Why did she keep thinking of Alex Burke? She was free of him at last, just as she had wished during all those months. She ought to be thinking of Uncle Charles, and of the days ahead when she would need every ounce of courage and strength to devote herself to his comfort and happiness. She ought to be thinking of Robert Mabry, who had paid such flattering attention to her on the journey to Calcutta, and who had promised to call on the morrow to see how she fared. Instead, unexplainably, unwillingly, her thoughts focussed on the one man she wanted more than anything else to forget. The question pounded in her head. Why, against all reason and inclination, was she haunted by the memory of his face, his touch, his voice?

After a while, Uncle Charles insisted that she go downstairs and dine, and she reluctantly agreed, promising to visit him again immediately afterwards. He merely nodded, closing his eyes wearily as she moved away from the bedside. But it was not only this display of sickly exhaustion which caused a troubled frown to shadow her face as she slowly descended the stairs. There was another matter on her mind, and it weighed heavy. Try as she might, she could not free herself from her relentless thoughts.

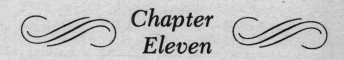

Chapter Eleven

After the first few days, life in Calcutta settled into a comfortable routine. Elizabeth took over the management of the household at her uncle's request, overseeing the activities of Freela, the Indian housekeeper, the French cook, Claude, whom Uncle Charles had lured into accompanying him from the Trent country estate, and the score of other servants, gardeners, grooms, footmen, and maids who composed the household. She managed easily. with a firm yet diplomatic skill acquired through years of living in a large household with numerous servants. Nyomi, the girl who had served her tea that first afternoon, became her personal maid, her impeccable service hindered only by a language problem. Elizabeth was untiringly patient, however, and attempted to learn a few words of Bengali even as she taught some English ones to her fascinated servant. Nevertheless, communication through gesture remained the order of the day.

Her mornings were spent with Uncle Charles in

his expansive bedroom suite, either talking or reading aloud. Elizabeth derived great pleasure from these visits, and from the many small services she could provide to ease his suffering. In the afternoons, though, her uncle generally slept under sedation, for by that time of day his pain increased nearly unbearably and he was only spared by the blessing of laudanum-induced sleep. Elizabeth often read or sewed during these hours, and sometimes she entertained one or two of the wives of other British personnel stationed in Calcutta. To her surprise, she found that Calcutta was a highly social city, where British society engaged in almost as much entertaining and gossip and scandal-mongering as their brethren in London.

There were carriage rides along the Course, and evening strolls upon the Strand Road promenade, a walkway especially created by Lord Hastings for ladies and gentlemen. There were splendid boating parties upon the Hoogly, magnificent subscription balls at the London Tavern in Vansittart Row, with dancing and whist and intense, wild gambling that lasted throughout the night. And there was theatre at the New Playhouse, built in 1772, where one could watch Shakespeare from the pit of the gallery.

This variety of entertainments increased Elizabeth's sense of wonder at the society in which she found herself. Calcutta was a land of dramatic contrast. The Hindus lived in squalid poverty in primitive, mud-thatched huts, eking out a vile existence with arduous labor, their lives brightened only by their quiet, somber religious reflection. Yet, beside the most pitiful poverty rose gleaming white mansions with marble stairs, and lovely gardens filled with orchids and fountains and wandering peacocks. The streets, reeking with cow dung, were crowded with rickshaws and bullock carts and fine, gleaming carriages, as unlikely a combination of simple and sophisticated as one could hope to see. While the British associated with the East India Company journeyed to parties and gambling dens dressed in their elegant silks and embroidered satins, turbaned Indians crouched in the streets in flowing white *dhotis*, smoking the hookah, or filling the air with the melancholy strains of a sitar.

Though by day the city enjoyed a bustling mercantile atmosphere, at night the encroaching jungle would not be forgotten. Tigers hungry for meat would carry off a helpless victim, thus serving as a grim reminder of its lurking, ever present savagery. Footpads and thieves abounded by night, and scavenging hyenas were often met on muddy, deserted streets. It was a wild, exotic land, filled with contrasts and eccentricities, and Elizabeth eagerly absorbed its rich flavor.

One of her favorite pastimes during the afternoons was to drive about the town with Captain Robert Mabry. Captain Mabry was tall, slim, and extremely good-looking, with curly, dark brown hair and warm, brown eyes. From the first moment they had met he had charmed her with his easy smile and polished manners. On that particular occasion he had just boarded the *Hornet* as its new commander and discovered her as one of Burke's prisoners. Mabry, under the command of Chief Commander Richard Perry, had instantly accepted her calm explanation of the circumstances of her imprisonment. Gallantly, he had insisted that she occupy Captain Burke's private cabin for the remainder of the journey, while he, the ship's new commander, would take over her quarters in the small, crowded cabin. It had been strange for Elizabeth to move her things back into Burke's quarters, knowing that this time she would be sleeping quite alone. The cabin had seemed unnaturally large and empty to her. Nevertheless, she had spent the remainder of the voyage in great comfort, and she had been grateful to Captain Mabry for his kindness.

Their friendship had developed rapidly. She found his attentions most flattering, for it had been a long time since a man had paid her lavish compliments and fussed over her with such great solicitude. Alexander Burke certainly hadn't! And Robert Mabry was handsome, as well as courteous. She found that she enjoyed his company more and more as they became better acquainted.

One blistering afternoon, about a week after her arrival in India, Elizabeth sat perched beside him in his carriage as they drove through the muddied streets. She studied his profile as they moved briskly past turbaned peasants selling everything from flowers to fish, and bellowing cows who ambled aimlessly about.

"Look at that!" he laughed, pointing with his whip even as he adroitly guided the horses past a wandering cow. Elizabeth glanced in the direction he indicated and gave a gasp of pure astonishment. An Indian boy, no older surely than Henry, was riding an elephant through the muddied street. The beast made loud, honking noises as it clomped along, and rickshaws and wagons pulled by oxen hurried from its path. The elephant passed close to a display of pottery lining the street, nearly knocking it over with his enormous, wrinkled trunk, and a Hindu merchant shouted angry curses as boy and beast continued on their unhurried way.

"I've never seen anything like that before!" Elizabeth exclaimed in delight.

"You'll never get used to it," he told her. "This is my second visit to India and I still marvel at everything I see and hear."

"Was your first visit a long one?"

"About a month." He glanced at her with a meaningful smile. "I hope this one will be longer."

Elizabeth pressed her muslin handkerchief to her face, daintily wiping away the perspiration induced by the hot sun. With her other hand she worked the beautiful, hand-painted silk fan Robert had given her that afternoon. "Indeed, I shall miss you when you leave," she replied demurely.

"Fortunately, that will not be for at least several weeks. There's been some delay in the preparation of the goods we're assigned to guard en route to England, so my ship must wait. The other two frigates, under Commander Perry, are departing next week."

"What about Captain Mills and the *Windhammer*? Will they set out soon?"

He shook his head. "No, Mills decided to wait and sail along with the other merchantman, the one my frigate's accompanying. After his last experience, he's anxious for the extra protection."

"I certainly don't blame him for that," Elizabeth said ruefully. She fell silent. She had learned shortly after her rescue by the British frigates of the circumstances which had led to her good fortune: three frigates had been assigned to accompany the merchantman, *Red Snow*, as it transported some extremely valuable cargo to Calcutta. Commander Perry had decided to dock at Madagascar to replenish supplies, and it had been pure accident, although a lucky one for her, which had brought the British to port at the very time Alex's privateer and the captured merchantman lodged there. A lucky stroke for her, but disaster for Alexander Burke! She realized with a start that he and his captured crew would soon be towed back to England with Robert's frigate and the two merchantmen. But that would not take place for several weeks. What was being done with the prisoners in the meantime? Where they still chained in that dark, filthy pit below deck? She wondered, and asked the Captain directly.

"Yes, indeed," Robert answered grimly. "Although the head of the British attache in Calcutta, Major Sinclair, is considering a more practical alternative, especially since it looks like we'll be here for the next few weeks. No use letting them rot away, after all, when they can serve a useful purpose."

"What do you mean?"

"Enforced labor. Calcutta's a growing city, Elizabeth. There are streets to pave, mansions to build for our personnel, and the harbor—well, you saw yourself, it needs improvement. The peasants are plentiful, it's true, but why not use all the manpower available? I think Major Sinclair intends to put our colonial friends to work for the next few weeks. Let them earn their bread and water."

A cold, sickly sensation swept over her; she clamped her hands together tightly, oblivious of the pain as her nails dug into her flesh. "He...he can do that, this Major Sinclair?" she asked, trying to keep her voice steady. "He must have a great deal of power."

"Of course. He's in charge of all military affairs in this part of the world. Directly answerable to Lord Hastings, as a matter of fact. Say," he broke off, pulling the team to a halt and leaning over her solicitously. "What's the matter? You look as if you're going to faint!"

"It's nothing. . .only the sun," she murmured weakly, furious with herself for this ridiculous reaction. Why should she care about the fate of the rebels? Just because they were still shut up in that hot, filthy hellhole. Hadn't they done the same thing to the *Windhammer*'s crew when they had been captured? And why should she object to enforced labor under British control? She herself had been forced to work hard and grueling hours under the iron rule of Alexander Burke! It was a fitting punishment for him, more fitting than any she could have imagined. She should be delighted, pleased with the idea.

"Robert. . .I'm terribly sorry, but. . . . Please, could you take me home now? I'm not feeling very well."

"Of course." His hand closed over hers momentarily, then he set to turning the horses. "We'll be home in no time."

Elizabeth wanted only to block all thoughts of the captured men from her mind, but it was not to be. Upon her return home she found a note waiting for her from Major Sinclair, requesting her presence at Fort William the following morning. She handed it over to Robert in increased agitation, but he merely smiled and assured her that it was nothing but a procedural matter.

"No doubt he wishes a statement from you about your capture and stay on board the privateer. He's already interviewed Captain Mills and the rest of the merchant crew, so I'm certain this will be only a formality. Don't worry, Elizabeth. Major Sinclair must be aware of how traumatic an ordeal you've been through. He'll no doubt make this as brief and painless as possible."

"Robert, will you accompany me tomorrow? I don't wish to go alone." She raised soft violet eyes to gaze beseechingly at him.

"I'll be delighted." He moved closer, his hands gently clasping her shoulders. Apparently he mistook the distress in her face as anxiety over the upcoming interview, for he continued in the same gentle, somewhat indulgent tone. "Do stop worrying, Elizabeth. This is purely routine. Why, Major Sinclair even spoke with Henry, the little cabin boy who's been following me about ever since that day we boarded the *Hornet*. He didn't have much to say and he was out of there in a jiffy. You will be, too."

Mention of Henry diverted Elizabeth's thoughts from the plight of the prisoners. She remembered how the boy had pleaded with Captain Mills to let him remain on the *Hornet*, begging to be allowed to wait on her as he had in the early part of the journey. The Captain had agreed, and Henry had remained, giving her quick, unfailing service, and at the same time, transferring his hero worship from Alex Burke to Robert Mabry. She had been amused at the way his loyalty could swerve from one person to another as she watched him trotting eagerly after Robert each day. Captain Mabry had attributed this to Henry's background.

"His kind know no loyalty," Robert had laughed. "He'd as soon stab you in the back as shine your shoes."

His words had irritated Elizabeth; she hadn't realized how long it had been since she'd heard traditional English snobbery espoused. In reference to Henry, the words grated; she had felt almost angry with Robert for his attitude toward the boy who followed him about so devotedly. Then she had shrugged. After all, Henry *had* transferred his affections with incredible abruptness—Robert's opinion was justified by the boy's own actions. Her anger had melted. Why should she let such a small thing mar her relationship with an altogether charming man?

Now she said, "Speaking of Henry, what has he been doing since we landed in Calcutta? Is he still dogging your steps?"

He grinned. "Indeed he is. When I'm at the ship, at least. Captain Mills has apparently instructed him to make himself useful in keeping the *Hornet*, as well as the *Windhammer*, swept and clean. He seems to be always hanging about, working on some chore, or following me and my men around."

"I hope you're kind to him. He's a pathetic little thing, and he's really very sweet."

"Since you've shown such a special interest in him, I've made it a point to be kind," he replied. His eyes shone as he smiled down at her. "Surely you must know by now that I'll do anything to please you."

"You're very kind," she murmured. His hands tightened on her shoulders, drawing her near.

"It's not kindness that motivates me, Elizabeth. I'm driven by another, stronger emotion." With those words, he drew her unresisting into his arms. His lips pressed against hers in a tender kiss. Elizabeth returned it, her heart beating rapidly.

"Oh, Elizabeth, my sweet. . ." he began passionately, but the study door opened just then, and Dr. Shifnal emerged. Instantly, they separated. Elizabeth felt a slow blush steal into her cheeks, but Robert appeared perfectly composed, and after greeting the doctor politely, turned to her with every evidence of cool formality.

"Then it is to be my pleasure to accompany you tomorrow? Excellent. I shall call for you at ten."

"Thank you. Good day, Captain Mabry," she replied, matching his carefully proper manner. Then he was gone, and she hurried upstairs, her thoughts concerned with the pleasure of that secret kiss. She forgot her worries about the fate of the prisoners and the upcoming meeting with Major Sinclair. She stared smilingly at the pretty silk fan as she laid it gently on the dressing table. Yes, Robert Mabry was indeed a most fascinating man. He possessed the strong good looks of youth, combined with the sophistication of a man experienced at lovemaking. She looked forward to the next day, when she would see him again.

"So you are Captain Alexander Burke," Major Sinclair said slowly, his cold blue eyes appraising the man before him.

"So you are Major Thomas Sinclair," the man answered mockingly.

Sinclair's flabby cheeks reddened; his soft, white hands clenched into small fists. He was a squat, pudgy man, with a sour, bloated face, and a head shaped rather like an egg, its shiny baldness covered by an elaborate, heavily powdered wig. His eyes were palest blue. It had often been remarked by the men serving under his command that those eyes were really chips of glass, for they were so cold and pale that they lacked human quality. Despite this appearance, they were indeed quite real. They missed nothing. Now, as he sat behind the heavy oak desk in his office in Fort William, Sinclair's eyes did not miss the dignified bearing of the prisoner before him. They took in every aspect of the man, from his filthy clothes and matted black hair to the bruise on his face and the heavy iron chains binding his wrists. The most striking thing about the prisoner, however, was not his dirty, bedraggled appearance, but his air of cool authority. He showed no fear, indeed, he appeared relaxed and at ease— almost bored. One would think that *he* was in command, interrogating a prisoner, rather than that he was the prisoner himself, flanked on both sides by muscular, close-faced guards with glittering swords. His demeanor annoyed Sinclair, as had his reply. If there was one thing he would not tolerate, it was insolence.

"Captain Burke, may I suggest that in the future you refrain from answering my questions with your own. Merely reply to the question at hand. Is that clear?"

Burke raised an eyebrow at him.

"Is that clear?" Sinclair's voice rose angrily.

"Of course." Burke replied with languid disinterest.

The major eyed him sourly, with open dislike. Arrogant dog! How he loathed these tall, handsome bastards who thought so highly of themselves! He'd seen Burke's kind before—the strong, good-looking men, the ones the women made such a fuss over!

He'd watched them at balls and parties, with their easy manners and smooth, smiling faces. And the women! Clinging to them like ivy, pressing up close against them, with seductive eyes and eager smiles! Did they ever look at *him* that way? Never! Only at the Adonis, the handsome bastards. . .like this Alexander Burke! Well, this was one interrogation he was going to particularly enjoy. A sadistic smile curled about the corners of his moist, fat lips.

"Do you admit, Captain Burke, that you, as commander of the illegal pirate vessel, the *Hornet*, did deliberately attack and imprison the captain and crew of one of His Majesty's trading ships?"

"You know that I did, Major."

"Simply answer the question!"

Burke sighed. "Yes."

"And you admit to forcibly kidnapping one of His Majesty's subjects, a young woman by the name of Elizabeth Trent?"

At mention of the name, Burke's eyes hardened. "She was on board the captured merchantman, Major. What did you want me to do, abandon my mission because some damned English bitch happened to be on the ship I captured?"

"Enough of this insolence!" Sinclair roared, pounding his fist on the desk. The guards closed in on Burke, one of them giving him a short, hard jab in the stomach, and as he doubled over, the other brought his fist down on the back of his neck. Burke crumpled to the floor, his breath coming in short, painful gasps while the guards stood over him, ready to strike again. Major Sinclair watched with satisfaction.

There was a knock at the door.

"Come in!" Sinclair barked.

The door opened. A girl stood on the threshold, her tall, slender body attired in rich, cream colored muslin, her blonde hair smoothly coiffed, a pearl drop clasped about her white throat. At her elbow, Sinclair recognized Captain Robert Mabry in his smart blue uniform. But Sinclair paid scant attention to the captain. His eyes fixed themselves greedily on the face and figure of the girl.

He was surprised by what he saw. He had been told that she was beautiful, and indeed, it was true. She had the cool, lovely beauty of a sunflower in spring. But it was not her beauty that surprised Sinclair. It was an undefinable quality in her eyes and in her bearing. The girl was barely nineteen, and he had expected her to be a lovely child, nothing more. Elizabeth Trent was a woman. Beneath the fragile, flower-like exterior, he perceived intelligence and an iron strength. As a rule, young girls held no appeal for him; they were such silly, giggly creatures. But this one was different. He couldn't tear his eyes from her as she paused in the doorway, all regal grace and soft, breathtaking loveliness.

She, in turn, was as oblivious of him as he was of Captain Mabry. Her violet eyes had widened with shock and horror as she had caught sight of the man on the floor.

"Ah, come in, Captain. . . .Miss Trent." Sinclair, noting her horrified expression, sought to reassure her. "Do not fear, Miss Trent, this criminal will have no further opportunity to harm you. My men have him well under control."

Burke raised his head with an effort and his eyes narrowed to grey slits as they fastened on Elizabeth. His mouth hardened into a grim line, and despite the effects of his recent beating, he suddenly looked quite dangerous.

"Come, come, my dear," Sinclair continued, with a hint of impatience seeping through his tone of kindly indulgence. "Come in, I beg of you. Believe me, there is no reason to be afraid."

Still she did not move. She appeared not to have heard. Her eyes remained locked with those of the prisoner.

Sinclair's shrewd eyes flicked back and forth between Alexander Burke and the girl. Something was going on here which he did not understand. The air was charged, electrical. It was almost as if burning sparks were being exchanged between the two sets of eyes. The color had drained from the girl's face; Burke was flushed, his breath coming in short, angry gasps which Sinclair suspected no longer had anything to do with the blow he had received. The major's icy gaze took in the situation, but he was at a loss to understand it. Why this powerful tension between the two? A suspicion flickered across his brain. Perhaps there was something more to the tale of the captured merchantman than he had been led to believe. Perhaps the story the girl had given Mabry was not the truth, or at least, the entire truth. Sinclair's mouth curled upwards. He would find out. Oh yes, he would find out.

Captain Mabry had taken her arm and was leading her into the office. She appeared dazed, as if in a trance. He was speaking to her in low urgent whispers.

"Elizabeth, what is it? He can't hurt you, there's no reason to be frightened. Elizabeth. . . ."

"Captain Burke!" Sinclair broke in, his dry voice deliberate and thoughtful. "Do you know of any reason why Miss Trent should respond so dramatically to your presence? After all, you claim she was well treated under your command. Her reaction suggests otherwise, does it not?"

"Why don't you ask Miss Trent that question, Major? I am not in the least qualified to explain her behavior. Nor is it of any concern to me."

At his words, and the bitter anger in his voice, the girl seemed to come to life. She stirred, and her hand reached out to clasp Captain Mabry's arm as if for support. "Alex. . .Captain Burke. . . ." The whisper was barely audible.

Burke cut her off harshly. "Please address yourself to Major Sinclair, Miss Trent. He is the one who asks the questions. As I have said, neither you nor your behavior is of any concern to me."

She stiffened; the guards grabbed the prisoner's arms and dragged him to his feet, holding him between them. "After all," he snarled, "you know what I think of spoiled society bitches! My opinion hasn't changed."

Now it was her turn to flush. The lovely blue eyes sparkled like firecrackers. "Neither have your manners, Captain," she retorted. Turning to Major Sinclair, she bestowed on him a brilliant smile and extended her hand. "Good day, Major. I must apologize for my behavior—please say you'll forgive me." At his nod, her smile glittered still more brightly. "How kind. You see, I *was* rather disconcerted to find Captain Burke here, for though he treated me well during my imprisonment, I'm afraid I must confess that I took a severe dislike to him." She might have been any high-born aristocrat discussing the shortcomings of an unfavored servant. She seemed to have forgotten the presence of Burke, standing between the two husky guards not more than three feet from her. She continued silkily, beguiling the major with her eyes even as her smile sought to soften his shrewd expression. "You must understand my dismay upon entering this room and discovering this man, whom I've held in strict abhorrence since the start of our relationship. Robert, you understand, don't you?"

"Of course." Captain Mabry moved a protective arm about her shoulders; his eyes flickered scornfully toward Burke, who was glaring at Elizabeth with unconcealed hatred. "It must have been dreadful for you, my dear, having to spend so much time at sea with a man like that. Your feelings are perfectly understandable. I'm certain the major agrees."

Sinclair responded with a curt nod, but the chips of glass that were his eyes had grown colder. "Do sit down, Miss Trent. . . . Captain Mabry," he drawled. "Guards, take this scum-rat away—back to the hold with the others." As the guards obediently hustled the prisoner toward the door, Sinclair saw the girl bite her lip and look away. Before the guards could drag him from the office, Burke shook them off with sudden, furious strength, and whirled to face the three people grouped about the desk.

It was the girl he addressed, his glinting eyes boring into hers unmercifully.

"You always did play the fine lady very well, Lizzie," he growled softly. "At least, almost always."

The flushed, sweating guards grabbed him again and thrust him roughly out of the room. Except for the muffled scuffling sounds coming from the hallway, there was silence.

Elizabeth Trent took a deep breath. Both Thomas Sinclair and Robert Mabry stared at her with varying degrees of curiosity, as if waiting for an explanation of Burke's final comments, but she merely shrugged.

"As you can see, Major, my feelings for Captain Burke are strongly reciprocated. You may well imagine that our journey together was a great deal less than pleasant for both of us."

The interview continued, with Major Sinclair asking all of the routine questions, and Elizabeth Trent answering him with calm and ready composure. However, the echo of Burke's final words still reverberated in the minds of the three people in that room, and although no further mention was made of them, they were not forgotten.

When Elizabeth Trent and Robert Mabry had left him, Major Thomas Sinclair leaned back in his leather chair and fixed his eyes on the panelled ceiling of his office. The suspicion which had entered his mind earlier sharpened as he mentally reviewed the recent meeting. A smile played about his lips. Once again, the face and figure of Elizabeth Trent floated before his mind. The smile deepened. "Soon," he thought pleasantly, "very, very soon, Miss Elizabeth Trent is going to be all mine."

Chapter Twelve

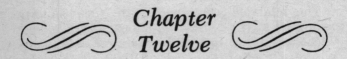

Sunlight fell in bright oblongs on the embroidered Persian carpet, making the golden threads glitter and dance; the silk curtains at the open window hung limply, unruffled for lack of a breeze; and the stifling heat permeated every corner of the room. But the hand-painted fan of Chinese silk lay unused on the dressing table as Elizabeth stalked nervously about her bedroom, too absorbed in her thoughts to notice the oppressive heat, or the perspiration beading on her brow.

Well, she had wondered about his fate and now she knew it. She had seen with her own eyes his thin, ashen face, the ugly bruise on his cheek, and the men standing over him with raised fists. Elizabeth cringed at the memory. Ever since she had returned from Major Sinclair's office late yesterday morning, the all too vivid picture of Alex at his capturs' hands had flashed before her eyes over and over again, until she wanted to scream with some strange, unnamed emotion bordering on hysteria.

Even the soothing voice of Robert Mabry as they drove home had not penetrated her rattled nerves.

"My dear, it's over," Robert had comforted her. "You'll never see that brute again—nor Major Sinclair. Try to put it out of your mind, Elizabeth. It's over."

But it was not over. She had to do something to help those prisoners—all of them. Despite the hateful way Burke had spoken to her, she could not bear to think of his suffering. And how could she blame him for the way he had acted? He had been beaten and degraded, while she had waltzed in on the arm of the man who had taken over his ship. Oh, why had she acted so stupidly, hurting him even more? She had behaved just like a spoiled society bitch, as he had called her so often! She couldn't even think about it without feeling completely ashamed of herself. But one thing was certain. She must do something to help him.

Elizabeth ceased her restless pacing and sat down abruptly on the edge of the bed, her hands twisting together in her lap. She knew what she must do. She must appeal for mercy to that unpleasant Major Sinclair.

She shuddered at the thought. Sinclair was a cold, unappealing man, with his short, pudgy body and those strange, pale eyes. Ugh! She had disliked him from the first, and she distrusted him, too. She would prefer never to see him again, but he was in charge of the captured privateers and he was the only one who could improve their situation. The beatings must stop, and the prisoners must be given decent food! She resolved to send a note that very day, requesting a visit with Major Sinclair.

Again, Alex's bruised, haggard face swam before

her eyes. She didn't understand why this vision upset her so greatly. She told herself that it was the others who really concerned her: Ben Tucker, who had been so kind, Simms, and the rest of them. Yet it was Alex's face which haunted her day and night.

A soft knock sounded on the door and Nyomi entered to inform her that Uncle Charles was awake and able to see her. She thanked the girl and hurried down the corridor to her uncle's suite. Uncle Charles's condition had deteriorated rapidly within the past week; Dr. Shifnal had warned her that the end was not far off. Elizabeth understood and accepted this prognosis. Seven months ago, in England, she would have been devastated by the news, but now she accepted it, however unhappily. Then she had been a silly, flirtatious girl who knew nothing more of life than parties and suitors and beautiful clothes. The girl who hurried down the candlelit corridor to her uncle's sickbed had seen brutality and violence, and hunger in a child's eyes. She had been raped and ravaged, and worked long, tortuous hours for her meager dinner. She had witnessed death and known despair. And above all, she had watched Uncle Charles suffer agonizing pain and courageously accept the knowledge of his own fate. No, though she grieved over his imminent death, the thought of it no longer made her feel as if the world were coming to an end. It would be almost merciful to see her uncle released from his prison of pain and helplessness.

"Elizabeth. . . ." His voice was a hoarse whisper. "Sit with me awhile."

"Of course," she replied in a soft, soothing tone, pulling up a chair beside the bed. Her hand gently clasped his dry, papery one. "I'm right here, and I shan't go away."

Dr. Shifnal, seated in a leather armchair in the corner of the room, his black bag beside him on a marble-topped table, nodded his approval. Elizabeth stroked her uncle's limp hand and spoke quietly of happy things, among them the kind attentions she had received from Robert Mabry. For although he was desperately ill, Uncle Charles's mind was still active and his wits sharp, and he seemed, during most of her visits, to be trying to glean from her some indication that her future would be assured. It seemed to make him happy to believe that she was in love with Robert Mabry, that they would be married, and she would be cared for after he was gone. Elizabeth saw no harm in encouraging this hope, although her feelings for Robert were far from developed. Nevertheless, if it eased her uncle's mind, she was more than willing to encourage his thoughts to travel in this direction.

"Captain Mabry will most likely come by to visit this afternoon," she told him quietly. "Perhaps he'll take me for a ride in his carriage. He drives the most beautiful pair of match bays you'd ever want to see, Uncle. And he tells me that they are mere nags compared to the pair he keeps in England. Very high steppers, I gather."

Charles Trent's watery eyes met hers. Despite his illness, they still glinted with intelligence. "Elizabeth." He spoke with an effort. "Are you happy, child?"

"Happy? Why, of course. Except that I wish with all my heart that you were well again."

"Hmmm. Is that it? I don't know. It seems to me

that there is trouble. Trouble in your heart. You've changed, girl." He coughed and continued thickly, "You're not the same little girl I left in England, you know."

"No, I'm a big girl now." She spoke lightly.

He shook his head. "It's more than that. I don't. . .understand it. The carefree, happy child is gone. You're a woman now, with. . .a woman's cares, I suppose." His hand pulled her closer. "Tell me, child, do you love this Mabry fellow? Is it love that is weighing with you so heavy?"

Color flooded her cheeks. She shook her head in confusion. "I don't know, Uncle Charles. I don't know."

"It's all right, child. Don't fret. Whatever man you pick is bound to be the best of the lot. I don't doubt your judgment one whit." He gasped with a sudden pain. "Just. . .be happy, Elizabeth. Remember to be happy."

Tears sprang to her eyes and for a moment she was tempted to blurt out the whole story. Oh, what a relief to sob out her unhappiness and uncertainty! But somehow she gained control of her frenzied emotions. Uncle Charles must never know the truth! His pain now was bad enough; how could she think to bring him more? Confession might ease her troubled spirit, but the burden would weigh even more heavily with him. No, she must continue to be strong; somehow, she must prove to him that she was happy. Forcing a smile, she turned the subject and talked on for a while in a happy vein, and had the satisfaction of seeing him smile occasionally at some joke or witticism. But soon his face became shadowed with pain, and finally, he cried out so suddenly that Elizabeth jumped up and Dr. Shifnal hurried over with his bag. While she talked soothingly and pressed a cold cloth to Uncle Charles's head, Dr. Shifnal removed the little bottle of laudanum from his bag. She watched as he measured four drops into a spoon and fed it to her uncle, who by this time was writhing in agony. It seemed like hours, but eventually the laudanum began to take effect. Charles's restless tossing and pain-filled moans ceased, and the watery blue eyes fluttered shut. His whole body relaxed. Elizabeth raised her eyes to meet the doctor's.

"He'll sleep for several hours. There's no reason you need stay."

She nodded and leaned down to kiss the ashen cheek, which felt as if it would crumple at her touch. She straightened, choking back tears, and avoided Dr. Shifnal's pitying gaze as she left the sickroom.

She was on her way downstairs to check on preparations for luncheon when the front doorbell pealed. Freela opened it, revealing the squat, uniformed figure of Thomas Sinclair in the doorway. Elizabeth continued her descent gracefully as the housekeeper admitted him, concealing her surprise and the involuntary shiver of dislike his appearance evoked. Well, it would save her the trouble of sending him a note.

"Ah, good day, Miss Trent," Sinclair said from the marble tiled hallway. "I hope you'll forgive this uninvited visit, but I must speak with you about an important matter. I trust I have not come at an inopportune time?"

"Not at all," she replied politely. He took her hand and raised it slowly to his lips, his eyes never leaving her face. Elizabeth controlled the shudder that went through her body at his touch and forced her expression to remain pleasantly impassive as his thick, moist lips brushed her hand. The skin on the back of her neck crawled, but she said with perfect composure, "I was just about to see to some luncheon. Would you care to join me, Major?"

"No, thank you. My visit must be a brief one, so I will not keep you long from your meal. Is there some place private where we may talk for a few moments?"

"Certainly," she replied, even more puzzled. "The parlor is this way, if you'd care to follow me."

She led him into the drawing room parlor, a spacious room containing an elegant blue velvet sofa and matching chairs, and heavily embroidered tapestries at the windows which blocked out the scorching Indian heat. While he carefully closed the heavy mahogany door behind them, her mind raced to discover the possible reason for his visit. She regarded him warily. Thomas Sinclair was not a man to make polite social visits; there was something on his mind, and instinctively, Elizabeth felt uneasy. She seated herself on the sofa and studied him as he settled into the blue velvet chair opposite. His relaxed, confident demeanor and the way his eyes bore coldly into hers did nothing to ease her nervousness.

"What is it you wish to speak with me about, Major Sinclair?"

"Ah, you're very direct, aren't you, Miss Trent? Good. I like direct women."

He caught her startled expression and his bloated face shook with laughter. "You think me impertinent? I beg your pardon. You must believe that my chief desire is to be in your good graces. Let me impress upon you, my dear, how greatly I admire you."

"Indeed," Elizabeth said coldly.

"Yes, indeed. But that is only part of what I have come here to discuss with you. I am preparing my report on the privateer incident, you see, and I thought you might be interested in my findings." He regarded her expectantly, but Elizabeth, hiding her growing uneasiness, made no reply.

"It is my conclusion that Captain Alexander Burke did indeed unlawfully seize the merchantman, *Windhammer*, and imprison her captain and crew, as well as yourself. That, as you know, coincides with the version you and certain others relayed to Captain Robert Mabry and myself." He paused, watching her face. "It is also my conclusion, Miss Trent, that the relationship between you and Captain Burke was more, shall we say, complicated, than you have led Mabry and me to believe. It is my opinion that you neglected certain details of your imprisonment on board the *Hornet*."

Elizabeth's heart had begun to thump uncomfortably in her breast. "I don't know what you're talking about, Major."

"Don't you? Allow me to be more explicit. It is my belief, Miss Trent, that you and Captain Burke were lovers. Ah, I see you are shocked."

"Shocked? Of course, I am shocked! I must tell you, Sir, that I find the tone and content of your conversation most offensive. If you'll excuse me, I refuse to listen to any more of your ribaldry!"

She started to sweep past him toward the door, but he jumped up suddenly and caught her arm in a pinching grip which contrasted oddly with the smooth cordiality of his voice.

"Not yet, Miss Trent. I have not finished. If you'll be so kind as to remain seated for a few more moments, I shall be happy to explain. Or would you prefer that I speak directly with your uncle instead?"

A sick little knot twisted in the pit of her stomach. She was beginning to understand. Without a word, she stepped backward toward the sofa and he released her, watching with satisfaction as she sank almost dazedly upon it.

"Yes, that's better," he said indulgently. "You see, Miss Trent, it was during our little interview yesterday that this theory occurred to me. I sensed some tension in the air when you entered and perceived Captain Burke." He held up a small, flabby hand as she started to protest. "Just a moment, please. You must realize, my dear, that I won't accept that silly story about how upsetting it was to encounter a man you despise. I caught the expression in your eyes when you first saw him and it wasn't fear or loathing. No, not by any means. That was when I became suspicious."

He paused to moisten his flabby lips. "I noted other things as well during that meeting which sharpened my suspicions. For example, I clearly remember that at one point you called him 'Alex'. That was hardly in keeping with the story of your professed abhorrence of the man. And he in turn, upon his exit from the scene, addressed you as Lizzie. He made some reference to your playing the part of the fine lady. 'Almost always,' I believe he said." Sinclair chuckled. "I took the liberty of interpreting those words for myself. Really, Miss Trent, the more I thought about it, the more obvious it became. A man like Burke would not scruple to take advantage of your charms. Why should he? And you, in turn, possess the poise and assurance one associates with a woman, not a silly little virgin."

He spread his hands, and smiled malevolently. "This is my evidence. Reasonable, is it not? Come now, why don't you confess the truth to me? Enough of this pretense."

Elizabeth wiped her clammy palms on her skirt and met his gaze defiantly. "Major, your evidence consists of nothing but conjecture and baseless assumption! You insult me! My relationship with Captain Burke was just as I told you—there is nothing more to be said or thought about the matter!"

"Shall we ask your uncle's opinion?" His voice was very gentle.

She stared at him mutely and read the smugness in his pale, icy eyes. They gleamed triumphantly. In that instant she knew, without a doubt, that he would not hesitate to explain his 'theory' to Uncle Charles. Thomas Sinclair was a shrewd, ruthless man—he would do anything, anything at all, to achieve his ends. Even if this included breaking the heart of a dying man. She swallowed and said tonelessly, "What do you want?"

He smiled widely. "Ah, now we are getting somewhere. Then you admit, my dear, that my 'theory' is correct?"

"I admit nothing! What do you want?"

"Like Captain Burke, I merely wish to take advantage of your abundant charms. You bestowed them on him, why not on me?" His voice squeaked with oily confidence.

"You must be mad!" Elizabeth sprang to her

feet, her eyes blazing, her heart hammering so loudly it seemed to her to fill the room. "Leave this house at once!" she stormed.

"Miss Trent, do not play this farce with me. I am not mad. On the contrary, I know exactly what I am saying. You see, I hold all the cards. You either do exactly as I say or I go immediately to your uncle and tell him that his niece is the lover of a colonial pirate. The choice, my dear, is yours."

"Major, you cannot mean this! You don't understand! I was raped! He. . . .he took me against my will!"

He shrugged indifferently and regarded her pale, horror-stricken face. "The choice is yours," he repeated.

Abruptly, she turned away from him and paced rapidly to the mantelpiece, resting her burning cheeks against the cold marble. Hot, silent tears spilled down her face. How had she come to this? For a moment her carefree London life flashed through a blur of tears and she compared the happiness she'd known then with the misery facing her now. To be Thomas Sinclair's whore! To sell herself for her uncle's sake! The bitter tears flowed faster. She knew Sinclair's words were a mockery—the choice was not hers to make. She had no choice. If Uncle Charles learned the truth, it would not only kill him as surely as a dagger's thrust, it would also break his heart. A lifetime of caring and loving would end in heartbreak and grief. Trembling, she brushed away the tears and straightened her back. She would not let that pig-bastard see her cry. She faced him rigidly.

"What do you wish of me?"

"Ah, you are sensible, I see. Very good. You will

not regret it, my dear. As a matter of fact, you will very probably enjoy it. I am no stranger to the art of love, you know."

"Merely tell me what you wish!" she snapped, her eyes icy and bright like diamonds.

"To begin with, I request the pleasure of your enchanting company tomorrow afternoon; my carriage will call at two o'clock." He paused and added in a voice which sent a chill down her spine, "Be ready. I despise tardiness." He held out a hand. "Come here, Elizabeth."

Like a zombie, she moved toward him. He took her limp, clammy hand in his and raised it once more to his lips, leaving a spot of wetness where his mouth touched it. Then he leaned over abruptly to kiss her mouth, but Elizabeth flinched automatically and turned her head, and the kiss fell instead on her cheek. Sinclair chuckled.

"That will do very well for today, my pretty one, but tomorrow, ah, that will be different. I look forward very much to seeing you then."

He departed without a backward glance, still chuckling.

Elizabeth collapsed in a heap upon the sofa and gave vent to her emotions, but she could not cry away the dread that engulfed her. And with it was rage, directed against the man responsible for her predicament. Alexander Burke! He had done this to her! A knot of hatred twisted inside of her and she found herself relishing his imprisonment and enforced labor. He deserved worse—much, much worse! Her sobs were loud and lengthy and when at last she staggered red-eyed from the room, the Indian sun had set, and the moon gleamed pale in an inky sky.

* * *

The following days were a nightmare. At any time she might receive a note from Sinclair, demanding that she meet him. His requests were frequent. At least once, sometimes twice a day, she was called away from whatever activity she was engaged upon. Once she was entertaining Mrs. Priscilla Richton, whose husband was a particularly close friend of Uncle Charles's. Elizabeth scarcely knew what excuse she made when the summons arrived; she only remembered Priscilla's shocked expression as she watched her hostess back embarrassedly from the room. Another afternoon it was Robert Mabry who was present to witness her confusion. This time the summons was in person. Major Sinclair himself appeared in the doorway, hat in hand, an expression of apology spread across his puffy face.

"Pardon me," he murmured, as Elizabeth nearly dropped her teacup. "I didn't mean to startle you, my dear."

Elizabeth jumped up. Mabry rose also, an expression of surprise crossing his handsome face. "What. . .what can I do for you, Major?" Elizabeth stammered hurriedly.

Sinclair smiled blandly. "Have you forgotten our engagement, my dear? You agreed to ride with me this afternoon, I believe. Or am I mistaken?"

"No, no. I beg your pardon. I'd completely forgotten."

The major's smile deepened. There had been no engagement. He seemed to receive great delight in discomfiting his victim. He turned amiably to Robert Mabry, whose surprise had become astonishment. "I do hope you don't mind if I steal your companion for a few hours, Captain."

"Of course not, Sir," Robert had said confusedly, flushing as he realized the impoliteness of this reply to Elizabeth. He added hastily, "Miss Trent must honor her commitments, of course, but I do regret the loss of her company."

Sinclair nodded. "Nicely put, Captain. Elizabeth, shall we go?"

At this show of familiarity, and the possessive way Sinclair took Elizabeth's arm, Robert's color had heightened still further. He took his leave hastily and spent the remainder of the day and evening puzzling angrily over the incident. Elizabeth's own mortification had increased tenfold the following afternoon, when he called to demand an explanation.

"What the blazes does it mean?" he asked angrily shaking her gently by the shoulders.

She had no answer for him, but her eyes swam with tears. His anger melted, and he kissed her forcefully. "Now, dearest, tell me what this is all about," he said in a gentler tone. Still she would not explain, merely shaking her head and begging him to forget the matter. Disturbed, he agreed, but it continued to gnaw at him, and when the same thing occurred two days later, with Sinclair appearing out of nowhere to sweep Elizabeth off, his anger exploded. The major merely smiled, and requested Elizabeth to choose between them for her afternoon's companion. White-faced, and with her eyes avoiding Robert's, she had chosen Sinclair. That was the last time Robert Mabry had called at the Trent house.

But these scenes were trivial compared to the humiliation she suffered when alone with Sinclair.

Much to her surprise, he did not attempt to actually make love to her. During their carriage rides, while the groom rode without, he would stroke and fondle her, his hands crawling all over her body, and his lips biting and sucking the flesh of her throat as they rode down deserted, dusty roads. She longed to push away his soft, flabby hands and drooling lips, but dared not. Instead, she would sit passively as he greedily fondled her, until he finally demanded that she respond to his caresses. Nauseated and terrified, she forced her lips to meet his, and at his insistence, reluctantly stroked the bulging organ beneath his breeches. He seemed to delight in the tears that spilled from her eyes on these occasions. Yet, so far, he had not violated her. She was in an agony of dreadful suspense as to when this would occur, but dared not question him. He seemed to enjoy the suspense he created in postponing her ultimate degradation. Every day he chuckled and promised that soon she would know infinite bliss. Elizabeth trembled with a combination of hatred and disgust, but said nothing, knowing that pleading on her part would only add to his lustful excitement.

About a week after this torment began, Sinclair changed the route of their ride. They drove up one midday, when the sun burnt orange in a vivid sky, and no wind relieved its oppressive heat, before a partially pillared structure where half naked men toiled wearily in the sun. Puzzled, Elizabeth dismounted from the carriage, squinting her eyes against the sun's brilliance. Then, as Sinclair led her closer to the toiling men, she began to understand. Their figures became clearer, and she recognized them. That was Ben Tucker, struggling painfully under a heavy load. Her heart pounding, she scanned the workers, and it didn't take long to discern the one she sought. Alex's hard, muscled body was bare to the waist, and sunburnt, and the raven black hair stuck wetly to his brow. He was raising a slab of stone to a man perched on the structure above him when his gaze fell on the visitors. He froze in mid-motion. Suddenly there was the crack of a whip, and Burke tossed the stone aside and spun about to glare at the guard who had struck him, a red stain seeping across his bare back. Elizabeth began to tremble.

"My dear, whatever is the matter?" Sinclair inquired benevolently.

She couldn't speak, but watched in sickened silence as Alex was struck down by two guards and ordered back to work. Sinclair led her closer, his arm tightly about her waist.

"Please," she begged. "Let us go away from here. I cannot bear it."

For answer, he pulled her into his arms and began kissing her: long, wet kisses, his hands tangling themselves in her hair. At first she shrank away, but he whispered harshly, "And how is your uncle feeling today, my pet?", and remembering, she succumbed, raising her arms about his neck in obedience to his panted directions, and returning his kisses with trembling lips. When he finally released her, she saw that all activity about them had stopped. They were the actors of a drama, it seemed, for all the men, including the guards, were staring fixedly at her. Alex looked like a stone statue.

"Come, my dear," Sinclair murmured. "I see we are distracting these men. They have a great deal of work to complete before Saturday. Yes, Saturday. Didn't you know? Captain Mabry has finally been given leave to sail, much earlier, I must say, than he anticipated. He and his men, with this motley group in tow, depart for England on Saturday morn. That's why I brought you here today; I thought you might want one last look at your former acquaintances."

It was on Friday afternoon that the note arrived. Recognizing the spindly handwriting, Elizabeth tore it open with customary dread. But this time the message was different. It didn't read: "My carriage shall call tomorrow at noon," or "I request your company later this day." It said:

"Tonight, my pet, you shall know the bliss I have promised you. My groom shall call for you at eight o'clock. Be ready. I have waited long enough."

Chapter Thirteen

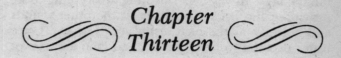

The carriage was damp and smelled of wet leather. Outside, a misting rain drizzled from the darkened sky and blurred a sliver of moon which faintly illuminated the deserted street. Elizabeth shivered slightly as she was jostled along the rough track, and pulled her shawl more closely about her shoulders. But it wasn't the cold that made her shiver, for in Calcutta even the moonlight was warm. Her chill came from within, where numbness had frozen her blood, and turned her hands to icicles. Yet she was calm. As the carriage plodded along the muddied road she wondered at her own stoicism, for despite the fact that her destination was a rendezvous with a man she abhorred, she could generate no strong feelings. Perhaps it was because all her tears had been spent, leaving her dry and empty—and far too weary to agonize over her plight. Besides, her fate was already determined. Tonight she would sleep with Thomas Sinclair. It was a fact: unavoidable, unchangeable.

She sat quietly as the carriage drew her ever closer to her destiny, listening to the mournful bellows of the wandering cows, the strange, chant-like Hindu words as a few hurrying peasants called to each other in the wet night. More distant, jungle noises assailed her ears, with the trumpet call of the elephant dominating, while occasionally some poor wild thing screamed as it became the victim of jungle law. Always, permeating everything else, providing the background for all the other sounds and noises, was the rush of the sea. The sea. Once it had seemed to her a prison, and land a haven of freedom. Now it called to her and she longed to be once more upon its waters, sailing far away from the horrors of her present. A tiny sigh escaped. The sea's beckoning calls were meant for others, not herself. With a pang she remembered that tomorrow Robert Mabry set sail for England, with the *Hornet* in tow. It had been a week since she'd last seen him on that horrid afternoon when she'd chosen Sinclair's companionship over his. He sailed tomorrow, and it was almost certain they would never meet again.

Then her thoughts shifted to Alexander Burke. It was odd how in her present numbed state, even her anger against him was suspended. She remembered his bloodied back when last she had seen him, and for the first time, a twinge of feeling pierced her heart, but she swiftly put that vision of him out of her mind. Instead, he loomed momentarily before her eyes as she had seen him so often on the *Hornet*, a dark, powerful figure with grey, gleaming eyes that bore straight through hers. She remembered the touch of his strong hands, often rough, some-times gentle, as they stroked and caressed her body.

To her shame, she still lay awake some nights, remembering the pressure of his body against hers, and his lips warm upon her flesh. It was wicked of her to desire him again, but she could not deny that many was the night she longed for him.

It was not long before she felt the horses slowing and the vehicle pulling to a creaking stop. She heard the groom hurriedly dismount, and a moment later the door swung open. Accepting the man's hand, she stepped down into the misty night.

The carriage had halted on a dark, cobbled street where leafy trees swayed overhead like ominous, black netted shadows, and large, ghostly houses loomed toward the inky sky. They stood before one such house, a rambling two-story mansion with white marble pillars guarding either side of the doorway. There were no lights to be seen on the main floor, but Elizabeth perceived two spots of brightness in separate upstairs windows. The groom hooked a thumb toward the house, and with a grinning, sidelong glance at her, turned back to the horses. She took a deep breath and pulled her shawl closer as she moved off slowly toward the house.

She had had no idea where Sinclair meant to conduct his rendezvous and had cared little. Now she realized that he intended to enjoy her in the comfort of his own home. She wondered how long it would be before he sent for her in daylight and paraded her before the servants. It didn't really matter, she supposed. Her reputation in India was tarnishing quickly: Robert Mabry now thought her a loose flirt, and Mrs. Richton, whom she had so rudely deserted one afternoon, was doubtlessly proclaiming her an unmannered chit. Elizabeth had no doubt that before too long she would be the publicly acknowledged mistress of Thomas Sinclair. It was inevitable. Her only consolation was that Uncle Charles would never know; no visitors were allowed to see him, so he would never hear the local gossip. Only Sinclair had the authority to demand entrance to her uncle's sickroom, and as long as she satisfied his demands, he would stay away.

With this small comfort, she had to be satisfied. She knocked softly on the heavy oak door, her heart thudding. The door opened almost immediately.

A dark, skinny Indian woman holding a long candle led her into the hallway, past several shadowed rooms where Elizabeth could barely discern the shapes of furniture. The impression she received was of great magnificence and grandeur; the pieces were large and heavy, and a pair of gold candlesticks caught her eye as she hurried past a parlor. Then they were at the staircase, a long, winding affair, thickly carpeted. She followed the woman closely, as it was difficult to see in the flickering candlelight. When they reached the landing, the Indian moved assuredly down the dim corridor to a door on the left and opened it quickly. Elizabeth stepped in. The door shut swiftly behind her.

The room in which she found herself was large and incredibly beautiful. Its most prominent feature was a huge bed facing the doorway where she stood. The bed was covered with a violet colored satin coverlet, and pillows of violet satin with pink lace trimming were piled neatly at its head. Violet draperies on the windows matched the coverlet, and a pink fur rug was soft beneath her feet. The room was brightly lit by pink candles in silver candlesticks. One large candlestick rested upon the blond wood night stand beside the bed; another many-branched one adorned the dressing table. Elizabeth moved slowly toward this piece. Its blond wood matched the night stand, but it was not the delicate beauty of the piece that drew her—it was the items atop it which attracted her notice. A lady's hairbrush and a silver comb sat on the smooth wood. A large bottle of perfume rested beside them, accompanied by a fine, violet lace handkerchief. A box of loose dusting powder, some rouge, and pearl hairpins completed the array. Draped across the chair in front of the table was a negligee of deep violet. It was very sheer and cut low across the bosom. Elizabeth fingered it slowly, raising her eyes to the mirror above the dressing table. Large, dark blue eyes stared back at her, and her blonde hair that had been carefully pinned was now damp and disheveled from the rain. The girl in the mirror seemed strangely out of place with this room; her blue muslin dress was sweet and girlish, the shawl over her shoulders looked old-fashioned.

As if in a dream, Elizabeth began unbuttoning her gown. She slipped out of it and threw it carelessly on the floor, then reached for the violet negligee. Her fingers slowly pulled the pins from her hair, and it cascaded golden about her bare shoulders. She sat down before the mirror and reached for the silver-handled brush; slowly she brushed the mass of gleaming hair, until it fell in soft, shining waves about her shoulders. Her eyes met those of the girl in the mirror again. The eyes were still dark and dreamy, but the girl seemed now to have changed. She blended perfectly with the sensual elegance of the room. The sheer negligee caressed

the length of her body, fitting tightly across her
breasts so that they swelled becomingly and the
nipples showed dark beneath the filmy gauze. Her
hair fell in a thick, golden mass about her creamy
shoulders, and her cheeks were tinged pink with
excitement. She looked utterly beautiful, like some
mysterous, sensual creature of the night. The room
seemed to have cast a spell upon her; desire stirred
in her blood, which coursed hot and rapid through
her veins.

As she sat there brushing her hair, sensuality
seeping through her like a wildfire, the door latch
clicked and opened. Thomas Sinclair stepped into
the room and shut the door very softly behind him.
His pale, bloated face fastened on Elizabeth with
eager, greedy delight. There was a strange glow in
his eyes, an excitement which penetrated even their
pale iciness. A slow smile spread across his face.

"My pet, you are lovelier than I had even imagined. Stand up, so that I might feast my eyes
upon your magnificence."

Abruptly, the spell shattered. With horror, she
found herself dressed like a strumpet, naked, save
for the worthless covering of the negligee. She
stood up, her knees shaking. All of the feelings
which had ebbed from her in the past few days,
leaving her in a stupor of hopelessness, rushed back
suddenly, pulsating through her body with powerful violence—the rage and revulsion struck her as
brutally as a blow, along with deep shame at her
appearance. Some of this must have shown in her
face as she stood, trembling, before Sinclair, for his
smile deepened as he watched her.

"What is it, my love? Are you embarrassed?
Come to me, we shall soon know an intimacy that

leaves no room for embarrassment. Come here."

She took a step backward, coming up against the smooth wood of the dressing table.

"Major Sinclair, please don't do this!"

"Very becoming, my dear. This modesty is most amusing. However, we both know it is only an act. You are, after all, an experienced woman."

"Alexander Burke raped me!" she cried. "Don't you understand? I am not the whore you make me out to be!"

"Whore? Nonsense. Does this room seem befitting to a whore? You are my . . . mistress. And as such, you shall reap the benefits of your position. Don't worry, Elizabeth, you shan't find me a stingy master. On the contrary, if you please me, I will be most generous."

He moved forward with hands outstretched, but Eliabeth darted to the far side of the bed, her breath coming in short, ragged gasps. How unbelievable that a short while ago she had been resigned to this fate; now it seemed unbearable, and she cast desperately in her mind for some escape, for some words that would distract him, delaying as long as possible the moment when he would press his sickening body against hers. She was intensely aware of her own nakedness beneath the filmy gown, and she felt more helpless than ever. Terror engulfed her, widening her eyes, and making her heart pound painfully in her breast.

She said desperately, "My . . . my uncle is worsening, you know. It . . . won't be long before he . . . dies. Then you will have no hold on me."

Sinclair laughed amusedly. "I doubt that. In the days to come it shall become increasingly clear to English society in Calcutta that our relationship is an intimate one. I've already dropped a hint to Mr. Richton, whose wife, I believe, observed your sudden departure one afternoon." He leisurely removed a snuff box from the pocket of his pale blue dressing gown, and opened it daintily. "Rest assured, my pet, that word will spread quickly— gossip always does, you know. Once the word is out, and your uncle dead, you will find it difficult to be accepted in society. I'm certain you'll see the wisdom of seeking my protection. I will provide for you most generously." He took a tiny pinch of snuff and replaced the box in his pocket, regarding her thoughtfully. "This room was formerly occupied by an Indian girl, a little older than you, a little more experienced, perhaps, but certainly not more beautiful. Do you like it? If you desire anything, do let me know at once, whether it be clothes, jewelry, perfume. I believe you will find my taste in such things quite exceptional." He began unfastening the dressing gown, adding approvingly, "The negligee is most becoming, my dear."

She ignored this, returning doggedly to the previous subject. "Indeed, sir, I shall not seek your protection when my uncle is dead. That would be the last thing in the world I would do! I will take the first ship to England and return to decent society! So you see, your hold on me is limited at best! Why not let me go now? Surely there are other girls who please you and who would come to you willingly? Why choose me?"

Sinclair advanced upon her, the strange glow lighting his eyes. His lips were curved in a dreamy smile. She retreated from him until the hard, pink and silver papered wall prevented her from going further. He closed in upon her and leaned down to blow out the candle winking on the night stand beside them. The room dimmed.

He reached out to finger a strand of silken hair. "Why have I chosen you, my pet? Because you are beautiful. And because there is something wild about you. Beneath your prim, ladylike exterior, it is there, some strange, untamed passion. Oh yes, I see it clearly. I sensed it from the first. Perhaps it was aroused by the presence of Alexander Burke that first afternoon in my office. I don't know. I do know that you have fascinated me since our first meeting. I wanted you then—and tonight I shall have you." His tongue licked the corner of his mouth. "As for your notion of sailing away after your uncle's death, well, all I can say is that you are delightfully absurd. You forget that I am in charge of the British attache in Calcutta. It will be a simple matter for me to issue directions that no captain is to permit you on board ship." He smiled indulgently. "Do you really believe I will let you go before I am totally bored with you? Ridiculous! And I have a feeling, my pet, that that day will be quite long in coming."

"*No!*" Elizabeth screamed. She pushed past him and jumped frantically for the door, but Sinclair leaped after her; his stubby arms wrapped themselves about her slender body and heaved her alongside of him onto the bed. Grunting heavily, he shoved her onto her back and climbed on top of her, his eyes lit crazily and saliva drooling from the corner of his mouth. She pounded ineffectually at his chest.

"So, you like it rough, eh?" he asked softly, and with the words hit her hard across the face with the back of his hand. Then he was upon her in a tangle of arms and legs, his immense weight pressing her into the bed as she struggled and sobbed beneath him. His thick, moist lips sucked greedily at the white flesh of her throat while his soft, flabby hands squeezed her breasts with painful ruthlessness. He panted obscenities in her ear, his heavy breathing hot on her neck, while she struggled frantically to free herself. Suddenly, in the course of the struggle, she brought her knee up to his groin with desperate, vicious strength, and Sinclair shrieked in agony, rolling off her, his face frozen in speechless pain.

Like lightning, she was up, reaching instinctively for a weapon. Her hands closed on the heavy silver candlestick, the candle now lifeless atop it. She raised it swiftly, even as Sinclair's arm reached out for her, striking him with all the force of desperation and rage. There was a sharp, sickening crack as the metal struck his head, then he dropped back onto the bed, a silent, unmoving figure.

Elizabeth saw with horror that blood trickled in a red, sticky stream from his forehead. Gasping, she leaned over him, placing her shaking fingers beneath his nostrils. His breath was faint, but warm upon her hands. Thank heavens she hadn't killed him! But she had no time to lose. At any moment he could regain consciousness. Her fingers tore at the negligee, then snatched up her blue muslin dress from the floor. She pulled it on hastily, grabbed her shawl, and bolted for the door.

The hallway was black as a pit. Cautiously she felt along the stone walls, until her trembling fingers found the stairway. Once she stumbled, but fortunately, the thick carpet padded the noise. She moved with frantic haste down the stairs and across the hallway, past the dim, shadowed parlor to the heavy oak door. No servants were in sight. Wanting to scream with the panic that welled inside her, she yanked the door wide and flew out into the night.

The misting rain had turned hard and driving, a forerunner of the approaching monsoon, but she scarcely heeded it as she fled headlong down the empty street. She had no idea in what direction she ran, or how to reach her uncle's house, but merely ran fleetingly as the terror and hysteria bubbled up within her. At any moment she expected to hear footsteps pounding after her, to hear Sinclair's heavy, panting breathing, to feel herself seized from behind. Driven by this horrible image, she raced wildly along the curving, muddied road, until eventually she noticed Hindu peasants, their heads veiled and bent as they moved along. She glanced urgently about for some clue as to where she was, but in her fear and confusion, recognized nothing. Then she spotted a wagon, drawn by two oxen, with a turbaned, olive-skinned Indian driving it. Piled in the wagon behind him were nets of fish, their odor thick and pungent in the wet night. Breathlessly, she ran to the wagon and, panting the few Hindu words she knew, begged the driver to take her to her uncle's address. Surprise and apprehension mingled on the Hindu's long, narrow face, but before he could stop her, Elizabeth jumped onto the seat beside him, still babbling the address, along with tearful, barely coherent pleas. Finally the man nodded, and spoke softly, uttering words which must have been meant to reassure her, but which she couldn't understand at all. He struck at the oxen, and the wagon rolled at a steady pace down the street.

Perched tautly on the seat, Elizabeth was oblivious of the overwhelming smell of fish, and of the rain that had soaked through her dress and left her hair streaming about her face. She was in a frenzy of fear that Sinclair might be after her and would find her at any moment, but at last, after what seemed like hours, the wagon turned onto the street she recognized and pulled up rather tentatively at her uncle's house. She had no money to give the man, but showered him with fervent, if somewhat incoherent thanks, which seemed to be all he desired, for he bowed his head slightly in acknowledgement and smiled at her most kindly. She leaped recklessly from the wagon and tore up the steps.

"Missy Elizabeth!" It was Nyomi who stood, her eyes wide with astonishment, at the head of the stairs, as Elizabeth burst into the house.

"Oh, Nyomi!" Elizabeth cried, sprinting up the marble steps as if pursued by demons. Then she stopped short, noticing for the first time that the girl's eyes were swollen, and her face shadowed with fear.

"What is it?" she cried hoarsely.

"Your uncle . . . General Trent. . . ." the girl spoke haltingly, in a hushed voice.

"What? Tell me!"

In answer, the Indian girl pointed silently to the door of Charles Trent's suite. Seized with a new horror, Elizabeth hurried toward it.

Dr. Shifnal sat at the writing desk, his pen moving swiftly, but he looked up when Elizabeth entered. She barely noticed him. Her eyes riveted on the bed, where a satin blanket completely covered the form of her uncle.

The doctor's chair scraped as he stood up. "I'm sorry, Miss Trent. It happened less than an hour ago."

Elizabeth walked dazedly toward the bed and gently lifted the blanket to reveal her uncle's face. Charles Trent's eyes were closed, his pasty skin was icy to her touch. The lines of strain about the mouth, though, were gone. He lay peacefully, empty of the pain which had tormented him in the past months. Slowly, dazedly, Elizabeth pulled the blanket back into place.

Charles Trent was dead.

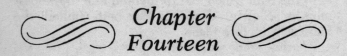

Chapter
Fourteen

The hold stank of sweat, human feces, and vomit. Through the heavy darkness, the black figures of men hunched on the floor were barely discernible. It was hot—suffocatingly hot—and the air was filled with the moans and grunts of suffering men. Alex sat wearily, his manacled hands draped over his knees, his dark head bowed. But for all this appearance of fatigue, he was alert, his ears straining for the sound he was expecting, and every nerve in his body tingling with anticipation. He had waited many weeks for this night. He only hoped that he and his men still had the strength to pull it off.

A chain rattled a few feet away. "Captain," came a hoarse whisper. "You don't think the boy will forget, or fall asleep, do you?"

It was Simms's voice, thick with fever.

"Don't worry," Alex answered grimly. "He won't."

He had experienced momentary doubts himself

this evening as he reviewed the plan. All depended on the boy. If, for some reason, he should be prevented from playing his part, the opportunity would be lost forever. But Alex had put aside his doubts. He knew Henry. The boy would find a way.

Burke leaned back against the damp wall, his thoughts traveling back to the afternoon of his capture, when Henry had been angry and rebellious.

"I want to stay with *you*!" he had cried. "I don't *care* if they lock me up!"

Remembering now, Alex grinned as he thought of Henry's flushed, angry face that day, though at the time he had not been amused.

"Listen to me, you young fool," he had rasped impatiently, shaking Henry by the shoulders. "There's not much time, dammit! Do you want to help me and my men, or not?"

Then he had explained his plan, while Henry listened with growing excitement. He had made it very plain to the boy that he must remain free, and above all, above suspicion. Henry must not visit the prisoners, or inquire after them, or show any interest at all. No, he must ingratiate himself with the British and become a familiar face among them.

Yes, it was a good plan—Henry could see that. It would work. But why couldn't it be done quickly, soon, within a few days?

Alex had shaken his head. The plan must wait until the evening before their departure for England. Whenever that might be. Any other time could prove disastrous, since the *Hornet's* supplies would not be replenished until directly before departure, and to escape on a ship without food or supplies would be suicidal. There would be no time to stop at Madagascar or any other coastal towns to stock up, for the British would no doubt be in quick pursuit. They must leave Calcutta with whatever provisions were necessary to get them across the ocean to America. Burke had stressed the point: under no circumstances must Henry seek him out before the eve of departure, for if he were caught, or even suspected of sympathy with the prisoners, his usefulness would be destroyed, and with it, the rebels' hope of escape.

Nodding solemnly, Henry had agreed. He would make no effort to approach Burke, or any of the others, until the night before sailing. In the meantime, he would attack himself devotedly to Captain Mabry and the rest of the British crew. In particular, he would visit frequently with the night guards on board the *Hornet*.

It was a good plan, Burke reflected, as all about him in the stifling hold, men groaned and sighed in the darkness. Hell, if only his body still had the strength for whatever violence was to come. The hardships of imprisonment had left their mark on him; he ached from the blows and beatings, and the endless days in the merciless sun, toiling beneath the whip. The meagre food and close, suffocating atmosphere of the hold had further weakened him. It had been a month since he had bathed or felt anything softer beneath his weary back than the hard wooden floor, and his hands were rough and bleeding from the stones he lifted and carried all day. His lean, muscled body, though, was stronger than ever; the grueling work had turned him to iron. If only he and his exhausted men could muster their strength for one all important effort, victory and freedom could be theirs. Tomorrow this time, they could be on their way home.

Home. He sighed, wondering what he would find if and when he returned. It was nearly a year since he had left Philadelphia, in June of 1777. Much had happened to him in that time and he knew well that even more had occurred in America. The war could be over, news of victory or defeat traveling slowly across the ocean. Or the battle might be raging still, savaging the land with blood and violence. His thoughts turned worriedly to Jenny. What of her, and little Sarah? He yearned to know how they were. Soon, if luck was with him, he would be on his way to them.

Despite the need for calm thinking, Alex fretted impatiently. He had been chained long enough—he was unaccustomed to being treated like a dog, and he was anxious to breathe the air of liberty, to be once more his own master and the captain of his ship. He wanted nothing more than to sail away from this infected island to the splendor of the open sea. Calcutta was a hellhole. There was nothing here that he would remember with anything but hatred.

Automatically, unwillingly, his thoughts turned to Elizabeth. That golden bitch, he thought viciously, his grey eyes hardening, his chained hands clenching into fists. She was the last thing on earth he would miss. He remembered her slim, lovely body, the flow of golden hair over her shoulders, her violet eyes flashing into his. Dammit! Women that beautiful ought to be hanged! He was ashamed to remember that once or twice he had thought himself fond of her. Fond—of that heartless beauty! At one point, he had even imagined that she felt something toward him. Hah!

What a fool he was! Women knew how to manipulate a man into thinking and doing the most ridiculous things. And Elizabeth Trent knew all the tricks. She was clever—dangerously clever. On some nights, when they had tumbled together in his big four-poster, he had come close to believing that he had awakened feelings deeper than lust in her. Once aroused, she made love like a wild animal, with fierce passion and energy. But sometimes it had seemed like more than lust to him. He had surprised a softened, dreamy expression in her eyes upon occasion, and sometimes she had murmured love words in his ear as their bodies mingled. But now he knew it was nothing more than his imagination, combined with her cunning. She was as treacherous and faithless as any woman, and more so than most. Jenny was the only one who was different. He should have realized that all along. Instead, he had allowed Elizabeth to make a fool of him. Bitterly, he prayed that she would never know her triumph. At least he had never betrayed the tender feelings she had aroused in him. She would never know her victory, not if he could help it.

A tiny sound reached his ears, and he froze, raising his hand to signal for silence. The hold became suddenly still, save for the lap of waves against the ship. In the silence, the reek of sweat and vomit seemed stronger, the air more unbearably stifled. The men huddled in the dark lifted their heads, their eyes gleaming like animals. There was a long, breathless pause. Then they heard it, distinctly. The sound of a key in a lock. With a soft scrape, the hatch opened and a thin shaft of pale moonlight streamed into the hold. A rope ladder, attached above, was lowered hurriedly, and the next moment, a small body swung into view. The hatch closed with a soft thud above his head, and the small figure descended with light feet into the pit of the dungeon.

"Captain!" Henry's voice whispered excitedly. "I got it! I got the key!"

A short time later, the iron chains lay in heaps on the floor. The men, flexing their aching muscles, grouped themselves at the foot of the rope ladder, with Burke at the head. Beside him, Ben Tucker, thin and sun-scorched, his sandy hair matted to his head with sweat and dried blood, listened intently. Henry quivered with excitement at his elbow. The other men had their eyes fastened on Alex with respectful attention as he issued rapid orders.

"You all know that speed and surprise are our primary weapons. Use them." There were nods all around. "Every man knows his job, so get to your positions—fast. Remove every obstacle quickly and silently. Do whatever you have to do. But remember, the most important thing is to secure this ship. Then, and only then, can we afford to take the risk of plundering those merchantmen." A grim smile crossed his face. "With any luck at all, we'll be on the open sea in a very short time—and we'll leave our friends something to remember us by."

As they made their way stealthily across the planked floor of the open deck, the men fanned out, disappearing into the shadows. Henry had told them the number and positions of the night watch; the crew would go about taking their customary places for setting the ship in sail, eliminating the enemy as they went along. Ben accompanied Alex in the direction of the quarterdeck companionway.

Both men moved softly, whatever sound they made hidden by the beating hum of a light rain and the swish of the sea.

Suddenly, the silence was broken by the scrape of a boot on wood. Coarse laughter followed. "Damn this rain!" a husky voice swore good-naturedly. "I always get the watch on wet nights!"

"You!" another answered. "I could have been bidding good-bye to my Indian wench in a dry bed, 'stead of bein' here. Don't tell *me* your troubles!"

The voices were loud in the hushed night. They were coming closer.

Alex and Ben exchanged glances, pressing themselves against the slippery wall. A moment later, two figures stalked around the corner into view, long-barreled muskets drooping at their sides.

Alex sprang forward, with Ben not an instant behind. The two men had time to do no more than exclaim in surprise. Alex's fist slammed into the larger man, a hulking, bearded brute with massive shoulders and a wicked-looking mustache. The man's exclamation was abruptly cut off by a smashing blow to his nose; he reeled, blood streaming from his nostrils, but managed to raise a huge left fist. Before it could connect, a lightning blow to his stomach knocked his breath away and he slumped to the ground. Alex wrenched the musket from his slackened grip and brought it down hard against the man's jaw. With a groan, his victim slouched forward into unconsciousness.

Ben's opponent, a short, brawny, leathery skinned fellow, was already prone, with a tricle of blood from his lip spattering the puddled deck. Ben grinned at Alex, saluting him with the guard's musket.

"Well done, you cocky rascal," Alex chuckled. "Don't forget to return just before we set sail and throw them overboard. I suppose they may revive when they hit the water and swim to shore, but at that point we'll be on our way. The main thing is that I don't want to be bothered with a handful of prisoners on this voyage. Understand?"

"Yes, sir."

"Good. Let's go on."

They had almost reached the stairway that led to the quarterdeck when the sound of voices reached their ears once more. They halted, listening intently. Two voices murmuring, their words unintelligible. One voice belonged to a man. The other, most definitely, to a woman. Ben's eyes grew saucer round; he clutched Alex's arm in a painful grip. That voice—he recognized it!

"Captain! It sounds like. . ."

"Yes, my friend, I know. It is she. The inimitable Miss Trent!"

Something in Alex's cold, glinting eyes made Ben uneasy, but Alex appeared to have forgotten him. He gripped his musket more tightly, and when he spoke, it was as if to himself.

"I hadn't thought it possible, but it seems I'm going to have the pleasure of seeing dear Lizzie once again. Yes, indeed, this is my lucky night. But not hers." He chuckled, a chilling, ruthless sound. "When I'm finished with her, she'll wish she'd never left London soil!"

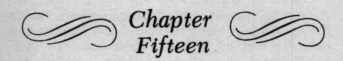

Chapter Fifteen

Robert Mabry paced restlessly along the deck of the *Hornet*, his cap pulled low over his eyes against the light rain which still fell. Earlier, the downpour had been quite heavy, but for the past half hour it had tapered off, giving him the opportunity to make a quick, last-minute visit to the ship he would be captaining home in the morning. He was anxious for the morning, anxious to sail. After a propitious beginning, his stay in Calcutta had not equaled his expectations. Damn it, it had not even come close! Instead of sailing away with a beautiful heiress as his fiancee, he was leaving as the second-rate suitor, rejected most embarrassingly for the attentions of a pudgy, middle-aged bureaucrat. He spat disgustedly into the swirling water.

When he had first met Elizabeth Trent, Robert had been taken with her beauty, her well-bred air. Never a man to neglect the ladies, he had paid her considerable attention on the voyage to Calcutta. It wasn't until later, through various conversations, that he discovered, most agreeably, that Elizabeth possessed wealth along with her other vitures. Then his attentions had become serious.

Robert Mabry was an ambitious man. He had gained a reputation as a bright, hard-working officer, but his ambitions were not satisfied with this station in life. Marriage, to either money or a title, had always been a consuming fantasy. With Elizabeth, the prospect had become tantalizingly real. Although it was unfortunate that Elizabeth Trent's family did not possess a title, she nevertheless moved in the first circles of London society. That, along with her substantial fortune, was certainly enough. Oh yes, quite enough. He began to court her in earnest, convinced that she would make a charming wife, as well as a convenient one. Everything had gone smoothly, too, until Thomas Sinclair entered the picture. Remembering, Robert grimaced. That bitch had chosen Sinclair's rank over his own good looks and affability. Women! As fickle as the weather. That he had been humiliated by Elizabeth's obvious preference for Sinclair, he did not deny. But the worst of it was that with her rejection of his courtship, his hopes for his future had been dashed. Like a tempting, delicious meal, he could almost taste the money and status marriage to her would have brought. On the verge of the feast, the meal had been whisked from under his nose, leaving only the fragrant aroma to torture him with what could have been. His hunger made him bitter, and angry. It was a dangerous combination.

The brisk clatter of hooves on the cobbled street leading to the harbor interrupted his deckside reflections, and he peered curiously through the mist.

Four horses and a carriage behind, from the sound
of it. Now who the devil would be driving about in
the rain at this time of night?

Robert watched as the carriage loomed into
view. The groom pulled the animals up a few feet
from the wooden-planked dock, but before the man
had time to alight, the carriage door swung open
and a shawled figure jumped out. Robert stiffened,
his eyes widening in amazement as Elizabeth Trent
reached into the carriage, pulling down a heavy
trunk, and then turned hurriedly to the groom, who
was now beside her. She pressed something into his
hand and waved him off, then turned her eyes toward the ship. When she saw Robert, a smile lit her
pale face, and she hurried forward, dragging the
trunk at her side, while the groom climbed atop his
seat and turned the horses back down the path into
darkness. Robert moved in surprise to greet her as
she hurried across the gangplank onto the ship.

"Elizabeth—Miss Trent! What is the meaning of
this?" he demanded, unsure whether to assume a
disapproving or solicitous tone. His anger with her
mingled with surprise at this unusual behavior.
What could it mean? Her response doubled his
amazement. She dropped the trunk and flung
herself on his chest, clinging weakly to him amidst
incoherent sobs.

"Oh, Robert!" she gasped. "Thank heavens I've
found you!"

He held her, confusion and doubt competing
with sudden, wild hope. "Calm yourself, my dear,"
he soothed her, stroking her damp, tangled hair.
"There is no reason to be upset. Why don't you tell
me what is troubling you?"

"You must . . . take me with you!" she begged,

staring up at him with huge, imploring eyes. "Say you'll take me with you!"

Could it be that the beauty missed him after all? Was it the prospect of his imminent departure that had caused this dramatic change? Mabry's ego weighed the likelihood of this, while his common sense sought a less romantic motive. Handing her his white handkerchief with the scarlet monogram, he smiled tenderly down at her.

"Elizabeth, please tell me why you're so anxious to accompany me. Surely, your uncle. . . ."

"He's dead. There is now nothing to hold me here. Oh Robert, you don't understand! I must leave . . . I must!"

Her voice rose to near hysteria, and he pulled her closer, wrapping his arms securely about her trembling body.

"Of course, Elizabeth. As you wish. But couldn't you try to explain? You're quite right, you know. I don't understand at all."

Sobbing, half incoherent, she did explain then, the words coming haltingly, in a pitifully breaking voice. She told him everything, about Burke, and Sinclair, the hideous blackmail, her rendezvous that evening, and finally, her flight from Thomas Sinclair. It was a relief to spill out all the shame and horror, to bare her soul to Robert, the one man who truly loved her, who treated her with tenderness and respect. She poured out her heart and then threw her arms about his neck, burying her face in his shoulder. Now everything would be all right. Robert would protect her, take care of her. He would take her away from this horrid island, back to England. Nothing, and no one, could hurt her again.

For a while, Robert did not speak. When he did, his voice sounded odd, rather taut and unnatural. "So that's it, eh?" he murmured softly.

"Yes." Elizabeth dabbed at her wet cheeks. "After I saw that Uncles Charles was . . . after I saw Uncle Charles, I just threw some things into my trunk, ordered the carriage, and went looking for you. At your lodgings, they told me you might be here." She managed a little smile. "I must say, they looked at me a little oddly when I knocked on your door, but I couldn't see any other way than to come after you myself." The expression in his eyes made the smile drain abruptly from her own. Something inside her went cold. "Robert, you do . . . understand? Don't you?" she whispered uncertainly.

He gave an ugly laugh. "Oh, yes, Elizabeth. I understand. I understand perfectly."

She stared at him in dawning horror as he continued in a harsh voice she scarcely believed was his own.

"I understand that you're a beautiful little whore. Oh, yes, dearest. High-priced, but a whore just the same. Tell me, how many men have you known in all?"

"What!" she cried. "I told you. Only Alex Burke, and I swear to you—he raped me!" Her voice rose dangerously. "Don't you believe me?"

He pulled her roughly to him. His face was very close to hers, his breath hot and rapid on her cheek. "I'll believe whatever you like, Elizabeth, my sweet. And I'll take you wherever you like. But I, too, demand a small price in return for these services."

Aghast, she tried to pull away, but his grip tightened painfully.

"Oh, don't worry, Elizabeth. It's only a small price. Marriage, my dear," he said in a calm, pleasant voice. "I will make a respectable woman of you —and you shall make a wealthy man of me."

She stared at him as if seeing a stranger. Gone was the facade of charm and congeniality. The face that stared back into hers was harsh, with gleaming animal eyes and a frightening hardness about the mouth. So Robert, too, was like all the rest. He didn't love her, he had never loved her. All he wanted was her fortune!

"No!" she gasped. "I won't marry you! I won't be tied to a damned fortune-hunting bastard for the rest of my life!"

"Very well," Robert snapped. "Then please remove yourself from my ship. I hope you enjoy your stay in Calcutta."

"You wouldn't leave me here!"

"No? I'm sure as hell not taking you with me. Not unless you agree to my terms."

For a moment she was seized with the impulse to scream, to shriek her frustration to the world. But the moment passed and the impulse faded; she faced Robert Mabry squarely, with narrowed eyes. Very well, she would agree. She would tell Robert he could have whatever he wished—once she was returned safely to England. But when they actually returned . . . that would be a different story. He couldn't force her to marry him. She would merely break off the engagement. And there would be absolutely nothing he could do about it.

"In case your're planning to doublecross me," he added smoothly, breaking into her thoughts and smashing her scheme to pieces, "just remember, I know all the details of your recent adventures. And

I would have no hesitation in bringing them to the notice of the World At Large, as they say in Londontown. Oh," he continued amiably, in the same voice he had used when inviting her for an afternoon ride, "you could deny everything, of course. But I daresay you would live the remainder of your life shrouded in scandal, creating gossip and doubt wherever you went. Not a very pretty existence, it seems to me."

"You stinking bastard!"

He smiled in acknowledgment. "Well, Elizabeth, what is it to be? Our lives joined in wedded bliss, or your permanent imprisonment in Calcutta with Major Sinclair?"

She raised her chin, her fiery blue eyes blazing venomously into his. "I'll marry you, you despicable snake. But I'll be damned if I don't make you regret the day you ever laid eyes on me!"

"Come now, why wait for the honeymoon?" he said, again pulling her to him, "I might as well enjoy the same pleasures other men have known." Then he kissed her playfully, teasingly, only to push her away as suddenly as he had grabbed her. There was laughter in his eyes as he grinned delightedly down at her.

How could she ever have thought him handsome, Elizabeth wondered, with an uncontrollable shudder. He now seemed a greedy, vulgar weasel of a man who would use a woman to gain wealth and position. He was revolting. She glared at him in contempt, oblivious of the rain which had quickened again, soaking her tangled hair and glistening on her flushed, upturned face.

Suddenly, there was a sickening thud, and Robert swayed and fell forward, hitting the deck hard.

Elizabeth jumped back and would have screamed in alarm, but a hand jammed cruelly over her mouth and at the same time, a strong arm wrapped itself tightly about her body. She found herself securely held, unable to move or speak. While she struggled in futile resistance, a figure stepped forward from the shadows. Ben Tucker peered down at Mabry's unconscious body, then patted the butt of his musket with satisfaction.

"Out cold," he announced.

Elizabeth appealed to him with her eyes. Do something, save me, she implored. Uncertainty shadowed his face.

"What are you planning to do with her, Sir?" He sounded as though he didn't want to know the answer.

"Do? Why, take her along, of course," answered a voice Elizabeth would have recognized anywhere. She struggled still more wildly, but her tormentor only laughed. "What's the matter, Lizzie?" Alexander Burke demanded mockingly. "Mad because I interrupted your *tete a tete*?"

His voice changed, becoming curt and businesslike. "Quick, boy. Hand me some rope and a strip of cloth. We've got to get her out of the way."

Ben hesitated, torn between conflicting desires.

"Did you hear me?" Alex growled impatiently, as Elizabeth's struggles intensified. "Rip your shirt to gag her, and find me some rope. Or would you rather I slug her with the butt of my musket as you did to Mabry?"

"But, Captain . . . need we take her along?"

"I'm in charge here, Tucker. I gave you an order and I'm not about to repeat it. If you wait any longer, we'll have the hole British force in India at our throats. Now, move!"

With a final, helpless glance at Elizabeth, Ben shrugged out of his torn, filthy shirt and ripped off a thick strip, which he handed to Alex. Then he hurried over to a coil of rope beneath the railing.

Elizabeth felt Alex's hand leave her mouth, but the next instant, the rough, dirty cloth was pressed between her lips and expertly tied. It fit snugly, and she tasted blood on her tongue. Despair choked her. She had fled from the hands of one hateful man into those of another, and now, a third, the worst of them all. For she knew just how ruthless Alex Burke could be, and anything, *anything*, was better than being at his mercy. But her struggles were in vain. Seconds later, Ben returned, and her wrists and ankles were tightly bound by rope which cut cruelly into her flesh. She could do little more than gasp at the pain before Alex flung her over his shoulder and stomped off in the all too familiar direction of his cabin. There he kicked open the door and lowered her from his shoulder onto the floor.

"I'll be back for you, Lizzie," he vowed. "The night is still very young." Then the door slammed shut and she found herself alone in the darkness, with the bite of rope at her wrists and ankles and the gag tight across her clenched teeth.

She lay quietly, knowing it was useless to struggle against her bonds. Alex had done a good job. Besides, after the harrowing experiences of the evening, she was far too exhausted to fight any more. A thousand questions screamed inside her head. How had Alex and Ben escaped? What exactly was going on? And what was to become of her? Too many questions, with no answers. And at this point, the answers probably did not matter much anyway.

She would wind up the victim of either Robert or Alex, so what difference did it make? Safety and security were gone—danger and deceit were her only realities, and this time alone was only a tiny pause in the dreadful tumult that her life had become. Soon, Alex or Robert would return, and it would all begin again.

Elizabeth had no clear idea of how long she lay on the cabin floor. She heard vague sounds from above—the scrape of a boot on wood, heavy jolts as objects were dragged. Eventually, she became aware of movement more intense than the mere jostling of the sea beneath. The choppiness of the stationary ship was replaced by a swift, gliding sensation. So they had sailed. To where, she wondered drearily, and with whom in command? Perhaps Robert had regained consciousness and summoned his men, crushing the revolt—if indeed, it was a revolt. But no, her confused mind corrected itself. It must be Alex. Robert would never have sailed tonight. He was scheduled to depart until morning. Unless it *was* morning. There in the dark, silent cabin she had lost all sense of time and perspective. Resignedly, she gave up. What did it matter anyway?

Heavy steps sounded outside and a key rasped in the lock. Then the door sprang wide and Alexander Burke's tall, powerful figure strode into the room, his dark hair a mass of damp, tangled curls, and his grey eyes glinting dangerously. He was not the same immaculate figure who had entered her room on the *Windhammer* that first night of her capture, splendidly dressed in black satin breeches and white silk shirt, with a sword at his side, but even now, clothed in filthy rags, and with his sunburnt skin grimy from dust and sweat, he was frighteningly formidable, a Hercules bursting with violence. He had her trunk, and set it down before closing the door behind him, carefully sliding the bolt into place.

Elizabeth lay motionless, watching him through bleary eyes. With three quick steps he was beside her, staring down. Never before in her life had she felt so naked and helpless as she did at that moment, which seemed to stretch into a silent eternity.

Then, Alex moved, so suddenly that she flinched involuntarily. With one swift movement he rushed to his writing desk and flung open the top drawer, returning immediately to kneel at her side. Elizabeth caught the flash of steel in his hands—a knife! Before she could blink he was sawing at her bonds, snipping them as quickly and efficiently as he had tied them, and removing the bloodied gag from her mouth. She tasted blood, and realized dully that her lips were bleeding. A glance at her numb arms revealed droplets of blood there, too, as well as at her ankles, where the rope had rubbed her skin raw. She felt faint and weak, and she closed her eyes. Distantly, she felt herself lifted and carried across the room and set down upon something soft. So . . . soft. She realized vaguely that it was the bed. Then all sensation ebbed as she gave herself up to the unutterable weariness, leaving pain and uncertainty behind.

When she awoke, the first thing Elizabeth felt was something cold and wet touching her lips, then her wrists. Her eyelids fluttered open. Alex was dabbing at her raw, bleeding wrists with a wet linen handkerchief, all the while swearing softly under his breath. She felt a trickle of life return as he worked, and she gave a sudden moan as a stinging sensation replaced the previous numbness. At the sound, he glanced quickly at her face. For an instant, Elizabeth thought she read concern in his grey eyes, and something that looked oddly like relief. Then a mask shut down over his features and he said grimly, "Ah, so you've come around."

Too weak to talk, she watched in silence as he turned his attention to her ankles, his fingers moving with gentle adeptness over her bloodless flesh. In addition to the uncomfortable tingling of returning sensation, her body felt stiff and ached dreadfully. Her throat was parched and hot, but she was too tired to request a drink. Alex, looking up suddenly from his efforts, seemed to read her thoughts. He brought over an earthenware mug and helped her to sit up. With his left arm supporting her, he raised the mug to her lips.

Brandy. Mmmm. She drank thirstily, letting the rich, strong liquid glide down her throat to spread its lovely, healing warmth throughout her body. She collapsed once more into the pillows and Alex silently returned the mug to the bureau and tossed the wet cloth aside.

"Th . . . thank you," she murmured.

He shrugged. "For what? For reviving you? I've told you before, Lizzie, you're no use to me dead."

"What . . . has happened?"

"My men have taken over the ship and sailed out of the harbor. It's nearly dawn, and we're making good speed. By the time your British friends come after us, we'll be beyond catching."

She digested this. Then she remembered something else.

"And . . . Robert?" she whispered weakly.

His face hardened. "We threw him overboard, with the others. He probably revived when he hit the water, and most likely swam to shore." He shrugged again. "Not that it would be any great loss if he didn't. Except perhaps to you, Lizzie. But that won't matter much anymore, my sweet, even to you. Either way, you won't ever see him again."

Relief washed over her. So the nightmarish prospect of a forced marriage was over. She sighed softly and passed her hand across her eyes.

Alex Burke turned away in disgust. "I realize you're going to miss your lover, Lizzie. Both of them, as a matter of fact. Or were there more than two? Perhaps Sinclair and Mabry were not enough to satisfy your seemingly insatiable appetite. However, I'm going to do my best to console you."

As he spoke, she stared at him in bewildered astonishment. Then she remembered. He had seen her with both Sinclair and Mabry. He thought. . . . Of course! She knew all too well what he thought.

"You don't understand," she said tiredly, but he cut her off sharply.

"Shut up! I don't want to hear any lies or excuses from you. What's it to me if you want to play the whore? But just remember, from now on, you're *my* whore!"

Tears stung her eyes. "You have no right to say such things to me," she quavered. "You have no inkling of what I've been through. . . ."

"What *you've* been through! You arrogant bitch! My men and I are the ones who've been chained up like animals and worked like pack mules from dawn to dusk! You've been gallivanting around, playing the elegant lady." The careful mask was gone; hatred was now stamped upon his face, and a fury more fierce than any she had seen before. Instinctively, she cowered against the corner of the bed, and seeing this, a cold, satisfied smile touched his lips.

"Yes, my dear Lizzie, you've known nothing but stuffed shirt military men for quite some time now. Clumsy, boring fools, aren't they? They haven't the least notion of how to satisfy a woman. So I'm going to refresh your memory of what it's like with a man who knows what he's doing."

He advanced swiftly upon her and ripped open the bodice of her gown. She shrieked, and delivered a stinging slap to his cheek, but he quickly pinioned her beneath him and continued ripping her garments from her body. Both desire and anger shone in his eyes as he raked her naked form.

"Damn you! How I've wanted this!" he muttered wildly.

"No! Please. . . ." she moaned, as his lips scorched the flesh of her throat and nuzzled agonizingly lower to her breasts. Suddenly, his stroking hands flew up to entwine themselves in her hair, and his lips crushed down upon hers with terrifying violence. At first, she resisted him with all that remained of her strength, but before she knew it, she was kissing him with the same savage intensity as he was kissing her, and her will to resist dissolved as she gave herself up to the simmering passion that could not be denied. Once again, her body was responding to his man, responding as it never had to any other. When Sinclair had touched her, her flesh had crawled; and even with Robert, while she had found his kisses pleasant, she had never experienced anything like this. Her skin tingled with delightful sensation, and her body instinctively melted into his. Eagerly, her lips sought his lips; their tongues waged their own secret battle. She became deliciously aware of the urgent pressure of his muscled body on her thighs, and when he spread her legs with his own, she did not resist. Her arms clasped him tightly to her, and she felt again the liquid fire seeping through her veins. When he entered her, piercing deep and hard, with searing, mightly thrusts, she cried out with wild joy, forgetting her shame at this reaction, knowing only the ecstasy of fulfillment as together their passion reached its glorious, dizzying pinnacle . . . and then another . . . and another. . . .

At last their thrashing bodies subsided. Alex rolled off her, propping up on one elbow to survey her better. The golden hair was tousled, her face damp and flushed, the eyes half open and dreamy, as he remembered so well. How he longed to kiss her now!

But for Elizabeth, the moment of joy had passed. Guilt, awful and weighty as an anchor, enveloped her, banishing the fire of a few moments before. It was true, she was no better than a whore. To be aroused by a man who cared nothing for her, who wanted only to punish her, and to use her body to satisfy his own lust! It was unbearable! Hot tears flowed silently down her cheeks.

Alex, seeing this, felt a knot tighten in his chest. He wondered suddenly if she had cried afterward with Sinclair, or Mabry. Probably not. She had chosen them willingly, invited them to be her lovers. Another thought occurred to him. Had she reacted with such passionate enthusiasm to *their* caresses? Has she kissed them with the same fervor that she had kissed him, devouring him with her lips, teeth, and tongue? His expression darkened. The very thought of her with those other men made him feel murderous all over again. With iron control over his renewed fury, he turned abruptly away from her, his clenched fist buried in the pillow.

"Go to sleep, Lizzie," he growled harshly. "Tomorrow there'll be more."

Chapter
Sixteen

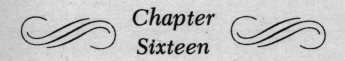

Looking back, the events of that crazy, chaotic
night in Calcutta were always to hold an aura of
unreality for Elizabeth. She remembered them as
one remembers a dream, or perhaps, a nightmare,
with a vivid sense of horror; yet, the events themselves were blurred and indistinct, as if they had
not really happened at all. But they *had* happened,
and their consequences were enormous and un-
deniable. They changed the course of her life, setting her in a direction she neither sought nor desired, for when that evening was over, she found
herself on her way, irrevocably, to America.

When Burke first informed her of this the morning following her abduction, she raged and stormed
at him in a tearful frenzy, screaming that he had
deliberately ruined her life, and throwing whatever
movable objects were handy at his imperturbable
head. He had merely ignored her until at last her
aim struck very near to home; the earthenware
mug shattered against the panelled wall inches

from his head. Then he had fixed those cold grey eyes on her panting, disheveled figure and bitingly informed her that any further displays would result in her immediate, forcible departure over the side of the ship. Although she did not for a moment believe he would actually toss her overboard, she refrained from throwing anything else in his direction, and when she discovered that her mingled tears and curses fell on deaf ears, she soon abandoned them, her hot rage cooling into frozen silence, occasionally broken by an acid remark. This set the tone of their relationship during the early part of the Atlantic crossing. While she maintained an icy demeanor, he treated her with open contempt, and the gulf between them widened with their seemingly mutual hatred.

Unlike their previous journey together, Burke no longer required her to toil on deck, but she was ordered to assist the cook in the galley, and to perform various other chores, such as mending torn sails and patching breeches and shirts. Aside from these duties, she was free to roam the ship, a privilege of which she gladly took advantage, often standing for hours gazing out at the unbroken blue of the sea, her thoughts thousands of miles away, dreaming of England and the home she would never see again.

One such morning, a fine, lusty summer's day, when the sun sparkled gold in a sky the color of blue silk, and the sea rippled as calmly as a baby's dream, Ben Tucker waved to her from the top of the foremast, where he was fastening a snagged sail.

"Ho, Lizzie! Beautiful day, isn't it?" he called cheerfully.

"Yes, lovely," she replied with an answering

wave. It was July, and the weather was deliciously
warm. Her hair was piled on her head in a tumble
of loose curls, allowing the breeze to tickle her bare
neck. She wore a man's blue linen shirt, with the
sleeves rolled up to her elbows, and a pair of baggy
blue breeches which reached her knees. Below this
point she wore nothing; neither shoes nor stockings
encased her slim legs and well-shaped feet. Watching Ben climb nimbly down from the topmast, Elizabeth giggled, wondering what her chaperone,
Mrs. Hampshire, would say if she could see her
now. No doubt that genteel lady would have dif-
ficulty recognizing the once proud, elegantly
groomed young lady she had accompanied to
London's finest soirees in this immodestly attired
hoyden who leaned against the damp railing and
breathed deeply of the salty breeze, relishing the
sun's warmth on her bare, toasted skin.

"What are you grinning about?" Ben asked, coming up to stand beside her at the rail.

"Oh, nothing." Her eyes sparkled. "I was just
thinking about my chaperone's reaction if she could
see me now."

Ben ran his eyes appraisingly over her. "You look
fine to me," he approved. "But then, I'm not a lady
myself, and I know they sometimes have different
notions."

"Yes, sometimes," Elizabeth agreed gravely, hiding a smile.

Ben surveyed her once more. "You know," he
said thoughtfully. "You've borne all of this pretty
well, it seems. I mean, you seem almost *happy*, despite the fact that you're going to a new country,
where you don't know anyone and where all the
people are at war with your own folk." He shook

his head. "Lizzie, you don't even seem *upset*."

"Don't I?" she asked confusedly, a blush stealing into her cheeks. "You mean because I've shed my silks and satins for these beastly breeches? Well, I'll tell you something, Ben Tucker! I may have had the sense to abandon propriety for the sake of comfort as far as my attire is concerned, but that doesn't mean I'm happy to be carried off by a ruthless barbarian to a country that's barely civilized! It doesn't mean I'm happy to be sailing on this filthy, stinking ship to a place I've no desire to go, and to keep company with a bunch of cloddish rag-tags who. . . ." She broke off in dismay, reading the sudden hurt in his usually merry blue eyes.

"Oh, Ben! I'm sorry!" she cried, clutching his arm. "I didn't mean *you*. Honestly, I didn't mean what I was saying. . . ."

"It's all right."

"No, it isn't. Those were wretched things to say, and I'm sorry. Truly sorry." She smiled beseechingly at him. "The truth is, I didn't want to admit it, but . . . I had some problems in Calcutta. And in a way, it was a tremendous relief just to sail away from there!"

"What kinds of problems?"

"Please, I'd rather not discuss it," she said, shaking her head.

"Okay." Ben patted her arm, accepting this answer with the easy-going serenity which made him such a dependable friend. There was a short, companionable silence as they gazed out at the placid sea.

Ben had spoken the truth, Elizabeth realized. She *was* happy. When she thought of the alternatives if she had stayed in Calcutta or sailed to England with Robert Mabry. . . . She shuddered at the thought. No, her present situation was infinitely preferable to either of those fates! Besides, she did enjoy sailing on the open seas. She could watch the ocean for hours—it was so changeable, so restless. One moment it might be dazzyingly clear and calm, and the next, churning with angry, white-crested waves which crashed and roared and gave her a pleasantly scared sensation. She felt healthy and alive, and despite the confinement of the ship, uniquely free. Yes, Ben was right. She was happy.

"Tell me about America, Ben," she said suddenly, breaking the silence.

He looked surprised. "America? What do you want to know?"

"Will I like it?"

He grinned. "Why not? It's a fine, lively place—especially with the war raging on. Let's see, Lizzie, it's July now, of 1778. That means we've been at war with England for almost exactly two years." He shook his head ruefully. "That's a long time for fighting."

"Just why *are* you fighting?" she asked. "I never did understand why the Colonies made such a fuss. All on account of some silly taxes."

"They're not silly," Ben replied grimly, his face darkened by a frown. "It started out as just the taxes, but then things got worse and worse—until they became unbearable! We've got rights, Lizzie, and your King George refused to recognize 'em!" He banged his fist heavily on the railing. "At first, we asked to have our rights recognized as British subjects. Why should we be taxed so heavily—and have British soldiers stationed in our towns, to boot —when we didn't even have representation in Parliament? Seems like a perfectly reasonable question to me."

"Yes, I suppose it is," Elizabeth answered uncertainly, a little abashed by his forcefulness.

"Well, the King didn't see fit to answer it. At least, not to our satisfaction. We tried over and over to get our fair rights as British subjects, but he sure didn't treat us like the rest of his subjects back in England. And things just kept getting worse. We didn't have any choice but to fight. If he won't give us our fair rights as British subjects, we'll have to get 'em as *American* subjects."

"Under what King?" she asked scornfully.

Ben shrugged. "Don't know yet. But we have a Continental Congress, which is like Parliament, and *they* are our representatives. Hey," he turned to her suddenly, "didn't they tell you anything about all this in London?"

"No one really talked to me much about the war, or the reason for it. Women aren't supposed to concern themselves with such things."

"Damnation! What *are* you supposed to concern yourselves with?"

"Fashions, parties, the theatre," she replied, not meeting his eyes.

Ben snorted contemptuously. "Well, you'll sure find it different in America."

"Really, Ben?" Elizabeth asked eagerly. "Do you mean that women are actually included in discussions of politics?"

"Sure. Just try to leave any Philadelphia woman out of anything, and she'll snap your nose off in a hurry!" His eyes twinkled. "Besides, war and politics are all that's talked about lately. We don't have time to worry about fashions or theatre and such stuff. There's a war on, girl, and like it or not, every one of us is involved."

When she returned to the cabin later, Elizabeth pondered his words. Despite her image of it as a wild, uncivilized land, America now seemed to her an exciting new world. Her pulse quickened with excitement as she thought of it, remembering how Thomas Penrith had laughed at her attempts to talk politics with him. She knew that he had thought it odd that she was interested in such a subject, and any Englishman would have agreed. Yet here was an American telling her that such interest was natural in America. It was a novelty indeed. Her thoughts turned with heightened interest toward her destination, and she determined to find out more about this rebellious, unorthodox land that was to be her new home.

A few nights later, she glanced up from darning a torn woolen shirt to study Alex's dark head, bent over some papers at his desk. "What will you do with me when we arrive in America?" she asked suddenly.

He looked up from his work, regarding her with that unreadable expression she longed to decipher. "I told you once before, Lizzie. We have prisons for enemies and traitors."

"Do you really intend to place me in some hellhole?" she cried angrily, thrusting the darning aside. "Is that to be your revenge for Calcutta?"

He smiled mockingly. "You wrong me, Lizzie. I seek no revenge." At her incredulous expression the smile deepened. "I didn't say I intend to place you in a prison hold. I merely said they exist. However, if you can convince me that you're not a dangerous enemy, I believe it's possible to find somewhere else to house you."

"You're ridiculing me. You hardly think me a dangerous enemy!" she retorted.

"On the contrary." The grey eyes pierced her like daggers. "I think you could be a very dangerous enemy, my sweet."

Their eyes met. His blazed with an inner fury she could not comprehend. Slowly, under her puzzled gaze, the anger died from them, and he spoke more normally.

"Don't worry, Lizzie. I have a feeling you'll like it in America. I doubt if I'll find it necessary to incarcerate you."

"What makes you think I'll like it?" she asked tartly. "I hear it's a wild, rowdy place."

"It is," he agreed. "Although not as barbarous as you undoubtedly expect. We have our landed gentry, the gentlemen with money and property and slaves. We have fine houses and fine ladies and handsome carriages, just as you do in England. But we've got something else. Life, and spirit, and ambition. In America, even the poorest farm boy, a lad like Henry, can make his way in the world, earning respect as well as money along the way. One does not need to be born into a noble family to be considered worthwhile by society." His eyes took on a thoughtful expression. "It is a mobile, restless society, where at birth one man is deemed equal to all others, and as he grows, he is distinguished from his fellows only by his own actions and abilities, rather than by the name of his father."

"Rubbish!" Elizabeth leaned forward. "What about the slaves you keep, the indentured servants who must toil away years of their lives? I've heard about *them*! Where is their equality, their opportunity?"

She had the satisfaction of seeing him flush. "It's

true," he admitted. "There is an inconsistency there. Many of my fellow patriots, particularly the farmers who depend upon mass labor for their profits, fail to see the hypocrisy. I would change it if I could, but you see, I am but a mere privateer, whose views, on this particular subject, are not shared by the majority."

"A mere privateer," she repeated skeptically, staring at him. As always, she was mystified and intrigued by him. He spoke as intelligently and articulately as a member of Parliament, and he bore himself with an air of authoritative dignity which not even iron chains could dispel, and yet. . . . He claimed to be nothing but a licensed pirate.

"Do you have any other profession?" she challenged directly. To her chagrin, Burke threw back his head and laughed.

"You must be ashamed of your background, since you won't talk about it," she jeered.

One black eyebrow lifted; the grey eyes fixed themselves, hawk-like on her face. "I live in the city of Philadelphia, Lizzie. More than that, you needn't know. You'll find out soon enough, for I'll probably bring you home with me—unless I change my mind, that is, and stick you in a prison hold after all."

With a malicious grin, he turned back to his paperwork.

"Bastard!" Elizabeth sprang across the room and slammed the cabin door behind her. She quickly mounted the steps to the main deck.

Above her, thousands of bright stars winked in a deep blue sky. She glared at them, trembling with anger and defeat as the night wind whipped at her hair and a spray of cold water struck her upturned face. A strangled sob escaped from her throat. Damn Alex Burke for being so mysterious, so maddeningly aloof! He was odious and insufferable and monstrously overbearing! She hated him! If only they had never met!

Of late, her curiosity about him had become almost overpowering, as if their reunion had heightened whatever previous effect he had had on her—an effect that had always been powerful. Now it was overwhelming. She was consumed with thoughts of him. She heard his voice in her dreams, saw his hard, handsome face in her imagination countless times each day, sensed his presence in a room before her physical senses were aware of him. He stalked her thoughts like a wild beast, preying on her in moments of sleep, as well as activity. Oh, damn him, damn him, damn him! Yes, she did indeed hate him.

Didn't she?

Elizabeth closed her eyes in desperation, squeezing all the confusing thoughts out of her head. When she opened her eyes a moment later, she saw something that made her stare.

A burst of pale blue light streaked through the sky for a blind, glorious instant and then disappeared in a shower of blue fire. A falling star. Falling so quickly that if she had blinked, she would have missed it.

At the same moment, she saw the truth. She was in love with Alexander Burke.

"Of course. Deep down, I must have known it all along," she whispered into the darkness. "Until this moment, I couldn't have admitted it to anyone —even myself."

She took a deep breath, aware that tears trembled on her eyelashes. How often she had heard it remarked that the division between love and hate was a thin line. More like a strand of thread! she thought wryly. But now that she realized she had crossed that line, what was she going to do about it? For she had fallen in love with a man who didn't share her feelings one bit. He treated her with contempt and coldness—except when they went to bed. Then he used her body shamefully to satisfy his own physical needs. While her heart was bruised and bleeding, his remained untouched. The situation was hopeless and she—she was doomed to misery.

With an abrupt movement, Elizabeth dashed the tears from her eyes. She stared out at the restless sea, filled with a new excitement. Who was she, anyway? Not some miserable, mealy-mouthed creature to be pitied and swept aside! She was Elizabeth Trent, and she was young and beautiful and smart enough to get what she wanted! *Whatever* she wanted! And that included Alexander Burke.

The same stubborn, indomitable streak that had set her on her journey to Calcutta in the first place against all warnings and restrictions now enflamed her spirit once more. She would win Alex's love if it was the last thing she ever did. She would *make* him love her, despite his maddening coldness and mysterious ways. Time and circumstance would throw them together and she would use every aid she could to conquer him.

Hope surged through her and she shed despair like a cloak in the summertime. In the starlight, her violet eyes glimmered. For a long time she stood there, dreaming and planning with quickened pulse, heedless of the chill wind and spraying water. At last she turned and moved slowly, thoughtfully, toward the cabin.

Part III.

Arrival

Chapter
Seventeen

Summer slid into autumn and autumn into the first chill days of winter. The wind turned cold and bitter and the ocean crusted over with ice. On many days snow blanketed the skies, slowing progress to a near standstill as the *Hornet* plowed its way through the leaden sea. The sailors bundled in woolen jackets and heavy breeches, and donned high, thick leather boots. They wandered about on deck with their heads bowed and their bodies bent nearly double against the force of the blistering wind.

With the passing of summer and fall, the high spirits of the company also waned. The days became as dreary and monotonous as the faded grey of the sky above, and tempers flared often. Even Simms, the good-natured, red-haired lieutenant, grumbled as he stalked about the ship, and the other men vented their unhappiness in bitter arguments among themselves, punctuated by colorful language which a year ago would have turned

Elizabeth's cheeks crimson, but now provoked only an amused laugh.

The men were anxious to be home. It had been a long, torturous voyage and they yearned to see their families and homeland again, to feel solid earth beneath their booted feet, and to eat good, thick meat, and not the dried out salted pork and fish of which they had grown heartily sick. They longed for their soft feather beds and fresh clothing, and more than anything else, for their women. "Home" dominated all of their thoughts, and as each day passed, their impatience grew.

Elizabeth, too, was caught up in this restless mood. Each day, cloaked in her soiled cape, she braved the wind and snow to perch at the railing, straining her eyes to catch a glimpse of land. Ben laughed at her and told her she could stare til she went snow-blind, but it would be a long while before she saw the coast. She snapped at him to mind his own business and turned angrily back to her vigil. Some days she thought she would go mad if she didn't see land soon.

One November morning Elizabeth was dusting and straightening items in the cabin when the door burst open and Alex and Henry entered, bringing with them a gust of freezing air which made her shiver. She cast a dark look in their direction and knelt to pick up a stray stocking.

"Miss, you'll never guess," Henry cried, breaking off his conversation with Alex to rush over to her. "Ben says I'm to come live with him and his ma and pa when we get to America, and the Captain says so, too. Isn't that something? Me and Ben'll be like real brothers!"

"That's wonderful." She managed a wan smile and leaned down to give him a quick hug.

"And then," Henry continued gaily, "I'll have a ma and a pa and live in a house and. . . ." A thought struck him. "Say, Miss, where are you going to live when we get to the Colonies?"

Elizabeth made no reply, but raised inquiring eyes to Alex.

"She'll be coming home with me, Henry," he replied easily.

Henry considered this. After a brief reflection, this plan gained his approval, for he nodded agreeably, and continued to outline for her all the delights awaiting him in Philadelphia, ranging from a new family to hot buttermilk biscuits for breakfast every day. Elizabeth listened absently, her mind on other things. When Henry was gone, she turned dejectedly back to her dusting.

Alex, leaning casually against the mahogany chest, watched her. Lately, she had been depressed and irritable. No doubt the endless days at sea were gnawing away at her nerves as they were at every one else's. He shrugged mentally. What could he do? It wouldn't be much longer before they reached home, and she would just have to cope in the meantime.

Elizabeth felt his eyes upon her and whirled suddenly, flushing as their eyes met. "What are you staring at?" she demanded.

His contemptuous smile was maddening. "Nothing, Lizzie. Nothing at all." He lifted his gold enamelled snuff box from the writing desk, dropped it into the pocket of his heavy black cape and strolled to the oak door. When he opened it, another gust of freezing air whipped through the room. Then he was gone, and the door banged shut behind him.

"Oh. .hhh!" Elizabeth gritted her teeth to avoid screaming in exasperation. Nothing, nothing had gone the way she had planned! All her efforts to win her black-haired privateer had proved fruitless. He returned all of her smiles with those infuriating, cold sneers, and none of her lures could coax from him a sign of tenderness.

She sighed. When they made love, she gave herself to him with complete abandon, and he responded with a violent passion which drove her wild. But aside from their bedding, he held himself aloof from her, with heartbreaking detachment. It seemed to Elizabeth that he was strangely fascinated by her, especially when she made a deliberate effort to be alluring, but that iron control which marked his personality always interfered when she seemed on the brink of success, and he regarded her almost warily, as an adversary to be carefully watched. She began to fear that no spark of love would ever touch his heart.

She had grown discouraged as much by the dreary length of days at sea as by his indifference. She felt trapped, like an animal, desperate for land and freedom. It was ironic that on the shores of Calcutta that last fateful night she had longed for the sea as her gate to freedom. Now it was her enemy, imprisoning, stifling. How she longed for land!

The days dragged by. Slowly, endlessly. It was always cold, no matter how many layers of clothing one donned, and the sun had become a pale watery glimmer in a faded sky. Day after day the picture was the same. Choppy grey ocean and washed out sky, dotted with endless fat snowflakes. But worst of all was the view of the horizon, dark and distant, and always landless.

The first week in December it stopped snowing. For a week they made good progress, and then on Monday, the second week in December, 1778, Elizabeth heard an uproar on deck—stomping feet, yelling and whistling. She grabbed her cloak and threw it over her shoulders as she raced out of the cabin and up the steps to the deck. Thick, lacy snowflakes were falling from the morning sky.

"Is this what all the excitement is about?" she wondered listlessly. "Because it's snowing again?"

Then she saw the rail crammed with pointing, shouting sailors. She fought her way through the pack and strained to see beyond. And then she saw. A faint, brown shadow in the distance, rising against the tip of the horizon. Land! Sweet, blessed land! She found herself cheering joyously with the others. Ben hugged her so tightly she thought her ribs would crack, and Henry's laughter rose above the men's wild shouting. She peered about for Alex, but he was nowhere to be seen in the wild, rowdy mob on deck.

"There," Ben said, pointing upwards to the quarterdeck. She raised her head to see Alex standing above them, magnificent in his swirling black cape and black satin breeches, surveying the scene with folded arms.

What kind of a man is he, Elizabeth wondered with a shiver, to maintain such calm in the midst of celebration? How can I love such a man, a man with icicles in his blood?

Suddenly, Alex's voice thundered above the general hubbub. "Silence!" he ordered, and at once the shouting ceased, and the men grew quiet, staring up at him.

"We're almost home," he announced. A cheer went up once more, but he raised his hand for silence. "That doesn't mean our troubles are behind us," he continued. "Who knows what we shall find when we dock in Philadelphia? Perhaps the war is over, and England has defeated us."

The men groaned and muttered uneasily as his words stung them. The festive atmosphere evaporated into a cloud of uncertainty.

"Or perhaps the war is still in progress," Burke went on calmly. "But Philadelphia may have fallen to our enemies. I don't know what has occurred during our absence, and neither do you. That's why I want to see Simms and Johnson and Tucker in my cabin on the double. They're going to head a scouting crew into the harbor by night to see how things stand. In the meantime, the rest of you must return to your posts immediately and keep your wits about you. There may be some heavy fighting ahead if the British are blockading the coast. On the other hand. . . ." He grinned wickedly. "If all is well, we'll have some heavy wenching to do when we return to our women!"

The seamen burst into applause and cheers, encouraged by this lighter note. They returned quickly to their positions on the ship. Elizabeth quietly watched Alex hurry toward his cabin, followed by Ben Tucker, Simms, and Ralph Johnson, a wiry stick of a man with eyes that shone like a wild wolf's. When they had disappeared, she made her way to the rail, fixing her eyes on that dark, distant shadow of land.

She felt very alone. For a while she had almost

forgotten that she was English, and these men around her rebels. Enemies. Her enemies. She wondered with a stab of fear how they would treat her when she arrived in their midst, these rebellious Americans. With hatred, suspicion? Would she be a prisoner? She regarded the dark shape of land on the horizon with a new trepidation.

As the day wore on, the coastline began to take on a definite form. They left the Atlantic Ocean behind, and sailed up the Delaware River at dusk, gliding past distant, twinkling lights on shore. They encountered no other ships, and when it was fully dark, dropped anchor, and the thirty foot cutter, with its crew of seven, headed by Simms, Ben, and Johnson, was lowered from the side of the ship and set off on its scouting mission. There was an undercurrent of excitement as everyone settled down to await the report.

The report, when it came, held good news. The war had not been lost, and though Philadelphia had been occupied for a time until the past June, under the command of General William Howe, it was once again the seat of Congress, and was being held against the British by Major General Benedict Arnold. General Washington, after a harrowing winter the previous year at Valley Forge, was in winter quarters in Middlebrook, New Jersey. Simms personally assured Alex that "all was well" at his house, and that preparations were in progress for his arrival.

"And," Simms added, "I was bid to tell you that arrangements will be made for the young lady."

Pleased with the news, Alex decided to sail into port under cover of nightfall the following eve. The seamen were in a fever of excitement as the time drew near, and even Alex seemed keyed up and restless. Only Elizabeth remained untouched by the mood of celebration, as her nervousness steadily increased. She kept to the cabin, busying herself with packing her portmanteau, and barely touched her food. Anxiety over her fate grew with each passing moment.

Dusk came, followed closely by the evening darkness. A few stars trembled in the sky, and snow was falling softly as Alex hustled her out of the cabin and up to the main deck. She watched as the ship sailed smoothly into the darkened harbor and halted with a gentle thud as it touched the moorings. The journey was over.

"Come on," Alex growled, pushing her ahead of him across the lowered gangplank. She barely had time to look about her at the crew working in swift, hushed silence to secure the ship, or at the wooden planked harbor on which she stood. Alex dragged her along with him, past other shadowed ships tied to their posts, past what seemed to be a large, ghostly shipyard alongside the dock. Suddenly a man loomed up before them, leading the tallest black stallion she had ever seen, with wide, gleaming sides and a thick length of flowing mane, which the beast tossed with great spirit as it pranced and snorted restlessly in the night air.

"Here you go, Mr. Burke," the man whispered in a dry, crackling voice as he sidled closer. "I've brought Moonfire, just as you asked. And allow me to welcome you home, Sir."

"Thank you, Walter. You'll find our baggage on the dock, ready to be loaded into the carriage." Alex took the stallion's reins and turned to Elizabeth. Without a word, he hoisted her roughly into the saddle and then vaulted up behind her. Then they were off, as the black stallion sprang forward into the night.

For Elizabeth, that journey was one of breathless excitement. The wind whipped through her hair as they raced along at a breakneck pace, through a silver maze of naked, icicled trees, while the moon peered luminously down from a sky of velvet blackness. She was glad of the cloak wrapped securely about her for the icy wind bit right through her woolen breeches and jersey.

"Where are we going?" she gasped once over her shoulder, but Alex answered only with a low chuckle deep in his throat as he urged Moonfire on even faster.

Elizabeth cursed him under her breath, but she was grateful for the pressure of his strong body close against hers as they plunged through the frosted night. She felt heady with excitement and nervousness.

Presently the wooded path gave way to a cobbled street lined with tall, snow-misted houses set well back from the road. Moonfire's hooves rang as he raced along the narrow, curving street. They rounded a curve at dangerous speed, clattered swiftly past what looked like a steepled church ringed with trees, and before Elizabeth knew it, were twisting right down still another cobbled lane. At the end of this street, Alex slowed the horse to a standstill. Elizabeth glanced about, shivering.

They stood before a curved carriage drive leading up to a three story red brick mansion adorned with a high, arched entranceway. Glistening trees ringed the drive in a graceful circle. Beyond, a single light shone in one of the lower windows.

As Alex swung out of the saddle, hauling Elizabeth after him, a stout, middle-aged man hurried up out of the darkness to take Moonfire's reins. Alex spoke to him briefly and then gripped Elizabeth's arm, pushing her ahead of him up the cobbled walk.

"Let me go, damn you," she panted, wincing from his grip.

Ignoring her, he knocked upon the beautifully carved oak door. It opened almost immediately and Elizabeth was shoved forward into soft light, while behind her the door thudded shut.

She found herself in an exquisite candle-lit hallway tiled in rose and cream. Rose patterned wallpaper adorned tall walls which curved into a magnificent arch above. Ahead, to her left, she glimpsed an elegant parlor where a hearth fire roared. But she paid scant attention to these details; all her attention was drawn toward the girl who stood before her, and the man two paces behind.

The girl was petite and charmingly pretty, with soft brown curls peeking from beneath a frilly white cap. She wore a cream-colored dressing robe edged with pink lace, which contrasted becomingly with her glossy dark hair and flushed cheeks. As Elizabeth watched, she hurled herself joyously into Alex's arms, and he opened them readily to receive her.

"What's this, Jenny? Did you miss me so much?" He inquired in a tone of amused tenderness.

Elizabeth felt as though she were on fire with rage and jealousy. Who was this woman? Surely, surely not his wife! Even Alexander Burke would hardly bring her home to his wife! Or would he?

Wild thoughts spun in furious confusion inside her head.

The tall man in the shadows stepped forward, revealing that he moved with a slight limp. "Welcome home, Alex. Pardon me for interrupting your reunion, but I believe introductions are in order. Don't you agree?"

"Ah, yes. You're right, Adam, as always." He disengaged himself from the dark-haired girl and turned back to Elizabeth, pulling her forward into the soft candlelight.

"Lizzie," he said, with elaborate politeness, "allow me to introduce you to my sister, Jenny, and her husband, Mr. Adam Warren." His voice grew heavy with mocking grandeur as he sweepingly indicated Elizabeth. "Sister and dear brother, I present to you Miss Elizabeth Trent of London."

Elizabeth flushed a deep scarlet, glaring at the three before her like a cornered lioness crouched to fight. Clad in breeches and boots beneath her cape, she presented an odd, striking figure, a wild, beautiful creature, despite her bedraggled state, meeting their scrutiny with angry defiance. It was Adam Warren who spoke first, breaking the silence with a gentle voice.

"It is a pleasure to meet you, Miss Trent. We had word that you were accompanying Alex and a bedroom has been prepared for you. And may I say that we're delighted to welcome you?"

"Yes," Jenny added quickly, sincerity sparking her voice. "We're very glad to have you, but you must be cold and nearly famished. Won't you come with me to your room, Miss Trent, and I'll have Mary bring you some warm milk and biscuits."

"You're . . . very kind," said Elizabeth uncertainly, still half-afraid.

"Not at all." Jenny shot a furious look at Alex and said with significant emphasis, "We'll talk in the morning, brother dear."

The echo of Burke's responding laugh followed Elizabeth up the rose-carpeted stairway. Jenny led her past the second floor landing and down a wide, spacious corridor lined with oil portraits. They passed a row of doors before Jenny opened one, beckoning Elizabeth to enter.

A short time later she found herself propped comfortably in a feather four-poster, covered by blue satin sheets and a plump, quilted comforter, balancing a tray of steaming hot chocolate and warm, buttered biscuits upon her lap. The maid, Mary, a fat, middle-aged woman, was tending a fire in the grate, supervised by Jenny.

A fire! How long it had been since she had felt the warmth of an open hearth! Already her frozen, aching muscles were relaxing, basking in the rosy warmth. She sighed deeply, hardly able to believe that she was really here in this warm, pretty room so charmingly furnished in pine, with blue silk curtains at the windows and a huge fluffy blue throw rug upon the gleaming floor. Things were happening so quickly, so unexpectedly. These people were treating her like a welcome guest, not like Alex Burke's strumpet, which was all she could expect after that humiliating introduction. She had looked like some seedy whore, and she knew it. Her cheeks burned as she remembered, and she stared at Jenny Warren, wondering why she was being so kind to her, even pampering her.

As if she felt Elizabeth's eyes on her back, Jenny

turned around, smiling. "There, now. I think that'll burn cosily enough through the night. Are you finished with your hot chocolate? Good. Mary, you may take it now."

When the maid was gone, Jenny blew out the candles in their brass holders and only firelight flickered in the darkened room. "Good night, Miss Trent," she whispered from the doorway. "Sleep well."

"Thank you." Elizabeth felt more bewildered than ever. Things were not going at all as she had expected. Kindness instead of scorn? Respect instead of distaste? Why?

Weariness crept over her like warmth from the fire, and though she knew she ought to sort out the variety of conflicting emotions and impressions she had experienced tonight, she felt too exhausted to try. Tomorrow, she thought sleepily, stretching out beneath the sheets, feeling the feather-softness caress her aching body. Tomorrow I will face it all.

Meanwhile, Alex Burke and his brother-in-law were sipping brandy before a roaring hearth fire in the parlor Elizabeth had noted branching off the main hallway. Alex sprawled carelessly in a tapestry woven easy chair, studying the colored liquid in his glass, while Adam watched frowningly from the mantelpiece by the fire.

"So that's the whole of it, more or less," Alex announced. "Adventures and misadventures."

"You seem to have had quite a time of it."

Alex grinned. "Indeed." He took a sip of brandy. "And you? How are things at the shipyard?"

Adam moved to a chair opposite Burke, limping slightly. He was a tall, straight man, with thinning dark hair and a narrow, bony, but not unhandsome face. His sober brown eyes were set above an aquiline nose, and the line of his jaw beneath long, thin lips was firm. He sat stiffly, as if in some pain, but answered steadily enough. "Business is booming. Of course, the snow slows us down, but the men are game enough, and we've got orders aplenty to fill. The Continental Navy keeps the pressure on." He shook his head. "They need the ships faster than we can build them."

"That's always the way. Have any messengers been through lately?"

"No. Washington's holed up for the winter, as you know, and there hasn't been too much naval activity lately. But come spring. . . ."

"Right. Well, now that my men are back, maybe we can speed things up a bit. Come spring, the Navy will need those ships."

There was a brief silence, then Adam cleared his throat. "Alex," he said suddenly. "About this girl. . . ."

"Yes?" Burke looked up, his grey eyes steely.

"Now don't look at me that way, my friend. You don't intimidate me. I'm going to say what's on my mind whether you like it or not!"

Burke grinned. "Go on."

"I don't like it, Alex. Not one bit. And Jenny was very upset when Simms gave us your message. What the devil made you bring her along? Oh, I understand that it wasn't your fault she was on that damned merchantman you captured in the first place. But you didn't have to kidnap her off the dock of Calcutta, did you?"

Burke's fists clenched. He jerked to his feet and strode across the room to the heavy draperies encasing the windows. "Yes, I did have to—at the time."

He turned back and his face was a granite mask: cool, controlled, revealing none of the tension which had provoked his sudden movement a moment before. "Forgive me. I don't wish to talk of it. She's here, and she'll remain. For my sake, treat her well."

"Treat her well! You're damned right I will, poor creature! I don't imagine she's had an easy time of it—not at your hands! In my opinion, you ought to be horsewhipped!"

Burke chuckled. "She's told me so herself a number of times!" There was another silence in which he drained his brandy glass and Adam watched him closely, both puzzled and concerned.

"You're not by any chance in love with the girl, Alex?"

"In love? With that yellow-haired witch? You know me better than that! I'm no fool to fall prey to some manipulating little beauty." He looked thoughtful. "She's a lovely one, though, and as spunky as a she-cat caught in the wild. With Lizzie, I never know what to expect next—whether she'll go off into one of her airs, playing the untouchable aristocrat, or fighting like a jungle cat." He broke off abruptly under his brother-in-law's stare, and changed the subject.

"Have you seen Granger lately? How is he?"

"He'll be by tomorrow, I imagine, to see you himself. He was here when Simms brought your message and promised to come again as soon as you returned."

"I'm eager to see him, but unfortunately I'll be gone myself in the morning. I must divide the spoils among my crew first thing, and then I wish to report personally to my friend, Captain Robbins, about my journey." He placed his glass upon the mantelpiece and moved briskly toward the parlor door. "I should return within the week, however, and will gladly see him then. In the meanwhile, give him my regards."

"And the girl?" Adam called after him. "Any message for her?"

"Tell her to console herself in my absence, for it shan't be long," he replied arrogantly, and with a grin he disappeared into the now darkened hallway.

Adam Warren stirred the embers of the fire for a while, lost in thought. He knew that Jenny waited up for him, but he was reluctant to leave this room. There had been some mystery touched on here which disturbed him, and he pondered his conversation with Burke for some minutes. Finally, he shrugged and gave it up. For all the years he had known him, Alexander Burke had always been a man of almost fanatic independence and privacy, one who kept his thoughts and feelings solely to himself. He wouldn't welcome meddling or questions. And he was more than capable of settling his problems himself.

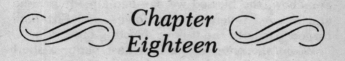

Chapter Eighteen

Elizabeth awakened in the morning to the sound of pouring water. She stretched, yawned, and sat up sleepily to see Mary emptying the steaming contents of a large earthenware pot into a shiny porcelain tub. Steam rose in a thick vapor, while just beyond, the fire roared merrily.

"Oh, Mary! A bath!" she cried in delight, hopping eagerly out of her bed.

"Yes, Miss." Mary tucked a stray grey hair into her starched white cap, smiling kindly. "Mrs. Warren thought you'd like a dip straight away, seeing as you've been on that dreadful ship and all."

The next quarter of an hour was spent in blissful luxury. Mary tempered the hot water with cold until the temperature was perfect, and Elizabeth soaked herself joyfully, rinsing away the accumulated sweat and grime, and scrubbing her hair and skin with delicious, lavender scented soap. Afterwards, wrapped in thick towels, she brushed her

269

long, tawny hair before the mirror framing the pine
dressing table. It felt wonderful to be clean and
sweet-smelling. She wondered how Alex would
react to her freshened state, but then remembered
how furious she was with him because of his hateful behavior last night. She cursed him under her
breath and turned away from the mirror to help
Mary, who was sorting through her wardrobe.
Somehow, the blessed woman had already pressed
and cleaned several of her gowns, and Elizabeth
turned busily to the task of selecting one.

When she entered the breakfast parlor a short
while later, dressed in a gown of pale, sea-green
muslin, with matching ribbons in her hair, she
found Jenny seated at a beautifully carved cherry-
wood table laden with hot, fresh-baked bread,
fruits, and a platter of cold meats.

"Good morning," she said rather shyly from the
doorway.

Jenny stared at her in amazement, startled by the
transformation in her appearance, for she looked
quite different from the bedraggled creature Alex
had dragged into the hallway. "Miss Trent! How
nice to see you looking so well!" she responded
warmly, when she could speak. "Won't you join
me for breakfast?"

Elizabeth accepted and seated herself at the
table, studying her hostess with great interest. Last
night she had received the impression of youthful
prettiness, and today confirmed it. Jenny Warren
was perhaps eighteen, dark-haired, and grey-eyed.
In the morning light which streamed in through the
wide bay windows, she immediately saw the resemblance between Alex and his sister, for she was
the soft, feminine version of his dark, handsome

masculinity. But despite the similarities of coloring and line, there was a certain contrast to their appearance, one which Elizabeth noted immediately. Jenny possessed a delicacy and serenity, a gentle peacefulness, which differed sharply from Alex's air of restless turbulence and power. He was a wild stallion chafing impatiently to be off; she a dove, comfortably nested. It was strange, Elizabeth reflected, that a brother and sister should be so alike, and yet so different.

"I hope you slept well," Jenny said, pouring coffee into Elizabeth's china cup.

"Quite well, thank you," Elizabeth replied. "And the bath this morning was wonderful. It was kind of you to think of it."

Silence fell. The two women sat stiffly, each desperately wanting to begin a conversation; neither knowing how. The uncomfortable nature of their situation made normal, trivial talk seem ridiculous, but neither of them knew how to broach the subject dominating their thoughts. At last, Jenny swallowed a gulp of coffee and began determinedly to speak.

"Miss Trent, I want you to know that I find my brother's conduct in abducting you and bringing you here completely abominable. It's difficult for me to express it properly, but. . . ." She paused, and then continued miserably. "When I *think* of what he's done I could wring his neck!"

"I've longed to do that myself! Quite often, as a matter of fact," Elizabeth answered wryly. "Tell me, where is your odious brother this morning?"

"Gone. He had errands that called him out of town, but he said he'd return within the week. Not that I imagine you're anxious to see him again!"

"Of course not." Elizabeth busied herself with buttering a slice of hot, fragrant bread, inwardly fighting back an instinctive wave of disappointment. So he had gone away, had he? Good! She'd be the last one to miss him. She glanced up to see Jenny watching her intently, and as violet eyes fastened on grey ones, she realized with a start that Alex's sister had the same unnerving ability to pierce one with her eyes as he could. In spite of herself, she felt herself blushing under that keen scrutiny.

"Mrs. Warren," she said hastily, in an attempt to divert attention from her own feelings. "Allow me to thank you for all your kindnesses to me, despite the fact that I've been dumped into your midst so rudely. You must think me quite. . . ."

"Please, Elizabeth, say no more! You mustn't think we blame you for this mess Alex has created! That would be absurd. All of our sympathies are with *you*, for it is quite clear that you have been grievously wronged—and I told Alex so this morning, before he left, and in no uncertain terms!"

At the mental picture conjured up by this statement of Jenny scolding her formidable brother, Elizabeth could not suppress a smile, and she found her hostess smiling back quite readily.

"There, now. We shall be friends, I hope. I insist that you call me Jenny—Mrs. Warren sounds quite stuffy!—and I shall call you Elizabeth—with your permission, of course."

"Of course. Please do—I'd like very much to be friends." Elizabeth found herself liking this charming, gentle-tempered girl. If only her brother shared a similar temperament!

After breakfast, Jenny led her on a tour of the

house, a three-story Georgian building furnished in what Elizabeth recognized as the highest quality of taste and elegance. The several spacious parlors boasted Chippendale chairs and richly embroidered damask sofas, with elaborate, embroidered tapestries and fine oil paintings gracing wood-panelled walls. Numerous Chinese vases, porcelain figurines, and silver candlesticks adorned finely carved maple tables, and an exquisite maple cabinet with tinted glass windows highlighted the main parlor, whose rose velvet sofa and matching Chippendale chairs rested upon an intricately designed Oriental rug. Elizabeth was too well-bred to exclaim, but she was highly impressed with the beauty of this house. She settled comfortably upon the velvet sofa and watched as Jenny picked up a basket of bright-colored needlework. Jenny's fingers worked with swift assurance as she worked blue thread in a neat, complicated design. And though questions buzzed in Elizabeth's head about Alex, the obvious wealth of this house, and the refinement of his sister, years of mannered training inhibited her from voicing them.

Her dilemma was ended when the parlor door opened suddenly and Adam Warren entered, his limp slightly noticeable as he crossed the room to bestow a kiss upon his wife's cheek.

"Good morning, ladies." He smiled at Elizabeth. "I hope you slept well, Miss Trent."

"Elizabeth, please. And yes, I spent an excellent night, thank you." She studied him as he moved stiffly to a small cherry-wood writing desk, opened a drawer, and removed an enamelled snuff box. He was a good-looking man in a quiet, unassuming way, quite different from Alex's overpowering appearance. He wore a simple dove grey satin waist-coat, a ruffled white shirt, and grey and white striped silk stockings above highly polished, silver buckled shoes. His brown hair was tied in a queue at the back of his neck and lightly powdered. A dependable man, Elizabeth thought, and there is kindness in his eyes.

"How are things at the shipyard this morning?" Jenny was asking. "Did you tell the men of Alex's return?"

"Yes, and they were heartily glad to hear it. Spirits soared, despite this confounded snow." Heavy brocaded draperies secured to the side of the rectangularly paned window revealed a snowy landscape where tall trees were heavily weighted by white mounds upon their branches, and heavy snow still fell steadily. Overhead, the sun glimmered in a pale blue sky, causing the snow on the ground to glitter like a sea of diamonds. But it was not the landscape which attracted Elizabeth's attention. She leaned forward eagerly to address Adam.

"The shipyard? Is that where you've been this morning?" Here at last was a clue to this family's background.

"Yes," he replied. "You must have passed it when you disembarked last night. To the right of the harbor."

"Yes, I remember it."

"Adam has been running things for Alex while he's been away," Jenny explained. "And I must say," she added, smiling up at her husband. "He's been doing a splendid job of it."

"I see," Elizabeth murmured. "Then Alex owns the shipyard?"

"Yes. His father left it to him—and a share to Jenny as part of her dowry. A booming business it is, too."

"Really? I'm surprised he abandoned it to become a privateer."

"Oh, Alex was always the adventurous type," Jenny laughed, putting aside her needlework. "Although at first, when he received his letter of marque from the Continental government, he never intended to sail off himself. He really meant to outfit the ship with men and arms and to set them on their way." She paused, seemingly about to say more, but instead pursed her lips together.

Adam continued for her gently. "Then, when I was wounded in action and had to return home, he saw a perfect opportunity. He could follow his heart's desire and commandeer the ship, leaving me to run the business in his absence."

"How like him!" Elizabeth cried. "I suppose it never occurred to him that you might need rest to get your strength back—that you might not want to tend to his stupid business while he went traipsing about making a fool of himself!"

There was a startled silence. Then Adam said quietly, "You're mistaken, Elizabeth. For one thing, since Alex and I are partners in the shipyard, I have a great interest in tending to its business, for my own reasons, as well as on his behalf. And for another thing, his decision to leave me in charge was based on the kindest of motives, not at all out of selfishness, as you suggest." He hesitated for a moment, his eyes meeting Jenny's briefly, and then continued in a quiet, steady voice.

"After I was wounded and unable to continue as a soldier in the militia, I went through a period of severe depression. It is difficult to explain, but I felt useless, as if I were a burden upon everyone. Alex sensed this and decided that by making me solely responsible for the supervision of the shipyard, he might help me to regain my self-esteem. Oh, it's true, the excitement of the journey lured him also, but he was primarily concerned with helping me. Which," he added, stroking Jenny's soft brown hair gently, "he did. He forced me to get busy and stop feeling sorry for myself, and he made me realize that I could still do a man's job and be a useful member of the human race, even though my leg injury resulted in permanent damage."

"Oh. I . . . see," was all Elizabeth found to say. It seemed that whenever she found Alex most hateful, most selfish and inconsiderate, she soon learned otherwise. He was more than ever a man of contradictions, totally unpredictable.

"Well," she at last remarked bitterly, "I'm glad he was able to help *you*. He's succeeded in ruining *my* life very nicely. And now I suppose I'll be scorned by the entire city of Philadelphia just because, through no fault of my own, I've been compromised by your dear, generous Alex." The words were out before she could stop them, but though Adam and Jenny looked concerned, they did not appear angry, and before she could apologize for her rude outburst, Adam put up a hand to prevent her from speaking.

"It's all right, Elizabeth. We understand, and believe me, we're very sorry for the predicament in which you find yourself. Alex, Jenny, and I discussed it at some length early this morning and we feel we've come up with a possible solution."

Elizabeth sighed resignedly. "Yes?" she asked.

"What is your solution?"

"We've settled upon a slight fabrication which may save everyone a great deal of embarrassment. You see, we're prepared to claim you as a cousin from New Jersey. We'll say that Alex visited you upon his return voyage, en route to Philadelphia, and found you in the midst of some family crisis—for example, your little brother and sister ill, and your mother anxious to send you away, lest you catch the fever. Upon hearing this, Alex brought you here for a visit with Jenny." He stared at her earnestly. "What do you think of it? Does it meet with your approval?"

"Have I a choice?"

"No," Jenny admitted frankly. "It's not a perfect solution, I grant you, but it will do. I don't think anyone will question you too closely, and claiming kinship with Alex will make your journeying together much more acceptable. Really, Elizabeth, I sincerely believe that this little story will make things easier for all of us."

Elizabeth stared from one to the other of them. It was true; this story, like that which she had told Robert Mabry when he had captured the privateers, would help save her reputation. She ought to be grateful for that. Yet she was so tired of the lies, the pretending. Why must she go to all these pains just to avoid offending society? Sometimes it seemed so silly.

"What of the seamen?" she asked wearily. "Won't they reveal the truth while talking with their wives and families? Gossip spreads quickly."

"Alex has sworn them all to secrecy under the most dire threats of restribution. I'll wager they'll hold their tongues." Adam rose and limped over to the window. "The only other people who know the truth are the four of us, and Granger. He was here the night Simms brought word of the ship. But don't worry about Geoffrey. He'll stand by the story we put about."

"Who is Granger?"

"Geoffrey Granger," Jenny explained, "owns the mill which provides lumber for our shipyard. He's also Alex's oldest and dearest friend. They grew up together. Many was the hour they spent swimming in the Schulykill, or racing their horses like demons. They were forever into some mischief! I think you'll like Geoffrey, Elizabeth. He'll probably stop by this afternoon to visit and that will give you a chance to get acquainted."

"Is he like your brother?" Elizabeth inquired, intrigued about what sort of man Alex would choose as a lifelong friend.

"I suppose he is, in some ways," Jenny answered thoughtfully. "You'll have to judge for yourself. He's quite gentlemanly."

In that case, Elizabeth decided privately, they must be vastly different indeed. Aloud, however, she said nothing. She already regretted her earlier criticism of Alex to his family and was determined not to hurt them again by her carelessness. Jenny and Adam Warren were good, generous people, and she had no right to take out her anger with Alex on them. Just because he had gone off and abandoned her as soon as they arrived in America, without a good-bye, or any concern for her welfare, or any thought for her at all, well, that was no reason to offend his relations, who were obviously devoted to him. No, she would take up her grievances with Alex in person at the first opportunity. It would give her great pleasure to tell him exactly what she thought of him!

Her thoughts were interrupted by the announcement of luncheon, and she followed Adam and Jenny into the dining room. The meal was simple yet delicious, with a tasty roasted chicken, hot buttered peas, a thick hasty pudding, and a large platter of delicately browned potatoes. Afterwards, Adam had to return to the shipyard, but Jenny led her upstairs to the nursery, where she was introduced to Sarah Warren, a lively child of three, with long, dark curls and chocolate brown eyes. The little girl greatly resembled her mother, but there was also something of Adam in the way her mobile eyebrows drew together in concentration, and lifted in surprise.

Elizabeth also met Hannah, a big-boned, jolly woman with a cloud of white hair and kindly blue eyes set deeply in a puffy, lined face. Hannah had been Jenny's nurse, and was now Sarah's, and seemed so comfortably settled in a rocking chair in the corner by the fire, with the little girl on her lap and her knitting basket beside her, that she might have been a part of the room itself, as warm and cozy as the nursery. Elizabeth spent the next few hours playing with Sarah, who was as bright and lively as a puppy, and chatting companionably with Jenny and Hannah. It was as pleasant a day as she had spent in a long time and she realized how sorely she had missed the company of women friends, of comfortable, idle talk, and of lazy afternoons before a fire. The memories of the cramped, freezing, perpetually rocking ship faded, and she felt herself already adjusting to this new, much more comfortable life. It was like being home in London again . . . almost.

It was later that same afternoon, when she and

Jenny were having their tea in the parlor, that she first met Geoffrey Granger. He swept smoothly in upon them, his full-length crimson great coat swirling about his black-booted ankles, an enormous cocked hat atop his thick brown curls, and a shiny black cane, its ivory tip polished to perfection, held carelessly in a gloved hand.

How like a cat he moves, Elizabeth thought instantly, struck by the magnificent, panther-like grace of the man. Jenny rose immediately and hurried to greet him, and Elizabeth gracefully extended her hand as introductions were performed. He lifted her fingers to his lips with easy assurance, and the soft tip of his brown mustache lightly brushed her hand. Then, as their eyes met, she felt an instinctive quickening of her pulse. There was something about this man, something vaguely familiar. Perhaps, she told herself, it was only his resemblance, in certain ways, to Alexander Burke. He was tall, approximately Alex's height, with the same big-shouldered physique and aura of power. His eyes were slate blue, lighter and cooler than Elizabeth's, like a crystal pond.

"Miss Trent, I'm delighted to meet you," he said warmly, smiling down into her eyes. "Although I wish the circumstances might have been different. It seems my friend, Alex, has been a trifle—shall we say?—rash."

Surprisingly, she felt no discomfiture at this reference to her abduction. Geoffrey Granger was a sophisticated man, and she no longer a virgin-child. She met his gaze squarely and answered with a composed smile.

"You're very kind, Mr. Granger. How nice to

know that Alexander Burke has such a gentlemanly friend."

Gentlemanly. Jenny had been right. It was precisely the word to describe him, Elizabeth mused, as he removed his cloak and hat, and deposited his cane in a corner. As he took a seat, and Jenny poured the tea, Elizabeth studied him, noting the fine cut of his black satin waistcoat and the perfectly starched ruffle of shirt at his throat and sleeves. His vest was embroidered in rose and gray and trimmed with small gold buttons, and his silver gray stockings fit snugly over supple, strong-looking legs. His appearance was immaculate, the first style of elegance, as only money and good breeding can assure. She could not help but compare him to Alex, who despite his aristocratic refinement, which she had noted from the first, possessed a personality edged with rough, volatile restlessness, an energy and strength that could not be contained. She admitted to herself that it was this roughness, this potential for explosive action, which most attracted her to Burke, even as it simultaneously repelled. Granger, on the other hand, as she observed him drinking his tea, his long, well-shaped fingers gripping the fragile Delft cup, lacked this roughened edge. He was all polish and politeness—totally masculine, yet with a friendliness and mildness of manner which denoted the finest breeding.

She watched him from beneath her lashes, wondering just why he attracted her interest so greatly, struck by a familiarity of appearance and gesture that nagged at her. At last, however, she gave it up. After all, he was a handsome man, smoothly polished and obviously wise in the ways of the

world. Naturally, she found him intriguing. That
was all there was to it.

"So Alex has run off again, has he?" Granger was
saying softly. "Quite unfriendly of him, Jenny,
don't you think?"

"Oh, Geoffrey, you know how he is. He can't
rest until he's divided the prize money with his
men. And then he felt obliged to report in person to
Captain Robbins."

"Prize money?" Elizabeth's eyes widened in surprise. "What prize money? Alex and his men barely
escaped with their skins from Calcutta, much less
bringing any British ships with them."

"They brought no ships," Jenny told her, "but
the night they escaped, Alex's men plundered the
merchantmen that were set to sail, and brought off
most of their goods, as well as a few sackfuls of
gold. Didn't Alex tell you, Elizabeth?"

"No, he never did," she murmured faintly. Then,
as the significance of this news dawned upon her,
she became angry. "Poor Captain Mills," she cried,
setting her cup down so abruptly that some of the
tea splashed over the edge. "He was all set to sail
for England in the morning. You can imagine his
predicament when he found his cargo plundered!
Oh, how despicable! To steal from innocent
people. . . ." She broke off abruptly, realizing that
to Jenny and Geoffrey Granger, Captain Mills rep-
resented "the enemy." She set her lips together in
silent chagrin.

"Elizabeth." Jenny's voice was gentle. "I know
it's difficult to understand, but in the end,
privateering hampers the British Navy, and that's
why it's necessary to attack merchant ships. Alex is
not a heartless man, nor is he a thief. None of us like

it, but then, war in itself is not very pleasant, is it?"

Elizabeth maintained a stony silence, looking at her hands. It was Granger who said, "It is always difficult to see an individual as one's enemy. How much easier to see only the swarming masses. But those masses are made up of individuals, no better nor worse than we ourselves. Believe me, Miss Trent, none of us likes having to injure individuals for the sake of our cause, but sometimes it is necessary in order to achieve our final goals."

"Then you believe that the end justifies the means?" she queried, her violet eyes dark and troubled.

"Yes," he answered firmly. "I do."

A chill swept over her. She didn't know why, nor did this response last long, but something within her rebelled against this philosophy.

A few moments later the incident was forgotten. They began discussing the tale to be circulated about Elizabeth's background, and Granger readily promised to uphold the story. Moreover, he expressed certainty that the instant Philadelphia cast eyes upon her, Elizabeth would become the toast of the town.

"Do you really think so?" Elizabeth asked thoughtfully.

"Undoubtedly. There's talk of a ball to be given sometime in the next few months, and I think I'd better reserve a dance with you immediately. May I have the honor?"

"Of course." She smiled, but seemed only to be half listening, as if her mind were on something else.

At last Granger rose to leave, declining Jenny's dinner invitation, but promising to call again soon.

"Miss Trent," he said, taking her hand in the friendliest manner. "May I say it has been a delight meeting you? Please excuse my impertinence, but I must add that I've been most pleasantly surprised. You are not at all what I expected."

She regarded him with a glimmer of amusement. "And precisely what were you expecting, Sir?"

"Certainly not a lady of quality. I had not thought Alex so great a scoundrel as that! But it does no good to talk of it at this point, so let me merely say that I am at your service, ma'am, at any time."

"Thank you. I'll remember that."

He bowed slightly and strode to the door, but turned back suddenly as if just remembering something. "Oh, by the way, Jenny, has a messenger been through lately?"

"No, though Alex expects one soon. We'll just have to bide our time."

"Quite right. I'm sure now that Alex is back. . . . Well, give my regards to Adam, and tell Alex to kindly stay put for a bit when he returns so that old friends might have a chance to visit! Good day, ladies."

He was gone in a crimson swirl of cape, closing the parlor door behind him. Elizabeth stared after him for a moment, wondering what he had meant about "a messenger." She debated over whether to ask Jenny, but then decided it would be rude to ask questions about a conversation of which she was not a part.

Jenny was chatting about preparations for dinner, and about Adam and Sarah, and other household matters, but Elizabeth scarcely heard. Her mind was on something else, something Geoffrey

Granger had said. About her becoming the toast of Philadelphia. His words of idle gallantry had triggered an idea in urgent need of development. And for the remainder of the afternoon, as she and Jenny talked casually of everyday things, her head was full of secret plans, weaving and spinning an intricate pattern of her own design.

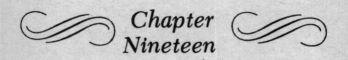

Chapter
Nineteen

On the following day, Jenny took Elizabeth for
her first carriage ride around the city. It was a cold,
December day, but the brisk air was invigorating,
and snow sparkled under a bright sun. Even the sky
blazed a brilliant blue, as if inviting one outdoors.
Comfortably ensconced on the upholstered seat of
the carriage, with Jenny and Sarah opposite, and a
warm blanket tucked snugly over her lap, Elizabeth
peered eagerly out the window. Jenny had lent her
a dark woolen cloak for the expedition, since her
once beautiful white cape was now far too shabby to
be seen in. She had also promised that she would
send for her own dressmaker that same afternoon to
fit Elizabeth for an entirely new wardrobe.

"We can't expect you to be the toast of Philadelphia in these few gowns you managed to bring
along!" Jenny had cried gaily during breakfast.

Embarrassed by this generous offer, Elizabeth
had tried to decline but Jenny had interrupted her
determinedly, with the information that Alex had

given her firm instructions about the matter.

"Alex had given you instructions? About me?" she faltered.

"He certainly has. You're to select whatever you like—cost is no consideration. Those are his words exactly." Jenny laughed. "Come now, Elizabeth, don't look so shocked. If my brother could kidnap you clear across the ocean, I think the least he can do is compensate you with a decent wardrobe! Surely you must agree."

True enough, Elizabeth had decided suddenly. And besides, a few beautiful new gowns would certainly help her new plan to succeed. So why not let Alexander Burke foot the bill for his own undoing?

Now, as the carriage clattered steadily along the cobbled road, Elizabeth watched with growing interest and amazement. Inundated with British rumor that the Colonies were wild and uncivilized, she was considerably startled by her first daylight glimpse of Philadelphia. From the moment they left behind the elegant residential neighborhood known, Jenny informed her, as Society Hill, where the Burke house stood amidst a little park of land, she watched in increasing wonder. She had imagined to find Philadelphia a rowdy little village, with dirty unpaved streets and small crowded buildings. Nothing that she had ever heard in England had prepared her for this lovely steepled city, with its wide, brick-paved streets crossing each other neatly at right angles, or for the profusion of elegant carriages and simple carts that traveled alongside each other through the town, or for the number and variety of gabled houses and shops lining the main streets. She listened delightedly as

Jenny pointed out places of interest. There, on
Chestnut Street, that solid, elegant structure with
the ornate clock steeple and weather-vaned tower
—that was the Pennsylvania State House, where
the Declaration of Independence had been signed
in 1776, and where the representatives of the thir-
teen colonies had met in the First and Second Continental Congresses. Around the corner, on Orianna
Street, was the home of Mr. Benjamin Franklin.
Past beautiful steepled churches and sturdy, two-
story brick taverns they trotted, while Elizabeth
drank in the marvels of this city. Jenny proudly told
her that Philadelphia was the leading colonial city,
not only the American political center, but also the
financial center. Due to its strategic location on the
Delaware River, the city was an invaluable port,
and its shipyard built vessels not only for the Pennsylvania State Navy, but for the Continental Navy
as well. Elizabeth was impressed. No wonder Alex
and his family lived so richly. Their shipyard was of
prime importance to the entire group of colonies, as
well as to the mother city.

"I never expected anything like this!" she exclaimed frankly. "What a beautiful, exciting
place!"

"It *is* exciting," Jenny agreed with a smile. "Especially since we're fortunate enough to entertain
some highly interesting visitors. The Marquis de
Lafayette was here a year ago, and I must say, he
hurried the beatings of many hearts!"

"Lafayette!" Elizabeth had heard of the wealthy
young French nobleman who had defied his King
to come to America and aid the colonists in their
struggle. He had been the talk of London in the
days before she'd sailed for Calcutta, and ev-

erybody had agreed that there wasn't a more romantic figure alive than the daring young Marquis.

"Did you meet him, Jenny? Was he very handsome?"

"Yes, I met him at a dinner party. He wasn't precisely handsome," she replied thoughtfully, remembering. "But I've never met a more charming young man. He began as a mere private, without pay, and quickly rose to the rank of Major General. And he became very good friends with General Washington almost immediately."

General Washington. Elizabeth had heard much about the tough, shrewd American commander. He was respected but bitterly cursed by Englishmen who wanted the war ended. Despite incredible odds, the man managed to hold together a rag-tag army, evading British traps, heading off advances. She wondered what he was like, and if she would ever meet him.

Suddenly, a wave of guilt washed over her. How could she sit here calmly admiring this rebellious city and discussing the Colonies' heroes? She was British, an alien here, an enemy. She ought to remain coldly aloof from the goings-on around her. But she couldn't. For some inexplicable reason, the moment she had set foot in this strange new country she had become involved, wanting desperately to know everything about it.

Perhaps I'm a traitor, she thought gloomily. Where in heaven's name is my sense of loyalty? I love England—it's my home, my homeland.

She lapsed into a troubled silence, which lasted for the remainder of the drive. Though Sarah giggled and babbled incessantly to her mother, Elizabeth scarcely heard, so immersed was she in her own disturbed contemplations.

The afternoon, however, left her very little time for guilt. The dressmaker arrived immediately after luncheon, a tiny wisp of a woman with silver hair and small, bird-like eyes, who scurried into the parlor where they were having coffee.

"I hurried right over, Mrs. Warren," she assured them shrilly, "as soon as I got your note. Is this the young lady I'm to outfit? Well, she'll be a pleasure to fit, let me tell you, not like these stout old dowagers who take it into their heads to wear the latest styles. Isn't that right, Carrie? You've seen them, you know what I mean."

The latter was addressed to a slender, pretty girl with long, auburn curls tied with a ribbon, who carried a parcel of boxes in the dressmaker's wake. "Yes, Miss Whigby," she replied obediently.

"I hope you don't mind," Miss Whigby hurried on, taking immediate charge of the parlor, opening boxes and spreading fabric over the sofa as she talked. "Carrie's learning the dressmaking trade from me, so I brought her along to help. You know Carrie, don't you, Mrs. Warren?" She raised her eyebrows significantly. "John Peterson's daughter."

"Yes, I know. How is your mother, Carrie?" Jenny asked gently.

"She's getting along nicely, ma'am, thank you."

Elizabeth, fingering some fine emerald green silk, noted the girl's quietness and caught a sense of sadness about her. She was a pretty thing, with soft, fawn-like brown eyes which held a frightened expression when she looked at Miss Whigby, who obviously intimidated her. Without knowing why, Elizabeth felt sorry for her.

"Now Miss . . . Trent, is it?" the seamstress continued. "Let me show you some of these treasures. Take this fabric for instance—fine linen, it is, you'll find none finer if you travel all the way to London or Paris. And such a pretty shade of blue; it would be lovely with your eyes. Don't you think so, Mrs. Warren? Carrie, *do* stand back, girl, so Miss Trent may see."

Miss Whigby chattered on in this vein, her fingers nervously patting and smoothing the fabrics, those dark, bird-like eyes darting critically over Elizabeth's face and figure. She had brought an ample selection and in no time at all Elizabeth and Jenny were caught up in the excitement of soft, beautiful fabrics and pretty colors. How long it had been since Elizabeth had had any new clothes! She selected the green silk for a riding habit, blue linen for a morning dress, some charming pastel muslins edged with lace, and a length of rich, dark blue satin for a new cloak. As an afterthought she selected some delicate, cream-colored Spanish lace for a shawl.

"Elizabeth, you'll need a ball gown!" Jenny exclaimed suddenly. "After all, Geoffrey Granger mentioned that there is talk of a ball. You must have something special for that."

Elizabeth remembered the silver gauze ball gown she had brought with her from England. Memories returned of her indecision over including the dress in her trunk. How long ago that seemed! Well, here at last was her chance to wear it.

Mary fetched the gown from her wardrobe and they all examined it scrupulously. It was still beautiful, the silver gauze netting delicate and lovely.

"I can see that you don't need a new gown, after all," Jenny admitted. "This is enchantingly pretty."

Miss Whigby began replacing the fabrics in their boxes, but Elizabeth glanced again at the silver gown. How sweet it was, how charmingly youthful. She remembered how once she had considered it the most beautiful gown imaginable. Now it seemed only a remarkably pretty dress, a dress for a carefree, innocent young girl. A dress no longer for her.

"Wait," she ordered impulsively, as Miss Whigby settled the lid on a box. "I want to see something else . . . something special."

The dressmaker's eyes lit up. "Yes, Miss. Of course." She snapped her fingers and Carrie handed over a large box. Miss Whigby withdrew a length of yellow organza. "Trimmed with beads, perhaps," she suggested eagerly.

"No." Elizabeth shook her head.

"What do you think of this silk, Miss Trent? It's the color of orchids. You could wear orchids in your hair. . . ."

"No." A corner of fabric caught Elizabeth's eye and she leaned across the dressmaker to pull aside a fold of tissue paper. There in a plain white box lay the most beautiful crimson velvet fabric she had ever seen. The color was deep, rich, and striking, the velvet soft as rose petals beneath her touch. It was exactly what she wanted. And she knew just what to do with it.

"Miss Whigby, will you design the dress according to my specifications?"

"Why, of course!"

"Excellent. I'll take this crimson velvet then, if you please."

Amidst the happy chorus of exclamations over the dramatic beauty of the material, a knock sounded upon the parlor door.

"Come in," called Jenny, rubbing the soft velvet against her cheek.

"Excuse me, ladies," spoke a self-conscious voice from the doorway, and Elizabeth whirled to see Ben Tucker step awkwardly into the room.

"Ben!" She flew to him and grasped his hands warmly. "How are you? You look wonderful!"

He did indeed, all strapping six feet of him. His thatch of curly blond hair was brushed neatly, and his mischievous blue eyes sparkled brightly in a flushed, healthy face. He wore a leather deerskin jacket over a white linen shirt and brown woolen breeches, all of which looked brand new. So did the shiny leather boots on his feet, Elizabeth noted.

"Much better than those ragged old things I've been wearing lately, wouldn't you say?" he grinned. He in turn studied her appearance admiringly. "You look pretty dandy yourself, Liz . . . Miss Trent." He broke off in sudden confusion, remembering all at once the other people in the room, the story he had sworn to uphold. His face flushed a deep red.

"Come in, Ben," Elizabeth invited, covering the moment smoothly by drawing him into the room. "You know Jenny, I'm sure, and this is Miss Whigby, and Carrie . . . Peterson, was it?"

The girl nodded, then dropped her eyes shyly.

"Oh, yes, I know the ladies," Ben began cheerfully, glancing from Jenny to Miss Whigby to Carrie, then suddenly back to the girl. "Carrie Peterson?" he exclaimed disbelievingly.

She lifted innocent brown eyes to his. "Yes, sir."

"I . . . remember you. Your father owns the bakery on Second Street. You were just a schoolroom miss the last time I saw you!"

"That was more than a year ago, Ben," Jenny reminded him, adding gently, "Unfortunately, Mr. Peterson was killed recently in a British raid on Mincock Island in New Jersey. He was enlisted in the militia, you know."

"Oh! I didn't know—that is, I hadn't realized. . . ." Ben stared at Carrie's bent head. She appeared to be studying the floor. "I'm sorry, Miss Peterson. I didn't mean to upset you."

During all of this, Miss Whigby studied him disapprovingly. A brash, impudent young man, she concluded, judging from the familiar way he had addressed Miss Trent and the rudeness with which he stared at young Carrie. Why, he hadn't drawn his eyes away from her since the moment they'd been introduced! Well, enough of this nonsense. She knew how to put an end to it!

"Mrs. Warren," she said primly, "I have other business to attend to, you know, so if this young man doesn't object, I'd like to begin fitting your cousin for her new gowns. The day *is* getting on, after all."

"Of course. You're quite right." Jenny turned to Ben, who was still staring raptly at Carrie. "Ben, was there some reason why you stopped by today?" she prodded, suppressing a desire to laugh.

"Oh! Yes!" he said, with a start. "I've just come from the shipyard. Mr. Warren sent me to tell you that he'll be staying late tonight and not to wait dinner for him. We're a mite behind schedule and he's aiming to catch up."

"You work for . . . my cousin, Alex, at the shipyard, then?" Elizabeth asked, fitting previously unknown pieces into a pattern.

"Yes, I'm a ship's carpenter, or at least, I was— until Captain Burke agreed to take me along as a privateer!" He grinned at her. "Things seem pretty dull now that I'm back. We had some fine adventures at sea!"

"I'm sure you did!" she murmured pleasantly, though a warning note hid beneath her casual tone. "I'm happy to say that my journey from New Jersey was quite tame."

"Yes, indeed!" Ben's eyes danced mischievously. "And a good thing, too. A fine young lady like yourself wouldn't have enjoyed some of our rough times one bit! A privateer ship's no place for a lady, that's certain!"

"Ben, I think you'd best be going now," Jenny said hastily, noting the cold, disapproving stare Miss Whigby was fixing him with, and fearful that his playfulness would result in an embarrassing slip.

"Yes," Elizabeth agreed. "I have no more time to hear of your exploits, Mr. Tucker!"

"Well, come by sometime to visit Henry," he called, as Jenny led him almost forcefully to the door. "He's up at our farm, near the banks of the Schulykill, and he's happy as a chipmunk, I must say. He wants to see you."

"I'll come by soon," she promised.

At the door, Ben paused, glancing hesitatingly over his shoulder. "Good day, Carrie." He said the name slowly, as if savoring it.

Carrie raised her eyes to smile shyly at him. "Good day, Mr. Tucker," she said in a sweet little voice which seemed to have a sudden, mesmerizing effect on Ben. Under his transfixed gaze, a blush rose in her cheeks.

"Good-bye, Ben," Jenny said firmly, pushing him into the hallway, and shutting the door quite determinedly upon him. She exchanged amused glances with Elizabeth.

"Miss Whigby, I'm very sorry for the interruption."

The dressmaker, her feather obviously ruffled, sniffed peevishly. "Hmmm! What an impudent young man! I don't see why you didn't give him a good setdown, Mrs. Warren, the way he barged in like that, taking up your time. He's a good example of how unmannerly young people are these days. . . ."

"Miss Whigby," Elizabeth interrupted coldly, "Ben Tucker is a most charming, polite young man, and moreover, he is a good friend of mine. Now, may we get on with the fitting?"

Miss Whigby clamped her lips tightly together and reached for a box of pins.

Later, Elizabeth and Jenny discussed the scene.

"I do think Ben was immediately struck with Carrie!" Elizabeth cried delightedly. "She *is* a fetching little thing. Yet she seems so unhappy."

"Her father's death was a great blow. Now her mother must support a family of five children, of which I believe Carrie to be the oldest. Poor child, I pity her all the more for having to work for Miss Whigby."

"Perhaps a strong, handsome young man will lift away some of her burdens," Elizabeth suggested, eyes sparkling.

"Such as Ben Tucker, I suppose? Do you think Carrie is attracted to him?"

"She'd be out of her head not to be," Elizabeth stated flatly. "He's certainly good-looking, and she must have noticed the way he stared at her, like a foolish puppy! Did you see the way she blushed? I believe they're both in love!"

"You're a hopeless romantic, Elizabeth!" Jenny laughed. "How do you know so much about love?"

Elizabeth made no reply.

"I'm sorry, my dear." Jenny reached out and touched her hand. "That was a tactless remark. Forgive me."

"Whatever do you mean?" Elizabeth asked airily.

"You know precisely what I mean."

Their eyes met; Elizabeth was the first to look away.

"I'll do whatever I can to help you," Jenny said quietly, but Elizabeth, wondering miserably if her feelings were really that transparent, merely shook her head and made no reply.

That evening she sat in the pine rocking chair by the window in her bedroom, gazing out at the fairy-tale scene below her. Soft white snow shrouded the earth, the trees were frosted silver, and a sliver of moon sliced the midnight sky. She watched that shining sliver of moon sliced the midnight sky. She watched that shining sliver of moon, thinking of Ben Tucker and the time they had spent together on the *Hornet*. She remembered the night he had kissed her beneath the stars last winter, a whole year ago. He had been infatuated with her then. How sweet and tender that kiss had been. There was no innocence about that night which made her sigh as she recalled it. And then she remembered what had come after: Alex finding them in each other's arms, his rage, his violent, passionate lovemaking. That was the night she had lost her virginity, and discovered the richness of passion deep within her. That was the first night she had felt his warm, devouring kisses, felt his hands caress her heated body. She flushed warmly, remembering. And she realized suddenly that she was grateful to Ben, grateful for that kiss under the stars. For it was that kiss which had led to Alex's raging jealousy, and that jealousy was now the key—the source of her plan. It was woman's ultimate weapon, the oldest most powerful weapon ever devised in the ageless battle between the sexes.

Elizabeth reviewed her plans. Here, in his own home, with his family all around him, Alex wouldn't dare molest her. She was free to do as she pleased, without fear of his reprisal, and she intended to use that freedom fully. She chuckled softly to herself. Perhaps only by driving him wild with desire, with jealousy, while impotent to do anything about it, could she force him to come to grips with his feelings toward her. If he didn't love her, nothing would help. But if, within the depths of his heart, he nursed secret, tender feelings, this course of action, if nothing else, would bring them to the surface.

She smiled, reflecting upon his previous jealousy. She would enflame him, drive him mad. What lovely revenge for all the sleepless nights he had caused her, nights when she had wept with grief and loneliness caused by his coldness. Yet, it was a twoedged sword, this jealousy. For it would work slowly, eating away at him until he could resist her no longer and must either claim her openly for his own or lose her to another, and yet, all the time she would be secretly hungering for him, suffering every bit as much as he. Even now, how she longed for him, longed to feel his strong, hard body beside hers, to kiss his lips, to run her fingers over the rippling muscles of his chest. She bit her lip, and wiped away a tear. Silently she cursed him for making her need him so. Somehow she must be patient, and very, very careful; the stakes in this game were frightfully high. If she lost this gamble, she lost everything.

Chapter Twenty

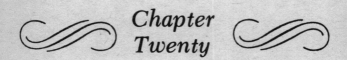

A howling wind screamed through the trees, whipping the thickly falling snow into a white, blinding whirlwind. The blizzard had been raging for the past three hours, suffocating the trees and paths in an avalanche of snow, blinding the lone rider who braved the furious onslaught, his horse knee deep in snow as it stepped tortuously through the drifts in search of a path. The rider, a black-cloaked figure bent nearly double over the animal's dark mane, cursed savagely as the horse nearly slipped, then he urged the beast on in a low, encouraging voice, which was swept away by the wind.

It was some time later when man and beast finally drew up before the three-story mansion, ringed by its graceful circle of trees, though they were barely visible now through the blinding frenzy of the blizzard. The rider dismounted, and with head bent against the wind, led the horse to the stable beyond the house. He fumbled with the latch, then the door slid open and a blinking, haggard face stared at him in astonishment.

"Mr. Burke!" the old man exclaimed, and behind him there was movement as another figure emerged from a stall to stand gaping at the tall, dark rider.

"That's right, you old fool. Step aside and let me enter! Moonfire's nearly frozen, and I'm not exactly warm and toasty myself!"

The two gawkers scrambled into action. While the younger took Moonfire's reins, the elder began brushing the snow from Alex's cloak.

"I'm all right, Walter. Dammit, see to Moonfire!" Burke shook them off and turned his attention to the horse. The barn was comparatively warm, lined as it was with stacks of hay and straw, and he watched as Jack and Walter, the same two grooms who had aided him a week ago when he and Elizabeth had arrived in Philadelphia, now rubbed down the shivering, half-frozen beast. They were good men, he knew, the best. All of the younger men servants had gone off to join the militia, but Walter and Jack were too old. They had worked for the Burke family nearly all their lives, since long before Alex Burke was born. He noted their expertness as they massaged and brushed the horse, fed him oats and a small amount of water, and threw a heavy wool blanket across his back. Gradually, the shivering ceased; Moonfire blew contentedly from his nostrils and nosed about in the oat bin.

"He'll be all right, Mr. Burke," Jack said cheerfully. "Better see to yourself. You look as if you could use a sip of rum."

Alex grinned. His unruly black hair curled about

his dark face, the grey eyes gleaming beneath thick black brows. He looked tired, his rugged, handsome face lined with fatigue, but the grin transformed him from a scowling, formidable figure, making him look suddenly boyish.

"You're right there; a pint of rum right now would just begin to warm me, Jack. But first, tell me, what are you two doing here at this hour? There's a blizzard raging, man! Why aren't you snug in bed with your missus?"

"On account of the visitors, sir," Walter put in, his thin voice dry and crackly. "We just came out to check on their horses, like Mr. Warren asked us to do from time to time."

"Visitors? On a night like this?" Alex frowned, noticing for the first time the three strange animals corralled alongside of the Burke family mounts.

"Yes, sir. Didn't you see the carriage outside? Two of 'em came in it, and a third rode alone. Came to visit the ladies, I guess, storm or no storm. Miss Elizabeth, in particular, if you know what I mean."

The grooms exchanged a wink and knowing glances. Alex's frown deepened. "Oh, they did, did they?" That was all he said, but he turned quickly for the barn door.

Outside, the fury of the storm had not abated, but he was so preoccupied with his own thoughts that he scarcely noticed its ferocity. With his head bent, and his chin tucked into the top of his cloak, he trudged against the wind to the servants' entrance at the rear of the house.

"So, she's made friends here already," he thought, scowling. He should have known. How silly to have felt any qualms about abandoning her the morning after their arrival; he'd known that Jenny and Adam would take care of her, and besides, Elizabeth Trent could take very good care of herself. She was a fighter, a survivor. What a fool he'd been to doubt that, to worry about leaving her. He had flattered himself that she might need his support. Hah! As if she needed anyone!

He let himself into the kitchen where Mary sat dozing on a bench by the open hearth. She woke up abruptly when the door opened to admit him, and a gust of freezing air and snow whipped through the room.

"Mr. Burke! My word!" she cried, jumping up and knocking a kettle off a shelf as she rushed to help him.

"Don't excite yourself, Mary," he said, brushing past her with a nod. "Where is my sister?"

"In the front parlor, sir, entertaining guests. Would you like some supper, sir . . . shall I bring you——?"

But he was gone in a swirl of satin cape, vanishing through the door and down the hallway leading to the front of the house. He moved with a single-mindedness that hesitated at nothing, his long, graceful stride marked with determination, yet the heavy boots making almost no sound on the richly carpeted floor.

As he approached the front parlor, the tinkle of feminine laughter mingled with husky male chuckling assailed his ears; he felt the warm, vibrant glow emanating from the fire even before he reached the open door and saw the cheerily burning hearth. Alex paused in the doorway, a dark, dramatic figure cloaked in black, his shrewd grey eyes taking in the scene before him. And what a very pretty scene it was.

Jenny, lovely in calico muslin, was seated in the rose patterned Chippendale chair opposite the fire, while Adam stood beside her, brandy glass in hand. The matching chair was occupied by a lady Alex recognized immediately: Miss Sally Herbert, a red-haired vixen with long, narrow green eyes and a deceptively sweet smile, whose marital claws he had been adroitly avoiding ever since her emergence from the schoolroom into polite society three years before. At nineteen, Sally Herbert was a seductively charming cat. His glance flitted over her briefly, then fastened on the form of Elizabeth, seated on the rose-colored velvet sofa, with one man beside her, and another standing at the mantelpiece, commanding her full attention as he recited an apparently amusing story. The words flowed unheeded around Alex; he was staring, hypnotized, at Elizabeth.

Never had he seen her look so beautiful, so soft and feminine. She wore a dress of muslin, the color a rich, blooming pink, edged with delicate white lace ruffles, its neckline cut fashionably, and most becomingly, low, revealing the creamy white mounds of her breasts rising and falling gently as she laughed at something the storyteller said. Alex felt a quickening of his pulse; he tore his eyes from those creamy mounds with an effort, letting them travel upward, past the slender, white throat where a pink velvet ribbon was tied, to her face, where milky skin glowed pink in the firelight. Her hair was swept atop her head, and fell in a shining mass of loose golden curls along the right side of her face. Her profile was exquisite: aristocratic, regal, beautiful.

It was Jenny who noticed him first. Glancing up from a selection of iced cakes, she gave a little startled exclamation, and leaped eagerly to her feet.

"Alex!" She rushed to him, while Adam limped forward, and the other occupants of the room hurried to greet him, all but Elizabeth, who remained indifferently upon the sofa.

"Why, man, you're nearly frozen!" Adam tossed Burke's cloak aside and drew him to an armchair by the fire. He pushed him into it and turned to pour brandy into a tumbler.

"Why, Mr. Burke, you poor thing. Did you ride through that awful blizzard to get here?" Sally Herbert hovered solicitously over the arm of his chair.

"Certainly, the same as you and your companions," he replied with a sardonic smile.

"But we only ventured a little ways, and John and I came in the carriage," she replied sweetly. "Edward did ride, it's true, but it's scarcely half a mile from his station." She laid a slender white hand upon his arm. "How many miles did you travel?"

He shrugged. "Several hours worth. But I must say, the journey was well worth the effort. I never dreamed of being received by three beautiful women."

He glanced involuntarily at Elizabeth. Violet eyes met his grey ones; a hint of a smile played at the corners of her mouth.

"Why, cousin, what kind words," she murmured. "Are you certain the cold has not affected your brain?"

The smile with which she uttered these words made them sound a joke, and everyone chuckled, although Jenny and Adam exchanged glances, and Sally Herbert glanced sharply from Elizabeth to Alex, whose outward composure remained unshaken.

"Thank you for your concern, *cousin*," he replied. "I assure you, my faculties are quite intact."

Elizabeth inclined her head slightly in acknowledgment of this remark, and then turned with a dazzling smile to the man on her right. "Edward, may I have another glass of hot cider? I feel a slight chill in the room."

"Of course!" Edward Langston was a chunky, agreeable-looking young man, attired in the smart blue uniform faced with red which signified his allegiance to the Continental Light Infantry Corps. Burke watched him coolly as he hurriedly poured the cider from its heavy pitcher.

"Alex, let me fetch you some cold supper from the kitchen," Jenny offered earnestly, fluttering about his chair like a mother hen. "You must be half-starved after that dreadful journey!"

"This brandy is all I need or want," he said abruptly. His keen gaze swept the room and rested upon the man by the mantelpiece, who also wore military dress. "A story was in progress when I entered," he drawled. "Pray do not let me interrupt. I believe you were speaking, Mr. Herbert."

John Herbert lifted his eyebrows, assuming an attitude of sophisticated *ennui*. "I was merely relating the latest tale about General Arnold and Miss Shippen," he said carelessly. "After all, that's all anyone ever talks of these days."

"Is it really?" Burke inquired, studying him impassively. John Herbert, Sally's brother, was a tall, thin boy with an abundance of curly red hair and a bony, freckled face. His brown eyes, like two huge freckles beneath narrow, arching brows, reflected boredom, and a trace of jealousy. Alex thought he could guess the source of the latter.

"Ah, then you're stationed under General Arnold's command?" he continued languidly.

"Yes. I trained under Baron Von Steuben at Valley Forge," the red-haired youth replied airily.

"I see. A good man, Von Steuben, so I hear. And you, Mr. Langston? Are you also stationed under General Arnold?"

"Yes, sir." Edward blushed, and appeared on the point of summoning his courage to offer a further comment, but was interrupted by Herbert, who leaned forward impatiently to address Elizabeth.

"Though all Philadelphia talks of the romance between General Benedict Arnold and Miss Peggy Shippen, I'm quite certain another topic will soon eclipse their appeal."

"Pray, what could that be?" Elizabeth opened her eyes at him, smiling coquettishly.

"Why, your own beauty and charm, Miss Trent, of course. Miss Shippen is reputed for her beauty, but may I say that she pales in comparison with your loveliness?"

"You may say whatever you wish," Elizabeth laughed softly. "But you run the risk of making me blush."

Edward Langston turned hurriedly to Elizabeth upon the sofa. "That is precisely what I told Miss Trent this afternoon," he announced breathlessly. "No lady in Philadelphia can hold a candle to her! Oh! Present company excepted, of course!" he added, flushing a deep shade of red as Sally Herbert set her lips together angrily, and a smothered giggle escaped Jenny.

"You know, it seems quite odd, Miss Trent," Sally Herbert drawled sweetly, "that you've never visited your Philadelphia cousins before. Precisely how are you related? Maternally, perchance?"

For a split instant there was a silence fraught with tension, and then Jenny said quickly, "Oh, no. Elizabeth is related to my father's family. Tell me, Sally, my dear, would you care for some more cider? Or some lemonade, perhaps?"

The uncomfortable moment passed, and Edward Langston and John Herbert began once more to shower their gallantries upon Elizabeth. But Alex had seen enough. He set his glass down abruptly on the mantelpiece and faced the company grimly, his lips set together tightly, and his eyes glinting.

"If you will all excuse me," he said coldly, "I will retire now. I'm beginning to feel a trifle weary of this long evening." He nodded stiffly toward the threesome grouped on the sofa, where Elizabeth was sandwiched prettily between the two military men, and then he turned to bow politely over Miss Herbert's extended hand.

"I do hope we'll be seeing more of you," she purred, her green eyes slanting up at him. "Now that you've returned from your adventures."

"It will be my pleasure," he answered grimly. With a brief nod to Jenny and Adam he stalked from the room, and heard the echo of Elizabeth's laughter as he closed the door behind him. Cursing her, and himself, and the two young fools dancing on her string like puppets, he strode angrily up to bed.

Elizabeth watched him leave the room with mixed emotions. Uppermost in her mind was satisfaction. Everything had gone splendidly! Despite Alex's outward composure, she knew him, knew that he had been discomfited by the scene in the parlor. Feeling weary, indeed! She had nearly laughed aloud in her triumph. He merely couldn't bear to see other men pay her their attentions!

Still, in spite of this triumph, she experienced a twinge of uneasiness. She studied Sally Herbert from beneath her lashes. That sly, seductive cat! Elizabeth had disliked her on sight, and now...well, she was entirely too interested in Alexander Burke. She would bear watching, that one, careful watching. And these two foolish puppies slobbering over her! Oh, Edward Langston was nice enough, though pitifully naive, but that John Herbert had the same sly look as his sister, a look she did not care for at all.

A faint smile touched her lips. How she had longed to run to Alex when he had entered the parlor, to help him with his cloak, to fetch his supper, and to warm him with her kisses! It had taken all the self-control she possessed to remain calmly seated while the others fussed over him. She sighed wistfully, wishing such control was unnecessary.

"Is something the matter, Miss Trent?" Edward Langston asked, leaning forward anxiously.

Elizabeth glanced about her and saw Jenny and Adam regarding her in silence, while John Herbert raised his eyebrows, and his sister watched sharply. "No, I'm terribly sorry, I believe I was caught up in a daydream," she explained with a slight, embarrassed laugh.

Mr. Herbert lowered his voice. "Really? Was I included in it, or is that too much to hope for?"

"I mustn't tell," she responded demurely, lowering her eyes, but she was thinking: that pompous young fool! I've never before heard such arrogance!

The guests stayed some little time longer, and Elizabeth flirted gaily, in a way she had not done since her London days, but her involvement was only superficial, and her thoughts kept drifting upstairs, to Alex Burke's bedroom.

The next afternoon she rode over to visit Henry in his new home with the Tuckers. The blizzard had subsided during the night, leaving the world wrapped in fresh snow, and the day was bright and brisk, perfect for a ride.

Jenny, who bought eggs and milk from Abigail Tucker, instructed Elizabeth in which direction to ride, and offered to accompany her, but Elizabeth begged to go alone. In England, girls were never permitted to go about by themselves, and upon finding this was customary in America, she'd been anxious to flutter her wings. Now, actually riding on a pretty, spirited little bay mare, clad in her new emerald green riding habit with the dark blue cloak flowing from her shoulders, she relished the luxury of riding alone. Following the wooded path Jenny had indicated, she urged the mare faster, oblivious of the chill wind which tore at her, knowing only the sheet joy of galloping through the winter woods undisturbed by a chattering companion.

She had a particular reason for wanting to visit the Tucker farm, aside from the obvious one of seeing Henry. She was anxious to meet Ben's mother, for she remembered a conversation with Ben one afternoon when they'd been scrubbing the *Hornet*'s deck, and he had repeated something his mother had said, something about Alexander Burke never taking a wife, "not after what he's been through." Elizabeth had never discovered the meaning of this statement, but she intended to do so today.

The peaceful solitude of her winter ride was broken presently by the shrill neigh of a horse and the unmistakable crunch of hooves on snow. Glancing behind her, she saw a tall, brown stallion bearing a familiar figure emerge from a path branching off her own, and she pulled the mare to a halt.

"Good day!" Geoffrey Granger called, riding up beside her. He was as immaculately attired as ever in his magnificent crimson satin cloak and cocked hat. The white ruffles of his shirt collar just showed above the gold brooch which secured the cape.

"It's a lovely day for a ride, isn't it?" Elizabeth smiled.

"Yes, indeed. I was on my way to see Alex," Granger replied. "I ran into John Herbert this morning and he told me Alex reached home last night. I trust he's well?"

"Quite well. At least, he was last evening. I haven't seen him today. Apparently he went straight down to the shipyard at an abominably early hour." She heard the annoyance in her voice, and tried to disguise it by adding brightly, "He hadn't returned when I left, but I'm sure Jenny will be glad to see you, and you can probably wait for him there."

Granger shook his head. "I wouldn't mind riding along with you for a bit, if you don't mind."

"I'd be delighted. I'm on my way to the Tucker farm. A friend of mine is living there now."

"Oh, yes, the cabin boy Alex brought from England. A clever little tyke, or so I hear."

Elizabeth laughed. "Oh, Henry is very bright, and very sweet. And he's very happy, too. You should have seen him when I first met him, a poor, little ragged creature, half starved."

They had turned their horses back on to the path Elizabeth was following and now continued at an easy trot.

"So he had a hard time of it back in England? I don't imagine the same was true of you."

"Oh, no. I had a wonderfully easy life, completely care-free. The only problems I had involved deciding which gown to wear to the theater!"

Granger laughed, and then asked casually, "Do you miss it?"

"Well, of course! That is, I miss my friends, and my chaperone, and all the familiar activities." She thought for a few moments, and then said suddenly, "But I've never felt so alive as I have since coming here. There's something about the Colonies. . .I can't explain it."

Granger's slate blue eyes watched her intently. "You like it here then?"

"I do. You know, Mr. Granger, I didn't always agree with the way things were in England. Why, I was even discouraged from discussing the war with a gentleman! It isn't like that here." She bit her lip, musingly. "And then there's Henry. In England, a boy like he has no chance at all to be anything in the world. But here. . .well, things are different. And I like it."

There was a brief silence. Then Granger remarked off-handedly, "So you side with the rebels now? You're no longer loyal to Britain?"

She flushed. "I don't see it quite that way. I love Britain. I'm not exactly certain whom I side with. I don't know enough about all the issues, only what I learned on the ship from Alex and Ben, but let's just say that from what I do know, I now have some sympathy for the rebel cause." She laughed embarrassedly. "You must think me a horrible traitor."

"Not at all." He returned her smile, and steadied the brown stallion as it stumbled over something beneath the snow. "It's good to know who's side you're on," he said.

They rode on together for a while, until they neared the road leading down to the farm. Granger pointed it out to her, then turned back up the path the way they had come.

"I'll leave you to visit with your friend, while I see if Alex has returned yet." He took her gloved hand and raised it to his lips. "You haven't forgotten the dance you promised me, have you?"

"Of course not. I'm looking forward to it."

"So am I. Good day, then."

She watched him canter back up the path until he disappeared into a web of snow-frosted trees. For some reason she could not quite understand, his questions had disturbed her. It had been almost as if he were testing or evaluating her. But why?

An answer eluded her. Shrugging, she spurred the mare down the sloping road toward the red brick farm building ahead, where white smoke curled lazily from the chimney against the backdrop of sapphire sky. Geoffrey Granger and his questions faded from her thoughts. She had a more important mystery to solve today.

Before she had more than slid from the saddle, a screeching yell sounded, and a small, bundled figure flew toward her. Behind him, grinning, stood a youth of about fifteen.

"Henry!" Elizabeth scooped the boy into her arms, kneeling to peer into his exuberant, red-cheeked face.

"I knew you'd come, Miss!" he cried triumphantly. "Ben told me he saw you, and that sure made me wish to see you, too. I know you wouldn't forget about me."

"Forget about you, Henry? Never!"

A woman's strong, slightly throaty voice interrupted from the doorway of the farmhouse. "Henry, don't keep the lady standing out in this cold! Where are your manners, boy? And you, too, Simon. Miss, won't you come in and sit by the fire?"

Elizabeth straightened, smiling. "Thank you, I'd like that very much."

It was indeed much warmer indoors, where in the kitchen a crackling fire roared in the hearth and the savory, delicious smell of beef stew filled the room, emanating, apparently, from the black pot which hung on a hook over the fireplace. An assortment of strawberry and raspberry tarts filled a shelf near the long, rectangular wooden table, lined by hard benches which would comfortably fit a family of ten. After hanging her cloak on a peg by the door, Elizabeth seated herself in a rocker by the fire, the rough wooden seat beneath her cushioned by a pretty embroidered pillow. She looked approvingly about her at the cozy, cheerful room, while Henry perched at her elbow, and Mrs. Tucker returned to the wooden counter where she had been kneading bread. Her strong square hands resumed their work upon the dough with practiced competence.

"You look wonderful, Miss," Henry told her admiringly, stroking a corner of the green satin fabric of her riding habit.

"And so do you! Philadelphia obviously agrees with you, young man." It was true. She had never seen him so healthy and bright-eyed. Was this stout, red-cheeked youngster the same ragged child she'd first met on that noisy, bustling London pier more than a year ago? It seemed impossible, especially when she remembered how subdued and frightened he had been then, pitifully terrified of the brutal purser. Now he seemed taller, and his face had completely lost that pinched, pale look. He might be any happy, healthy youngster, bubbling with a child's limitless energy. He also, it seemed, now possessed undaunted courage. He was telling her proudly how wonderful his new home was, and exactly what he would do if any Redcoats dared to cross his path, or tried to take him back to England.

"Very brave!" she applauded, trying hard not to laugh.

Mrs. Tucker glanced over her shoulder at them. "Now, Henry, that'll be enough of your tales," she admonished firmly. "You'd best be getting back to the barn, to give Simon a hand with the milking. Miss Trent and I will have a nice chat, and I'd be mighty pleased if she would help herself to one of my tarts and let me fetch her a glass of cider."

Henry looked longingly at the row of tarts, but the woman shooed him off with a laugh. "You'll have one at supper if you behave yourself!" she called after him as he scampered out the kitchen door.

Elizabeth accepted both the tart and the cider. She had grown accustomed to the scarcity of tea in

Philadelphia, a result of the war, and had developed a real fondness for the refreshing flavor of spiced apple cider, a beverage served frequently at meals and in-between. Now as she sipped her drink, she studied the woman kneading bread. Abigail Tucker was a big-boned horse of a woman, with lined, leathery skin, and a thick mane of graying black hair beneath her starched white cap. She wore the simple calico dress and patched apron of the farmwife, and both showed signs of having been mended many times. Surprisingly, she moved easily for such a large woman, and there was a comfortable confidence about her that was becoming. Elizabeth marveled at how quickly her square brown hands worked the dough, and then her gaze traveled upward to be confronted by a pair of shrewd blue eyes. Abigail Tucker appraised her critically for a mong moment. Then she nodded.

"So you are Elizabeth Trent," she remarked.

"It's a pleasure to meet you, Mrs. Tucker. Ben is a good friend of mine."

"Yes, I know. He told me."

Elizabeth started to speak again, but the older woman suddenly dropped the blob of dough on the counter with a soft thump and turned to face her squarely, wiping her hands on her apron. "I declare," she announced in her strong, husky voice. "That Alexander Burke must be out of his head."

Considerably startled, Elizabeth stared at her. "I beg your pardon?"

"Come on, girl. Don't play games with me. I know the truth. About you, that is. The way he carried you off—clear across the ocean. You're no more his cousin than I am!"

For a moment there was dreadful silence as Elizabeth stifled a gasp. Finally, she spoke, barely able to contain her anger. "Who told you?"

Mrs. Tucker chuckled.

"Who told you?" Elizabeth demanded again.

"Now, girl, just calm yourself. Don't go into a fret. Henry let it slip t'other night, quite by accident. Heavens, Ben was fit to kill him, and the poor child turned red as a radish. He just about burst into tears. But don't you worry, nobody heard except me and Sam, Ben's pa, and we're not going to tell no one. Why should we?"

Elizabeth regarded her uncertainly. There was kindness in the blue eyes which returned her gaze. Something about the woman implied that she could be trusted. Elizabeth relaxed slightly in her chair.

"Now, you finish your cider," Mrs. Tucker instructed, sitting down upon a three-legged stool. She began peeling potatoes on the table before her, throwing the skins into a short wooden barrel as she talked. "It's none of my concern if Alex Burke wants to behave like a crazed idiot, and I don't see why it should be anyone else's either."

"Thank you. I appreciate your discretion, Mrs. Tucker. Really, I do."

"Pshaw, child. Don't think on it. Though I must say, when I first heard of it, I scarcely believed it myself. I didn't think Alex such a fool, nor such a scoundrel." She continued thoughtfully, running her gaze over Elizabeth appraisingly. "But now that I've met you, I can understand it a mite better. Alex must be out of his head. . .in love."

Despite herself, Elizabeth blushed furiously. "Hardly," she replied, with an attempt at airy composure. "He despises me, as a matter of fact."

"Pshaw, girl. I know Alex Burke. He's never

done anything this foolish in his entire life. Specially where a woman is concerned. Normally, he keeps his distance from them like they had the plague." She chuckled. "Not that they don't make a fuss over him. Why, Sally Herbert's had her eye on him since the day she left the schoolroom! And she's not the only one!"

"Yet he avoids them?" This was what she had come to investigate. Elizabeth leaned forward eagerly in anticipation of the response.

"Oh, he's had women enough, from tavern wenches like Cass Morgan to fine ladies, but he never cared a shilling for 'em. He just plays with them until he breaks their hearts. When they start getting serious, or making demands, that's when he takes off." Mrs. Tucker lowered her voice conspiratorially. "I'd have bet my last potato that he'd never marry. . .until now, that is."

"Why did you believe this?" Elizabeth pressed. "Why does he despise women?"

"That's a long story, Miss." The farmwife shook her head sadly. "And not a very happy one. It all has to do with that mother of his. Laura, that was her name. Laura Burke. A devilish beauty, that girl, with all that black hair and dark eyes. A witch, a beautiful witch, that was Laura Burke."

"What has that to do with Alex?"

"Plenty, my girl. You see, that mother of his was just as wicked as she was beautiful, and that's the truth. She was a restless, flighty thing, never able to settle down. John, Alex's pa, thought the world of her, gave her everything you can imagine and more, but it wasn't enough for her." She lowered her voice again. "She took lovers. Lots of 'em. Any man with a handsome face and an easy manner found his way to her bed. One summer afternoon, though, she got caught—by young Alex.''

Elizabeth gasped.

"Yes, miss. I remember it clearly, it being about a week before my wedding to Sam. Alex was only a child, barely more'n Henry's age, when he discovered 'em. And right behind him came his pa.''

There was a silence. "What happened?'' Elizabeth asked fearfully.

"From what I heard, quite a scene. Laura tossed her head and packed her bags and ran off with the fellow, a traveling doctor or some such thing. John was left alone to raise Alex and Jenny, who was little more than a babe.'' She sighed. "He never got over it. My stars, how he loved that woman. The whole thing broke his heart—heaven knows he was never the same afterwards. And Alex? Well, he never forgot it either.''

"He never saw his mother again?''

"No. We heard about five years ago that she'd been killed in New York, over some kind of lover's quarrel. But that was all. She never wrote, or visited her children. I think it hurt Alex most of all, since Jenny was just a babe and didn't really know what happened. But Alex, he grew up with a distrust and hatred of women that is pretty powerful.'' She shook her head regretfully. "It was quite an ugly scandal at the time, but most folks have probably forgotten all about it by now, and even if they haven't, I don't think they made any connection between that little episode and Alex's nasty ways with the ladies. But I've always thought it due to that black-haired witch, and no one will convince me otherwise.''

Elizabeth stared at her hands. Ben's mother was

probably right. Imbedded in Alex Burke was a deep-seated hatred of women, a distrust that originated early in his childhood. After having been hurt once so deeply and permanently, was it any wonder the little boy had grown into a man who despised women, using them only for his lust and pleasure, erecting barriers to guard him from ever being hurt again?

She sighed. "I see. Thank you for telling me all this."

Abigail Tucker patted her hand. "Don't let it fret you overmuch, miss. I think there's hope for that young man. I never would have thought it before, but when I heard how he brought you clear across the ocean. . . ."

"That was done out of spite, Mrs. Tucker."

"Maybe. Maybe not. I didn't know Alex ever to act *that* crazy before. It just could be that you've gotten through to him."

But Elizabeth shook her head. "Please. I'd rather not talk about it any more."

"Suit yourself." She stood up heavily and carried the peeled, sliced potatoes in the skirt of her apron over to the hearth, where she dropped them into the simmering pot. "I'm mighty glad you stopped by, though. Been wanting to meet you, after hearing so much about you from Henry and Ben."

"I think you're wonderfully kind, Mrs. Tucker, for taking Henry in the way you have. Not many people are so generous."

"Nonsense, girl. I'm used to having a pack of children around. And since my eldest girls have gone off and married and now have little ones of their own, well, this old house just misses the sound of wild young voices." She chuckled, then added more seriously, "I don't want you thinkin' it's any kind of a hardship, either, having Henry here with us. No, Alex Burke took care of all that. He insisted to my Sam that he would be financially responsible for the boy. You know, he pays for his food, clothing, and the like. Says he wants to make sure Henry goes to school and gets a good education."

"I've heard that he's a very good, very generous man," Elizabeth said almost dazedly, thinking of what Adam Warren had said about him.

"That he is—none better," the farmwife answered firmly. "Now, Miss, would you care to stay for supper? I know Ben would be happy to see you, and I've got a beef stew and fresh bread and puddings. You're most welcome to join us."

"Thank you, but I must be going. Jenny is expecting me." Elizabeth rose, reaching for her cloak.

"Well, I'm sorry to hear that, and I'm sure Ben will be, too. Although, come to think of it, he'll be late coming home for supper tonight." She smiled in her blunt, friendly manner. "That sweet, foolish boy! What do you think he must do with some of that prize money of his? Got it into his head to buy me a fancy new bonnet! He insisted! Drove me into town the other day to pick out ribbons and such at the dressmaker's, and today he's stopping by Miss Whigby's to fetch it for me. Have you ever heard of such a good, thoughtful boy?"

Elizabeth hid a smile and answered properly, bidding a most pleasant farewell to Ben's mother. She found it amusing that this shrewd, solid woman who seemed so knowledgable about everything knew nothing of what was going on right beneath her nose. It was obvious to Elizabeth that Ben Tucker was using the bonnet as an excuse to visit

Miss Whigby's shop, no doubt in order to see Carrie Peterson. Good for Ben, she thought triumphantly. He must be in love with the girl. Well, no doubt Mrs. Tucker would find out soon enough.

She stopped at the barn to say good-bye to Henry before leaving, and then rode swiftly for home. The afternoon chill had increased, and it was beginning to snow again lightly. But it was not the weather which occupied her thoughts.

Mrs. Tucker's revelations about Alex filled her with compassion for him, but they also increased her sense of uneasiness about the plan she had concocted. To incite jealousy in the heart of a man who already distrusted women now seemed madness; and her role of the irresistable *femme fatale* might remind him all too painfully and disastrously of the mother who had deserted him. Once again she found herself pricked by doubt, uncertain which course to follow.

The sun was a dripping buttery ball in the western sky when Elizabeth dismounted in the cobbled drive beside the Burke house. She led the mare past the house in the direction of the stable, but upon nearing this building, noticed something that made her stop and stare. A strange horse was tethered to a lone post behind the house, near the kitchen door. The animal, his head lowered, blew white steam from his nostrils, while his hoofs pawed impatiently at the snow. There was sweat on his body.

Now who would leave their cold, tired horse outside on a day like this, instead of bringing him into the stable to be tended? The answer was obvious. A man in a hurry, one who isn't staying long. But why would such a man bring the animal to the rear of the house, instead of leaving him tethered in front? It was as if the horse were being hidden from view.

She asked old Walter about it when she turned her mare over to him, but he just shrugged his drooping shoulders and claimed to have no knowledge. There was a glint in his eyes however that belied his words.

Pondering this mystery, Elizabeth approached the house, walking past the unfamiliar horse to enter by the kitchen door. She waved to Mary, who peered up from her steaming soup pot in surprise, and continued thoughtfully toward the front of the house. Upon nearing the front parlor though, a man suddenly swung around the doorway as if in a great hurry, colliding with her heavily. The force of the collision knocked Elizabeth into the opposite wall. Considerably startled, the man threw her a hasty, mumbled apology over his shoulder and hurried past, one hand holding his tricorn hat upon his head as he sped along the corridor, his boots thumping softly on the carpet.

"What in the world. . . ?" she said indignantly.

"Who's there?" Geoffrey Granger's voice boomed from the parlor.

"*I* am here," she replied irritably, crossing to the doorway. "And I would like to know just what is going on—"

She broke off abruptly, staring not at Granger, who stood before her, but at Alex, who had paused in the act of placing some papers in a safe above the mantelpiece. The painting which normally occupied the space had swung aside, revealing a small, hidden valut. With a black frown darkening his features, Alex quickly completed his action, setting the papers inside and then shutting the safe's door with a resounding thud. The painting swung back into place.

"What are you doing here?" he demanded of Elizabeth angrily.

"I was making my way toward the stairs when some clumsy fool stumbled into me," she retorted. "What is going on here? Did that man belong to the horse I saw hidden in the back?"

Burke and Granger exchanged glances. It was Granger who said in a lowered tone, "I think we'd best tell her, Alex. Living here, she's bound to find out sooner or later. This way, we avoid a lot of potentially dangerous questions."

Burke transferred his gaze to Elizabeth, his grey eyes very light and cold. "Very well. Come in and close the door behind you."

She obeyed, wondering what was going on. It seemed that mystery always surrounded Alexander Burke.

"Won't you sit down, Miss Trent?" Granger suggested politely.

"Thank you, I prefer to stand."

There was silence. "Will one of you please tell me what this is all about? Or need I ask Adam and Jenny?"

"That's enough!" Alex grated harshly. "I see I have no choice but to tell you—a little, at least—of the truth. So be quiet and listen!"

"I'm listening."

Granger moved to her side, gently touching her arm. "Miss Trent, the man you saw was a messenger. A spy, you might say. He brought us some information, some papers, and in turn, we passed some news on to him."

"A spy!" she gasped. "You mean, working against the British?"

"Of course, you fool," Alex answered, his lip curling derisively. "This house has long been used as a stopover point for 'messengers,' where they can pass on information or receive it. We've even hidden a few hotly pursued men when necessary." His gaze bore into her. "Adam and Jenny know, of course, and the servants. It would be pretty difficult to live here and not get an inkling sooner or later of what is going on, which is why I decided to tell you." He paused and his expression hardened. "I'm assuming you can be trusted, Lizzie."

The name rankled, but she ignored it, merely lifting her chin.

"You *can* be trusted, can't you?"

Still she said nothing. With a flash, his hands shot out and encircled her throat, the strong fingers closing in an iron grip. "Answer me," he ordered in a deadly voice.

Elizabeth felt, rather than saw, Geoffrey Granger's shocked reaction and she trembled with anger. Her violet eyes ignited into blue fire.

"Let me go, you bastard," she hissed.

The pressure of his fingers increased. She felt herself gasping for breath as a tide of pain washed over her.

She heard Granger say, "Now, Alex, really," in a shocked voice which sounded far away.

"Can I trust you?" Alex's voice hammered in her ears, between waves of pain.

"Yes." She managed to gasp the single word.

"Good." He released her suddenly, and she would have collapsed if he hadn't caught her. He held her tightly, staring down into her pale, dazed face.

"That is a sample of what will happen if you betray me," he said coolly. "Now, I think you'd better go upstairs and compose yourself. I do hope there won't be a bruise."

Elizabeth shook free of his hold, raising her hands to her throat. She stared at him for a long moment, an expression of fury in her eyes, combined with something else, a kind of hurt that had nothing to do with physical pain. When she whirled and stumbled out the door, Alex glanced at Granger, and then lowered his eyes. He stared down at his hands, cursing himself silently.

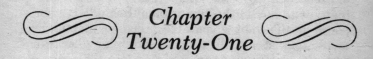

Chapter
Twenty-One

Philadelphia was abuzz with activity and speculation in the weeks that followed. General Arnold and Miss Shippen still dominated the tongues of the gossipmongers as their romance blazed on, unhindered by the rumblings of disapproval among certain members of polite society. General Arnold, it seemed, had raised the ire of many Philadelphians, in particular, the Council of Philadelphia. It was rumored that he was employing his military aides in achievement of personal gains, and that he misused the Pennsylvania militia to his own advantage. Many resented the airs assumed by the one-time hero of the Battle of Saratoga, evidenced by his engagement of a housekeeper, groom, coachman, and several other servants, not to mention his handsome coach, fine-stepping horses, and elegant mansion. The military hero seemed determined to prove himself one of the social elite, and Peggy Shippen's relationship with him only served to increase the Council's discon-

tent. It was widely known that she had been the
toast of the town during the British occupation of
the city, and whispers abounded that she had distinctly Loyalist sympathies, and many friends
among the British officers. Still, Arnold appeared
captivated, courting her openly, in defiance of public opinion.

Toward the end of December there was a flurry
of excitement as it was rumored that General Washington was due in the city to plan the military cam-
paign for the coming year. He did come, meeting in
secret and at length with Philadelphia's leaders,
and when he finally departed to rejoin the army in
New Jersey, he left behind a trail of praise and pre-
dictions.

January arrived, and with it, news of a more disturbing tone. A messenger en route from New Jersey had been attacked in the woods; the secret
documents in his possession had been stolen, and
the agent had been killed. In the ensuing weeks,
news of this nature became more frequent. Documents were misplaced or stolen, Continental military attacks mysteriously anticipated by the British.
A flutter of nervousness ruffled the surface of Philadelphia society as it became apparent that a leak
existed somewhere. In the taverns and meeting
places people whispered apprehensively and shook
their heads.

Gloomy thoughts faded, however, as January
slipped into February, and then March approached. Everyone, from the blacksmith to the
head of the Council of Philadelphia, talked of one
thing and one thing only: the public ball to be giv-
en on the fifteenth of March.

The Burke household was no exception. Jenny
and Elizabeth talked of little else, and busied them-

selves with preparations. There were ribbons and stockings and sequined shoes to purchase, and Elizabeth's dress to be sewn by Miss Whigby under its designer's strict supervision. Even Adam got into the spirit of the occasion by purchasing new silver buckles for his shoes. Alex Burke marched determinedly about his business, indifferent to the preparations for sartorial splendor, but Jenny whispered, giggling, to Elizabeth, "Don't worry. Alex always looks magnificent when he attends a ball. You'll see, no one will compare to him."

Several weeks before the ball, Elizabeth had learned that it was Carrie Peterson who would be sewing the intricate crimson lace ruffles on her gown, as she had a delicate touch which excelled at such painstaking work. Elizabeth had taken advantage of this fact to present Carrie with a gift of appreciation for the work she would be doing: the silver gauze ball gown was pressed upon the girl as an advance thank-you. Though Carrie had at first tried to decline the gift, Elizabeth, suspecting that the girl would be unable to afford a new gown otherwise, had insisted, and finally had been rewarded by the warmest gratitude, marked by happy tears. It was all set: Carrie would wear the gown to the public ball. Elizabeth was delighted, certain the girl would look charmingly lovely on Ben Tucker's arm.

The day before the festivity, Elizabeth was driven into town by the groom, Jack, to collect her completed gown from Miss Whigby. Telling him to wait, that she would be out directly, she entered the dressmaker's tiny shop, hearing a bell tinkle softly overhead to indicate that someone had entered.

Miss Whigby looked up from arranging some

cambric cloth on a shelf, and a smile fluttered on her thin lips.

"Why, Miss Trent! Good afternoon! My, you're looking well." She came around the counter to lead Elizabeth to a yellow damask sofa and urged her to seat herself. "I do hope Mrs. Warren is well, and that darling little Sarah. Such a pretty child! Well, Miss Trent, what do you think of this weather we've been having? Have you ever seen a winter this mild? It hasn't been cold since January, and Mrs. Gates says it should be a right early spring, and she should know, her husband is a farmer, after all. . . .Well, now, I suppose you're here to fetch that ball gown. A lovely thing, simply lovely. You know, you have superb taste, Miss Trent—"

"Thank you," Elizabeth interrupted smoothly, containing her impatience at the woman's chatter. "Is the gown finished?"

"Of course it's finished. Although, as a matter of fact, Carrie just completed the ruffles this very morning, not more than two hours ago. So slow, that child! Although she does exquisite work, I must admit that. And the stitching those ruffles required was exceedingly tricky. Yes, it was indeed, but she did a beautiful piece of work on it, and that there's no denying."

The shop door opened just then, admitting a stout, well-dressed dowager of whom Elizabeth had slight acquaintance. They exchanged nods, while Miss Whigby jumped up eagerly to greet the newcomer.

"Ah, Mrs. Holcomb, what a pleasure to see you!" Her beady eyes darted confusedly between her two customers as she became aware of a dilemma. "Oh, dear. I was just about to fetch Miss Trent's gown for her."

"I can get it, Miss Whigby." Elizabeth stood up, smiling. "Please don't trouble yourself. I'd like a word with Carrie, anyway."

"Well, if you're sure. . . .Very well, Carrie will be happy to assist you. Now, Mrs. Holcomb, what can I show you today?"

Elizabeth stepped quickly through a narrow doorway at the rear of the shop, entering a small room strewn with fabrics and gowns in all manner of construction and design, and scattered with tiny dolls fitted out in assorted apparel. A long work table and bench ran along the center of the room, and at the end of it sat Carrie Peterson. Her head rested on the table; her auburn curls were a tangled mass. When Elizabeth entered, the girl glanced up fearfully, revealing reddened, swollen eyes. Tears glistened on her pale cheeks.

"Carrie, whatever is the matter?" Elizabeth hurried to her side in alarm.

"I beg your pardon, Miss Trent," she answered, rising to her feet rather unsteadily. "You won't tell Miss Whigby, will you?"

Elizabeth glanced briefly at the pile of unfinished work on the table and then returned her gaze to Carrie's face. "Don't be silly. I've no desire to cause trouble for you. But I would like to help. Won't you tell me what is troubling you?"

Carrie shook her head and made no reply. She began folding the length of brown muslin fabric on the table beside her. Elizabeth hesitated, caught between a desire to help the girl, and a fear of intruding. Obviously Carrie didn't wish to talk about her problem—or else she was too shy to burden another with it. Impulsively, Elizabeth said, "Is it Ben Tucker?"

"What?" Carrie glanced quickly at Elizabeth. "How did you know?"

"It was just a guess. What has Ben done to make you so unhappy?"

"It's not Ben," the girl whispered. "At least, it's not his fault."

Elizabeth sat her down upon the bench and handed her a handkerchief. "Why don't you tell me about it, Carrie? Perhaps I can help."

"There's nothing anyone can do." Carrie dabbed at her eyes as fresh tears welled up. "Ben's lost his job. Mr. Burke fired him from the shipyard."

"What!" Elizabeth struggled to take in what she had just heard.

"It's true. And it's partly my fault!" She turned to Elizabeth miserably. "We. . .Ben and I, met early this morning for a walk before we went to work. We try to spend as much time as possible together," she explained shyly.

"I understand."

"Well, this morning we lost track of the time. You see, Ben asked me to marry him."

"Carrie! That's marvelous! This should be the happiest of days for you."

"It did begin that way, but then. . .well, before we knew it, Ben was late for work, and I nearly was, too. I ran all the way! But Ben. . . ." She broke off despairingly.

Elizabeth stared at her in astonishment. "You can't tell me that Alexander Burke fired him just because he was a few minutes late this morning!"

"It's true, Miss Trent. It *has* happened once or

twice before, but Mr. Burke never seemed to mind much. Lately, though, Mr. Burke's been under a lot of pressure, according to Ben. I guess the shipyard is struggling to keep up with the government's requests for ships, and Mr. Burke has been working the men pretty hard." She shrugged, wiping her eyes again with the handkerchief. "At any rate, he dismissed Ben this morning—in front of all the other men. Ben is furious! He vows he wouldn't go back to work for him if Alexander Burke begged him on his knees! But now," she took a deep breath. "Now we'll have to postpone our marriage plans. Ben says he's going to find another job right away, but times are not easy." The tears began to fall again, and she hid her face in her hands. "Miss Trent, I don't know what we're going to do!"

Elizabeth patted her shoulder. She had grown very quiet while Carrie had been speaking, but now she said crisply, "Carrie, I want you to stop worrying. Everything will work out."

The girl stared at her through swollen, disbelieving eyes.

"I promise you. Everything will work out," she repeated firmly. "Now, wipe your eyes, and let me have my dress, if you please. I have some important business to see to this afternoon."

She left the shop with cheerful assurances to Carrie that everything would be fine, but she knew the girl didn't believe her. Once outside, Elizabeth dropped her heartening attitude and let the trembling anger possess her. She entered the carriage without a word to the groom and sat in fuming silence all the way home. It was almost dinnertime when she arrived and she knew exactly where she would find Alex. He always spent the hour before

dinner in his library, reviewing the day's paperwork.

She rapped sharply on the library door and,
without waiting for an answer, opened it and
stepped inside.

"What is it?" Alex was seated behind the sturdy
walnut desk, his black hair rumpled and falling
over his forehead in an untidy fashion. He looked
tired; the grey eyes had lines beneath them, and his
mouth formed an impatient scowl. "What is it?" he
repeated, glaring at her.

Elizabeth firmly closed the door and approached
the desk, her hands on her hips in a challenging
position.

"You look tired. Did you have a difficult day?"
she asked in a steady voice.

"As a matter of fact, I did. We're extremely busy
now at the shipyard. We're overworked and under-
staffed, and short of time," he answered wearily.

"I see. Is that why you fired one of your best
men?" This time her voice came out as stinging
acid.

There was a silence, while they glowered at each
other, and Alex's eyes narrowed dangerously.

"So that's it," he growled. "You've come to
plead for him, have you? I should have known. Is
Ben Tucker one of your lovers, Lizzie? You always
were fond of him, weren't you?"

"That's right, you cursed fool! Fond of him! And
nothing more!" She was breathing hard despite her
determination to remain calm. "I suppose friendship is something you can't understand. Well, that's
not important now. I want to know why you dismissed one of your most trusted men when you've

just finished telling me that you're short of help and time."

"He arrived late this morning. It's not the first time. And there is no excuse for it."

"He was arranging his betrothal."

"What!" Blood darkened his face and he surged furiously to his feet. "Betrothal? To you?"

Suddenly Elizabeth burst into laughter. "Don't you ever listen to what I say? Ben is my *friend,* and that is *all* there is between us. He is betrothed, as of this morning, to Carrie Peterson."

"Peterson? John Peterson's girl?"

"That's right. I just spoke with her and you may like to know that you've made her abjectly miserable on a day which should be one of the happiest of her life. And Ben, too."

Alex sat down again abruptly. He ran his fingers through his tangle of black hair. "Damnation!"

"Exactly." Elizabeth seated herself in a wing-backed chair opposite the desk and studied him. "Why in the world did you fire him over such a little thing? Surely it doesn't happen *that* often."

He sighed. "No. It doesn't. It was just. . .well, I was on edge today—we're having trouble meeting our schedule, and I'll be gone in a few days."

"Gone?" The word came out more sharply than she had intended. "Where are you going?"

"I only learned of it yesterday. I'm taking the *Hornet* around the eastern coast on a privateer mission. Specially requested. Simms and a few of the others will be coming along, as well as some new men. We'll leave the day after the ball, but only for a month or two. It seems the Continental Navy needs some diversionary activity."

"It sounds dangerous."

He shrugged, and a hint of a smile played around his lips. "Don't tell me you're worried about me, Lizzie?"

Elizabeth tossed her head. "What do you think?"

There was another silence as he tried to read her eyes. Finally he gave it up and said with a bitter smile, "I think I'd best solve this problem with Ben before I go."

"What are you going to do? According to Carrie, he was furious this morning and swore he wouldn't come back to work for you if you begged him on your knees."

Alex laughed. "Did he now? Well, I'll wager I can persuade him. I had no idea the boy was going to take a wife. I believe an increase in pay may be in order."

"Alexander Burke," Elizabeth accused suddenly, "I believe you regretted firing him the moment it was done! Admit it!"

The grey eyes held a laughing light. "You're right, Lizzie. I never would have done such a damned thing if I hadn't been so worried about leaving for a month." His tone changed. "One never knows what state things will be in when one returns."

Elizabeth had the feeling he was talking about something besides the shipyard. His keen eyes bore into hers as if searching for something. She stood up abruptly and started for the door, fearful of betraying herself.

"Lizzie." His voice stopped her. She turned around.

"I trust you will save at least one dance for me at the ball tomorrow night."

"Why, Alexander." The name sounded sweet and lilting on her tongue. "Is that a request?"

"Damn you, yes! It is!"

"Well, then, I'll see what I can do," she promised, violet eyes alive with laughter. The door closed gently behind her and Alex stared at it for a moment, half smiling. He found himself looking forward to the ball.

That evening Elizabeth lay in bed lost in dreamy anticipation. Tomorrow night. . .at the ball. . . . Unlimited possibilities opened before her, among them the chance that Alexander Burke's cold reserve would finally melt, that he would succumb to her allure. She knew the crimson velvet gown would be ravishing, and she had special plans for her hair. And with the effect of the music, the dancing, the lights. . .such magic could be very powerful. Perhaps Alex would be caught up in its spell.

If not—She dared not think of that possibility. She knew he was leaving early the next morning, and the knowledge distressed her more than she cared to admit. She would miss him achingly, that was certain. A month, perhaps two! It sounded like forever! And if after tomorrow night she had not moved nearer to winning his heart, well, she might as well give it up. The separation caused by his journey would only widen the gulf between them, making it impossible to reach an understanding upon his return.

One fact remained, and one fact only. All depended upon the ball tomorrow night.

Chapter
Twenty-Two

The morning dawned with a spring-like breeze tickling the tree branches, and the sun a golden brooch in the blue silk sky. Elizabeth sat up, stretching, as Mary bustled briskly about, tending the fire. She sipped hot chocolate in bed, and nibbled on tiny buttered biscuits warm from the oven.

Jenny's head peeked in the door. "Good morning! Why don't you just relax today and spend the whole morning preparing for your bath? I'll have lunch sent up for us in my sitting room and afterwards, we'll take our time dressing. Doesn't that sound nice?"

"It sounds heavenly!" Elizabeth smiled. "Isn't it sinful to be so lazy?"

"Probably." Jenny shrugged. "But I've always thought a little luxury before a ball quite in order." Her head disappeared and she shut the door softly behind her.

Elizabeth spent the day in peaceful relaxation. She had a lovely warm bath in the white porcelain tub, soaking luxuriantly in the scented water and washing her long blonde hair with an elaborate amount of lather. After rinsing thoroughly, she stepped into a thick towel and wrapped another turban-style about her head. Her skin glowed pinkly as she dried herself and donned a blue satin dressing robe. Then she sat down at the dressing table in front of the mirror and began to brush her hair. It fell in long yellow strands around her shoulders. She brushed slowly, patiently, until it was nearly dry, feathering softly about her face and shoulders with golden silkiness. Delightedly, she shook her head, watching it swirl and shimmer.

Luncheon, with Jenny and Sarah, was a merry affair, with cold meats and hot soup, and some delicious iced pastries served with coffee. Afterwards, she took a nap, drifting off to a light, dreamless sleep on clean satin sheets, with a quilted comforter pulled up to her chin and the fire crackling softly in the grate. It was late afternoon when she awoke, time to begin dressing for the ball. With quickened pulse and a sense of heady anticipation, Elizabeth removed the crimson velvet gown from her wardrobe.

It was not more than an hour later that she surveyed the results of her efforts in the long mirror above the dressing table. She nodded, well satisfied. A smile curved her lips. Just let Alexander Burke try to resist her tonight!

Downstairs in the front parlor, Alex and Adam were sipping brandy when Jenny entered, looking lovely in apricot satin, with her bronze hair gleaming and her wide dark eyes glowing with excitement. Her husband, handsome and reserved in a brown satin waistcoat and silk knee breeches, kissed her, and exclaimed admiringly that he would be the luckiest man at the ball.

"Wait until you see Elizabeth!" Jenny interrupted. "I caught a glimpse of her on my way down. She's gorgeous!"

Alex drained his glass, and his sister glanced at him appraisingly. Yes, he did indeed look splendid, just as she had assured Elizabeth he would. A black velvet waistcoat, expertly cut, fit firmly over his broad shoulders, and white ruffles showed at his throat and wrists. His breeches were of black satin and his silver-grey silk stockings emphasized his muscled, powerful legs. On his right hand glittered the emerald ring which had been a gift from their father. He looked extraordinarily handsome and aristocratic, yet as rugged and masterful as ever. Jenny could not help thinking what a striking couple he and Elizabeth would make tonight.

A step sounded on the stairway and all three of them ambled into the hallway expectantly. There they stopped, staring up in awe at Elizabeth, who was descending the winding stair with slow, regal grace.

Alex watched her with devouring eyes. She was breathtaking, a rich, sumptuous vision in crimson velvet, the magnificent gown setting off her figure to perfection. It was cut in a low V, revealing a daring amount of tempting white bosom, and the velvet was gathered tightly at the waist, accentuating its slenderness, then billowing into a full, graceful bell. The sleeves were off the shoulder, falling gracefully into fashionable fullness, layered at the ends with rich red lace worked in a cunning design. Rubies gleamed at Elizabeth's white throat, and dangled from her ears, and her golden hair was held in place atop her head by an ebony comb studded with the same winking gems, permitting only a few sausage ringlets to dangle enticingly about her ears. Her violet eyes shone in an oval, ivory-skinned face as she descended with floating grace. Sensuality clung to her like a subtle perfume.

Alex longed to reach out and pull her into his arms, to feel her soft, yielding flesh beneath his hands. He wanted to bury his face and fingers in the silkiness of her hair, to tear away the restricting comb and let the golden strands tumble in rich profusion. He struggled for control of his feelings as years of guardedness warred with his instincts. There was danger here—the one peril he truly feared.

With a supreme effort, iron control returned, and he clamped it desperately over his weakened instincts. Idiot! he lambasted himself silently. You mustn't betray yourself to this witch! She'll only use her powers to destroy you! His mouth tightened grimly. He had watched Elizabeth Trent these past weeks and months; he had seen her ensnare the hearts of numerous suitors, men too weak or naive or foolish to resist her lures. He had watched them dangle like puppets on a string, dancing to whatever tune her whim fancied, and he'd turned away in disgust. Jealousy had twisted his heart when he'd seen her smiling attentions centered on those others; that he could not deny. But even more powerful had been his determination to avoid the trap of his fellows. He's play no puppet, dance to no tune! No woman would play Alexander Burke for a fool! He'd managed to treat Elizabeth with cold civility, to avoid her whenever possible, and somehow his resolution had remained intact. But now. . . . He fought his weakness with all the control he possessed, thinking angrily of how he'd looked forward to this night, especially after the way she'd teased him yesterday afternoon. No, it must not be! Tonight, of all nights, this woman was dangerous, a goddess of loveliness seething with sensuality, a temptress with soft eyes and white skin, outwardly cool and composed but inwardly glowing, ready to ignite at a touch. Alex's hands clenched at his sides. Fear of his own peril gave him strength as Elizabeth reached the last step and paused at his side.

"Well, well," he grated at last. "Tell me, is it whore or goddess I see before me?" He was painfully aware of the delicate scent of violets from her hair.

There was a gasp from Jenny, and Adam shot him a startled, frowning look. But it was Elizabeth he watched. She stared at him mutely as if he had struck her.

He forced a laugh, hoping it sounded mocking and amused. "No retort, Lizzie?" he goaded. There was safety in this angry mood. The magnetic spell had been broken.

"We have nothing to say to each other, Mr. Burke," she replied in a low voice.

"We really must be leaving," Jenny said hurriedly.

"Yes, do let's go." Adam hastily took her arm and led the way to the door.

Alex glanced down at Elizabeth. With mock gallantry, and a harsh smile on his lips, he offered his arm, but she turned from him with an abrupt swish of velvet and lace, following Jenny and Adam into the mild March night. Alex felt a wave of relief. Good. A barrier of anger stood between them. He must not let it fall.

During the carriage ride to town there was a marked silence, broken only by intermittent, strained attempts by Adam and Jenny to make conversation. After a while, however, they gave it up, realizing that they could not compete with the electric tension between their companions, or fill a silence brimming with unspoken thoughts.

When they finally arrived, the clamor of the ballroom provided a striking contrast to the silent carriage ride. The ball was being held in a town meeting-hall, a long, high-ceilinged room which had been transformed into a most spectacular ballroom for the occasion. Giant chandeliers gave off an abundance of candlelight, reflecting brightly off the immaculately polished hardwood floor. Blue silk embroidered sofas and tall, green potted plants lined the room, and at one end, a long table covered with a silver cloth was laden with plates of sliced roast turkey and kidney pies. Wine flowed lavishly. The strains of music floated through the room, and couples already swirled gaily about the floor in a rich variety of color and fabric. The sound of laughter greeted Elizabeth and her party as they entered the hall, breaking in upon their mood of angry silence. Immediately upon their entrance they became the center of a swarming group as Elizabeth's suitors descended like a cloud of locusts.

"Miss Trent, may I say that you've never looked so beautiful?"

"Miss Trent, would you honor me with a dance?"

"Miss Trent, may I bring you some refreshment?"

Elizabeth responded with flirtatious gaiety, but her coquetry disguised a churning upheaval within. Ringed by her admirers, she had become separated from Alex and Jenny and Adam. Peering about, she saw them at the center of another group, led by Geoffrey Granger and some other families of their acquaintance. Alex looked coolly bored. She watched with a knot in her throat as he sauntered across the room, deftly avoiding the dancers.

"Thank you, Edward, I'd love to dance," she replied automatically, and permitted Edward Langston to lead her to the center of the floor. She paid no heed, however, to her flushed, excited partner; instead, her eyes followed Alex across the room. Seeing his destination, Elizabeth stifled a gasp of dismay. He paused formally before Sally Herbert and bowed. Then he was leading her onto the floor, while she, a striking figure in rich green silk, her red hair arranged in soft, loose curls, gazed up at him with her most provocative, green-eyed smile.

Elizabeth turned hurriedly away, a dazzling smile upon her own lips. "Edward, you're a charming dancer!" she cried.

"Th. . .thank you, Miss Trent. I feel like I have two left feet!" he confessed, blushing.

Her laughter trilled. "Nonsense. You're doing splendidly!" She felt herself growing breathless and dizzy from the dance, and wished she could keep spinning forever.

To Elizabeth, the evening seemed to drag interminably. She danced, and drank wine, and flirted with every man in the room, a smile pasted brightly on her face. Inwardly, though, despair possessed her, a tight, aching knot torturing her heart. She had lost, she knew it. Those few derisive words from Alexander Burke at the start of the evening had sealed the hopelessness of her cause. The barrier he had erected between them was permanent and unmovable, and the sooner she accepted it, the better off she would be. The knowledge had a strange effect on her, though. It made her giddy, reckless; she felt a compulsion to keep moving and to not give herself an opportunity to think. Whirling about the ballroom, flushed from the effects of the wine, she felt driven and somehow wild. She couldn't stop, couldn't miss a dance. Her partners changed, a succession of strong arms and eager eyes, but she seemed barely to notice. Her smile glittered for them all, her arms encircled their necks as they sailed in a sea of dance, but to Elizabeth their faces were all the same, a nondescript blur, meaning nothing.

She received and declined a proposal of marriage from Edward Langston, and laughed almost hysterically upon Geoffrey Granger's arm. He studied her closely and suggested that perhaps she'd had enough wine. No, not nearly enough, she'd giggled, blinking back the silly tears.

In this ballroom setting, richly attired in blue velvet only a shade deeper than the slate blue of his eyes, Geoffrey Granger seemed even more naggingly familiar to her. When she told him this, he threw back his head and laughed, saying, "Now I *know* you've had too much wine!"

Ben Tucker approached her, requesting a dance. Carrie, he explained, was deep in conversation with his mother and father.

"Oh, are your parents here?" Elizabeth cried, as Ben's arm went around her waist. "I'd love to see them!"

"Fine, Lizzie, but perhaps you'd better come back down to earth first."

At the stern note in his voice she laughed. "Aye, aye, Sir!"

"Now, Lizzie, get a hold on yourself," Ben hissed in her ear. "I've never seen you like this before!"

"I've never felt like this before!" She giggled, but there was despair in her eyes. "Oh, Ben. . . ."

"It's all right. I understand." He said nothing for a moment. All around them was laughter and merriment, but a moment of quietness enveloped them as they moved automatically in the rhythm of the dance. "I have to thank you, Lizzie, for fixing things between Mr. Burke and me."

"He told you?"

"Yes. As a matter of fact, he *persuaded* me to return to work, at a rather nice increase in salary, I must say."

"Oh, Ben, I'm glad." This time her smile was genuine.

"And Carrie told me how nice you were to her, too—and how you gave her that pretty dress she's wearing. Now, Lizzie, I want you to know I'll do anything, *anything at all*, to help you. After all you've done for me."

"Ben, you're very sweet, but there's nothing you or anyone else can do."

"Is it that bad?" His usually merry blue eyes frowned.

She took a deep breath. "Yes, I'm sorry to say. But for heaven's sake, don't worry about me. I'm the belle of the ball! Haven't you noticed?" The mask of gaiety was back in place.

"Yep, I've noticed. I've also noticed that you're doing a pretty good job of trying to appear happy. But I know you better."

The music stopped. "I guess you do," she said softly. She looked up into his eyes and saw the worry there. "I'll be fine," she assured him brightly, but there was an emptiness in her voice.

They were interrupted at that moment by John Herbert who approached with a confident swagger. "Miss Trent, may I beg another dance?" he inquired, bowing low over her hand.

"Why, of course!" Elizabeth flung a last smile at Ben over her shoulder and followed John onto the floor. But they only remained there briefly before she realized that he was leading her toward the curtained double doors which opened onto a little terrace at the far side of the hall.

"Where are we going?"

"Onto the terrace. I desperately need a moment alone with you!"

"Why, John!" She smiled teasingly up at him through her lashes, recklessly allowing him to lead her through the curtained doors. It was cool outside, and quiet, a welcome relief from the noise and confusion of the ballroom. The night was calm and mild, more like April than March, with a faint, sighing breeze ruffling the still empty tree branches. Several feet away, Elizabeth discerned a rabbit twitching its ears. Suddenly it darted away into the shrubbery beyond.

"Was there something you wanted?" she purred, turning with a smile to her companion.

"I want you," he answered huskily, with a faintly demonic light in his eyes. Elizabeth thought how like his sister he looked: so sly and clever. Even in his smart blue military uniform, with his red hair powdered and tied in a queue, he seemed only a pompous, scheming youth certain of getting his way.

"I'm flattered, naturally," she remarked.

He took a step closer and put his arms boldly about her waist. "Marry me, Elizabeth," he whispered urgently.

She drew back her face from his kiss. "I'm of course gratified by this proposal, John," she began automatically, "but—"

"I don't want to hear any buts!" He held her more firmly and quickly planted his lips upon hers.

"John!" she cried irritatedly, twisting in his embrace. "Let me go at once!"

"Cajolery is useless with you!" His low laugh sounded smug. "So I've elected the opposite approach. You're a beautiful woman, Elizabeth—but you need a strong hand." He pulled her closer and began nibbling her ear in a supposedly romantic fashion. But John Herbert had underestimated his beloved.

"Let me go, you mannerless ape!" She shoved him away from her with all her strength and glared at him angrily.

Herbert recovered his balance, gaping at her in surprise. He'd expected a little modest resistance, but not this. She was apparently stronger than she looked, and a great deal more determined. He began to flush with anger and embarrassment.

"I made you a respectable offer!" he protested.

"In a most unrespectable fashion!" she retorted. She was breathing rapidly and her eyes glittered like diamonds. Well, at least the impudent fool hadn't disheveled her hair! She gave a short, contemptuous laugh and turned away from him, back to the ballroom. It was her second proposal of the evening, and she'd received as little satisfaction from it as from the first.

It was then that she saw the tall figure blocking the doorway, the curtains parted behind him. She stopped short. Alex Burke lounged languidly in her path, an expression of cool boredom resting on his handsome features.

"Good evening, cousin." He nodded to her and then let his gaze wander to John Herbert, crouching against the terrace railing like a cornered fox.

"Ah, Mr. Herbert," he drawled, and there was the faintest note of scorn in his voice. His eyes had taken on a steely quality.

"Good. . .evening, Mr. Burke," Herbert managed through clenched teeth. "I was just. . .that is, we were. . . ."

"Indeed." The single word contained unlimited contempt. Alex turned lazily back to Elizabeth. "I believe you promised me a dance, cousin?"

She nodded, her manner as cold and distant as his own, allowing him to lead her back into the hall and to the center of the floor. The first lilting strains of a minuet drifted in the air.

"You're apparently irresistable this evening," he said, his arm circling her waist in a strong grip.

"Some people think so," she replied, her eyes stabbing him like dagger points. "Must you hold me quite so tightly?"

"Yes. I miss having my arms around you." He grinned. "I miss the pleasure we used to know together when we lay in that big bed in my cabin, squirming about beneath the sheets—"

"Stop it!" she hissed up at him. "Must you be so

crude and monstrous even *here*?"

He shrugged. "When I saw you sailing down the stairs tonight—it brought back memories. You looked so aroused. . .and arousing. Even now, with your eyes feverish from the wine, and your face flushed. . . ."

"How dare you!" she stormed, and she would have broken away from his embrace had he not tightened it almost painfully.

"Now, Lizzie, you don't want to make a scene in front of all these interested people," he chuckled.

She glanced about her. It *did* seem as though people were watching them intently. What in the world were they looking at? she wondered crossly. Her gaze fell on Jenny across the room, talking with a stout, matronly dowager whose silver-grey hair, styled in the latest mode of fashion, resembled a beehive. Elizabeth smiled rather wanly and received an answering wave from Jenny.

"Why do they all seem to be watching us?" she managed through clenched teeth.

"Perhaps because we make such a charming couple."

"Really," she said coldly. Avoiding his gaze, she stared about her once more. It *was* possible that he had correctly guessed the reason for all the attention they seemed to be enjoying. In a way, she could understand it. They must present quite a dramatic appearance: Alex so tall and rugged, with his raven-black hair and glinting grey eyes, and she, slender and blonde on his arm. How greatly they contrasted, she realized. Yet, despite appearances, she knew they had much in common. They both possessed more than their fair share of indomitable pride, as well as stubbornness and a restless, volatile nature. Not to mention violent tempers. She sighed. No wonder they couldn't get along; their own blazing personalities thrust them into continual conflict. She should have realized long ago that she and Alexander Burke were hopelessly mismatched.

The minuet ended. They stared at each other for a moment, and Elizabeth was intensely aware of the pressure of his arm about her waist. Then someone coughed softly beside her and an eager young voice spoke hopefully at her elbow.

"Excuse me, Miss Trent. May I have the honor of the next dance? I believe it's a Virginia Reel."

She recognized the speaker, Lewis Watson, the son of the dowager with the beehive hair. He was a fresh-faced boy, no more than eighteen, and she found his youthful naivety curiously touching.

"Of course." She turned quickly away from Alex.

"One moment, if you please," Alex said smoothly. "Permit me to take this opportunity to bid you farewell for a time, cousin. As you know, I depart at dawn."

"You're leaving the ball already?" she faltered.

He nodded. "Miss Herbert has permitted me the honor of escorting her home."

"I see." She bit her lip and valiantly forced herself to smile. So, it was truly over then. She had lost. "I wish you a most pleasant journey, cousin." The words came out stiffly, sounding absurdly formal. Not daring to meet Alex's gaze, Elizabeth took the arm of the patiently waiting boy beside her. "Mr. Watson, I believe the Reel is beginning."

He broke into an excited grin and led her with awkward care toward the line of dancers. Elizabeth was smiling brightly, to all appearances delighted

with the prospect of the dance. It was a lively frolic,
absorbing the vigorous attentions and energies of
the dancers. Everyone was exhausted by the finish.
No one noticed that beneath Miss Trent's brilliant
smile her skin was pale and her lips dry. Neither did
they notice that her eyes were unusually bright and
moist. No one knew that the unquestionable beauty
of the ball longed brokenheartedly for the solitude
of her room, where she could weep away the throbbing pain in her heart.

It must be nearly three o'clock, Elizabeth decided, as she lay twisting and turning in her downy
bed, too restless and miserable to even close her
eyes, much less sleep. The ball had seemed interminable, a nightmare of forced festivity, but the
hours since her return home sometime after midnight had not offered any solace. Her pillow was
damp with the tears she had shed, but she was far
from comforted. Alexander Burke left on the morrow and she knew she had lost him. He had made
painfully clear his contempt for her, and demon-
strated once and for all that the barrier between
them was impregnable.

One thought seared her mind, hurting perhaps
more than anything else. Tonight Alex was undoubtedly bedding Sally Herbert. *She* was enjoying his caresses and kisses, and knowing the ecstasy
to be found in his arms.

Elizabeth's only comfort, bitter as it was, came
from the knowledge that Sally Herbert would not
be able to pierce that iron shield any more than she
had. She might know his lust and enjoy the pleasures of his masculinity, but she would not succeed
in touching his impenetrable heart. No woman

could, thanks to his mother.

Sitting up, Elizabeth tossed the quilted comforter aside and scrambled out of bed. Sleep eluded her, and wrapped in a cloak of despair, her restless energies sought an outlet. The comfortable bedroom seemed stifling, and she could no longer bear the confinement. Barefoot, clad only in the loose muslin nightshirt she had worn to bed, she padded across the room and eased open her bedroom door.

It was still mild outside, with starlight softening the shadows, and a faint breeze blowing her nightshirt about her bare knees as she crossed the grounds and slipped toward the stable. The night was quiet, save for the sounds of wild creatures rustling and scurrying through the brush. A rabbit darted across her path, and as she neared the stable door, an owl hooted from a naked tree. The moon above cast a long luminous shaft of light as she gently eased open the door, and this pool of moonlight dimly illuminated the stable's interior, revealing the drowsing horses in their stalls, the floor lined with stacks of hay. Quietly closing the door, Elizabeth tiptoed to the center of the stable, breathing deeply of the pungent, hay-scented air. She sank down in a corner of the stable, burying her face in a pile of soft, sweet-smelling hay. Once more the tears began to flow and she lay there racked by sobs of uncontrollable misery. Never had she felt so lonely, so desolate.

She did not hear the latch click, or notice the stable door opening, sending a beam of moonlight along the dusty floor. Alex Burke silently framed the doorway, his eyes narrowed as he studied the girl weeping in the hay, her hair a tangled mass of curls the color of ripened wheat, swirling loosely about her shoulders; her slender, curved figure visible beneath the thin muslin nightshirt. Her legs and feet were bare. She looked delicate and vulnerable, like a golden flower, and he felt a lump in his throat as she stirred, still sobbing, on her bed of hay.

He shut the door softly behind him, but this time Elizabeth heard the noise. Her head came up and she gave a gasp of fright.

"Have no fear," he assured her in an odd voice.

She covered her tear-stained face with her hands. "What are you doing here? Get out! Can't you leave me in peace?"

"But you're not at peace. What's the matter, Lizzie?"

She merely shook her head wildly, refusing to look at him. "Go away!"

He took a step closer. The scarlet dressing robe he wore was open to the waist, revealing his broad, hairy chest. Black hair fell untidily over his brow and his grey eyes pierced her searchingly.

"Lizzie. . . ."

"Stop it!" The words came out in almost a shriek. Elizabeth raised her head, glaring at him. "What are you doing here? How did you find me?"

He shrugged. "I followed you."

"Why? Do you plan to rape me again? Well, don't count on it! I'll scream to wake the dead—and your family and the servants will come running. You can't use me any more as you did on your precious ship, Captain Burke!" The words spilled out venomously. "Besides, haven't you had enough tonight? Or didn't Sally Herbert satisfy your craving?"

A grim smile touched his lips. "My, you *are* the shrew tonight, aren't you?" he remarked.

Fresh sobs shook her. Why must she always battle with him? The man brought out the worst in her! And now, for him to see her like this . . . reduced to tears at his feet! It was unbearable!

"Lizzie, tell me the cause of all this! Right now!" he ordered tersely, looming over her.

Hysterical laughter threatened to overcome her. "Is that an order, Captain?"

"It is."

Suddenly, her mood changed. A sense of unutterable weariness overcame her, banishing all pride and pretense. She no longer had the strength to play her role, to continue this dreadful charade. An uncontrollable urge to admit the truth possessed her, dominating her being, and chasing away the last, clinging remnants of pride. She peered wretchedly up at him through a blur of tears.

"I love you," she whispered.

Shock, amazement, and disbelief all reflected themselves in his features. He stared at her with eyes that seemed to pierce her very soul.

A bitter smile fluttered on Elizabeth's lips. She nodded, and whispered again, "Heaven help me, I love you." Then she buried her face once more in the hay, consumed by agonized sobs.

The next thing she knew, he was kneeling beside her, his arms lifting her to him, cradling her, while his lips bruised hers in a fierce, brutal kiss.

"No! Stop!" She struggled to break away from him, pleading, "I'll not have you use me again! How can you be so cruel? You're. . .torturing me!"

Again his lips crushed against hers, smothering further protest. Then his voice sounded in her ear, husky and strangely tender. "No, Lizzie, I'm not being cruel. I'm not using you."

She felt, as always, her limbs grow weak from his caresses; she fought for self-control. "Please," she begged, squirming in his iron grip.

"Ssh." His lips silenced her once more. There was a pause while she lay motionless in his arms, eyes closed, as the blood coursed hotly through her veins. Then he whispered very softly, "I love you, Lizzie."

Her eyes flew open, staring into that lean, tanned face so close to hers.

He smiled, and the grey eyes shone with a tenderness she had never seen there before. "It's true, my love. I've fought it for too long." With the words, his lips found hers in a kiss that was fierce and tender at once.

She found herself returning it, matching his fervor, draping her arms about his neck in a feverish embrace, as if trying to hold on forever to something that could vanish in an instant. He loved her? Dare she believe it? Could it really, possibly, be true?

For a moment reason battled with emotion as she tried to sort out the confusion in her mind, but then, all thought vanished in place of sensations that left no room for reason. His hands tore the thin muslin gown from her body, and slowly began their delicious exploration. Her nipples grew erect with pleasure as he fondled her breasts, teasing her with his tongue, letting her feel the powerful hardness of his masculinity between her thighs. His lips scorched her flesh, alternately demanding and gentle, and she returned his caresses and his kisses with an equal ardor as a wild abandon engulfed her, sweeping everything aside but the joy of these moments, and the knowledge, certain now, that he loved her.

Afterward they lay exhausted and peaceful in each other's arms, with Alex's scarlet robe draped across their trembling bodies, and the sweet-scented hay soft and warm beneath them. Eventually they talked in gentle whispers. Elizabeth now found it easy to tell him all the things pride had not let her say before. About Robert Mabry, and Thomas Sinclair. Of how they had tried to use her, against her will.

"You're the only man I've ever loved," she murmured almost shyly, gazing into his eyes. "And the only one who has ever made love to me. I've had no other."

Alex noted how her eyes glowed softly violet and her hair shimmered in silken strands about her bare shoulders and breasts. He pulled her close and once more kissed those pink, yielding lips. He smiled at her.

"About Sally Herbert. . . ." he began, but she stopped him, her eyes clouding over, one finger to his lips.

"Please, I don't want to hear about her."

"My darling ninny, there's nothing to tell. The damned girl cornered me into driving her home, but that's all. Oh, she invited me to stay awhile, and no doubt the invitation in her eyes promised other things as well, but I wasn't interested. Damn it, Lizzie, you're the only woman I want to make love to—the only woman I've ever *loved*."

Lizzie. She remembered as if from another century how she had abhorred that name when he first began calling her by it. Now, she heard tenderness and love in the syllables, and thrilled to the sound. She buried her face in his chest, scarcely believing her own happiness.

After a while, they made love again, more slowly this time, with long, languid caresses full of pleasure. Much later, they slipped on their garments and he scooped her up in his arms as if she were a doll, carrying her across the grounds and into the house, up to her bedroom. It was there that they spent the remainder of the night, falling at last into the depths of sleep. Just before they slept, however, Alex leaned close, wrapping his arms about her as he whispered in her ear.

"Lizzie?"

"Mmm. Yes?" she murmured drowsily.

"I must depart in the morning, you know. As a matter of fact, in a few short hours from now. Do you realize that we've made love nearly throughout the night?"

"Mmm, I know. Nice." She snuggled closer.

"When I return, we'll announce our betrothal. I want to marry you as soon as possible."

She smiled at him through half-closed eyes. "Yes, as soon as possible," she whispered happily.

He kissed her eyelids and settled down beside her. Elizabeth lay in pleasant drowsiness, enjoying the peacefulness of his presence, relaxing more completely than she had in months. Suddenly, though, a chill seemed to touch her: she shivered as if an icy finger had slid down her spine. A premonition of something unknown and frightening disturbed her tranquility, lasting only a moment, then disappearing into nothingness. It was like a shadow, blocking the moon. Was it a nightmare? she wondered.

She opened her eyes, gazing at Alex asleep beside her. How wonderful to lie here with him. She moved even closer, revelling in the strong, solid presence of his muscled body. Everything was perfect. They had found each other at last, and had overcome all the barriers, proving their love beyond words, beyond doubts. And when he returned, they would be wed.

What was there to worry about? What could possibly interfere?

Chapter Twenty-Three

Somewhere overhead there was a splash of color and a burst of song as a robin plunged through the cloud-streaked sky. Elizabeth watched it swoop onto a tree branch beside the road, a twig in its beak to be added to the already plump nest in progress. Little ones must be on the way, she thought, smiling to herself.

She had good reason to smile. It was late April and wild flowers were blooming everywhere; and the scent of honeysuckle was rich and pungent, and the trees were sprouting lovely green buds. And tonight, Alexander Burke returned from his privateer mission.

She was in a fever of impatience for his return, longing to see that lean, handsome face, to press her lips against his. The message had come three days ago, indicating that this was the day of his arrival. Probably after dark, so don't wait dinner, the message had read. She hummed a little tune to herself as she strolled along the wooden path, anticipation of their reunion sending her spirits soaring. She had missed him dreadfully, all the while trying to hide her powerful feelings from Adam and Jenny, determined not to let on the change in their relationship until he returned and they made the formal announcement as planned. But it had been terribly hard not to continually sigh over his absence.

All that was behind her now. Only a few more hours and they would be together again, proclaiming their love to the world.

Elizabeth smiled to herself once more. She felt a tingle of excitement at the special news she had to tell Alex tonight. Her whole being glowed with pleasure at the thought of it.

She was with child.

It was still early in the pregnancy, too early for anyone else to detect. Her figure was as slender and graceful as ever; only the happy glow that seemed to envelop her, and the shining healthiness she projected, would provide a clue to the perceptive observer.

Ambling along the wooded track, stopping only occasionally to gather lilacs from their wild bushes, she wondered vaguely why Geoffrey Granger wanted to see her today, and more especially, why he had insisted on secrecy. She had encountered him in town yesterday, while purchasing some hair ribbons for Jenny, and he had told her that there was something important, but very private, that he had need to discuss with her.

"Very well," she had answered, smiling. "Shall we walk together? I've nothing pressing to do at the moment."

"Unfortunately, I have some business to attend

to," he had replied regretfully. "I detest troubling you this way, but perhaps we could go for a drive tomorrow afternoon?"

She had agreed, inquiring at what hour he would call.

"Miss Trent, I do apologize for all this inconvenience, but I'd prefer to meet upon the road. I'd rather that Adam and Jenny didn't know about our discussing this matter. It concerns Alex."

Considerably surprised, she had assented, agreeing to meet him at half past three on a particular shaded lane not far from the Burke house. She had promised not to mention anything to Adam or Jenny, but she could not help wondering what he had to discuss that was so urgent and so private.

Her curiosity had set her out early today. It was barely three o'clock when she left the Burke home in a soft blue muslin gown, her hair trailing down her back in soft gold ringlets. The morning had dawned overcast, with the threat of storm clouds shadowing the horizon, and a warm, muggy feeling in the atmosphere. It had grown even warmer in the afternoon, and now as Elizabeth walked she felt the results of her exertion. Her hair clung damply to her face, and her dress was sticking to her back. Well, that would teach her to be more patient, she scolded herself silently. Instead of meeting Granger at the appointed place, she had taken it upon herself to walk the quarter of a mile to his house. But now, in the heat of the afternoon, and with dark clouds looming in a grey sky above, she regretted the impulse. She decided to rest on a shady bank of grass, beneath a towering elm tree set off from the road, hoping she would have time upon returning home to have a nap and a bath before

Alex's return. She wanted to be fresh and beautiful for him.

She had barely seated herself with her back against the sturdy elm when the pounding of hooves assailed her ears. She peered around the tree to see the passersby, wondering if it were anyone she knew. But the two men converging upon each other from opposite directions were unfamiliar, and something about their appearance made her remain perfectly still, obstructed from their view by the rolling bank of grass and the tree's thick trunk.

The riders paused a short distance from her, greeting each other with coarse familiarity. The first, a hulking brute with a broad, flat face, wore a tricorn hat and dusty clothes. He was perspiring heavily, sweat glistening on his black-bearded face and along the sides of his arms where the sleeves of his soiled linen work shirt were rolled to the elbow. The other man was swarthy and lean, moving with quick, nervous gestures. His voice, reaching Elizabeth's ears clearly, had a curious whining quality.

"Everythin' set?" the swarthy man grated.

"Yep. He's sure a cool one, calmer than a turtle in a shell. What time's Burke due?"

"After dark." The swarthy man spat, and his hands moved restlessly over the reins of his skittish horse.

Elizabeth tensed, suddenly fully alert. Who were these men, and why were they discussing Alex? Her throat went dry as she strained to catch their next words.

The hulking one was speaking, his voice deep and slow. "You're sure there won't be no trouble with the Trent girl? She'll cooperate?"

"She'll cooperate," his companion rasped. He chuckled dryly. "When I get through with her, she'll be like molding clay in our hands. You can bet on that. Tomorrow this time Burke'll be dead and no one the wiser. Our only problem will be to keep Cass from dancin' on his grave." He spat again, wiping his mouth on the sleeve of his jersey. "Now, Thorne, you hurry on to the inn and make sure his lordship's set. We'll catch hell if there's any trouble at either end."

The big, sweating man nodded and raised his enormous hand in farewell. Then he spurred his dappled mount among the road which Elizabeth had just traveled, while the other man galloped off in the opposite direction. Only a cloud of dust remained where they had met.

Elizabeth crouched in frozen terror, her thoughts churning. It was a plot against Alex—involving her! She struggled to make sense of what she had heard. *Tomorrow this time Burke'll be dead.*

She had to get help. Geoffrey Granger would help her. He was Alex's oldest and closest friend. She must go to him!

She scrambled to her feet and began to run, heedless of the raindrops now drizzling from the murky sky. Granger's house was not far, just around the bend. Damp, panting, she ran on, stumbling once over a jutting tree root in the road, but continuing doggedly, fearful to pause for even an instant. Whatever was going to happen, it would be soon, and that meant that she and Geoffrey did not have much time to stop it.

As she neared Granger's two-story stone mansion, she wondered fleetingly if this were not the very reason Granger wanted to speak with her. Perhaps he knew of the plot and wanted her help, not wishing to alarm Adam and Jenny. There was no time, however, to reflect on this possibility. Staggering up the steps, she leaned on the door peal, clutching her hands to her heaving sides. It seemed an eternity, but at last the door opened and a portly butler eyed her disapprovingly.

"Yes?" he droned.

Elizabeth pushed past him, shouting, "Geoffrey! Geoffrey! Come quickly!"

Footsteps sounded above and Granger appeared at the head of the stairs, dressed for driving, his ivory handled cane in hand.

"Miss Trent!" He was by her side in a moment, and dismissed the butler with a wave of his hand. "I was just about to set out to meet you. Whatever is wrong?"

"I. . .must talk with you!"

"Of course. Come into the study and have a glass of wine. My dear, you're soaked!"

She allowed him to lead her into a large, spacious study lined with books and candles. He poured two glasses of wine from a crystal decanter, and then insisted that she sit down on one of the plush blue satin chairs while he leaned against the marble desk, studying her speculatively.

Elizabeth gulped the wine quickly to settle her frazzled nerves, hoping it would stop her hands from trembling so noticeably. Then she set the glass down abruptly on a maple table beside her.

"Geoffrey, you must help me! There is a plot afoot, involving Alex. Someone wants him dead!"

He stared at her. "Calm yourself, my dear."

"But. . .you don't understand. It's true. I overheard two men talking on my way here. . .just a few moments ago! They're planning to kill him!"

A frown creased his brow, and he took a slow sip of the Madeira. "What exactly did you hear?"

"Not nearly enough!" She took a deep breath. "Only that everything was arranged; that tomorrow this time he'd be dead, and that somehow, I'm going to cooperate! I have no idea what they're talking about!" Her voice shook. "Geoffrey, I'm frightened."

"Don't be." The slate blue eyes studied her, their expression unreadable. "There is no reason to be afraid. As long as you cooperate, you're in no danger."

"Cooperate. . . ?" She repeated dazedly. "What are you talking about?"

She saw it then. Incredulity flooded her features. "You. . .you're involved in this. . . ."

He nodded calmly.

She blinked, still unable to believe what he was telling her. Her frightened mind struggled to sort out the pieces.

"But you're Alex's friend—his best friend. Why would you want to harm him?"

Granger crossed leisurely to the decanter, refilled his glass. "More wine? No? Well, to answer your question, my dear Miss Trent, I don't *want* to harm him—it's merely necessary."

"I don't understand." Fear and hatred underlined her voice; her nails dug into the sides of the chair.

He shrugged. "We're on opposite sides. You see, Elizabeth, my loyalties are with the mother country. Unfortunately, yours and Alex's are not."

"You're a traitor!" She accused contemptuously.

"No. I'm completely loyal to England."

"You're betraying your friends!"

Again he shrugged. "Necessity compels me. I have a greater duty than to the yoke of friendship."

She remembered then something he had said to her once before. They'd been discussing privateering. *None of us like having to injure individuals for the sake of our cause, but sometimes it is necessary in order to achieve our goals.*

"So the end justifies the means," she spat. "Even if it requires murdering your friends."

"Even that." He set his glass down on the desk beside him. "Tell me, Elizabeth, aren't you even curious to know how you fit into this plan?"

She remained silent, though the pounding of her heart seemed to fill the room. He was toying with her, enjoying this game. She wondered why she had never noticed the coldness in those slate blue eyes before, never distrusted that purring voice.

"I was going to meet you this afternoon as we agreed, and then bring you here. You very cooperatively saved me the trouble." A smile twisted his lips. "From this point on, everything will follow the original plan, up to and including the conclusion you overheard on the road: Burke's death, with your help."

She started to interrupt him, but he held up a manicured hand. "Just a moment, please. Let me explain in full." He produced a sheet of paper and a quill from the desk drawer, and set them down. "You're going to write a note—a rather incriminating note, I'm afraid. In it, you will reveal that you've stolen documents from Burke's hidden safe and are prepared to pass them on to your accomplice, to whom the note is addressed." As she half rose from the chair he came forward and pushed her back with effortless strength. "In the note you will also set up a time and place to meet, more particularly, at midnight tonight by the old Cobb wishing well in the woods. There you will supposedly pass on the stolen papers." He smiled almost fondly. "Your being British helps a great deal, you know. It adds considerable credibility to your involvement. And the fact that I stole the documents myself at a convenient moment, and have already passed them on, will only add to the evidence against you."

"Go on," she prompted through clenched teeth.

"The note conveniently will be lost and I will most conveniently discover it. You, by the way, will have mysteriously disappeared." Granger shook his head with a rueful smile. "Knowing Alex, he will fly into a black rage and vow to have your blood. Naturally, he'll plan to arrive early at the appointed spot in order to apprehend you and your villainous accomplice, and I will offer to accompany him on this perilous mission."

"You bastard," she said in a low, agonized voice.

"As you wish. At any rate, my accomplices will be waiting when we arrive sometime before midnight, and together we will, ah, eliminate Alexander Burke."

"Why must you kill him?" she began desperately. "You have the papers you want."

"Yes, this has been an ideal arrangement for me. I've been the key agent, setting up the attacks on messengers en route to and from Burke's, obtaining top priority documents. But you see, Elizabeth, sooner or later, Alex and others would become suspicious; they would begin narrowing down the number of people who have access to the information that permits the set-up. Eventually, they might expose me. This way," he raised his glass to his lips, eyeing her with satisfaction, "blame for all of the past information leaks centers on you, the missing British heiress. Oh, yes, I am sorry, Elizabeth, but the true story will have to come out in the investigation: your British ties are exceedingly relevant. It's quite a shame, really. I had at first hoped you would be a valuable aid to me—and a most willing one. But after our conversation in the woods that afternoon, when you revealed your shifting loyalties, I realized that any assistance from you would have to be of an unwitting nature."

Elizabeth leaned forward in her chair. "You still haven't answered my question. Why must you kill Alex? Isn't framing me enough? It will distract attention from you, and I'll go away! I promise! There's no need to kill him!"

"My, you are devoted to him, aren't you? I suspected as much. Not that it matters. Alex never trusted a woman in his life, and with all the evidence against you, including your own signed note. . .well, he'll accept it readily enough. To answer your question, though, Alex's death has been ordered by my superiors. They seem to think that it will disrupt colonial intelligence if one of their chief supporters is destroyed. It will appear, naturally, as though you and your accomplice killed him and fled, a report to which I will most obligingly testify."

He grew thoughtful. "No doubt after this piece of skullduggery, Philadelphia's other citizens will think twice before offering their homes or businesses as meeting places for rebel spies. After all," his voice went on mockingly, "if a man like Alexander Burke can get killed, how much more dangerous is it for the average dullard?"

Her eyes glittered furiously. "You're despicable!" she flung at him. "And if you think I'm going to lift one finger to help you, you're insane!"

A peal of thunder split the air, breaking the intense silence which followed her outburst. Rain driven by a moaning wind, hammered at the draperied windows. Inside, the stillness was charged, electric.

Granger fingered the note paper and quill. "You're going to write this letter," he said calmly, his head tilted to one side, watching her.

For answer, Elizabeth's fingers closed about her wine glass, and with a lightning movement, she sprang from the chair and dashed the contents in his face. She flew to the door and yanked it open, only to find her path blocked by the swarthy man she had seen on the road. She screamed, trying to shove past him, but he grabbed her easily and dragged her back into the study, one hand twisting her arm painfully behind her back, the other snaking across her throat to hold her against him with brutal force. Gasping and sobbing, she struggled to free herself, but to no avail; the man's grip was cruelly unbreakable, and it was all she could do to stay on her feet, fighting the searing pain in her arm as he twisted it viciously.

Granger strolled to the door and composedly shut it, while the swarthy man brought her to the center of the room, apparently waiting for further orders.

"As I said, Elizabeth, you *will* cooperate," Granger drawled lazily. He returned to the decanter, poured himself another glass of the Madeira, and stood sipping it as he watched her.

"Please, let me go," she begged, barely able to gasp the words. Pain washed over her in a breaking tide. "Stop him. . .please."

"Ah, then you consent?"

"Damn you, no!" Somewhere she found the strength to hiss those words through trembling lips. "I'll never agree."

At a nod from Granger, the swarthy man suddenly released his hold on her throat, his hand dipping downward for a flashing instant, but before she could react, it returned, only this time it bore the glint of steel. A knife. Elizabeth shuddered uncontrollably, feeling her knees grow weak.

He wouldn't. This was incredible. Half fainting, she wondered dimly if this were a nightmare from which she would any moment awaken. Yet, another part of her knew that it was not. This was reality. Danger, more intimate and potent than any she had ever known, threatened her now, threatened her and her baby. Alex's baby. Through the blur of tears and pain, her mind groped for answers. She had to protect more than herself in this situation, more, even, than Alex. She had to think of the unborn child within her, the child which could be lost any moment due to the pain and trauma she was undergoing. This new terror was greater than all the others, even the knife, and she knew what she must do. Vaguely, as if from far away, she heard Granger's voice, bland and impassive, saying, ". . .if necessary, though it would be a shame to mar such beautiful features. Why don't you save yourself the agony."

"All. . .right." It was a whisper, a moan, barely audible, but Granger must have heard it, for he held up his hand and her tormentor released her abruptly. He pocketed the knife, grinning.

It did not take long to write and sign the hated note, though the quill trembled in her hand. When it was over, Elizabeth collapsed, weeping wretchedly.

"Well done," Granger approved briskly, removing the note from between her fingers and staring down at her. She presented a pathetic appearance, her blonde hair damp and bedraggled, the blue muslin gown she wore full of wrinkles and torn at the shoulder where Rollins had wrenched her arm. He stroked her head sympathetically.

"No need to worry about anything now, Elizabeth. You'll be quite safe."

She didn't answer, but continued crying.

"Rollins here will take you to the Golden Horseshoe Inn. There's someone there whom I believe you will remember and he's quite anxious to see you again. In fact, he plans to keep you with him for a time—at least until he tires of you—so, have no fear, your life is safe."

She regarded him through bleary eyes. "What are you talking about? Who. . . ?"

"You'll find out in good time. Rollins. . . ."

As the swarthy man closed in upon her again, Elizabeth cringed in her chair, but he merely laughed and grabbed her wrists.

"Please excuse this discomfort, but believe me, it is necessary. You must not be discovered en route to the inn, or upon entering it." As Geoffrey Granger spoke, Elizabeth realized what was happening. Rollins was binding her wrists with rope.

"Oh, no—please," she implored weakly, but Granger cut her off.

"It is necessary." There was no arguing with the

ruthlessness she heard in his voice.

When her wrists and ankles were securely bound, Granger produced a white linen handkerchief, and before she could protest, he fastened it securely to gag her. Then she was lifted in Rollins's sinewy arms and carried out of the study.

Elizabeth stared wildly about as she was borne through the house, past several uniformed servants. They all appeared deaf and blind to her predicament: they were all involved in this conspiracy, every one of them. Hatred shone from her eyes; she wished them all a bloody death.

Rollins carried her through a rear door in the kitchen, out into the storm. Rain fell upon them as he set her beside a shabby wagon to which a rather bony horse was hitched, its head lowered miserably against the wetness. Reaching into the wagon, Rollins drew forth a large, stained potato sack. The last thing Elizabeth saw was Geoffrey Granger silhouetted in the doorway. Then the sack was thrust over her head and body, blotting out all vision.

She was heaved into the wagon, and she heard the sounds of Rollins mounting the driver's seat, clicking the horse into motion. The wagon rolled forward, jostling over the wet, uneven track.

"Heaven help me and my baby," Elizabeth prayed. She felt as if she were stifling inside the sack; the air was dank and close, and she felt both warm from the confinement and chilled from the rain which had soaked her to the skin. Bound and gagged, unable to move or speak, her already bruised body was jarred painfully as the wagon made unsteady progress along the rough road.

She was headed for the Golden Horseshoe Inn, a

meeting place, she knew, for sailors and travelers and merchants. Dimly, she wondered the identity of the man Granger had mentioned, the one who planned to "keep her." Fear for her life and for the life of her baby enveloped her, but could not erase the overwhelming dread in her heart.

Alex. He was in danger—terrible, imminent danger. And the worst part of it was that he would die believing she had betrayed him. Hot tears slid down her cheeks. If only she could have spared him that pain—so much worse than any other Granger could devise. The pain of betrayal.

Oh, love, she prayed silently. Forgive me.

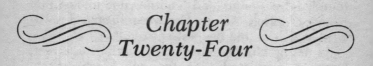

Chapter
Twenty-Four

Alex swore softly as Moonfire stumbled in the soggy earth. Burke hauled him upright and gave the beast an encouraging pat. Somewhere nearby a wolf howled. The night was filled with the rustle of rain on leaves and the sighing of the wind through the glistening, shadowed trees. Overhead, a black gauzy sky swirled with the ragged remnants of ghostly grey clouds, obscuring the moon so that the darkness was deep—nearly impenetrable.

Geoffrey Granger glanced momentarily at the man riding beside him, reading easily the signs of Burke's suppressed fury. Though Alex sat Moonfire with his customary ease, Granger saw the tautened body, coiled like a spring braced for release. Alex's lips were clamped tightly together, giving his face a grim, hardened expression, but it was his eyes, grey and glinting, narrowed hawk-like, which made him look truly dangerous. They were the eyes of a man not only prepared to kill but eager to do it. Mercilessly, they stared straight ahead, piercing the murky darkness of the drizzling night: there was no trace of compassion or kindness in them.

Granger smiled inwardly. All was going exactly as planned. Consumed by fury with the English girl, Alex was riding straight into the trap which had been prepared for him. No doubt his surprise would be unbounded when, instead of finding his traitorous beauty and her accomplice, he was surrounded by Rollins and Thorne, not to mention Granger himself. Ah yes, Granger reflected shrewdly, that will be the deepest cut of all.

Trotting alongside Alex through the forest, Granger admitted to a twinge of conscience. Friendship was not an easy thing to put aside, after all. But his friendship with Burke had not been the same since hostilities began between England and the Colonies. He had lost respect for Alex after hearing his foolish rebel beliefs. Burke favored "independence" and "liberty." Hah! The man could not see that the road he followed led to anarchy and chaos. He had grown foolish and sentimental. And too dangerous for his own good. Alex's privateering activities, as well as his connections with colonial intelligence agents, had sealed his fate. He could not be allowed to continue his rebel activities.

It was a shame about the girl, though, Granger thought regretfully. How he would have relished her for himself! That slender, tempting body, golden hair, and those unforgettable violet eyes! He sighed. Perhaps Richard could be persuaded to share her—even only for one night. But he knew that once he had tasted that sweet, tender flesh, he would be hard put to give her up. She was a woman who would haunt a man. Either way, he reflected wryly, the loss was his, for she now belonged to another.

"We're getting close." Alex's whisper broke the silence between them. He pulled his pocketwatch from beneath the folds of his heavy black cloak. "Nearly eleven-thirty. We'll have plenty of time to ready ourselves."

Granger nodded, thinking again how well everything was going. And why not? It had been a well-laid trap, the product of extensive, clever planning.

A muscle twitched in Alex's jaw as he recalled the scene of pandemonium and confusion he had encountered upon arriving home. He would never forget Jenny's pinched, white face, or the way Adam's shoulders had sagged. Or Geoffrey Granger's frown, his eyebrows drawn together in deepening concern as Burke stood in the doorway demanding to know where Elizabeth was. Enough! He thrust from his mind the memory of how they had told him about Elizabeth's disappearance and the note she must have misplaced, the one Granger discovered in the parlor. No, he must not think of it. Or he would stir up the embers of his fury beyond all control. And that was something he could not afford to do—yet.

He gritted his teeth. They were almost at Cobb's wishing well. All his nerves and senses sharpened, keyed to the slightest noise or movement as they emerged through a cluster of trees into a small clearing. There, in the center of the clearing, ringed by a fringe of ancient trees, stood the old brick well, long abandoned, covered by crawling green ivy. It was a favorite rendezvous for lovers—but not to-night.

Alex rode to the center of the clearing, halting just before the well. He wheeled Moonfire to face Granger, who had stopped at the edge of the clearing and was watching him intently.

"Shall we tie the horses behind the trees to the right?" he suggested.

"I don't think so, Alex," Granger replied slowly.

"No? You have a better plan, Geoffrey?"

At that moment, movement exploded on either side of him. Two men jumped out from the circle of trees, wielding long heavy muskets pointed directly at him. Geoffrey Granger reached into the folds of his cloak, drawing forth a large, silver-barreled pistol which he held loosely, almost playfully, though a sad smile twisted the corners of his lips.

"I'm sorry, Alex," he said, shaking his head. "You must understand, this is absolutely necessary."

Alex did not move. He regarded Granger with unruffled calm. "Perhaps you'd best explain, my friend," he said grimly.

"Ah, yes, an explanation," Geoffrey drawled thoughtfully, reminding Alex of a cat toying with a mouse before the kill. "I'm afraid it's going to be necessary to kill you, Alex. I've had my orders, you see."

"British orders?"

"Yes, British orders. I suppose you think badly of me for not having openly admitted my Loyalist sympathies, but in truth, Alex, can you blame me? I saw what happened to those unfortunate fellows who did admit their ties with England: the tarring and feathering, the rocks through the windows of their homes. No, I did not care for any of those disreputable fates. Besides, I was much more valuable to my country this way, as a trusted confidante of the rebels. My information and activities have been invaluable to the Crown."

"And I'm sure you expect to be heavily rewarded," Alex's voice was thick with undisguised contempt. "So it was you who stole the missing papers." It was a statement, not a question.

Granger nodded. "In case you're wondering, they've already been passed on to another agent." He leaned back in the saddle, relaxing. "Yes, Alex, I regret to say that you've been totally outwitted. This game is slightly different, though, from those childhood ones we once played, isn't it? For one thing, the stakes are higher. As a matter of fact, you will pay dearly for this loss." He lifted the gun, pointed it at Burke. "You will pay with your life."

Alex shrugged. "So it seems." He allowed his gaze to wander to the two men on either side of him. One was a big, hulking brute, the other a dark, nervous man who was licking his lips in obvious enjoyment of the situation. Alex's hands clenched into fists at his side. Not yet, he told himself.

"What have you done with Elizabeth?" he asked casually, forcing himself to sound calm, almost indifferent. But Granger wasn't fooled.

"Ah, yes, the lovely Miss Trent," he remarked musingly. "She's quite a treasure, Alex. But then, you know that, don't you? Have no fear for her safety, though; she's in very good hands. The gentleman who has her now was most anxious to bed her, and intends to keep her for some time. You'll be happy to know that he is quite well off and can afford to maintain her most comfortably." He paused, tilting his head to one side thoughtfully. "I always thought she'd make an excellent mistress—her beauty is quite unsurpassed. I'm sure she'll get on famously once she becomes accustomed to her new station."

Alex felt sweat on his palms, knew a rush of color darkened his face. He struggled for control. "Where is she?" he rasped.

Granger waved the gun carelessly. "In another's bed, at the moment, I'm certain," he laughed. "I intend to ask if I may borrow her myself for an evening, since I'm certain she'll provide great sport. The girl has rather a lot of spirit, and bedding such a fiery wench should be most amusing. She put up quite a fight when it came to writing that little note you saw earlier." He nodded toward the dark, swarthy man. "I'm afraid Rollins here had to get a bit rough in order to. . .persuade her."

At these words, and the mental image they conjured up, Alex's last thread of control snapped. His rage surged to the surface in one powerful explosion, consuming him in a savage frenzy. "Damnit, now!" he roared in a voice which split the night like thunder. At the same instant he charged forward on Moonfire straight at Granger who, taken by surprise, had no time to protect himself before Alex lunged at him and hurled him to the ground, leaping on top of him before he could roll aside.

Suddenly the night was filled with shots, and shouts, and the smell of gunpowder and blood. Rollins and Thorne fell forward, and their muskets, which a moment before had been pointed at Alex as he tackled Granger, struck the earth with a dull thud. Rollins, moaning piteously, stretched out a trembling hand for the weapon which lay just beyond his grasp. His fingers brushed it, grasped, then suddenly went limp. He was dead, like his companion, a bloodied figure in the mud.

Ben Tucker and Adam Warren stepped out from their hiding places behind the trees, surveying their handiwork with solemn satisfaction. It had been difficult waiting for Alex's signal before taking care of these brutes, but they had followed his instructions to the letter. A perfect plot within a plot. And it had worked. They turned grim faces toward the two desperate figures struggling a few yards away. Burke and Granger were fighting furiously, like crazed animals, their breath coming in ragged, heaving gasps; grunts and groans punctuating their battle. Their blows connected with sickening impact as they engaged in their deadly ballet. The watchers tensed as Granger's fist slammed brutally into Alex's jaw. Ben took a step forward, his musket levelled at Granger's swerving, ducking figure, but Adam stopped him with a hand on his arm.

"Let them finish," he said grimly. "Alex wanted this."

"Did you really think I'd fall for your filthy trap?" Alex grated, his breath coming in short, excruciating gasps. "I knew Elizabeth. . .would never. . .betray me—and that left only you!" He hit Granger in the jaw, a blow that sent him reeling backward. "You stinking traitor—who so *conveniently* found that trumped-up note! What have you done with her, damn you? Tell me!"

But even as he followed up his advantage, moving in close for a body punch, Granger kneed him, aiming viciously for the groin. With needle-sharp reflexes, Alex managed to sidestep, and the blow struck the inside of his thigh. He tackled Granger with renewed fury, and both men went down, rolling and grunting in the mud. For a moment, Ben and Adam could not tell who was on top, there was such a confusion of capes and flying mud and hoarse groans. Then a faint glimmer of moon showed briefly between the rolling concealment of the clouds, casting down a pale whisper of light, just sufficient to enable them to discern Alex astride Granger's heaving body. Burke's muscled arm was wedged against the other man's throat, pressing, squeezing relentlessly. Granger flailed uselessly, unable to throw off his opponent, helpless beneath that powerful weight and the awful pressure at his throat. He struggled, gasping and wide-eyed, for breath.

"Please," he wheezed, half sobbing.

"Where. . .is. . .she?" Alex's breathing was labored also; sweat poured freely down his face. But the pressure on Granger's throat did not waver.

Granger had never heard his voice so deadly, so full of murderous savagery. Above him, the world spun, blurred; his eyelids fluttered with the effort of reply.

"At the inn. . .Golden Horse. . . ."

"The Golden Horseshoe Inn?"

He managed to nod. It was over now; Alex would kill him, break his neck, and be done with him. Granger welcomed the thought. If only he would finish it, and stop this terrible pressure, the unbearable pain. . . .

Suddenly it stopped. Alex removed his arm, heaved himself to his feet. Granger found himself alone on the oozing mud. Gasping and sobbing, he watched Alex stagger away, toward Ben and Adam and the horses. Then he remembered the gun. . .it had gone flying. . .it must be here somewhere.

It was Ben who saw the flash of silver. He jerked his rifle upward, shouting, "Alex, look out!"

Burke whirled and fired, using the little pistol he

had tucked into his breeches. It was a straight shot, and an accurate one. Granger's arm sagged, and the silver-handled pistol sank into the mud.

There was silence, save for the rustling of the leaves, and the sudden, incongruous song of a nightingale.

"So, my friend, you would have shot me in the back," Alex muttered. He stared for a moment at the lifeless body of the man who had been his friend. Then he tucked the pistol away, and turned wearily back to Ben and Adam. "See to them." He jerked his head toward the corpses.

"Where are you going?" Adam asked sharply.

Alex's voice rang with steel as he vaulted into the saddle and gathered the reins. "To the inn," he said grimly. "There is more blood that demands shedding this night."

Then he spurred Moonfire, and they were off, charging with reckless speed through the twisting track, while overhead the moon disappeared once more behind a sea of misted clouds.

Chapter
Twenty-Five

It was hot in the room—stiflingly hot. Elizabeth
lay perfectly still, too exhausted to struggle. She
was bound and gagged, just as Rollins had left her
when he had dumped her onto the bed and then
left, locking the door behind him. Struggling would
only waste whatever little energy she had left and
something told her she must save her strength for
whatever was to come.

From below she could hear the strains of music
and snatches of bawdy songs sung by deep voices.
The clamor of men's uproarious laughter drifted
upward, occasionally accompanied by the shrill
giggle of a wench, or the clink of glasses. The smell
of ale and tobacco permeated even this little room
above the tavern, seeping beneath the heavy
wooden door.

With an effort, she raised her head and peered
through the dimness at her surroundings. She was
in a small, windowless room, furnished sparsely,
with bare wooden floors, and an ash-filled, unlit

corner hearth. For the rest, it contained only a shabby pine bureau, a scratched night stand beside the bed, one old rocker chair with a worn cushion, and a single candle sputtering in its tarnished wall-bracket. The candle provided all the light in the room, which was not very much at all, giving the chamber a gloomy, eerie quality. Only the bed on which she found herself indicated any concern with comfort; it was a soft, plump four-poster covered with a brightly colored patchwork quilt. For all its downy softness however, Elizabeth remained far from comfortable. The rope cut painfully into her wrists and ankles and the gag across her mouth made it difficult to swallow. Her entire body throbbed with soreness suffered at Rollins's hands, and by the grueling, jostling wagon ride. But mental anguish tortured her far worse than any physical pain she experienced. Her frantic mind seethed with visions of Alex's prone, lifeless body, and she shuddered uncontrollably, knowing the trap laid for him and helpless to prevent it.

"I'll never see him again," she thought miserably, as tears slid down her cheeks. She couldn't envision life without him. His strong, handsome face and tall, lithe body were a part of her, an extension of her own being! Closing her eyes, she could see him clearly, his grey eyes smiling at her with that special, tender light, as they had that final night when they were together. She heard his murmuring voice, felt the fire ignited by his lips. Only to be in his arms once more!

But that would never be. Alex would die, and with him, the love he had felt for her. He would die hating her, believing her to have betrayed him. All their love and passion, their dreams and desires, would vanish like smoke, replaced instead by the acrid stink of hatred. When she thought of what could have been. . .what *would* have been. . . . But it would never be. Cruel fate had wrenched them apart even as they tottered on the brink of happiness.

A key scraped in the lock, and Elizabeth stiffened, her heart beating wildly in her breast. The door opened: it was the girl she had seen earlier when Rollins had removed that beastly sack and thrown her over his shoulder, carrying her up the rotted back steps of the inn. A door below had opened suddenly, revealing a noisy, smokey world of laughter and shouting and drink: the tavern. The girl had shut the door abruptly behind her, jerking her head in Elizabeth's direction without surprise.

"That her?"

Elizabeth remembered how her black eyes had gleamed maliciously.

"No, it's me grandmaw," Rollins had retorted sarcastically. "You can tell him she's here. And bring her some food, Cass. Granger's orders."

The girl had nodded and whirled, returning to the tavern, her long, shiny black hair swirling behind her. Elizabeth had forgotten her until now, when she entered the dim chamber balancing a tray of food.

Cass kicked the door shut and crossed the room, setting her burden down upon the dusty night stand. She folded her arms, staring at Elizabeth with an expression of curious dislike on her round, rosy face.

She was a large, buxom girl with the air of the country about her. She had a gaudy prettiness, accentuated by her white ruffled blouse, cut low to show off full, ripe breasts, and the brightly colored skirt of blue and green and red swirling about wide, rounded hips. There was a hardness in her face, however, which detracted from her simple country prettiness; what could have been charm emerged instead as tough vulgarity, unsoftened by any evidence of sweetness. There was a harshness about the wench's full mouth, a coldness in her eyes that instantly discouraged whatever hopes Elizabeth had briefly nourished that here was a possible ally. She would find no compassion here.

"So you're the English bitch his lordship's been hankerin' for," Cass sneered. There was jealousy in her black eyes as she critically surveyed Elizabeth. "You're comely enough, I'll grant," she added reluctantly. "Let's see if you've got any sense."

She reached into the sash of her skirt and brought out a glinting knife which made Elizabeth stiffen in terror. But the girl merely threw back her mass of long black hair and laughed, a full, chortling sound reverberating throughout the tiny room.

"I'm not goin' to cut you," she promised mirthfully, "unless you do somethin' foolish. I'm goin' to cut these ropes here, so you can eat. But one move and I'll let you have it." A spiteful smile curled her lips. "I learned how to use this knife when I was no more'n ten years old, and I'm good with it. I'll cut you if you try anything."

Deft fingers removed the gag, and Elizabeth swallowed convulsively, testing her sore, bleeding lips with her tongue. She remained motionless as Cass cut away her bonds, then slowly, moving carefully so as not to alarm her captor, she brought her wrists in front of her and began rubbing them gingerly, helping the circulation start again.

Cass nodded and stepped back a few paces to sit down upon the rocker, fingering the knife and never letting her eyes stray from Elizabeth.

"May I. . . ." Elizabeth found her voice cracking in a most humiliating way. She swallowed and tried again, angry with herself for giving this chit the satisfaction of frightening her. "May I untie my ankles?" she asked, more strongly.

The girl shrugged, but eyed her warily, suspicion edging her voice. "All right, but don't get off the bed. I mean it, I'll cut you into little pieces if you make a wrong move."

Elizabeth nodded, stilling the pounding of her heart. It was a relief to free her ankles from their bonds and to stretch her weary muscles. She glanced at the tray of food beside the bed. It contained a plate of roast mutton, a chunk of bread, and a glass of ale.

"I'm not hungry." The sight of the food made her feel slightly sick.

"If I were you, I'd eat it," Cass advised bluntly. "It's all you'll get tonight, and besides," her eyes took on a knowing sparkle, "you'll need your strength when his lordship gets here. He's been hot to bed you for months, and most likely he'll keep at it all through the night. He's like that, I know." Her eyes shone with remembered pleasures.

Elizabeth could not suppress a shudder. She wanted desperately to know who "his lordship" was, but wasn't certain how such a question would be received. At last she took her courage in her hands and said, in a voice she hoped was steady, "Would you be so kind as to tell me the identity of this person you're talking about?"

Again the girl threw back her head in laughter.

"Would I be so kind, is that it? My, we *are* the fine lady, aren't we?" The harshness in her features deepened and her voice was gloating. "I've had my orders not to tell you, and I'm goin' to stick by 'em. He wants it to be a 'surprise.' So just eat your supper, my fine lady, and don't fret over what you can't change. He'll be here soon enough and he's bound to have you, and so he will. Better just relax and enjoy it."

Wordlessly, Elizabeth reached for the tray, drawing it onto the bed beside her. She felt no hunger, but she knew she should eat, for her baby's sake if not her own. When she had finished and had pushed the tray aside, she asked Cass the time, trying to make the question appear casual.

"Near midnight," the girl responded. "Guess you know what that means. Mr. Alexander Burke is just about breathing his last."

Her words were like stakes driven into Elizabeth's heart. But somehow, instead of demoralizing her, they had an opposite effect. A spark of anger ignited deep inside her; the flame caught and held, glowing strongly. Perhaps it was Cass's arrogant heartlessness that goaded her, or maybe the effects of the ale she had drunk with her supper which revived her spirit, making her want to fight. She only knew that she had never been one to accept defeat, and this time was no different. She set her lips together. It might be too late to save Alex, but she would not let him die alone. She would see him avenged, even if she had to do the killing herself. Anger licked through her veins, warming her. Yes, she would do the killing herself.

"Do you know Alexander Burke?" she questioned softly.

"You bet I do!" the girl spat, and with a little shock, Elizabeth noted the hatred in her voice. "My name's Cass Morgan—did he ever mention it to you?"

Elizabeth shook her head.

"I figured not," Cass remarked bitterly. "When I first started working here, he came in sometimes and bought me drinks. Was real nice to me, you know what I mean? And him bein' so handsome, too. I fell for him, like a squirrel in a bear trap!" Her voice shook with suppressed fury. "He wasn't my first man, you understand, not by a long shot. But he was sure the best." Her eyes glistened. "Never met a man like him before. Fool that I was, I took it seriously." She began to rock vigorously in her chair, scowling wrathfully.

"What happened?" Elizabeth prompted.

"I'll tell you what happened," the girl rasped. "He was just playin' around! I didn't mean a damned thing to him! That bastard! He stopped coming around, and then I heard he'd taken up with a bitch at another tavern. And later on it was a 'lady of quality,' as they say. And then another." She laughed mirthlessly. "But he dropped them all, same as me. None of 'em meant a thing to Mr. Alexander Burke." She stopped rocking and leaned forward, smiling with deep satisfaction. "And now, you see, I'm goin' to have my revenge. He's goin' to pay dearly for how he hurt me. He's goin' to die!"

"I. . .see." Elizabeth did see. It was apparent that Alex's careless use of women over the years had earned him a dangerous enemy in this girl who had nursed her pain into murderous hatred. She felt pity for the girl, understanding a little of what she must have suffered, but the fact remained: she was a conspirator, one of those responsible for Alex's murder. She would have to pay like the rest.

Elizabeth's gaze swept the room, questing for a weapon. The room was almost bare save for the minimum of furnishings. She eyed Cass's knive. That would be difficult—and risky. She weighed the odds, seeking in her mind for a plan.

At that moment, however, footsteps sounded on the landing outside, and before she had time to do more than swing her gaze in that direction, the door burst open and a man framed the entrance-way, his eyes glinting with pleasure.

Despite her newfound purpose, and the cold determination that had possessed her, Elizabeth gasped. Her mind had prepared itself for mayhem, for murder, and for grief, but somehow this face from her past squeezed through her defenses and penetrated her anger, threatening to replace it instead with instinctive fear.

Lord Richard Milburne towered in the doorway, clothed in deerskin jacket and breeches, a sword at his side and the bulge of a pistol at his belt. He looked rugged and suave at the same time, exactly as she remembered him on that dreadful night when he had molested her in the garden during the Carrington ball. Now, seeing him again in America, she felt dizzy with shock and a kind of numbed terror. Her memories of his strength and ruthlessness crowded in upon her.

"Well, well, well—Miss Elizabeth Trent," he drawled from the doorway, and his gleaming eyes explored her body with piercing interest. It was as if she were naked beneath his gaze.

Cass sidled up to him, her hand touching his arm. "My lord," she began provocatively, but he brushed past her into the room, saying curtly, "I'll see you on the morrow, Cassandra. Be a good lass and take this tray away so that Miss Trent and I may, ah, renew our acquaintance."

The girl scowled, her black eyes stabbing Elizabeth jealously, but she tucked the knife back into her sash and moved obediently to gather the tray. She hesitated for just an instant at the door, but Milburne was already approaching Elizabeth on the bed, and with an angry toss of her head, she left, slamming the door loudly behind her.

In the room it was very quiet. Elizabeth crouched motionless, unable to tear her gaze from that handsome, ruthless face. Lord Richard Milburne! So, he too was involved in this treacherous plot. From somewhere came an instant of startled recognition, a familiar image clicking into place. "Granger!" she gasped. "I knew he looked familiar! You're related to Geoffrey Granger!"

He nodded, smiling indulgently down at her. "He's my cousin, Elizabeth," he acknowledged. "You do remember that shortly after our little encounter in the Carrington garden I sailed for America, to visit my Yankee cousin and aid him in his activities against the rebels? Well, Geoffrey Granger is that cousin." He grinned at her. "You may find this difficult to believe, but I've been posing as a fur trader all this time. Quite a change in station, eh? You see, it allows me great freedom to come and go as I please, gathering information and passing it along. For the most part I've been lodging at this very inn, where I've become almost a part of the scenery, you might say, and where I've been receiving the most gratifying attention from the staff."

"Cassandra Morgan, you mean," Elizabeth corrected coolly. Her temporary intimidation had passed. Perhaps the Elizabeth Trent he had known in London would have cowered before him, pleading for mercy, but she was no longer that same girl. She was no frightened innocent defending her virginity, but a woman, wise now in the ways of men, familiar with their weaknesses. She had her own weapons, far more subtle than the weapons men employed, but equally dangerous. Her mind raced, planning, plotting, but she talked quietly, stalling for time in which to organize her thoughts.

"Why do you do it?" she asked, meeting his gaze squarely. "Why go to all the trouble to pose as a trapper, and go traipsing over the countryside, when you could be comfortable and safe back in England?"

"Why, for the sheer fun of it!" He laughed at her baffled expression. "It's adventure—it's danger! Those are the things I seek from life. I want excitement, not boring tranquility. This situation in the Colonies offers a perfect opportunity for someone of my restless nature. I couldn't pass it up."

"So you are involved in this conspiracy against Alex Burke?" she queried.

"Oh, yes, indeed," he returned, his eyes glowing like embers. He reached down to finger a stray curl trailing over her shoulder. Elizabeth managed to refrain from shrinking at his touch, instead meeting his gaze unflinchingly.

"You may imagine my surprise, Elizabeth, when you arrived in Philadelphia," he went on, and there was a hint of mocking laughter in his voice. "My cousin informed me immediately, and I must tell you, it was a great revival to my spirits. I came to

America seeking adventure, but things were comparatively dull until you and Mr. Burke arrived on the scene. Then things livened up considerably. And I must admit, Elizabeth," his hand strayed downward toward her breast, and began to trace lightly over the creamy flesh where the gown was cut away, "I had a double incentive in helping to plan Burke's downfall. One was the service of my country and the aid of my cousin, and the other reason was you." He cupped her breast in his hand, squeezing slightly, his fingers playing with her nipple through the thinness of the muslin gown and the sheer chemise beneath. "You were my promised reward, and I must say, it was well worth the effort and the wait. You've become even lovelier, my dear. I'm going to enjoy showing you off as my mistress when we return to England."

So that was his plan, was it? Elizabeth allowed herself to smile at him, hoping she looked docile and obedient. She had already noted the pistol at his waist. Now it was a matter of luring him closer. The gleam of growing desire burning in his eyes told her this would not be difficult. She spoke then, her voice soft and seductive.

"I hope you'll be kind to me, my lord," she purred. "It's obvious that struggling will not help me. Pray tell me, if I am willing and try to please you, will you be gentle with me?"

Milburne chuckled and sank down beside her on the bed. His arms enfolded her in a crushing grip, and his lips seared the flesh of her neck as he pushed her head back and kissed her brutally. "Ah, my dear, you beg for bruising, masterful love," he whispered in her ear. "It's impossible to restrain my passion to mere tenderness!" His hands began their greedy massage of her breasts, and Elizabeth leaned against him, murmuring as if with pleasure. She forced her revolted body to relax, to melt into his embrace, at the same time opening her lips to his kiss. Milburne's mouth tasted of ale and tobacco and she fought back nausea. After what seemed like an eternity, the kiss ended. His lips began travelling down her throat and bosom while his hands clawed at her clothes. Giggling softly, Elizabeth pushed him gently down on the bed and observed how flushed and feverish his face appeared as he looked up at her, his eyes burning with a powerful lust. She let his hands play with her breasts as she began to run her own hands sensuously over his body. She traced his shoulders, his chest, the bulging muscles on his arms, down to the lean, narrow waist. . . .

Her fingers closed on the pistol and in a flash she had whipped it from its place and bounded backward off the bed, aiming the weapon with both hands at the man who still lay there, startled into immobility. This condition did not last long, however; Milburne's features darkened with rage, and he shot up, only to freeze at Elizabeth's harsh warning.

"Don't move, my lord, or I'll shoot you dead," she ordered, and from the tone of icy hatred in her voice he knew that she meant what she said.

Milburne cursed. "What game are you playing, bitch?"

"No game, sir. I mean to kill you. And your little plaything, Cassandra. And your dear cousin, Geoffrey Granger. Everyone who was involved in this stinking plot to kill Alex." As she said the words, she realized with a heart-rending jolt that at this very moment, Alex probably lay dead. Vengeance!

What good would it do her now? No matter how many she killed, it would not bring Alex back to her. She began to cry, bitterly, grievously, the gun shaking uncontrollably in her hands. Suddenly she wanted nothing other than to escape this place, to go somewhere quiet where she could be alone with her grief. She began backing toward the door, only dimly aware, through the blur of tears, of Milburne's angrily flushed face glaring at her.

From below came a sudden roar of laughter, and Elizabeth glanced instinctively at the floor. It was all the chance Milburne needed. Like a bolt of lightning, he dove off the bed straight at her, and though she hesitated only an instant before firing, it was an instant too long, for even as she pulled the trigger he was upon her, and the shot went wide as he grasped her wrist and nearly broke it in a brutal attempt to wrest the weapon away. Elizabeth screamed, and the gun went skittering across the wooden floor; then she and Milburne went down in a tangle of arms and legs and crashing bodies. He was upon her in a flash, his weight pressing her cruelly into the hard floor, his hands pinning her wrists above her head in a grip of unbreakable iron. He was breathing heavily and his face was still flushed, but with fury now, as well as desire. Elizabeth fought frantically, helpless beneath his heavy body, her hair tangled about her face and throat, tears pouring down her face. She cried aloud as his fingers bruised the tender flesh of her wrist, and Milburne's eyes lit with cold satisfaction.

"You're a wild one, all right," he grunted, leering down at her. "I like a wench with spirit, Elizabeth, but I think you have too much for your own good." He laughed heartlessly as she bucked in vain, trying to free herself. "No, my beauty, you won't escape me again, not this time. Not ever. I'm going to teach you to obey, and by the time I'm finished with you, you'll be as tame as a lap dog." He snickered, an ugly sound. "And your lessons begin right now."

He grabbed both of her wrists in one of his, clamping them together securely, and raised his other hand to strike her.

Elizabeth screamed, and cringed futilely from the expected blow. But the blow never came. A commotion sounded outside the door and suddenly it crashed open. Milburne froze, his heavy body still astride her, hand poised to strike. There was a shocked silence while Elizabeth dazedly twisted her head in a vain attempt to see the newcomer. Her breath was coming in ragged sobs; she was damp all over with perspiration. Moaning softly, she strained to turn her head. But the newcomer stood behind her and she could not see who had entered. She only knew that Richard Milburne seemed to have been turned to stone.

"Cass Morgan fled when she saw me, but you shan't have the opportunity to do the same," a voice said coldly from the doorway. "Get up and prepare to die!"

Elizabeth recognized that iron voice with a rush of mingled joy and incredulity. Again she desperately twisted her head, gasping, "Alex. . . ?" The name came out weakly, barely audible, but amazingly the voice responded.

"Yes, my love. This swine will do you no further harm."

She began to sob again, tears of joy and relief which flooded her eyes and wracked her body.

Milburne hadn't taken his eyes from the figure in the doorway.

"You! How can. . .this be?" he croaked hoarsely.

"I told you to get up!" There was a terrible deadly quality about Alex's voice which Elizabeth had never heard before. It had its effect on Milburne. Slowly, he heaved himself to his feet, legs apart, standing over her. Free of his weight, but too weak to rise, she turned and began to crawl toward Alex.

His gaze flicked briefly over her and he said with that same deathly calm, "Lie still, my dearest, and have patience with me. There is something I must do before I soothe your hurts."

She understood then. Somehow she managed to drag herself to the edge of the wall, leaving a direct path between the two men. Their eyes bore into each other. Milburne's hand groped nervously for the sword at his side, then hesitated, loosely grasping the hilt.

Like a flash, Alex's hand went to his hip and drew forth his own sword, a lustrous, gleaming blade. "Excellent, my friend," he mocked, brandishing the weapon with easy assurance. "You have chosen the method of your own death. Now let us get on with it."

Milburne swallowed, eyeing his opponent with rising anger. He jerked his sword out of the scabbard, and as he weighed it in his hands, his confidence seemed to grow. Milburne was an accomplished swordsman; his reputation in England was widely known.

"*En garde*," he hissed, lunging at Burke with his outstretched sword.

Alex neatly sidestepped the lunge and brought his own sword to the ready. Milburne wet his lips with his tongue, swearing softly over this first unsuccessful gambit. The two men began to circle each other, both moving with panther-like grace in the wildly dancing light of the flickering candle. Then Alex struck, attacking with lightning speed, but Milburne parried strongly, mounting a concentrated defense. Attack, defend, parry. Retreat, attack. Feint, attack. Parry and attack again. And so it went.

Elizabeth, huddled on the floor against the wall, watched the battle with terror-stricken eyes. Each time Milburne's sword threatened to penetrate Alex's defense, she felt as if the life were draining from her own body, and then when Alex parried, and matched the blow with a cunning one of his own, relief engulfed her in a drowning wave. Around and around the room they fought, slashing and hacking in a dance of death. Sweat poured down their faces and both men were breathing hard. They wielded their swords more heavily now, as if the weapons had increased in weight, and their movements were labored and slow where before they had been blindingly quick. Elizabeth reliazed that strength and endurance were now the key. The opponents had proved themselves equally expert with a sword, and the outcome hinged on who could outlast the other. With her damp palms pressed to her cheeks, she searched Alex's face, noting sinkingly the signs of strain about his eyes, the weariness around his mouth. A low whimper of fear escaped her.

And then it happened. Milburne stabbed at Burke's chest, a blow Alex parried roughly and followed up with an attack of his own. He lunged his sword straight at Milburne's heart. Milburne raised his sword to block the thrust, but weariness slowed his reaction and the parry came too late. Alex withdrew the weapon instantly and stood back as Milburne uttered an outraged groan, then sank to the floor, dead. Alex tossed his bloodied sword to the floor, and gathered Elizabeth into his arms.

He held her so tightly she thought her bones would be crushed, but she clung to him, crying over and over, "My love, my love, my love."

"It's all right, sweet, really it is." He kissed her upturned lips and stroked the tousled hair with a strong, tanned hand. "You're all right, my darling, and no one will ever hurt you again."

"I thought. . .you were supposed to be. . . ."

"I know. But Granger's plan backfired." He laughed shortly. "You see, he didn't take one thing into account. I love you. And I trust you. I never doubted you for an instant, my sweet. And so his plan shot wide of the mark—fatally wide, for Geoffrey."

"Oh, Alex. . . ."

"You're all that matters, Lizzie," he whispered and his arms drew her closer. They seemed unaware of their surroundings; all that mattered was that they were together against all expectations.

"We must be married very soon," he murmured huskily in her ear.

Then Elizabeth remembered the child she carried. She raised her eyes to his like a startled doe and her mouth flew open. He was to be a father, and he did not even know it!

"What is it, love?" he asked amusedly, the grey eyes gleaming.

Elizabeth felt suddenly shy. She lowered her gaze to her belly and unconsciously placed her hands there. Then she smiled sweetly up at him and Alex noted for the first time the special glow in her eyes.

"I am with child," she whispered softly, unable to control the lilting happiness in her voice. "I carry our babe, my dearest love."

Alex's grey eyes widened. He glanced swiftly from her face to her still slender belly and his voice, when he spoke, was hoarse with joy. "Are you sure?"

Elizabeth nodded happily. "Quite sure, dearest. Does that please you?"

For answer, he gathered her into his arms once more in a crushing embrace, then seemed abruptly to remember her delicate condition. His hold became suddenly tender, as if she were a doll made of fragile glass. She laughed, and kissed his hair, that unruly thatch that insisted on falling over his brow.

"I see you are pleased," she smiled mischievously. "I assure you, my relief is heartfelt." Her violet eyes sparkled as she went on teasingly. "After all, I didn't know quite what to expect. Ruthless privateers are *so* unpredictable, you know."

Alex grinned. "And spoiled society bitches are *so* silly," he retorted.

He took her gently into his arms and got to his feet. "And now, Lizzie, I think it's time to get you home and to bed. In the morning you'll begin ordering your bridal clothes, and I'll see to the other arrangements. Ben Tucker and his Carrie shall not be the only lovers wedded next month." He carried her toward the doorway, but when she protested that she could walk, he cut her off abruptly. "Silence, wench. You'll do as you're bid. You've had quite enough exertion for one evening."

"Yes, Alex," she replied meekly enough, inwardly amused by his sternness. She leaned against him as he carried her down the stairs, thinking peacefully, "For tonight he can have his way. We have a whole lifetime ahead of us in which to dispute." A smile curved her lips and with this happy thought she snuggled closer against the chest of her future husband as he carried her out into the rain-washed night.

Epilogue

From within the borning room came the sounds of pain: moaning, a stifled gasp, low, breathless sobbing. Alexander Burke stared at the door to that room as if by piercing it with his eyes he could see what was occurring within. After a moment, he turned away from his scrutiny of its impassive wooden panels and resumed his pacing, his boots making only a dull thumping sound on the carpet as he walked back and forth before the door.

Adam Warren limped slowly up the flight of steps to the landing, his brown eyes glimmering with sympathetic amusement as he offered Alex a glass of brandy, and watched him down the contents as eagerly as if he were a desert wanderer come at last upon an oasis.

"I know precisely how you feel, my friend," Adam assured him. "When Sarah was born, I nearly wore a hole in this very carpet."

Burke scowled. He knew that Adam was trying to reassure him, but he cared not the least about the experiences of any other man. This situation was different. That was Lizzie in there, giving birth to *their* child, and no words could soothe his nervousness. All he wanted was to have the damned thing over with, and to see his wife and child. He groaned and ran his fingers through his black hair. Just to know that they were well and healthy!

Adam patted his shoulder. "She's been in her labor time for some hours now," he said. "It should be soon."

Burke nodded, then whirled to face the door as sounds of renewed activity seemed suddenly to burst from the room. He could hear the low, excited murmur of voices—Jenny's and Hannah's and the same midwife who had helped bring Alex into the world—along with an anguished shriek that he recognized as Elizabeth. He paled, and would have charged into the room, but for Adam, who grasped him firmly by the arms.

"Alex, be sensible, man!" he pleaded, shaking his brother-in-law desperately. "Don't add to the confusion like a damned fool! It will all be over soon!"

Alex grimaced. Adam was right, of course. Somehow he managed to contain his anxiety, and refrained from bursting into the room. But as sounds of activity and excitement from within increased, so did his nervousness. It seemed like a century passed, but at last he heard the sound his ears had been straining to catch. A wail pierced the air, loud and furious. Alex knew that sound. There was no other in the world quite like it. It was the lusty cry of a newborn babe.

Shortly afterward, the door opened and Jenny smiled out at him, looking tired but overwhelmingly happy.

"Come in," she whispered, beckoning with her finger. "But you mustn't stay long. She needs to sleep."

Alex rushed straight to the bed, where Elizabeth smiled wanly up at him, her face flushed and damp, violet eyes glowing proudly. Her hair was a tangled mass on the satin pillow, but to his eyes she had never looked more beautiful.

"You have a son," she whispered joyously.

And beside her on the bed lay a scrawny, wrinkled pink babe, his tiny bald face puckered with the beginnings of another wail.

"He's hungry." Elizabeth drew the baby lovingly to her breast, where he eagerly began to suck. Alex watched wondrously, kneeling beside her to grasp her hand. He could not rid himself of the feeling that he was witness to a miracle.

Elizabeth watched them both, a sense of warm, glowing happiness settling peacefully over her. Never had she imagined that life could hold so much joy. Everything she wanted in the world was right here with her in this room.

And so Stephen Charles Burke was born in the city of Philadelphia, a living symbol of the timeless, infinite love between his parents, a love which grew ever stronger and more beautiful with the passing of the years.

There are a lot more
where this one came from!

Don't Miss these Ace Romance Bestsellers!

_____ **#75157 SAVAGE SURRENDER** $1.95
The million-copy bestseller by Natasha Peters,
author of Dangerous Obsession.

_____ **#29802 GOLD MOUNTAIN** $1.95

_____ **#88965 WILD VALLEY** $1.95
Two vivid and exciting novels by
Phoenix Island author, Charlotte Paul.

_____ **#80040 TENDER TORMENT** $1.95
A sweeping romantic saga in the
Dangerous Obsession tradition.

Available wherever paperbacks are sold or use this coupon.

ace books,
Book Mailing Service, P.O. Box 690, Rockville Centre, N.Y. 11571

Please send me titles checked above.

I enclose $. . . . . Add 50¢ handling fee per copy.

Name . . . .

Address . . . .

City. . . . . State . . . . Zip . . . .

74B